RIPPLES IN THE CHALICE
A TALE OF AVALON
BOOK II

Adam Copeland

For My Mother Gayle, My Sister Annette, And My Aunt Catherine...You Are All My Talisia.

Acknowledgments

I wish to thank all the people in my life who made this work possible, whether they knew it or not. You were the influencers, the motivators, the believers, the task masters, and the contributors. I thank you all. Here is a short list of you (in no particular order), and if I left you out, know you are no less important to me. You are a part of the most important story of all...my life.

Adam Copeland.

Sarah Cypher, Jennifer Thomas, Dan Dreier, Will Hertling, Jaymi Elford, Cheri Lasota, Auburn Seal, Gretchen Grey-Hatton, Paul Smith, David Greene, Amanda Washington, Roslyn McFarland, Ripley Patton, Maria Lee, Alexis Mason, Mark Kellar, Lisa Shah & Larrie Noble Sr., Ingrid Wolf, Jason Cortlund, Norman Gouveia, Terese Thompson, Dregam, Ammie Hague, Chris Yee, Craig Hurley, Caitlin Diehl, Dheyrdre Machado, Nicole Gress, Patrick Timm, David Drazul, Andreas Gustafsson, Brian Tashima, Courtney Pierce, Brad Wheeler, Michele Freeman, Shannon Coon, and Stephen Merlino.

Prologue

They say when you're dying, your life passes before your eyes. They're right.

What they don't tell you is that life mocks and lectures you while it's happening.

Sir Patrick Gawain did not need that. Not now. Not when a sword was about to strike him at eye level.

He noted its wide, swinging arc. The blade seemed to slow down the closer it came to his head. Indeed everything began to slow down, taking on a dreamlike, or rather, nightmarish quality —as if the world had plunged into a sea of despair, where grief hindered all movement.

To his left, Greensprings burned. The central keep tower guttered like a giant candle whose flame licked at low-hanging dark clouds, giving them a brimstone glow.

To his right, flanks of a group of enemy horsemen disappeared into the forest beyond Greensprings. In the dream-motion, the earth their horses kicked up hung in the air, gently rolling in suspension. The horsemen pursued Aimeé, who held the object of all their troubles—and their salvation. They followed much closer than Patrick wanted. He had hoped to give her a much greater head start, but even that had not gone according to plan. The enemy would catch her soon, and her only protection would be her one-time rapist with whom she rode.

Around him the battle raged. The combatants danced the deadly dance, a thousand rising arms and falling bodies in tune to the music of clashing steel. Men's cries of pain and anger formed the song.

Movement may have been dreamlike, but it only gave him more time to see his friends and comrades dying.

Nearby Sir Corbin spun with a long sword in each hand, surrounded by opponents. Sir Peredur struggled to get free as an attacker palmed his face into the water of a deep puddle. Sir Waylan and Sir Brian fought back to back, running out of precious space to maneuver. Four enemies forced another Avangardesman, his identity obscured by the press of attackers, to his knees. They held his arms out to the sides while a fifth pulled his head back to expose his throat and run a sword blade across it.

A mob of attackers pulled down the last of the mounted Avangardesmen, horse and all. Even before the knight hit the ground, his attackers struck with sword, axe, halberd, and maul like farmers threshing wheat.

Patrick realized it had been raining for some time now. The odd slowing of time enabled him to see the drops of rain, blood, and flying sweat as they hung trembling in the air.

His heartbeat drummed louder.

How did things go so horribly wrong? How did it come to this? Were not the righteous supposed to prevail?

He'd caused all this. Things could have been so different if he had only made different choices; one choice in particular, so long ago, and none of this would have happened. The consequences of his action lay all around him in the mud, the blood, and the fire. Now the grand experiment known as Greensprings on the island of Avalon collapsed into a bloody ruin. And once they captured Aimeé with her precious charge, the world would never be the same, either.

Patrick would not witness any of this because death had arrived, brought to him by the hands of his own brother. Patrick's sword arm dipped. His brother's blade came within inches of his face now, moving so slowly it may as well have stopped. But it did not, for he could see its sharpened edge pass through a fat raindrop, slowly parting it like a quivering bead of quicksilver.

As he watched the drop separate on the blade, Patrick noticed his reflection in the metal. In the reflection, he could see a figure at his back walking towards him. Another attacker coming from behind? This figure moved at a normal pace, not in slow motion. Once right behind him, Patrick recognized the face.

The sword truly did stop moving now. The parted raindrop froze in place.

"Rise, Patrick," the voice said.

Patrick came to a standing position from his knees and turned to face the newcomer.

"You," he said.

Before him stood a mirror image of himself, though rain and sweat did not plaster his other self's dark shoulder length hair against his scalp. Nor did he wear Patrick's torn and bloodied black Avangarde surcoat with the white swan emblem on the chest. He did not have rent armor with loose chain mail links spilling from threads. The Other's face, with its high cheekbones and light complexion, was clear of cuts, blood, bruises, and mud. His own hazel-green eyes, with a hint of gold circling the pupils, peered at him intensely.

Once, Patrick referred to him as the "Apparition" because when he came during his silent, unsettling visitations he wore a deeply cowled robe. Nowadays, he came wearing a sort of simple cassock of a forgettable color and made no attempt to obscure his face. The visitor still preferred to wear gloves, though, which Patrick noticed when the Other hooked his thumbs in his belt. Also, the Other no longer remained silent. Though Patrick often wished he did.

"Have you come to save me at the last moment, again?" Patrick asked.

"No," the Other responded, gesturing with a nod towards where Patrick had sat on his knees moments before.

Patrick frowned and looked in the direction. To his surprise, he saw he still knelt there, the sword dangerously close to his head. All frozen in time.

Patrick staggered back and looked down at his hands. He still wore his bloodied and muddied gauntlets, but he held no sword. He gasped and patted himself down, confirming the solidness of his body.

"Well, this is a new one," he said. "What does it mean? Am I dead, then?"

The Other shook his head. "You will be, though, unless you do something quick."

Patrick shrugged. "So do something. Step in as you did when I fought Loki and he had the upper hand."

A sneer, ever so faint, curled on the Other's lip. "I'm here to help you help yourself this time," he responded. "Just moments ago you lowered your sword arm. You weren't even trying."

Patrick sagged and ran a hand through his hair, leaving a streak of grime.

"Why? Why do you care? Who are you? *What* are you? Why won't you tell me?"

The Other approached the frozen, still-kneeling Patrick and bent over to scrutinize his face as if fascinated by an insect.

"Much rides on your success here," he said at last. "You must hold on as long as possible."

Patrick chuckled without mirth. "Define success. Look around! It is over! I held on as long as possible, and they're still dying!"

The Other broke his gaze away from the kneeling Patrick. "It is not over. You must continue the fight."

Patrick staggered a few steps in the direction of the keep and looked at a particular spot of ground before the gate. His jaw muscle moved as he ground his teeth.

"I'm so sorry!" he shouted at the spot. His eyes glistened with tears though none fell to his cheeks. He pulled his gauntlets off and stared at his hands, turning to the Other.

"So much blood," he spoke softly, rubbing his fingers along a scar that ran the length of his right palm. "It flows from the people who trusted me. Believed in me." He wrung his hands in an attempt to make them clean. "I can't get it off. I can't get it off!"

"Get a hold of yourself!" the Other shouted, displaying for the first time something resembling emotion. "You must be strong. You must follow through. You've come so far and taken such great steps. Don't stop now."

"Why?" Patrick asked, meaning more than just the immediate inquiry.

"These people followed you onto the battlefield because they believed in you," the Other replied. "If there is any chance of their surviving and changing the course of history, you must believe in yourself as well. You must fight until the end."

"Even if it looks hopeless?" Patrick whispered.

"Especially when it looks hopeless," the Other whispered back, then gestured to the still frozen Patrick. "And now it is time to return and raise your sword."

"What? That's it?" Patrick glowered at the interloper. "That is your sole purpose for being here? That is all the aid you have to offer—" Patrick waved his hands at the spectacle around them, scowling "—just to say, 'You must hold on?' How does that help?"

"What more do you want from me?" the Other asked, glowering back.

"I want to know where I went wrong! I want to go back and change things! Surely if you can stop time, you can reverse it?"

The Other shook his head gravely. "I did not stop time, merely took you out of it for a moment."

"Then what good are you?" Patrick kicked at a dirt clod.

The Other stepped closer, almost nose to nose.

"Would it motivate you to raise your sword arm one last time if I showed you that you did nothing wrong? That your guilt is an illusion?"

"Yes," Patrick said without hesitation.

The Other reached up and touched Patrick's face, the glove rasping against the skin of his temple.

"Then see," he said.

Patrick's vision suddenly narrowed to a dark tunnel. He gasped and almost lost his balance.

"What do you see?" the Other asked.

"I-I'm high above, in the dark, looking down on a boat on a river, lit by lanterns," Patrick responded. "I don't remember this. What am I looking at?"

"You are looking at the whole story. All the choices leading to today. Did you really think this was all your doing? Everyone has to take a share of responsibility. Now, watch."

Chapter One

After many hours, the rhythmic creak and gentle splash of the oars had become hypnotizing. All on board fell quiet, lost in their thoughts. This included the young King Henry Salian, fifth of the name, who found his thoughts wandering to old lessons from his father's tutor. Henry hadn't liked the man, and certainly resented the many hours spent indoors learning trivia just as easily referenced by any number of counselors at a moment's notice. He still rankled at the knowledge of having been robbed of a significant portion of his childhood. Children should play. But the elder Henry—Emperor Henry—felt otherwise. He had insisted a leader must project intelligence and wisdom, not just power. Plus, it just wouldn't do to turn constantly to advisors amid negotiations.

As the younger Henry grew into manhood, especially tonight, he had to admit that some of his father's advice rang true. Tonight he needed to project a certain image to ensure the placement of an important game piece on the playing board.

There were plenty of other lessons, however, whose truth Henry was not willing to concede. The young king set his jaw firmly at the thought. Tonight would be the beginning of asserting himself.

Project that, *Father*.

He placed a foot on the boat's gunwale, leaned forward, and prayed that his memories of those childhood history lessons would be sharp. Perhaps something in all that trivia would be useful tonight. Though he doubted anything useful would come from knowing that people often referred to the River Tiber, upon which they floated, as *flavus*—the blonde—because of its yellowish color.

It didn't look yellow to him, even in the day's last light as they departed shore. Just dirty. In the dark it looked black. Gray-brown in the light of the boat's lanterns. Initially, Henry had questioned the wisdom of having lights at all, considering their clandestine mission. Those of his men who had traveled here before, as well as their boat-guides, cautioned most large boats on the river had lanterns and it would actually draw attention if they hadn't. Henry relented, and also agreed to dress down for the occasion. The only thing betraying their status was the craftsmanship of their weapons. Those his escort would not part with, to Henry's relief.

"We're almost there," one of the oarsmen said, from what Henry could guess from his Italian. The hired boat-guide pointed. Rowing proved unnecessary as they traveled from north to south with the river's current. Returning upstream to the outskirts of the city, where the horses and carriage waited, would be a different matter.

"Will he be there?" Henry asked, turning to Gustave.

The large burly man stood next to the young king and stroked his thick brown beard.

"You can count on it, Your Highness," he grunted. "They can't pass up an opportunity such as this. If conditions permitted it, I'm certain they'd have a red carpet laid out from the Castel to the basilica just for you."

Henry knew the answer, but liked reassurance just the same, which is why he also asked, "And the owner of our transportation and his crew? I trust they will keep our comings and goings private?"

Again Gustave grunted, passing a glance at the nervous oarsmen.

"A substantial sum will assure secrecy—that, and the fact that we greeted them with their family names and what villages they come from, with hands on sword hilts."

Henry nodded, smiling. Though officially his father's man, Gustave had proven loyal to the younger Henry's cause. Gustave also had grievances against the emperor and had been instrumental in showing Henry that one need not be a victim of the established order of things.

The young king took in the scene as they approached their destination.

For many leagues the countryside had been mostly dark and empty. Now the buildings became more frequent, larger in size, and made of stone. The docks were larger, as were the boats— some with sails. Shrubs and weeds replaced trees on the cramped shoreline. Before long, the left bank disappeared altogether and the buildings formed a wall extending below the waterline. Ancient, red-tiled roofs sloped down from at least three stories above. The walls' stones had been re-mortared by countless generations. From the Roman Empire foundation stones, to the trellised windows of the Visigoth Occupation, to the Italian city-state rain gutters, these buildings reminded Henry how short-lived were men and their plans.

A huge wall slowly curved in from the west and asserted itself closer and closer to the water as the boat made its journey. Soon it dominated their right flank, almost as high as the buildings to their left, fashioned from huge blocks of pale stone streaked with age. Its age did not compare to a rapidly approaching bridge made of similar stone. Flat with no curvature, four major arches supported it over the water, with a series of smaller ones disappearing into a mound of earth rising from the river's west bank. An oarsman pointed to a gate sitting almost hidden in scrub. It would have been easy to miss if torch light from both the bridge and wall hadn't illuminated the area.

Beyond the gate and wall sat a huge drum-shaped fortress.

"Rome," Henry whispered, taking in the stout buildings clustered around it.

"Ja," Gustave responded. "Some of it, in any case. The city proper is to the east, and huge. This here to the west is mostly the Leonine City, surrounded by the Leonine Wall."

"Right," Henry mused out loud, remembering more history lessons. "Some old pope named Leo tired of Saint Peter's Basilica getting sacked every time barbarians came to town, so he extended Rome's walls around it."

Gustave laughed. "It's funny, don't you think, those barbarians were our own forefathers?"

Henry chuckled at the idea and puffed up with a little pride.

"Turns out, it wasn't a bad idea to build the wall," Gustave added, seriousness creeping into his tone. "Not long before you were born, I was here with your father laying this very place to siege. That pompous old man, Pope Gregory, refused to recognize your father as emperor. Refused to perform the coronation on him. All attempts to drag him out of that fortress to make him perform his duty failed. He and his cronies hid behind those walls like cowards."

"I have to admit, Father's solution had a certain audacity to it," Henry said.

"Ja, I'll give him that," Gustave conceded, some mirth returning to his voice. "If you don't like the rules, break them and make your own. Grabbing another pompous old man, making him pope, then having him make you emperor will work. But by doing so you won't have the support of all the people. You never will, but it's important to get as much support as possible."

"Which is precisely why we're here," Henry nodded. "Honey attracts more flies than vinegar."

Gustave placed a hand on Henry's shoulder and squeezed.

They came to the shore just below the little gate. From here they could see the foundations of the bridge supporting the arches in the low September waters. They gave the impression the bridge had feet.

"I hope you're right. This way cannot possibly have any worse an outcome than your father's," Gustave said, then jumped into a familiar tirade. "Shortly after he was crowned emperor, we fled Rome as Gregory's supporters from the south came to his rescue. It was shameful, running from a city that, by all rights, was ours. The only consolation we had was that their rescuers, the southern Normans, so ravaged the city in the process that the local nobility chased Gregory out of the city as well."

"And years later Gregory's successor sits here in Rome again, living like some sort of emperor himself in the Lateran Palace, and we sneak about like thieves. The papacy still refuses to recognize my father as emperor," Henry added, stoking his companion's fires, though by now he didn't need to. Gustave had proved fully committed to Henry's plan long ago.

"And there is nothing but war because of it," Gustave continued. "Too many popes and too many nobles use that fact to choose whichever side they want to further their own ends. Your father spends all his time and energy quashing rebellions."

"And murdering his own family," Henry added, his face contorting into a mask of anger. "It is too much. Conrad was a fool to covet Father's throne so openly, but he did not deserve this."

"Ja, it was his murder that opened many eyes," Gustave agreed. "I loved your father. Trusted him. But he swore it was a natural sickness that took your older brother's life. He lied to my face."

"A 'natural sickness?'" Henry scoffed. "What sickness has the audacity to leave a garland of baby's breath stuffed into Conrad's mouth as a message?" Henry's eyes squeezed shut, his head drooped, and his fists shook with outrage. "Well, I got the message. But not the one my father intended: if you're going to covet the crown, do it quietly. Certainly don't start by smearing your father's and stepmother's names by calling them perverts. And don't switch your allegiance to an opposing pope by announcing it in public, let alone acting as his lackey. Could you believe it? He actually led the man's horse around as if he were a servant."

Gustave shook his head. "Conrad may have had all the cunning of a gourd, but you are right, he should be alive today. You, on the other hand, will survive. You are not so headstrong. You are smarter. Now that you are next in line, the world will become a better place on the day your father falls from power."

"Agreed." Henry's chest puffed. "And I thank you for believing in me and my plan. Tonight we will make the first moves of the game—quietly."

The boat bumped against the marshy shore. An oarsman jumped out to steady it, indifferent to the water and mud. Judging by the smell; it wasn't all mud. Placing a hand on the willing shoulder of one of the commoners, Henry made the leap from the boat to the dry riverbank. One of his escorts shared a few words with the boat's captain, no doubt planning the return trip.

Gustave landed next to him and led the way up the hill toward the gate.

"Too many popes, indeed," Henry picked up their conversation. "Too many rebellions. That all must end. There must be one pope, one emperor, one empire."

A path of sorts led them up a steep hill, making them sweat even more. Henry threw open his cloak, grabbed the edges of the fabric, and fanned himself, not caring if he exposed his sword.

Gustave paused ahead of him. He turned, and while jerking a thumb in the direction of the gate said, "You sure you want *that* pope to be *the* pope?"

Henry paused, took a breath, and fanned himself more.

"A chessboard has many pieces," he replied. "The more you position in the right places, the better your chances of success. Some of the pieces won't survive. Doesn't matter, so long as the final objective is accomplished. And what pieces remain on the board when it's all said and done will be very, very grateful pieces. Besides, Conrad made the mistake of conspiring with the wrong pope. I am collaborating with my father's own pope, and should a rumor start, it won't be so damning."

Gustave looked Henry up and down with approval. Smiling, he gestured to the last few steps through some scrub trees to the gate.

It revealed itself as a sort of postern gate with thick double wooden doors, perhaps as high as two and half men, and one wide. It most likely served for quick entry and exit of messengers.

"Very well then," Gustave said, reaching up to one of the huge iron rings. "Let's accomplish in one night with a little honey what your father couldn't in many months with vinegar and an army: gain audience with a pope in the Leonine City."

Gustave banged the ring on the wood. The noise sounded thunderous.

A moment passed, then the door's peephole slid open. A shadow appeared behind an iron grate.

"Quo vadis?" came a young man's voice.

Gustave replied, "In nómine Patris et Fílii et Spíritus Sancti."

A pause followed while all held their breath.

"Bonum!" came the positive response, followed by the peephole slamming shut.

When the door started to swing open, Henry's escort jumped in front of the young king, hands on sword hilts, though it proved unnecessary.

Standing in the doorway, a lone figure bid them to enter quickly. The man was slightly built and wore a black cassock, and when he had finished locking the door behind them, the dim torchlight revealed him as someone not much older than Henry's own fifteen years. Unlike Henry, however, this fellow managed to grow a thick and well-manicured goatee. Its dark color matched his wavy hair.

"Willkommen, König Heinrich Salian, der König der Römer," he said in German with only a hint of an Italian accent.

Pleased, Henry responded in German, "Thank you for making the effort to accommodate my language, especially the proper form of my name 'Henry,' and for properly addressing me as 'King of the Romans.' Few these days are wont to recognize that."

The man touched his breast with a hand and bowed.

"Ours is to serve, Your Highness. I am Victor, attendant to His Eminence Cardinal Teodorico, soon crowned this night pope, loyal to the empire. He charged me with conducting you with safe passage to the basilica. He wished me to convey his gratitude for your presence at his coronation ceremony."

We'll see about that, Henry thought, but only smiled.

"You are alone?" Gustave asked, looking around nervously, hand on hilt. His tone conveyed both surprise and suspicion.

Victor remained calm, almost smugly so. "I was confident His Highness would bring sufficient men for his comfort. Any men I might have brought may have disconcerted you."

"Still, there is some risk in what we do tonight, and you walk the streets alone?"

"Paschal and his anti-imperialist supporters are safely behind their walls on the other side of Rome. As for the streets, they pose no threat to one who is familiar with them. I assure you we will be safe on our way to Saint Peter's."

He motioned for them to follow and they moved away from the gate, paralleling the river separated by the Leonine Wall. Now Henry saw the fortress sat a good distance away from the wall. He strode down a cobblestone street between the wall and the place his father had attacked many years before. Seeing it this close, with its massive walls and gate, he understood why his father's siege had failed.

"Sì," Victor said, noting Henry's interest in the structure. "Castel di Sant'Angelo. Many a pope has hidden there from the people's armies. A proper spiritual leader shouldn't have need of castles to hide, not from his own people. He should be among them, about the Lord's work. Something we hope you can help make happen, mein König."

Henry grunted his acknowledgment, but did not pursue the discussion. He would discuss such things with Teodorico himself, not his servant.

As they walked, the wall and street diverged and the street became populated by buildings. First there came small shops with red-tiled roofs, then the large, crowded buildings typical of Rome.

The occasional lit window among the tall stucco structures punctuated the empty street. Though only a little more than half full, the moon was bright enough to make shadows.

"I must warn you," Victor said, turning and making a point to look directly at the king. "When you take audience with His Eminence, he will be surrounded by his supporters who've also come to witness his coronation and make oaths."

Henry scowled at the man, barely believing his audacity. He gripped his sword hilt so tightly the leather creaked.

"That was not the agreement," Henry said, coming to a complete stop. "There will be no oaths from me. I offered promise for promise, as my correspondence with your master stated, and I insist on a private audience. As I can see you have no intentions of honoring the agreement, I see I wasted a trip!"

Henry turned his back on the open-mouthed servant, but made sure Gustave saw his wink as he walked away.

Gustave smiled nervously and ordered the rest of the entourage to follow.

Henry did not smile. He squeezed his eyes shut, set his lips into a grim line, and raised his fist to gently beat his breast, keeping count. By the count of two, he realized he did not breathe.

"Apologies," Victor called after the group, arrogance drained from his voice. He chased after them.

On the third beat of his breast, Henry exhaled and his eyes snapped open, smiling. By that time Victor positioned himself in front of the group, bowing deeper than ever.

"I am merely passing along a message," Victor continued, frantic. "His Eminence is perfectly aware there will be no oaths from you. As for the others in the room, a notable presence is necessary for confirmation of the ritual. All those present are ardent supporters of my master—and you, my highness. In fact, they will be eager to make oaths to *you*."

Henry stared impassively at the servant until satisfied with the man's squirming.

"Are there any other surprises?" Henry asked.

"None, I swear."

With a dismissive huff Henry gestured Victor to lead on.

With a sigh of relief, Victor urged them in the direction of a building looming in the distance. As Henry calmed his beating heart, he wished not for the last time they rode on horseback and were not walking like commoners. The closer they came, the more they needed to zig-zag through smaller streets and alleys, as no direct path presented itself.

At last they opened upon an expansive plaza, and directly across from them loomed Saint Peter's Basilica, Western Christendom's most holy site and the place where emperors and popes were made.

From here, the building appeared to be a series of square columns assembled like building blocks, ornately carved in incredible detail. Smaller buildings surrounded the central structure, some of them full-sized churches, but they were dwarfed in comparison.

Despite the late hour, plenty of people were about. From this distance, next to the building, they looked like ants.

Henry gawked. He knew past generations had built Saint Peter's over the tomb of its namesake, but he had always imagined a chapel built about a gravestone. The Castel Sant'Angelo could almost fit inside this structure.

"So big," he said in wonder, forgetting himself.

Victor smiled, no doubt enjoying Henry's moment of amazement. "Your first time?"

Henry quickly closed his jaw and grunted in the affirmative.

"Wait until you see the inside," Victor said with a note of returning pride.

They mounted the steps, the exertion bringing out more perspiration, and came to three giant bronze doors the size of castle gates.

"Under normal circumstances," Victor said, "the coronation would take place here, on the platform in front of an adoring crowd," he said waving a hand over the plaza, imagining a sea of spectators. "But these are desperate and uncertain times."

Henry nodded. "When it comes time for your master to perform my imperial coronation, I expect it to be here, in public view."

Victor nodded as well, turned on a heel, and led the band through the massive doors into a dark atrium.

Inside lay a courtyard open to the sky containing a well-landscaped garden bathed in moonlight. Beyond rose the front of the immense facade of the double-tiered basilica proper.

"Popes, emperors, kings, and queens are not unlike architecture," Victor continued, gesturing to the many columns. Paths wound through the garden, but Victor took them to the right, toward a lantern-lit colonnade.

"They need to be built up, and supported from beneath. They are only as strong as their base," Henry responded, eager to show he understood the metaphor. He did not care for this servant's attempt at philosophizing. It sounded too much like lecturing, which did not sit well with Henry.

As they traveled the corridor, Victor said, "Consider the keystone." Victor did not notice or care about his guest's agitated tone. "It hangs precariously from the center of an arch at its apex. If it weren't for the support of the stone to its left and its right, it would slip and fall."

When Henry responded indignantly, he had to speak a little louder as they passed two fountains gurgling in the courtyard, and night birds flittered noisily from well-pruned tree to well-pruned tree. The largest of the fountains was in the shape of a bronze pine cone, green with age. It sat nested upright beneath a bronze cupola supported by many columns. Water flowed from its top, spilled over the ridges of the cone, and splashed into a waist-high, box-shaped pool.

"Without the keystone, the whole arch collapses."

"Precisely," Victor said, pleased.

They approached five wooden doors, banded and studded with iron. Victor took them to the center and greatest of these. Two armed men in full armor stood guard, and Victor spoke to them in quiet Italian.

Gustave leaned close to his king and whispered, smiling, "Ja, but who is the keystone? That is the question."

Henry smiled only with his eyes and said nothing.

The guards opened the ponderous door.

If the outside of Saint Peter's surprised Henry, the inside shocked him.

Before him stretched a cavernous space difficult to imagine being built by man. He had heard stories of the sheer size of the Coliseum, but had yet to lay eyes on it. He had learned of the Great Pyramids of Egypt in his studies. But this... Darkness filled the square cavern, but just enough moonlight pierced the upper story windows of the structure that he could make out a forest of giant columns, supporting a shelf of intricately carved marble. Expansive sections of more marble surmounted the shelf, with colorful frescoes of biblical scenes, past popes, patriarchs, and prophets covering every inch. Atop these marble sections rested the gabled roof, constructed with crossbeams whose single pieces of solid wood had to have come from monstrous trees. The beams hovered so high off the ground, if Henry had had a bow, he would have had difficulty reaching one with an arrow.

While he gaped, Gustave gently took Henry by the arm and guided him down a short flight of steps, making sure to keep up with Victor.

"Impressive, no?" Victor said over his shoulder.

Henry swallowed before answering, not wishing to have Victor catch him as slack-jawed again.

"Of course it is."

Victor waved a hand over the expanse of columns, saying, "A testament to Christianity's victory over the ancient Roman Empire. That fact and the fact this holy place has stood for close to eight hundred years is also a testament to His everlasting glory."

"That's all very fascinating," Gustave said impatiently, "but if I may remind you we must leave before sunrise. We don't have another eight hundred years."

Beyond a massive arch and resting in a well-lit chamber, a small structure nestled against the back of the basilica, beckoning them.

A building within a building? Henry thought.

During the long approach to the little square building made of blue-veined marble, Henry studied the painting on the curved wall above it. There a colossal Jesus floated in a blue celestial gallery of stars, apostles, and sheep while making a sign of peace.

Henry's gaze flickered back to the top the structure where sat the church's altar under a bronze canopy that dangled a crown of flickering votive candles.

An enclosure of marble walls and spiraling columns surrounded the building, complete with an iron gate. A group of robed men knelt just inside the gate at the base of the stairs to the altar, chanting. Incense joined their song, rising to the heavens.

Victor turned to the Germans and whispered, "This is where the coronation will take place. These priests are preparing for the ceremony."

Henry nodded, assuming they would enter the gated area, but Victor circled around to where the sanctuary met the basilica wall. There, an entry led to a flight of stairs disappearing beneath floor level.

Twenty steps led to a terracotta chamber dimly lit by candles. Incense, smoke, musky sweat, and an earthy damp mildew odor pressed around a group of robed and hooded people.

Victor lead the Germans through the crowd toward a man in a simple white robe. He was kneeling in prayer on the packed earthen floor. Politely Victor paused behind him.

Henry and his men waited at the front of the crowd, silent in the twenty-odd crowd. Chant and incense filtered down to them from the priests praying above. He realized the sanctuary building above served as a shell covering this place: a place once open to the elements and graffiti-writing pilgrims on a windswept hill, holding the mausoleum of a man who once followed Christ. Ate with Him. Prayed with Him. Died for Him.

Henry did not count himself a religious sort, but even he had to admit the antiquity of the place evoked a feeling of reverence.

At last Victor leaned forward and whispered in the man's ear, who turned his head slightly and nodded an acknowledgment. Slowly, stiff from hours of prayer, he rose to his feet with the aid of his attendant.

He was aged, though not elderly, and crowned by a full head of gray hair well on its way to turning white. A square jaw, lined with time, sat beneath a sharp nose. With his back to the candlelight, his eyes were dark.

He smiled congenially and approached, opening his arms in welcome. His body was lanky, straight, and healthy.

"Welcome, King Henry, to the Confessio of Saint Peter," he said in German. "I cannot tell you how pleased I am someone from House Salian is attending my coronation, hmm?"

They bowed to each other, as did the others in Henry's entourage.

The man, Cardinal Teodorico, stood much taller than the King, almost as tall as Gustave.

"I regret my presence couldn't be more official, but as I'm sure you know, my oath as King of Germany is that I would not interfere with my father's greater empire," Henry responded, his lip curling ever so slightly at the last part. "You are correct, however, that a Salian should be present for your coronation. My father saw fit to make your predecessor a pope, and he should be here to see you enthroned as well. One of many areas we disagree."

Teodorico shrugged slightly. "To be fair to your father, this occasion was not necessarily expected, hmm? We had expected my predecessor to recover from his long sickness, yet he passed rather suddenly. Also, this occasion was not necessarily advertised. The invitation list was short, hmm, yes?"

Henry paused in thought, and he said, "Your willingness to take on the mantle of antipope is commendable, but I must say I am surprised at your choice to keep your election secret. Your letters said something of a 'greater plan?'"

"Becoming the Pope of the Opposition, or 'antipope' as you call it, is only the beginning, hmm?" Teodorico said. "My predecessor Clement made little headway towards uniting Christendom under one papal rule. I have no intentions of being just as ineffectual, hmm? From what I gather from your letters in our correspondences, you feel similar about your father's difficulties in calming civil strife in the empire? What if I offered a path that unites us all, hmm?"

"One empire, one emperor, one pope," Henry stated, nodding. "How does keeping your election secret further that?"

"On occasion, especially when a Church official is in a hostile environment," Teodorico explained, "it would not be safe or expedient for a priest's elevation to the position of cardinal to be publicly known. Once identified, his enemies will try to eliminate him, hmm, yes?"

Henry nodded, adding, "Like taking out the leaders on the battlefield."

"Precisely!" the cardinal said enthusiastically, gesturing at Henry as if encouraging a bright student. "Such cardinals are called '*Cardinalis in Pectore*'—Cardinal in the Breast, or 'Hidden Cardinal.' Likewise, I plan on being '*Papa in Pectore*', hmm? Hidden Pope, until I am secure from a position of strength. I will initially accomplish more as a secret pope, procuring that which I need to reveal myself from a position of such strength, nobody will deny I am the one, true pope, hmm? And I will be free to perform a coronation on a one, true emperor, hmm, yes?"

Teodorico gestured at the young king with open hands.

At this moment Henry realized two things. One, Teodorico's speaking proclivity was a stutter of sorts, and stutterers always made him laugh. And two, Teodorico's revelation, after all the vague statements and insinuations in their correspondences to date, finally confirmed what he had hoped: Teodorico belonged to him. If he played his pieces right, that is. Which he fully intended on doing to ensure positioning this piece in its proper place. The latter fact kept Henry from laughing and ruining their negotiations. Henry did smile though, pleased at what he heard, and amused by how he heard it.

"And what do you plan on doing to secure your position of irrefutable strength?" he asked, curious.

Teodorico drew in a breath as he drew up his height.

"Coronations, crowns, thrones, and crosses... These are all symbols giving strength to those who bear them. They *are* power," he said, approaching Saint Peter's tomb, raising his hands reverently at the stone wall. Turning back to Henry, he added, "They give meaning and purpose. They are beacons to the people, who are comforted by them and follow them without question. Bear the right symbol, and the people will follow you to the ends of the earth. It is why your father went to such great lengths to be crowned emperor by a pope, hmm, yes?"

Teodorico took quick steps towards a little window from which wafted the chants and sweet smelling incense. He stabbed a finger at it.

"There, across the river, sitting in luxury in the Lateran Palace, is Pope Paschal the Second," the cardinal sneered. "Why is he there, presiding over the Cathedral of Rome, hmm? And my predecessor, the previous antipope, died outside walls that should have been his, hmm? And my coronation is being held in darkness, hmm, yes?"

Henry realized the questions rhetorical and patiently waited for the answer. Though he had a difficult time not smiling as the cardinal's stutter became more pronounced the more excited the man became.

"Because *his* predecessor held a symbol legitimizing his party's claim to the papacy," Teodorico's voice fell almost to a whisper.

"Jerusalem," Henry whispered back.

"Sì," Teodorico said. "Jerusalem. Pope Urban managed to reclaim the Holy Land from the heathens with an army of crusaders. Therefore, Urban's papacy was perceived as the righteous one. So the people follow his successor today. Their party isn't more righteous, more special. They merely hold a symbol, hmm, yes?"

"You plan on performing a greater victory?" Henry asked.

"No," Teodorico responded dramatically. "I plan on possessing a greater symbol."

The cardinal returned to the red wall, placed a hand gently on its surface. The glow of the candles on the shelf rimmed him in light.

"What do you know of the Isle of Avalon?" he asked.

He kept his back to the king, waiting for a response.

"The Britannien island from the stories of the Knights of the Round Table?" Henry said, unable to keep his brow from knitting in confusion. "It is a legend. A place full of Valkyries that took König Arthur to his final resting place."

Teodorico faced the young king, smiled slyly, and said, "Not a legend. A very real place. One of the British Isles, though secret and hidden—much like everything we talk about tonight, hmm?"

The cardinal approached Henry and stood uncomfortably close, his gaze serious and his height intimidating. Suddenly he didn't seem like such a silly old man with a stutter.

"I guess by your reaction you also do not know of the Greensprings School, hmm, yes?"

Henry shook his head. None of this sounded familiar and it angered him that he felt at a disadvantage.

"Your father has been keeping secrets from you," Teodorico wagged a finger at him. "As emperor, he and other rulers have been sending young nobles to a secret school on Avalon."

"I doubt it," Henry scoffed. "He wouldn't—couldn't—keep such a secret from me. He was so high and mighty on my own education, he definitely would have sent me to such a special school."

"Not this school," the cardinal almost laughed. "This school was meant to teach peace and cooperation. Things your father viewed as soft and weak. He had no trouble sending his enemies' children there. Make them more submissive, hmm, yes? But not you. He would not want that for you. Not his son."

Henry froze, not sure what to think. Now that he thought about it, his father was perfectly capable of keeping secrets from him, as he was obviously capable of far worse. What surprised him was that his father might have believed in his skills as a future king.

He resisted the temptation to turn to Gustave and angrily ask, *Did you know?*

Instead, he hid his feelings and addressed the cardinal crisply.

"How is it you would know of such things, but not the son of the emperor?"

Teodorico wisely chose to remove the gloating from his voice. "Privately I may be a loyal imperialist, but publicly I do serve my cardinal duties for Paschal and his reformers, hmm? How else can I remain in Rome? Therefore, I am not only aware of a certain department within the Roman Curia that oversees this school, called the Board of Benefactors, but I am the appointed cardinal who oversees the overseers, hmm, yes?"

Henry frowned. "If they believe so much in their mission, why keep the school secret?"

"That many noble eggs in one basket would tempt a fox to come along and snatch them up, yes?" the cardinal said. "Therefore, it is a school *in Pectore*, watched over by a *Cardinalis in Pectore*. The island hides behind a miraculous mist that is next to impossible to navigate. Also, the students are housed in a mighty fortress, the Keep at Greensprings, guarded by an order of knights called the Avangarde."

Henry felt his eyes narrow. "I still don't see how an Avalon compares to a Jerusalem."

"It's what's in Avalon that I seek, hmm?" Teodorico explained. "The symbol of symbols, that will make reclaiming the Holy Land look like child's play. One of the Avangarde is a crusader who went on quest and brought back with him a wondrous cup that performed miracles, hmm? Understand, yes?"

Henry's teeth ground. He did not like being led like an ass by the nose.

"I understand I'm losing patience," he said levelly.

The cardinal made a conciliatory gesture as he continued. "Don't you see, hmm? The legends are true: Avalon is the place where the Holy Grail resides. The Cup of the Last Supper. The Lord's Cup. The vessel that caught the blood of Jesus Christ as it spilled from the wound in his side."

Henry felt muscles relax in his face as the implication dawned on him, but then just as quickly disappointment settled in his gut.

"A crusader?" he almost scoffed. "That is not surprising. The country overflows with veterans of the war coming home from the Holy Land telling fanciful tales. They bring tales of Saint George and dragons."

"Agreed, hmm?" Teodorico conceded. "But many witnesses saw this crusader, this Avangarde, place the contents of the cup to the lips of a dead woman and bring her back to life before the altar in the church. The Greensprings annals document this, naming the knight by name: one Sir Patrick Gawain, hmm, yes?"

Henry remained silent for a moment, mulling his thoughts. "And what if it is true? May I remind you my father already possesses the Spear of Destiny—the very relic that caused the blood of Christ to flow into the cup in the first place—yet, despite the legends surrounding it, he has not been able to put down all rebellions or further his empire. What would the cup accomplish?"

"Your Highness is most astute, hmm?" Teodorico's confident smile almost lit up the chamber. "Firstly, your father indeed holds the Spear of Destiny in his treasury. But it is incomplete. It is missing its tip and therefore the legend that any ruler who possesses the weapon will stand undefeated in battle is only partially fulfilled. A situation you only stand to inherit unless something changes, hmm, yes?"

Henry shifted uneasily at the accuracy of the statement.

"Secondly, the Cup of the Last Supper is a vessel of healing, and it is complete." Teodorico continued. "He who holds the cup will be viewed as God's chosen leader of the Church, hmm?"

"And you plan on keeping the cup for yourself. I see," Henry concluded. "How does this help me?"

"It is my firmest belief God intended for the mighty Empire to hold the spear to protect God's flock, and for the loving Church to hold the cup to nurture, hmm, yes?"

Henry's heart leaped with possibilities, but he maintained his composure.

"Keep the flock in line and docile," he summarized, nodding.

"Another way of putting it, yes, hmm?" Teodorico agreed. "With your support I will be a most grateful ally doing his part to keep the flock docile. With a symbol like the Cup of the Last Supper in my possession, we can be united as a family. One empire, one emperor, one pope. Everyone happy and benefiting, hmm, yes?"

Henry fought to keep from chewing his lower lip. His eyes ached. He could find no hint of deception in the cardinal's reasoning.

Though the discussion did not transpire exactly as Henry pictured it, and he certainly resented the old man's pretensions, their meeting was going well. After some thought he had to admit the cardinal's plan had merit. In fact, it rather pleased him. He just didn't want to appear cowed into it without first obtaining essential concessions of his own.

Do not behave the rash fifteen year old everyone believes you to be, he reminded himself. *Chief among them, your father.*

"Indeed, everyone must benefit," he said rigidly. "Your plan shows promise, but first let us be clear what those mutual benefits might be."

"Very well, hmm?" Teodorico smiled, exhaling his own apprehensions. "I will remain supreme pontiff, hmm, yes?"

"Of course," Henry conceded, "but your papacy, and indeed all bishops in the empire, will be staffed by those who meet my approval. Future popes will be of my choosing alone."

Teodorico hesitated momentarily, putting on the pretense of considering some response other than the one Henry knew he had to make for these discussions to move forward.

"Absolutely," the cardinal said at last. "I agree with you and your father in this matter. It is no accident that kings and emperors are worldly leaders of God's people. It is by divine appointment and it only makes sense their leadership should decide who guides their people spiritually, hmm? It is a travesty Paschal and his party insist otherwise, perpetuating the conflicts tearing the empire apart, hmm, yes?"

Henry allowed himself a smile as he sensed the playing piece taking up its position on the board.

"However," Teodorico added, "those individuals who present themselves with proper credentials and meet our approval can purchase their positions, hmm, yes?"

Henry licked his lips, savoring the idea of future revenues for his coffers. "So long as we share equally in the purchase price."

Teodorico smiled and inclined his head in agreement.

"Finally," the cardinal said, "you will uphold the institution of clerical marriage."

Henry shrugged, saying, "I care not what men of the cloth do beneath the covers, I care more from what cloth they are made. You may keep your concubines."

Teodorico made a face and tsked.

"'Concubine' is such an unpleasant word. I merely suggest men of the cloth are granted access to the worldly pleasures all men deserve. After all," the cardinal said and gestured with his chin at the red wall, "even Peter had a mother-in-law, proving holy men could and should marry."

A pause followed, and the chanting above came to a halt, filling the chamber with silence.

"We are in agreement then?" Henry stated at last.

The cardinal inclined his head.

"As overseer of overseers, I imagine it should be a simple matter for you to obtain this cup?" Henry asked.

Teodorico pursed his lips, replying, "Though I may be the shepherd, the sheep are numerous and have a tendency to stray, hmm? It won't be a simple matter, but I assure you the cup will be mine soon enough, especially if I have certain resources at my disposal, hmm, yes?"

Henry resisted rolling his eyes. Of all things to happen this night, it was the most expected of things, but still the one that galled him the most. "I trust that a large donation to the Church, in your keeping of course, will suffice to secure these resources—and the cup?"

"Absolutely, your highness," Teodorico purred.

Just then Victor, who had slipped out unnoticed earlier, returned and made a sign to the cardinal.

"Ah, the timing is divine," the cardinal said. "It would appear all preparations for my coronation are in place. Now, if you will all allow me a final moment with Saint Peter, I will join you above soon."

The robed crowd began to shuffle about and ascend the staircase.

One figure approached the cardinal, removing her hood to reveal a stunningly beautiful woman. Henry blinked. She stood almost as tall as the cardinal, with long dark hair that glinted auburn in the candlelight. Her skin glowed with an olive tone, and her sharp features accompanied a regal nose—all indicating some indistinct Mediterranean heritage. Her thin eyebrows, almost appearing painted on her, delicately arched over her wide brow. Her eyes glittered clear and amber in the darkness.

Judging from her body language and the proximity to which she stood next to Teodorico, she held a special place with the cardinal.

"Why, Your Eminence," Henry said, taking a step forward to join the couple. "Your lady is quite lovely."

The young king kissed the woman's hand as she offered it up in greeting. As she curtsied, Henry couldn't help but notice the hand looked like that of someone much older. He would have guessed her to be in her late twenties, maybe early thirties at most, but the hand curled almost crone-like. Maybe the poor lighting in the chamber only gave that impression, because a closer examination showed the skin on the hand and forearm to be smooth and strong. Her long fingers ended in sharp, well-groomed nails.

"Yes, hmm?" Teodorico beamed with pride. "Your Highness, may I present to you the Lady Lilliana Vergoza de Aragon."

"Pleased to meet you, Your Highness," the Lady Lilliana said. Her voice was deep, but smooth like warm molasses. Her accent intrigued, proving just as indistinct as her heritage. She boldly made eye contact which made the young man feel like the center of the universe, but also gave him the impression she looked right through him with those luminous eyes.

"The pleasure is all mine," Henry replied. "I would count myself the luckiest man in the basilica if you were to be seated next to me during the ceremony—with your permission of course, Cardinal?"

"What better escort, hmm?" Teodorico agreed. "But allow me a private moment, first, hmm, yes?"

"I'll await you above." Henry smiled and turned to leave with his entourage. He turned back with an afterthought. "Cardinal, out of curiosity, what name have you chosen to use under the papal mantle?"

"Theodoric," the cardinal responded.

Henry smiled and said, "How very German."

"I thought you might be pleased, Your Highness," Teodorico replied with his congenial smile.

Henry grunted something in agreement, turned on his heel, and left up the staircase in a flutter of cloaks.

#

After he had left and the cardinal and Lilliana stood alone, Teodorico turned to the beautiful woman.

"That could not have gone better, hmm?" he said. "He is much more clever than I thought. Until this evening I was certain his advisors were writing his letters, hmm, yes?"

Lilliana turned to the older man and stroked his face. The candles began to burn low in the now-quiet chamber.

"Yes, very clever young man," she responded, "but not clever enough to learn that the tip of the spear had been found recently in Antioch—though is mysteriously lost again."

Teodorico took her hand and kissed the inside of her wrist. "Yes, shame that, hmm?"

"All is going according to plan." Her voice flowed as dark as their surroundings. She cradled his face and peered long into his eyes. "Gain the cup, and all will be yours."

"Yes, my love," he replied without a stutter.

They kissed, long and passionately. Her eyes flickered open and in the fading light they flared with a light of their own. She blinked, and her pupils turned into feline slits.

Chapter Two

Patrick paused in his unpacking when Aimeé shot up with knife in hand and gazed out into the darkness. She froze, listening intently.

"What is it?" Patrick whispered, also freezing where he stood.

"I thought I heard something." Her hand tightened around the knife handle.

Patrick squinted into the forest. He dropped the bedroll he had been unraveling, placed a hand on his sword hilt, and walked a short distance away from their campsite. With his back to the fire and his eyes adjusting to the darkness, he looked about. He took another step and a flurry of birds erupted from the brush, disappearing into the night.

Exhaling loudly, Patrick slammed his partially drawn sword back into its scabbard.

Aimeé giggled. "Not exactly goblins or bandits, now were they?"

Patrick smiled wryly and returned to spreading out their bedrolls.

"No," he agreed, "which is fortunate. My country is not exempt from those who would take a shortcut to wealth by taking it from us."

"I wouldn't have guessed it. Your people have been lovely so far," Aimeé said, returning to her work at the fire. She sliced at links of sausage with the knife in one hand and a large double-pronged fork in her other. "Especially at Ga—? Gail—?"

"Gaillimh," Patrick said the word with a roll of his tongue, then translated, "Galway."

"Gal-way." Aimeé tried the word out with a tongue habituated only to French. She frowned. "Isn't that where you are from? Why are we still traveling? I thought for sure when our boat landed there I could say goodbye to my seasickness."

"All the land hereabouts is actually considered Galway," Patrick replied, sweeping an arm across the darkness. "It is a county in the Kingdom of Connacht in Eire. That village at the river mouth was only a trading post, though I can't believe how much it's grown since I was last here, with a fortress being built and all."

"I would have thought that was your home, the way you jumped from the boat and buried your face in the sand."

Patrick laughed as he smoothed out the last of the blankets and propped up his saddlebags as pillows. "Aye, it was close enough to thank God. I promised Him if I survived the Crusade, and I ever saw home again, I'd pray the minute I touched Irish soil."

"I must admit I rather liked your display of a little emotion," Aimeé said, smiling as she threw the sausage into the frying pan. She started cutting the onions as the links sizzled. "So where exactly is your home, then, Patrick?"

"Over yonder." He pointed down the road next to which they camped. They had been traveling on it for the better part of the last day. "In the middle of nowhere, north of the Slieve Aughty Mountains, west of the River Shannon, and south of Loch Riach."

Aimeé made a face. "Oui, that all makes sense to me."

Patrick chuckled and clarified. "We are close. About another day's travel."

"Will you be just as emotional when we arrive at your village proper?" she asked, throwing the onions into the pan. "I'd like that. You are quite handsome when you smile."

Patrick scoffed, waving off the compliment. "Don't get used to it. Just because I now have reason to be happy—having finally been accepted as full Avangarde, regaled as a hero, given leave to visit family, and bagged the prettiest lass on all Avalon—I'm not prepared to give up my title as 'Sir Silence.' I have a reputation to keep."

"'Bagged!'" Aimeé cried, eyes flaring. She wagged the fork at him. "Look here, Sir Knight, no one 'bagged' me. I might be a commoner, but I am a free-person of Aesclinn with no need of taking up the company of pompous arses. My place in the world is quite secure with or without you, so do not make me sound as if I were a prize duck won at a festival."

Patrick struggled to keep a straight face. "Your point?"

"Watch your mouth, Sir Silence, or else!" A smile threatened to crack her facade of anger.

A warmth loosened his chest. "Or what?" Patrick crossed his arms, also struggling to hide a smile.

What she said about his past quiet behavior rang true, but being with her, even during banter such as this, he felt joy. It opened his eyes to the little details he may have otherwise overlooked. It came easily to admire the curve of her smile, and certainly all her other curves, but now he noticed little gems such as the mischievous glint in her eyes, or her tendency to crinkle her nose at him.

Aimeé stabbed a piece of sausage from the pan, held it up, and expertly sliced it in half with a slash of the knife. "Or else they'll be calling you Sir Lacking."

"Oh no you don't!" Patrick rushed forward and swept her into the air. The dam holding in his happiness broke, spilling out as laughter.

Giggling, she mock-struggled only for a moment before giving into a rain of kisses. Then she looked into his eyes and stroked the side of his face.

"I mean it. You really are a different person when you smile," she said. "From the moment you touched the shore and met your countrymen, you were far from being 'Sir Silence.' Speaking your own language for the first time in years was like watching a crippled man walk for the first time."

"There is some truth to that," Patrick agreed, reaching up and pressing her hand to his face. He kissed her wrist. "I felt free, like I could fly. Normally I have a difficult time with the Irish tradition of storytelling about the bonfire, but not that first night back when they demanded stories of my adventures."

"Yes!" Aimeé's eyes widened with her smile. "I've never seen you so animated. Though I didn't understand the language, I could tell you're quite the storyteller!" Her smile diminished some. "Despite not knowing the language, I still noticed you didn't mention Avalon, Greensprings, or Loki. Why is that?"

He set her down gently and crouched next to the fire, turning the links. "Plenty of people would believe me fighting for God on crusade, but few would believe I was on the fabled Isle of Avalon fighting gods," Patrick explained, "and I am under strict orders to keep Greensprings and the school secret. My adventures there, too."

Aimeé ran her hands along the surcoat on his chest, tracing the outline of the gold dragon on a field of green. He'd had to take off his Avangarde one before departing Avalon.

"Aye," Patrick said, recapturing her hands and holding them against the dragon, "we must maintain the ruse, even with my family, that I am a knight employed on an English estate. I have plenty of tales of my journeys to the Holy Land to keep all entertained."

From the darkness, a horse's whinny caught Patrick's attention.

"Speaking of being entertained, Siegfried doesn't seem too pleased to be tied up alone," he said. "I'll pay him a visit after dinner."

"Are you well with that?" Aimeé asked, drawing Patrick's attention back. Concern crept into her voice. "Talking about the Crusade, I mean? You—always hesitate."

He looked down into her sweet face framed by a wild mane of honey colored hair, gazed into her green eyes, and put on a brave smile. He winced, however, as he felt a spasm of twitches above his right eye. His fingers moved from Aimeé's and began a familiar rubbing about his temple as the sounds of clashing steel and people's cries echoed in his mind.

"I had demons," he said, "but they are gone now. I told you once about the specter that followed me? The thing I called the Apparition? When exposed it was merely my own face. Well, this Other me is gone now. I haven't seen it for some time. If that is not proof my demons are gone, I don't know what is."

"Then why do you still cry out in your sleep?"

"I thought I slept rather well," Patrick said, genuine surprise in his voice.

"No, you don't," she pointed out, and took his hand. "You kick and flail, you call out names... You almost attacked me once."

Patrick's mouth dropped. "I— I'm so sorry. You're the last person in the world I want to hurt."

Aimeé kissed his fingers. "I know. I only blame what's inside you."

This didn't comfort Patrick and his mirth evaporated. Siegfried whinnied again from the dark.

"I call out names?" he said.

"Oui," she replied, "Philip. Paulette. Who are they?"

Patrick felt the twitching above his eye again, but refused to acknowledge it. "I couldn't say. Philip was a common name. You couldn't pick up a rock and throw it in any direction and not hit someone named Philip." He allowed humor back into his voice. "And don't get me started on Henrys and Roberts. It was extremely confusing."

Aimeé latched onto the humor in his voice and asked in mock agitation, "And Paulette?"

"That I have no idea," he replied in all seriousness, shrugging. "There weren't many women around, let alone any of that name."

Aimeé assessed his veracity with a probing stare. "Very well, Sir Knight, you shall get off easy this time," she said, a smile cracking her withering gaze, "but there shall be no Paulette coming between us."

Patrick kissed her just as Siegfried called for attention yet again.

"However a certain horse just might," Patrick said. "I best go visit him."

Aimeé giggled and turned to retrieve something from her cooking bag. "Here, take a carrot. He likes those."

When she bent low, her head passed through the vapors of their cooking meal and she stood suddenly and took a shuddering step from the fire.

Patrick came to her side as she became violently ill, vomiting into the grass.

"Aimeé, are you well?" he asked as he rubbed the back of her cloak, bending over to look into her face.

Aimeé stood, wiped her mouth, and exhaled loudly. "Still seasick, I think. I just can't seem to shake it. If I ever see a boat again, it will be too soon."

"It's been days since we left the ocean."

"Something I ate then," she replied and moved back to the frying pan, dismissing the matter.

"Perhaps I should cook from now on then," Patrick suggested, laughing.

Aimeé's eyes flared as she flung the carrot at him. "Go attend to Siegfried or that carrot will be all you eat on this trip."

Patrick caught the vegetable and laughed as he turned toward Siegfried. He hadn't gone more than a few steps when he heard Aimeé making a muffling sound.

Thinking sickness had overcome her again; he turned back— and saw his world turned upside down. The bottom fell out of his stomach.

A man in soiled clothes covered Aimeé's mouth with one grimy hand while holding a rusty knife blade to her throat with the other. Two more men stepped out of the shadows, also dressed in rags and holding equally weathered weapons.

Patrick fixated on the blade scraping against Aimeé's white throat. He froze as he never had before. His breath caught in his chest, yet his heart quickened to maddening speed.

"Drop yer sword belt," one of the assailants said with a mouth mostly missing teeth. He waved his warped sword at Patrick. "If you do, your lass there just might come out of this alive."

With his sword still sheathed and a useless carrot clutched in his sweaty grip, helplessness and rage warred inside him as he realized he could not save her.

Aimeé, however, did not wait to be saved. Her arm rose from underneath her cloak to reveal the cooking fork gripped in her fist. It came down and sank solidly into her attacker's leg, causing the man to scream in pain. His grip faltered, and she slashed at him with the cooking knife in her other hand.

Patrick made his move. The carrot made an effective weapon after all as he threw it with force at the nearest attacker's face, distracting the man long enough to reclaim his own sword.

In three successive moves he slashed the third attacker, spun, and ran carrot-face through with his blade. Withdrawing his weapon, Patrick ran to Aimeé just in time to see her assailant roll off her body.

"Aimeé!" he cried.

She sat up and kicked away from the limp form. The man's glazed eyes stared skyward. A gaping wound in his throat pulsed blood.

Hands shaking, Patrick helped Aimeé up and brought her into the firelight. There, panic washed over him anew.

Blood covered her from head to foot.

A pain like a hot poker shoved into his temple, driving him to his knees. He dropped his sword and gripped his head as he stared at her. His vision swam and the image of a blood-covered blond woman seared across his eyes—was it Aimeé? This woman's deep blue eyes stared sightlessly.

"Patrick!" Aimeé cried, reaching for him. "It's not my blood. It came from him!"

"Get away!" Patrick screamed, scooting away.

Confused, Aimeé stopped her advance and stared.

"Patrick, what is wrong?"

Patrick stared for a few more heartbeats, then shook his head as if clearing water from his eyes. He looked around. His swimming vision coalesced: a campfire, three dead bodies, Aimeé covered in blood, her green eyes imploring for an explanation.

"I-I'm sorry," he said at last, coming forward and gathering her into his arms. "I just don't know what I'd do if I lost you. Again."

#

The following morning Aimeé regarded Patrick from her pony as they traveled the road, leading her to an uncertain destination. Not just a new town, but a new future. Siegfried, Patrick's giant black warhorse, must have felt more conversational than he did, periodically nudging her cheek with his snout.

It would seem Sir Silence had returned, if only for the moment.

"Go on, say it," Patrick said, as if feeling the weight of her gaze.

"Say what?" she asked.

"I let bandits creep up on us unnoticed, and more, I froze when they attacked," he replied. "You almost died because of me."

Aimeé touched his leg. She admired his long dark hair moving in the breeze. His high cheekbones moved as he ground his teeth.

"You did nothing wrong. You're my hero. If you recall correctly, it was I who was distracting you," she soothed. "That is not what troubles me, though."

"What is it then?"

"How you behaved when it was over."

"I cannot explain that," Patrick replied quickly, rubbing his temple. "I guess seeing you covered in blood like that startled me beyond measure. I... You..."

He seemed to choke on his words and his throat bobbed furiously. He took her hand on his leg and squeezed it.

She squeezed it back. Under the best of circumstances, his reserved nature made it difficult to guess his feelings. When he had invited her on this journey to his homeland, to allow her behind the veil of the mystery shrouding him, he had made no promises. Made no declarations of love. Aimeé accepted that, content to wait until he felt ready. After last night's attack, however, that possibility now looked distant. For similar reasons, she put off asking what they intended to tell his family about their relationship. She clutched her pony's reins a little too hard, telling herself it would all work out.

"You really did marvelously," she said, choosing to focus on something positive. "I've never seen you in true battle. Very impressive. A true knight." She shook his hand for emphasis, leaning forward in the saddle to look him in the face to make her point.

Patrick beamed an exaggerated smile at her. At least he was trying. "You did well too. Very brave," he said. "You probably could have handled all three by yourself."

"Undoubtedly," she sniffed with as much humor as she could muster, shaking her lingering anxiety from the ordeal. "It's the least I could do after you suggested you do all the cooking."

Patrick snorted a genuine laugh.

"Your secret is safe with me," she added. "Your fellow knights needn't know you were rescued by a maidservant. You will still become Captain of the Avangarde before long."

"Captain of the Guard? I don't know about that," Patrick responded, a scowl developing across his brow despite his smile. "I was almost cast out for my disagreeable nature, remember? I feel lucky just to be allowed into the Order, so I'm not about to rush things. Besides, I don't think I'd care for the burden of leadership. Being willing to die as a soldier is one thing—but commanding others to their death is quite another."

"Well, I think you'd make a fine leader," she insisted.

"A fine leader wouldn't have let a kindly old priest bully him into going against his better judgment," Patrick countered.

"You mean the cup? I'm sure it will be perfectly safe in the church, and many people's faith will be strengthened because of it, just as Father Hugh hopes. What harm can come of it?"

Patrick sucked in air. "That's what I'm afraid of. I promised the guardians of the cave I'd return it."

"But you didn't say when," Aimeé reasoned.

"A nuance I'm sure will not go unnoticed by the guardians." Patrick's grip on Aimeé's hand tightened. "Which means what exactly? I don't know. My guts tie into knots the more I think about it. I should have returned the cup right away. I shouldn't have listened to Father Hugh, but his plea to let the people adore it as a miraculous object of God was convincing."

"You worry too much," Aimeé said, and kissed his hand. "It will be fine. As soon as we return, you can fulfill your promise."

They rode with only the sound of plodding hooves to pace the time. They passed among rolling dales and oak groves suffused by sunlight. The light rendered every possible shade of green, almost matching the surreal brilliance of Avalon.

The road crested a dale and they entered into a circle of monolithic stones, the sort that also populated the Isle of Avalon. Or perhaps, Aimeé thought, Eire had the same mysterious stones as Avalon. Which came first? Where did they originate? Who erected them?

She posed these questions to Patrick as he dismounted to pray before a stone cross that dominated the center of the ring.

"I'm not sure," he replied as he knelt and crossed himself before the elaborately carved Celtic monument. "They say they've been here before time, even before my people. Legend says it was the Fair Folk who raised them with magic, or grew them from the earth like trees. Other say they are giants turned to stone by magicians."

Aimeé bit back her next question while Patrick fulfilled his crusade promise to pray before every holy shrine between the coast and his home. She noted that once this place must have been a true ring; the long stones littering the ground had rested atop the standing stones. She also noted their voices echoed inside the circle.

"Then why is there a Christian cross here?" she asked when he finished and mounted Siegfried.

"They say Saint Patrick came here and upturned the sacrificial stone and with just the power of his voice in prayer, carved the stone into a cross with its images," he replied.

"What do you think?"

"I think after all I've seen on Avalon I can believe anything now."

They moved beyond the stone giants, and Patrick sighed and stated it wouldn't be much longer. "We've been very fortunate," he added, laughing away the last of the previous night's trouble. "The weather has been very agreeable. You're going to be left with the misconception it's always sunny here."

Aimeé breathed in the summer air and fluffed her cloak, thankful for the warmth of the day drying the last of the dampness from the garment. The blood had washed out readily in a stream that morning. If only the memory would clean away as easily.

In another hour Patrick stiffened in the saddle and looked intently ahead. A village came into view. A handful of buildings surrounded a church adjoining a square with a central well. To one side, a low stone wall enclosed a spacious area. The buildings were of the same gray stone and roofed in thatch. Green grass sprouted from them, and oddly, a goat stood atop one of the buildings, grazing.

Aimeé loved it immediately.

Patrick drew in a nervous breath and grabbed her hand. "Almost there," he said.

"What is it called?" she asked.

Patrick shrugged. "Nothing really, just the Gathering Place. Few people truly live here. It is merely the place we gather to shear the sheep, attend Mass, and celebrate."

"Where do you live, then?"

Patrick gestured with his chin. "Another hour down the road."

Patrick led them into the square near the church. Though the largest building in the village, it comprised little more than a stone-fenced corral, clay-packed wattle walls, and a thatched roof. Its stone facade was decorated with some modest carvings and a pair of stout oak doors.

After dismounting and transferring his shield from his back to his saddle, Patrick helped Aimeé off her pony.

By now people came out of the buildings and children quickly surrounded them to gawk at the knight, his giant warhorse, and his lady. Many of them approached the French girl and tittered questions at her, pulling on her dress.

She looked down at their little dirty and smiling faces and said, "I'm sorry, I don't understand."

"They're asking if you're a princess," Patrick said, securing their mounts to a hitching post.

She laughed. "What will you tell them?"

Patrick smiled at them and said something that seemed to leave them confused, but they flittered excitedly around her just the same.

"I told them you're *my* princess," he said.

Aimeé glowed.

"Patrick?" a man's voice came.

Through the crowd an elderly man in a brown robe approached. With big eyes he took in the sight of the tall knight.

Patrick, just as excited, embraced the man and exclaimed, "Athair Caraig!"

They exchanged many words, but before long Patrick pointed to Aimeé.

The man—the parish priest, Father Peter—greeted her with kind words she did not understand. While doing so, however, his attention suddenly returned to Patrick and he exclaimed something, putting his hands to his face as if just remembering something. He looked between Patrick and the church, speaking excitedly.

Patrick's brow furrowed and he grunted a question as if looking for confirmation.

Father Peter nodded and pointed to the church and again said something sending Patrick into an excited frenzy.

Patrick raced for the church doors and Aimeé followed with an excited crowd.

He flung the doors open and entered with his cloak flapping wildly behind him.

Despite the bright midday sun, darkness reigned inside with only some candles to give context to the simple chamber. A lone figure knelt before the altar in prayer.

Her head was bowed beneath a veil, but at the sound of the doors, she lifted her head in their direction and shielded her eyes against the onslaught of daylight. Patrick paused, his shadow falling across her.

"Máthair," he said.

The woman rose, eyes growing big with disbelief.

"Patrick?" her voice came out a whisper, then she squealed with delight as she ran forward.

They met halfway and embraced so strongly Aimeé thought Patrick might crush the petite woman. He let her go long enough to bend down and raise her skyward by the hips and twirl her about, shouting with joy. The woman cried out in surprise at the move.

For the briefest of moments Aimeé felt an irrational twinge of jealousy at the display, but it faded as her eyes adjusted to the darkness.

The slender woman's veil fell away like a leaf floating on the wind, exposing long dark hair with a streak of silver down one side. Crows feet lined her eyes, and many years of tedious work had gnarled her wrists and hands.

At last Patrick put her down and a flurry of words passed between them. Her eyes sparkled and she refused to let entirely go, clinging to him.

Eventually Patrick led her back toward the entrance and brought her into the sunlight before Aimeé and the curious crowd.

As he introduced Aimeé to her by name, Aimeé had a better look at her. She was shorter even than herself, and petite, but strong in a sinewy way. Aside from the silver streak, she had the same raven-black hair as Patrick. Her eyes, an extreme version of Patrick's sitting in a beautiful porcelain face of sharp features, struck Aimeé the most. Whereas Patrick's had gold flecks floating about the pupils in a sea of hazel, hers had a distinct gold halo surrounded by stark green, almost unsettling in their alien beauty.

"Aim-ai..." the woman sounded the name out slowly, trying out the syllables. She smiled and looked Aimeé up and down in a fashion only one person in a man's life possibly could.

"Aimeé, my mother, Talisia," Patrick said, almost nervously.

Patrick's nervousness became contagious. Aimeé drew in a breath and her stomach turned into knots when she greeted the woman, "Bonjour."

Talisia embraced her and responded with soft words Aimeé did not understand. She also stroked her face, looking into her eyes, and oddly, touched her stomach.

Shortly thereafter, the crowd of people pushing to gather around Patrick separated them and Aimeé bided her time with the curious children. While doing so she saw Patrick for the first time in his element, among his people. He had friends, family, and no language barrier. She knew when this moment came she would be put aside, if only temporarily. Still, now that the moment had come, she felt alone and wondered if this is how he had felt this past year at Greensprings. What a lonely man he must have been.

She sighed and patiently waited until Patrick said his goodbyes and made his promises to the villagers of returning later. With that, he climbed into Siegfried's saddle and surprised his mother by bending down and lifting her into the saddle in front of him.

Aimeé climbed into her pony's saddle, and to the sound of Talisia's joyful laughter, they left a crowd of waving villagers behind.

#

Patrick's home was part manor house, part castle, part long hall, and part farm. It sat between green pasture lands dotted with sheep and fields of golden wheat.

A Celtic cross topped the apex of the manor's stone facade. Thatch, suspended by stout beams of oak, sheltered the buildings. Many windows offered light and air, but thick wooden shutters and iron-banded doors provided defense.

Smaller encircling buildings, made of the same local stone and thatch, created a common ground where many chickens, geese, pigs, and goats roamed.

Several children in wool tunics paused in their tossing grain to the animals to watch wide-eyed the approaching knight with Talisia held captive in his saddle.

Half ran to meet the approaching group; the other half ran inside shouting.

Once arrived, Patrick quickly led them inside. Fresh rushes covered the floor of packed earth, the furniture simple but sturdy wood, a few tapestries hung from the walls with a large wolf pelt, and little else. A plethora of candles and the red glow of embers from a sizable fireplace provided illumination in the rooms, which had a cave-like air despite the sunny day.

People came from every room, their excitement matching that of the children. They all but mobbed Patrick and much talking ensued as Aimeé again hung back, patiently watching the reunion.

Two girls, both around seven years of age, approached and looked up at her with grimy but smiling faces. Their hair would have been a fiery strawberry blonde if not for all the moss and twigs knotted in them. Despite their disheveled appearance, Aimeé never saw two happier children.

They grabbed Aimeé by the hands and intoned questions at her.

She beamed at them. "I'm sorry, I don't understand you."

Their eyes widened and they suddenly ran to one of the women surrounding Patrick.

"Maman! Maman!" they shouted in French, while pointing to Aimeé.

With a curious look in her face the woman came to Aimeé, dragged by the girls. She shared the same fiery red-gold hair as the children, though immaculately kept. It hung about her head like a curly nimbus of dawn.

"Française?" she asked.

Aimeé nodded, delighted, "Oui! Vous êtes aussi?"

"Non," the woman responded, continuing the conversation in the language Aimeé understood. "I am Breton, from Brittany. My name is Beatrix, and you? I'm sure Patrick would have introduced you, but obviously he has his hands full."

Aimeé understood Patrick's preoccupation, but was happy to have someone to talk to. She examined Beatrix, a full-figured woman whose bright hair and freckles looked very much out of place among the dark and willowy Gawain family. Her accent, though similar to Patrick's when he spoke French, had a different flavor to it. Everything about her made Aimeé curious.

"I am Aimeé de la Chasse," she responded.

Beatrix appraised her, not sure what to make of her.

"I'm afraid I am as common as grass and sunlight." Aimeé answered the unspoken question, removing as much awkwardness as possible.

Patrick strode over and embraced her with a single arm and turned her to the assembled crowd. He spoke her name and talked for a bit, which brought the briefest of pauses, but quickly gave way to excited chatter. They surrounded her and greeted her with many hugs.

Talisia broke through the crowd, took Patrick by the hand, and led him down a hall. A hush fell over the crowd and a procession followed after them, sweeping Aimeé along.

Talisia paused at a door, said some quiet words to Patrick, then bid him to enter.

As the door swung open, Patrick approached a bed where a man lay asleep in the dark room. A candle on a nightstand illuminated the scene just enough for the silent spectators in the hall to watch. Patrick gently nudged the man to wakefulness.

At first he did not respond, even when looking Patrick full in the face, but then struggled to sit up in shock. Though very sickly and not well, Patrick vainly tried to hold the man down, but they eventually settled into a tight, rocking embrace.

"Daidí, Daidí," Patrick wept.

The man wailed, repeating, "Mo buachaill!"

A loud commotion came from the front of the house, and a man's loud voice called out in a questioning tone. Beatrix responded, and Aimeé followed her, not wishing to be alone while Patrick remained occupied.

As they entered the main living area a very large man stood with hands on belted hips. Though not dressed in knightly garb, the sword at his hip and the steel vambraces on his wrists left no doubt his status as a warrior. He had Patrick's eyes, which glittered in the dark, and Patrick's cheekbones protruded from a well-groomed beard. A shorter, darker man with similar facial features, but with a wild beard, accompanied him.

The giant newcomer spoke with some consternation, but stopped suddenly when he laid eyes on Aimeé. Confused, or curious, he grunted a question and Aimeé didn't need to speak the language to understand what he asked.

Beatrix put a protective arm around her and said her name, followed by some words and the name Patrick.

The man blinked. "Patrick?"

As if his name conjured him, Patrick entered the room and the two men faced off for a tense moment.

Finally, they embraced fiercely like men who hadn't seen one another for a long time, pounding each other's backs.

#

The next few weeks flew by, but their first evening, spent mostly at the dinner table, was long and memorable. Though the Gawain family owned land as nobility, they were humble. They had plenty of sharecroppers and servants to herd the sheep, but no servants within the household, and therefore dinner fell to the women. They excluded Aimeé from duties that first evening, but following evenings she happily helped out, glad to avoid the awkwardness of being waited upon. The women treated the kitchen as their personal kingdom, banishing men from it.

The first several dinners, over trenchers of soda bread filled with lamb stew and sausages and boiled greens on tarnished-but-ornate plates, Aimeé came to know the family. Beatrix acted as a great resource, filling in tidbits of information about the family members.

At the head of the table, helped to his seat from his sickbed by his wife and sons, the elder Gawain presided over his family. Aimeé was very surprised the kindly Shannon Gawain was a smallish man, not at all tall like Patrick and certainly no giant like his eldest son, Sian. She imagined in younger and healthier days he was tough and wiry in a manner like his second son, Domhnull. Domhnull was surprising to Aimeé in that he was dark complected with blazing blue eyes. He did, however, have the raven hair and high cheekbones common to the family that must have come from Talisia. Shannon's eyes were gray as stone.

Beatrix's redheaded girls, the chatty Mayana and Maria, could almost pass for twins. So too could Patrick's dark-haired elder sisters, Dierdre and Catha, who could also pass for younger sisters of their mother. They had Talisia's fair complexion, sharp features, and fiercely noble faces, but they were taller and stronger. Catha had almost-black eyes promising trouble if you trifled with her. Beatrix later explained Catha was aptly named after Badb Catha, the Irish goddess of battle. Literally, her name meant "Battle Crow," which also matched her glossy hair.

At the far end of the table sat the youngest Gawains. Domhnull, who didn't seem to adhere to any rules, sat wherever he pleased and lately he sat with nine-year-old Conor, making him laugh by howling like a wolf and generally carrying on like a child himself. His antics drew scornful looks from Sian, but that only encouraged him.

Aimeé found the family conversations boisterous, including frequent heated discussions. Talisia kept things from truly getting out of hand, but her brood still managed to throw food at one another.

Naturally Patrick and his news received most of the attention those first few nights. As he had mentioned earlier, they had to amend their story. The story he told was largely true, but with enough alterations to maintain the secrecy of Avalon and Greensprings. Patrick told his family they both served in a castle in the land of the Angles where Patrick battled and defeated a nobleman who had been trying to usurp the authority of the castle and lands. Having proven himself in battle, Patrick petitioned the lord of the castle for leave from his duties to visit his family.

Patrick told how he had thrashed a fellow knight who had assaulted Aimeé. When he did, she waited for him to elaborate on their relationship, but either he did not elaborate or she lost it in translation.

When that happened, the hint of a shadow crept into her soul. Little things that had troubled her grew larger in her mind. Was he more distant since his odd behavior after the bandit attack? Was he a little too quick to agree to his pious mother's insistence they sleep apart in the household? Yes, ever since his last adventures in Avalon, Patrick himself had become more pious. He prayed regularly and lived the life of a true Christian knight, which meant he limited how he expressed his physical affections for her, but recently even his kisses and touches felt faraway.

You're just being silly, she told herself. *After all, did he not bring me to his homeland to meet his family? What more should I expect from someone whose strength is not speaking his heart's desires?*

Even as she told herself this, her stomach turned, but she did her best to attribute it to the new food and the lingering seasickness. Even so, one evening she ran behind the manor to the privy and became violently ill.

When she had finished and turned to leave, she came face to face with Talisia, who watched her with concern.

Talisia touched her brow with the back of her hand, and did that odd thing where she touched her stomach. Upon doing so, Talisia's luminous eyes flared slightly in the dark. She led Aimeé back to the kitchen and prepared her a soothing tea. Beatrix entered and she and Talisia spoke some.

"She was concerned you had the sickness," Beatrix explained after Talisia left the room. "A year ago, a terrible illness swept through the land and made many a widow and orphan. Shannon is still recovering from it."

Aimeé gasped. "Do I have it?"

"No, you are not sick," Beatrix replied, but would not elaborate and bid her goodnight.

Days later, she and Beatrix sat on a hill having a blanket lunch while watching the men shear sheep. Even though a long-lost son, Patrick did not escape family duties. He, Sian, Domhnull, and even little Conor worked shirtless in the hot sun with the shepherds.

"So our Patrick is a true knight now," Beatrix mused out loud. "We had our doubts."

This surprised Aimeé, who asked, "Why is that?"

Beatrix shrugged. "There are no lack of warriors about, but to go through all the training to be dubbed a knight, the expense of it all, plus to find someone who is willing to squire you in this area—

it is very difficult. But Patrick was determined to make it happen. He proved us all wrong."

"If few people do it in these parts, what drove him?" Aimeé asked.

"Patrick is the third son and not likely to inherit much," Beatrix explained. "Patrick's options, like all younger sons, were limited. He chose to become a knight, to have a skilled profession, and find his own way in the world. His Uncle James, Shannon's brother, is a knight and squired him as a lad. After many hard years, he finished his training and service and was dubbed a knight. It was the happiest day of his life, until..."

Her voice trailed off and she picked at the grass, avoiding eye contact with the French girl. Aimeé waited patiently for her to pick up with the story.

"Until his love put him aside. Patrick was convinced once he proved himself a knight, the girl of his dreams would agree to marry him. She agreed at first, but then said she wanted to devote her life to God, to become a nun and enter convent. Brokenhearted, Patrick respected her wishes."

"Then she changed her mind and married another," Aimeé finished, familiar with the basics of the story.

"Aye," Beatrix nodded. "Not long after that, a missionary came to town, ringing a bell and proclaiming the pope in Rome had declared a Crusade to oust the heathens from Jerusalem. Patrick wasted no time heeding the call. We thought we would never see him again, but there he is, alive and whole."

"His body is whole," Aimeé said after a long pause, "but his heart is still troubled. He... won't talk about it. He has nightmares."

"And it eats him from the inside out," Beatrix added, nodding. "He was always that way. Too strong for his own good. Sian is the same way, but tries to bluster his way through things whereas Patrick merely endures in silence."

"Why do we put up with such things?" Aimeé asked, a quiet frustration in her voice.

Beatrix rubbed her shoulder. "Because we love them."

Aimeé took her hand and squeezed it, thankful for her presence.

Beatrix squeezed her hand back. "Be of good cheer. He is out of harm's way, has patronage and protection in an English lord's castle, and is a knight and a hero who rescues maidens."

Despite her words of encouragement, Aimeé still felt a shadow upon her soul.

"Beatrix, you know as well as I that I am a maidservant, and no maiden," Aimeé said. "The story he told—about the knight insulting me—it was worse than that. Though it was incredibly pleasing to know he thrashed my assailant in the keep courtyard in front of God and everyone, it happened... after the fact."

Beatrix gave her a knowing nod, and her face was sad. "No matter, he must care for you very much to have done that, and to bring you all this way."

Yes, but was it out of guilt? Aimeé thought, tendrils of doubt spreading in her gut, then added out loud, "Just the same, I wish he would tell me so."

"Sian is the same way. They are very much alike, those two, though they don't always want to admit it. They are men of action. They do, they don't just talk about it, and Patrick is more reserved than most. He cares for you, I can tell."

But how much? The tendrils spread.

Aimeé shook herself, put on a smile, and decided to change the subject to lighten the mood. "And Sian, how did you meet?"

Beatrix smiled broadly.

"Well, he did no heroics, after the fact or otherwise," Beatrix explained, "but he did show up larger than life. He was loud and boisterous and made me laugh. That is all I needed to be swept off my feet. My father is a Breton merchant. From Brittany, to Cornwall, to Limerick, to Galway he traded timber and wine for wool and metals. The Gawain family is one of what they call the 'Tribes of Galway,' the merchants' guild operating out of the trading post on the coast, at the mouth of the River Corrib."

Aimeé remembered the first village at which they arrived when first coming to the shores of Eire.

"It was his turn to negotiate with the ship captains. I was with my father on my first trip. Sian fell in love instantly. Me, not so much. But he persisted, serenading me from the shore every night until I gave in, came off the ship, and went walking with him.... chaperoned, of course."

"Sian? Singing romantically?" Aimeé said, trying hard to picture the big man doing such a thing.

Beatrix nodded vigorously. "He's actually quite good."

Just then, Mayana and Maria who had been playing nearby came running over and exclaimed, "Look, maman! A rainbow! Can we go look for the pot of gold?"

Beatrix's brow furrowed. "Absolutely not. Never go chasing rainbows, you hear me? The Fairy Folk put their treasure at the end of rainbows for a reason... so you'll foolishly chase after it and be led astray. You can never catch a rainbow. The harder you try, the further you get from home, and the next thing you know you're lost and at the mercy of the Fairy Folk who'll exact a dear price from you. Instead of finding treasure, you'll find you're giving up your own as a ransom."

As a shiver came over Aimeé as she contemplated the idea of chasing beautiful yet unattainable things, Beatrix pulled her children down to the blanket and hugged them to her bosom.

"Not all Fairy Folk are bad," Mayana said as she turned over to lay her head on her mother's lap.

Maria did likewise. "Uncle Donnie is a gruagach, and he is not bad. We like him. He plays with us."

Beatrix snorted a laugh. "Who told you such a thing?"

"Daddy," the girls said as if it were the most obvious of answers.

"Gru-gie?" Aimeé asked, trying her best to pronounce the word correctly.

Beatrix laughed. "A gruagach is a kind of fairy who does manual labor and other basic things; they are not of the royal caste. They're more like a goblin of sorts. Leave it to my husband to tell his children their Uncle Domhnull is a goblin."

"Daddy also says he's a changeling," Maria added.

"Oh, for heaven's sake." Beatrix shook her head in exasperation.

"Changeling?" Aimeé made a questioning face.

"Another sort of fairy tale," Beatrix offered. "It is said that malicious fairy folk will replace a human newborn with a magic rock. The rock grows into a child, but it is dull-witted and a burden to the family, while the real baby is a slave back in the Otherworld. Again, you can tell my husband likes to entertain his children at his brother's expense. These Irish are especially disturbed by changelings.

"Your Uncle Donnie is not a changeling. You can spot a changeling a mile away," she said in all seriousness to her children. "They are round of eye, slack of jaw and have webbed hands and feet."

"But he is a gruagach, then?" they persisted.

"There may be some truth to that." Beatrix rolled her eyes. She addressed Aimeé while picking at the grass and leaves in the tangled mat of her girls' hair. "He is a peculiar sort who prefers the wilds to the house. The girls love their Uncle Donnie and he often brings them home dirtier than when they left. I'm afraid someday he is going to take them into the wilds and never come back."

Beatrix hugged the girls tighter. Aimeé sensed a hint of seriousness in her voice.

"Grandmère Talisia is no gruagach," Maria said proudly. "She's *Daoine Sidhe*. She's a fairy princess."

Aimeé smiled at the innocent sweetness of the children.

Then Beatrix surprised her by saying, "No, it's true."

"Tell us the story, maman," Mayana pleaded. "Tell us the story of grandpère and grandmère."

"Oh very well," she said and Aimeé listened intently, curious.

"Long ago before you were born," Beatrix began, "indeed, before your dadda was born and your grandpère Shannon was a young man, he went a-hunting with his brother James in the misty mountains where they meet the great River Shannon, after which he is named. He became lost, separated from Grand-Uncle James. The dark fairy folk, the drow, and every spiteful pixie and sprite led him astray with the intent of leading him in circles until starved or frozen to death. But Shannon knelt at the river's edge and prayed to the Christian God. And lo and behold, Talisia came out of the water..."

"'...naked as a newborn babe!'" the red headed children said together, giggling.

"Yes, she heard Shannon praying, and came from the fairy world under the water, drawn by his words. She asked, 'To what god is this you pray? I've never heard such words. Tell me more.' Now, the last thing Shannon thought to see in the wilderness was a beautiful naked woman, so naturally he thought the evil fairy folk were playing a trick on him. But Talisia persisted, wanting to learn more about this Christian God. So Shannon told her what he could, but then said, 'Guide me out of here, and I will tell you about His son, as well.' She agreed. Shannon put his cloak about her and she led him out of the wilderness. He took her home to a priest who also thought it was a trick, but she asked so many questions and learned so fast. She learned all the prayers—and in Latin no less—and then became baptized. She married Shannon, had many beautiful children..."

"...and they lived happily ever after!" the girls added.

"Well, it's mostly true," Beatrix said, noting Aimeé's incredulous look. "Shannon Gawain did bring home a strange, beautiful woman one day from a hunting trip. Her language was different, she knew very little of the ways of the common folk, and she had an insatiable appetite to learn all things, especially about God. The priest was a superstitious sort, even more so than the people, and put her to many tests before becoming convinced she was as human as the rest of us. Even to this day, Talisia goes out of her way to know more than the average person about scripture, and I dare say she spends more time in that church praying than Father Peter does. All this she does to ensure her children are not perceived as demon spawn. She even tried directing Patrick toward the priesthood, teaching him scripture and letters in Latin. Well, we know how that turned out."

Aimeé shook her head, surprised at the revelation and even more surprised Patrick hadn't said anything. She knew he could read and write, rare skills, but he had never explained why. He often hid the fact as he felt it would alienate him from the brotherhood of knights, who were largely illiterate.

"Surely, she is merely a foreigner like you or me," Aimeé said.

Beatrix chewed on her lip thoughtfully, saying, "Her language was different, but still of Eire. The old timers say it was a form of *ancient* Irish, and she said her tribe was the *Tuatha*, which simply means 'The People.' Shannon finally convinced Father Peter she was just from a secluded tribe, hidden away in the mountains. But then came the wedding, and that only started the fairy rumors again."

"Why's that?" Aimeé asked.

"Her people came for the ceremony alright, but they were a strange sort. Half were tall and willowy like Patrick, with Talisia's blazing eyes. Their clothes appeared to be spun from fine metal wire with the symbols you see everywhere on the stones about Eire. Their weapons were of the finest craftsmanship. They were no country bumpkins from some hidden village in the mountains. The other half, you could believe were from a primitive tribe. They wore animal skins, and their weapons were made from shaped flint. They were short, dark and weathered. It sounds like they were more like Domhnull in appearance. They were a quiet bunch, so I'm told. They were very sad to see Talisia marry an outsider, and even sadder to see her take up a foreign god, but they respected her wishes, kissed her goodbye, and haven't been seen since. Even so, Talisia has had to endure much to convince the community she is no evil fairy bent on harm."

"They think she's a selkie," Mayana explained.

"A water spirit who appears as a seal, but turns into a woman on land," Beatrix answered the confused look on Aimeé's face. "They marry mortal men, have their babies, then take them back to the water with them."

"Now you tell us story, Aimeé," the children pleaded.

"Me?" she said, not sure what to say.

"Yes! Story! Story!"

After a moment of gathering her thoughts she said, "How would you like to hear a story about your Uncle Patrick?"

"Yes!"

"Very well, then," Aimeé began. "You know your uncle is a knight, right?"

The girls nodded eagerly. "Well, what you may not know is he is a knight of the Isle of Avalon, do you know where that is?"

"It's where King Arthur went after his last battle," Mayana said.

Maria added, "And where the Lady of the Lake comes from. She gave him his magical sword, Excalibur."

"Very good!" Aimeé said. "Patrick is a knight sworn to protect a castle on Avalon that is full of lords and ladies, and he's sworn to protect the secrets of the isle. In fact, I shouldn't even be telling you any of this, but because you're his nieces, I guess there's no harm."

The girls giggled.

"One day," Aimeé continued with a flourish of her hands and wide eyes, "an evil lord came to Avalon, seeking the secrets of the isle so he could rule the world. Little did anyone know, but this lord was actually the trickster god, Loki, in disguise..."

Aimeé proceeded to recount how Loki had used Avalon's secrets to access the realm of Faerie, kidnapped a princess in the process, and how Patrick had been the lone knight capable of pursuing him.

"It was I who spied Loki in the distance running away with the princess," she explained. "I went to Patrick to tell him what had happened, but just as I did, Loki's servant shot me in the back with a crossbow bolt, right here." Aimeé turned slightly on the blanket and pointed to a spot on her back, her finger making a circle in the wool of her dress.

Aimeé finished the story of how she had died, how Patrick had entered into Faerie to defeat the dark lord and rescue the princess, and how he had brought back a magic cup and used it to bring her back to life.

The girls clapped their hands.

"You must be much more beautiful than the princess," Maria said, "for Uncle Patrick to pick you over her."

"Oh, trust me, he struggled over it, but eventually he made the right choice." Aimeé did her best to laugh at her own words, but it came out nervously.

"Avalon?" Beatrix said. "You have a gift for storytelling."

"My manner, or my content?" Aimeé asked.

Beatrix responded, eyes narrowing thoughtfully. "Both, but more so the content, I think."

The girls rose from the blanket to tackle her and shout, "Play! Come play with us!"

Aimeé laughed in mock protests as one pulled on her arms while the other pushed from behind. In the process, the collar of her dress momentarily slipped down her back to reveal a terrible round scar.

#

That evening, thunderclouds rolled in and heavy rain pelted the house as she and Patrick ate dinner with the family.

"Now you get to see real Irish weather," Patrick said at table. "I hope the roads won't be too bad tomorrow when we go to the festival at the Gathering Place."

Later, he bid her goodnight with a kiss as usual by lantern light at her chamber door and ambled towards his own room.

She let out a deep breath, watching his light fade the farther he walked away.

Soon afterward she let the pitter-patter of rain against the window shutters lull her to sleep.

She didn't feel she had been sleeping long, however, when a disturbance in the hallway woke her with a start. People ran and shouted. A similar disturbance outside the house also drew her attention. She put on a robe and joined the throng of panicked family running for the main entrance, thinking maybe a fire had broken out. Outside, in the lead, Catha held up a lantern to reveal Sian and Patrick in the driving rain. At first Aimeé thought the two brothers fought, but a second glance showed Sian putting out his hands, speaking soothing words she did not understand. Beatrix and Talisia stood nearby with wet hair plastered against their faces, doing the same. Patrick moved erratically in circles shouting, though Aimeé could not understand what he said. The family gathered around to watch the spectacle, concern drawn in their faces.

When Beatrix noticed Aimeé, she came to her. "He woke us, shouting into the darkness in French, though he is not making any sense. He won't listen to us."

She urged Aimeé towards Patrick, who now shouted in Gaelic.

"Patrick, what is wrong?" she called over the rain and his shouts.

Soaked in a muddy nightgown, his head jerked in her direction when she spoke. His eyes widened and he backed away.

"No, get away! I didn't mean it! I take it back!" he shouted in French.

Then, raising a knife she hadn't noticed until now, he staggered towards her shouting in Gaelic.

Gasps erupted from the crowd and Aimeé slipped in the mud as she tried to back away. Her world shattered with confusion. Patrick stood over her with the knife, railing to the night, to the rain, and back to her. Wild-eyed, he thrust his hands out to her, palms up with the knife balancing precariously in one, and made a questioning statement in Gaelic. When she did not answer, he took the blade and sliced it across his palm, creating a thread of crimson flowing with the rain down his wrist.

"No!" she cried.

Sian leaped over her and planted a fist across his brother's face, sending him with a splash into a puddle, where he lay motionless.

#

The following morning, Aimeé awoke to the sound of giggling children and a light touch on her face.

"Girls, please," Aimeé pleaded, rolling over in her bed.

The laughter came again, but fainter as if from down the hall, but the touches on her face gently caressed her again. First they traced her brow, then her cheek, and finally her lips.

She sat up in bed and opened her eyes to an empty room.

"What the..."

She rose from the bed and entered the hall to look in either direction.

No one was there.

Her stomach twisted into knots, and she recalled the events of the previous night. She moved to dress herself and go find what had become of Patrick. After the incident in the yard, they had placed him on the dining room table where Talisia spent careful minutes sewing up his hand. When it was apparent Patrick was out cold for the rest of the night, Aimeé had gone to bed.

In dressing herself she paused, however, when a wave of nausea overcame her and she ran to the room's bedpan to empty her stomach.

#

The family did not let the previous night's incident interfere with preparations to take the wool to the Gathering Place. As Aimeé understood it, all the local families would be doing the same and there would be a festival, as well.

The household buzzed with activity. Aimeé searched for Patrick. She came across an unusually quiet Sian who pointed down the garden path behind the manor and urged her to follow it.

"Patrick and mama," he said. His eyes lingered on her as if she might have a better explanation as to what had transpired in the rain.

Not sure what to say, she thanked him, picked up her skirts and ran down the path into the grove.

Flute music wafted on the breeze. By the time she arrived at its source, singing followed it: a beautiful yet mournful tune in the language Aimeé had come to recognize as classically Gaelic. Talisia paused and raised the flute to her mouth again. Aimeé noted the flute hung around Talisia's neck by a string. Closer examination revealed the flute was actually the crucifix Talisia wore about her neck, hollow and fashioned with little holes.

Patrick sat on the ground at her feet, his upper torso hunched forward with his head in her lap. The slump of his body and the rhythmic rise and fall of his back indicated he slept peacefully.

Beatrix sat next to Talisia on the bench and motioned Aimeé forward, assuring her she did not trespass into a private moment... or perhaps invited her into one.

Aimeé sat and the three women crowded on the small seat. Talisia stopped her singing and flute playing. Patrick snorted in his sleep and moisture beaded his brow.

Talisia asked something quietly, directing it towards Aimeé as she stroked Patrick's hair.

"Can you tell me what happened last night?" Beatrix translated for her.

"I don't know exactly," Aimeé admitted, and told her all she knew about his restless sleep, his crying out names, and the Apparition—the Other.

Talisia remained quiet for a while after Beatrix had finished the translation.

"The war follows him," she said eventually. "His soul is wounded. Fragmented."

"Is there anything we can do?" Aimeé asked, her brow creasing with concern.

After another long pause and several more strokes of his hair, Talisia replied, "When he was a child and his troubles became too much, he would come to me like this. I would sing for him. Play music for him. It would help guide him to a peaceful place, and from there he could heal."

"How long does it take?" Aimeé asked, wanting to reach out and stroke Patrick's hair as well, but refrained, not wishing to intrude on a mother's touch.

"From taunting boys?" she said, raising the flute to her mouth. "Not long. But from the scars of war?" She gave a slight shake of her head before she whispered the tune through the flute. When she paused again, her own brow creased in concern. "I'm afraid it will take much more time than he has with me, and for some reason he is resisting, though he is not quite aware of that himself. It will take some time. It will be up to you."

Aimeé blanched. "Me? I can't sing. Certainly not as beautifully as you."

Talisia smiled as she removed the necklace and handed the instrument to her. "You can play. Here, I'll show you."

Aimeé gingerly took the tiny wood instrument that barely fit in one hand and bunched her fingers about the holes as she put it to her lips.

After Talisia had shown her the pattern her fingers should follow, she gave it a blow. At first the tune came crudely, but took on form. Talisia smiled encouragement, but then quickly stopped Aimeé's fingers when she attempted to pick up speed once her confidence grew.

"That is a different tune," Talisia warned. "That one is not the healing tune, but more of a call for help."

A breeze moved through the grove, swaying the tree branches. A flurry of birds buzzed the clearing, fluttered about the women's heads as if searching for something, and then just as quickly departed.

"You must practice the correct tune," Talisia admonished, smiling at the birds as they left, "and be careful of using that other tune on Avalon. There is no telling what manner of creatures will show up if they heard it."

"Avalon?" Aimeé tried to pretend ignorance, shooting a glance to Beatrix who looked down.

"It was not Beatrix who let slip the knowledge," Talisia explained. "Patrick finally admitted it to me. A son cannot keep secrets long from his mother. Fortunately, this music will be even stronger in a place like Avalon."

Patrick snorted and his head jerked up. He looked around blinking.

"Oh, hello," he said. His Adam's apple bobbed in his throat and at first he would not make eye contact with her. He raised a hand to rub the sleep from his eyes. When he did, she noticed the bandage on his hand. A thin stretch of red stained the white cloth. "I guess I was sleepwalking bad last night, and I owe you an apology. I'm very sorry. I didn't mean to frighten you." He rubbed his jaw where Sian had struck him.

"Patrick, your mother says you should listen to her music and song," Aimeé said, concern in her voice. She reached out and took his bandaged hand. "It will help you..."

"I have. I'm fine now," Patrick almost snapped, frowning as he stood stiffly. He withdrew his hand. "I have listened and slept well. I feel much better."

"Patrick..."

"It was only sleepwalking. A nightmare. It's over," he said dismissively. "I must go help prepare for the trip to the festival."

He kissed Aimeé on the head, said something to his mother and sister-in-law in Gaelic, and left.

"Don't let him ignore it," Talisia insisted, her eyes following him. "Play for him every chance you can."

She closed Aimeé's fingers about the flute, indicating she should keep it. Aimeé protested at first, but relented at Talisia's urging.

Yet worry gnawed at her.

Before reaching the house, Patrick paused to sit next to his father who reclined on a chaise in the garden. The two men reached out and took each other's hand and sat for a good long time, not saying a word.

#

That evening, the population of the Gathering Place swelled a hundredfold and the area filled with animals, wagons, tents, and bales upon bales of wool.

After Mass, the people of Galway gathered for a lively dinner held about a massive bonfire followed by singing, storytelling, and dancing.

After an exceptionally boisterous dance, Aimeé begged pardon from the heat and exertion, and Patrick led away from the fire.

"Are you well?" he asked, brow furrowed with worry.

"Oui," she waived his concern off. "Too much food, too much drink, and definitely too much dancing. I just need a rest is all."

Sian arrived then with a tankard in hand and called Patrick over to join him and a group of men.

"Go on," she encouraged him. "I understand, the menfolk call. Go enjoy yourself."

Patrick kissed her brow and left.

When he left, Aimeé noted Talisia nearby with Shannon and a group of older men. Her luminous eyes glittered in the dark. Aimeé moved to wave a greeting, but doubled over, clutching her stomach. Thankfully, she did not vomit, but came close.

Talisia rushed over. Aimeé tried to wave her off, but Talisia gripped her strongly by the wrist and peered into her face, not maliciously, but sternly. Aimeé yielded to her will and let herself be led to the well where Talisia applied a damp cloth to her forehead and made her recline on a bench.

"No more dancing," she said in broken French.

She left briefly and came back with Beatrix, with whom she exchanged words. Beatrix smiled and nodded knowingly. The elder women sat on either side of her.

"You don't know, do you?" Beatrix asked.

"Know what?" Aimeé said, struggling to keep her head back and the cloth on.

"That you're with child."

Aimeé's head snapped up and the cloth fell into her lap.

"That can't be!" she exclaimed, almost standing, but the women held her down.

"You are," Beatrix insisted.

Aimeé's mouth dropped, though no words came out. She looked to the thoughtful face of Talisia and blushed. The Gawain matriarch reached over and stroked her hair and said some gentle words.

"I understand how the world works," Beatrix translated for her, "and you and my son are young and beautiful."

"But, but..." Aimeé stammered. She held her stomach, disbelief and a storm of emotions raging through her.

"But we... oh," Aimeé started to protest, but realization dawned on her as she remembered a certain night after a festival not so long ago. A festival not so different from tonight. She blushed again and stammered, "It's not what you think, yes there was some drink involved, but it was only once. Your son has been more than respectful and a good Christian knight and..."

Beatrix translated, and halfway through her nervous defense Talisia held up a halting hand. With a girlish smile she reached out and cradled Aimeé's face, kissing her.

"There is no need to explain. I know my son. Besides, 'Uncle Ale' and 'Auntie Wine' have been the godparents of many a child and have brought many a gift into the world that otherwise may not have come on its own. I am happy for you."

Aimeé relaxed and allowed the women to hug her.

She pulled back and rubbed her stomach and the warmth she felt radiating within.

Moments later, however, an icy cold extinguished that warmth and her hands jumped from her body as if stung by frostbite.

The women looked at her with concern.

"The noble who attacked me..." she said, looking sadly at her stomach. Her hands hovered over it, fingers curling and uncurling, as if trying to decide whether to caress it or tear it apart.

Realization dawned on the elder women and a collective gasp issued from them.

"It was about the same time?" they asked.

Aimeé nodded, despair falling over her like a pall.

Talisia bent to a knee, touched Aimeé's stomach and placed her cheek against it, murmuring words as her eyes closed.

After a moment, Aimeé looked to Beatrix for understanding.

"She says a mother knows her own blood," Beatrix explained, then she frowned as she continued the translation, "...but there is something shrouding this child. Something obstructing her Sight." An uncharacteristically puzzled look crossed Talisia's face when her eyes opened. "She cannot say it is not Patrick's, but cannot say that it is," Beatrix continued. "It is beautiful, no doubt, but something hides it. There is..." Beatrix's and Talisia's brows creased with concern. "...a darkness. There is danger."

Talisia rose, still staring at Aimeé's belly, still holding it as if her touch could protect it from future woes.

"No matter what happens, we are here for you," Talisia assured Aimeé, "but you must talk to Patrick."

#

Before searching Patrick out, Aimeé spent some time alone, alternating between feelings of lightness as if she might float away with the surreal situation, and collapsing under the weight of a millstone around her neck.

A baby? she thought. *Whose? Patrick's beautiful green-eyed child, or Geoffrey's brown-eyed monster?*

Initially, the idea of the latter made her ill and want to tear her belly open and sit in a swift flowing river to cleanse her womb.

No, she told herself eventually, *it is not the child's fault. It is from God, not Geoffrey. It will need loving. Otherwise, it will become another Geoffrey walking through this world and that won't do.*

She clung to that notion and her hands rubbed her stomach, pressing harder as her resolve grew.

She found Patrick deep in conversation with a couple, and when he saw Aimeé approach, an odd mix of relief and anxiety filled his face.

The man he spoke to was a short rotund fellow with an affable face and receding hairline. He held a young boy, perhaps two or three years old, by the hand. The woman had thick dark hair and sparkling blue eyes. Once, she must have had the sort of beauty that would have made Aphrodite jealous, but now she had the full-figured maternal beauty that comes with having had several children.

Patrick introduced Aimeé by name, then said stiffly, "Aimeé, this is Malcolm O'Connor, and his wife... Kellie."

His former fiancée. Aimeé blinked, and awkward cheek-kissing ensued, followed by a lengthy dialogue that Aimeé could not follow. She could only tell all felt very uncomfortable. Kellie regarded Aimeé with a woman's combination of surface politeness and subdued hostility.

Fortunately, the child saved them all by crying, at which point the O'Connors begged off to attend their child. Patrick happily let them go.

Later, Patrick and Aimeé found themselves at the well where Patrick splashed water in his face.

"Are you well?" she asked.

Patrick shrugged, saying, "That went better than I thought."

"You still care for her?" she asked, not as an accusation, but as a genuine question.

Patrick sat next to her on the bench and took her hand.

"No, and I thank God for that every day. I wish her the best, I really do. I just don't want to see it firsthand. Old wounds still hurt when poked. At least now I know they're healing. They just need more time."

Aimeé squeezed his hand back. The time had definitely not come for bringing up world-shattering news.

#

The following day, after the business of sorting the bales of wool, arranging them for transport to Galway, and picking the year's representative to negotiate their sale, Aimeé and Patrick found some time alone on a hillside to have a blanket lunch. From there, they could watch the continuing festivities.

He then shared news of his own.

"We'll be returning to Greensprings soon," he said.

"So soon?"

"Aye, I promised Sir Mark and Father Hugh we'd be back by the time the new flock of Guests arrives. That should be happening soon as the season changes. Besides," Patrick added with a wistful smile, "if I stay any longer they will expect me to help with the harvest, as well. I'm supposed to be relaxing."

Not sure how to break her own news, she started with some other innocuous conversation while she buttered her bread.

"Why is it that Dierdre and Catha are not married? They are older, no?"

The wind blowing through their hair also swept patterns in the grass. White fluffy clouds drifted through the air like sky castles.

"Dierdre is twice widowed," Patrick replied, picking up the butter knife to examine the butter still clinging to it. "Both her husbands died in unfortunate accidents."

"That's horrible," Aimeé said.

"Aye, and now everyone thinks she's cursed. Despite her beauty no man is in a hurry to be the third." Patrick meticulously wiped the knife against the lip of butter pot, then laid it across the mouth of the pot at its exact center.

"And Catha?"

Patrick smiled. "She almost killed the last man who tried to court her. She is no man-hater, but she is much too wild to be tamed. I imagine when the right man comes along she'll let it happen."

Aimeé swallowed hard, and after a quiet moment of mustering her courage, she asked, "And us? What are your plans for us?"

After readjusting the position of the knife across the mouth of the pot, Patrick leaned over and kissed her lightly on the lips, and replied, "I was hoping time will tell. My family likes you very much. That was the first thing I needed to know. In a little more time, God willing and I don't drive you crazy, we can discuss... more."

Aimeé closed her eyes. Disappointment roiled through her body. She had hoped for a clearer answer from him, not an itinerary of one of his calculated plans. She knew better than to ask him directly if he loved her. On top of being a man, he was Patrick, and most likely would withdraw into an awkward silence. She also knew better than to corner him into consenting to a hypothetical marriage by posing the question if she were hypothetically pregnant.

Instead, she just said it. "Patrick, I'm with child."

The wind picked up as he stared at her for a moment.

"You're certain?" he asked at last.

"Yes. Your mother and Beatrix pointed it out," she answered. "I imagine if anyone would know such things, it would be them."

"But it has been so long. How is it you're just now learning of it?" he asked, brow furrowed . Perhaps it was a natural reaction in men to find a better alternative to a surprising problem.

"I thought I was seasick this whole time, and my natural rhythms disrupted by the stress of travel. It all adds up now," she replied.

"But..." Patrick stammered.

Aimeé could not believe he was still trying to reason the child away.

"Obviously you don't know women's bodies as well as you thought," she said with not a little sarcasm, "and there is that small matter that I died for a short while—on enchanted Avalon—and who knows what kind of disruption to the natural order of things that could have caused."

Patrick stood and looked down upon the festival at all the people going about their normal lives as if the most earth-shaking news hadn't just announced itself. The wind ruffled the sleeves of his shirt as he begun to pace with his hands on hips.

"Well then, it's settled," he said at last. He stopped his pacing to address her, doing his best to conjure a smile. "Marriage it is! What good chance it is we're here with my family. We can plan immediately. Mother will be very happy, she will want—"

"Patrick," Aimeé said quietly, "I may only be a commoner who should be ecstatic at the idea of marrying up in the world, but I do have some measure of pride. It was my hope you would be happier than this. That you would want to marry me because you loved me, not out of some sense of honor and duty."

"But I do!" Patrick said. "It's just a surprise. I wasn't expecting it so soon. I—"

"Stop!" Aimeé shouted. She wanted all the facts known before he said too much too soon. "There is more."

He spread his hands, a look of anticipation on his face. She rose from the blanket and stood under his gaze. The wind whipped her hair.

"The timing. It could be Sir Geoffrey's. Yet another reason I was not certain of my own condition: I had thought the trauma of his attack had disrupted my cycles. In any case, I do not know for certain, and even your mother says she cannot tell. She does say, however, trouble follows the child. There is a darkness."

Patrick swallowed hard, his open hands closed into fists and she knew if Geoffrey stood there now he would have been a dead man. Most telling, however, behind the rage surfaced a look of crippling uncertainty. And maybe it was her imagination, but she thought she detected a hint of relief in his eyes. The possibility of escape.

It's just my imagination, right?

Patrick sat down hard. After a long moment of silence and frowning thoughtfulness, he took her by the wrist and drew her down beside him.

"No matter," he said, staring off into the distance. "I will not leave you alone in this. I will take care of you both. I will marry you."

"Did you hear what I said?" she asked, wanting to be certain he knew what he said. "It could be Geoffrey's, and your mother says—"

"My mother says many things," he almost snapped. "It's like this business with the flute. Stories for a child."

"You don't believe your mother has..." Aimeé struggled for words. "Skills? Knowledge?"

Patrick scowled. "You mean do I think she has fairy magic?"

"Don't you?"

Patrick remained silent for a while, grinding his teeth. "After my experiences on Avalon, I know she does. I understand my heritage better now."

"Then why don't you believe?"

Patrick growled and made a dismissive gesture. "My point is that I don't know what to believe anymore. I felt she was always hiding something from me. Telling me half-truths to protect me. I'm an adult now and don't need protecting. Her saying there is a 'darkness' over this child is her way of protecting me from the possibility it is Geoffrey's. I don't care. I will marry you and take care of it and you."

"Take care of me?" It was Aimeé's turn to scowl at his presumptuous and dismissive tone. "I don't want your protection. I want your love. We will need it if there is a shadow over this baby."

Patrick grabbed her wrists and pulled her towards him. His eyes turned intense and strange. "There is no darkness! Just things needing sorting out! I will sort them!"

"Patrick..." Aimeé writhed in his grip that started to hurt.

"There is nothing here I can't fix! There is—"

"Patrick, please, you're hurting me!"

Patrick froze. His eyes cleared and he looked down at his hold on her. Blood leaked from his bandaged hand and smeared her wrist. He shook his head as if waking from a dream, released her, and gazed at his shaking hands.

"I'm the darkness," he whispered, a far away look in his eyes. He slumped and rubbed at his temple. "Everything I touch goes to hell. You were raped in the first place because of me. Loki had you killed because of me. I'm a danger."

Aimeé wanted to reassure him, but realized she had instinctively pulled away when he had released her. She found herself protecting her stomach.

"I don't know the answer to these things," Aimeé said at last, "but perhaps we should take our time before making any decisions."

Patrick's distant gaze evaporated. "What do you mean?"

"We should hold off on marriage—no, don't argue. Let us, as you say, sort this out, but slowly," she responded.

Patrick protested just the same. "If you doubt I love you, then I will prove it to you over time."

"Perhaps," Aimeé said, "but even before your outburst, your love did not shine brightly. You brought me to Eire out of guilt because of how you treated me before my death. You brought me back to life so you could balance the scales, not because you loved me. Not the kind of love I yearn for."

"I'm willing to try," he said, brows knitting over his eyes. "I can't leave you alone in this."

Aimeé shook her head, responding, "You won't be, and if nothing else I have my people and support back in Aesclinn. I will not be the first commoner to bear a child alone."

Patrick got to his knees and held her tightly, his throat constricting as he said, "Please don't do this."

"Please let me," Aimeé responded, embracing him just as tightly. The clouds had blotted out the sun. Fat raindrops started to soak them. "I do not have name, title, or land. You have your honor and duty. I only have my pride. It is all I have. If you truly love me, if only a little, you will let me keep it."

The rain came down harder and the wind swept their blanket and meal away in a sudden rush.

#

Days later, Patrick watched Aimeé say long tearful goodbyes to Beatrix, in which she called the Breton woman her "angel." The rest of the family took turns in the yard to have their private moments.

The night before he and Aimeé had talked long into the night with his parents and Beatrix about their decision. Though greatly saddened by the uncertainty, they respected Aimeé's wish to try motherhood on her own, and all agreed it probably best to keep the news secret from the rest of the family for the time being.

"Besides," his father had said, taking his mother's hand, "you never know how these things turn out. God has a way of answering your prayers in the most unexpected of ways."

Despite the wise words, Patrick's mind and soul were banked in fog. His joyful homecoming had turned into more anxiety. Because the Other had disappeared, he had thought his past troubles gone, but nothing could be farther from the truth.

He rubbed at his temple, trying to vanquish the pain there and the remembered sound of cries and combat. Something lingered at the edge of his mind like a word on the tip of his tongue. He wondered what vexed him more: seeing ghosts, or this nagging inability to remember something important.

"You must let her play the music for you," his mother told him as he saddled Siegfried.

He suppressed a scoff. "Mother, please."

"You liked it enough as a child," she said, her beautiful eyes turning sad.

"Why didn't you tell me?" he asked, his tone speaking of another matter.

His mother looked away. "When you were little, you came running home one day. Black eye. Tears streaming down your face. The boys at the Gathering Place had been particularly cruel to you that day. They called you 'demon' and 'changeling.' Because of me." She turned back to Patrick and moisture glistened in her eyes. She reached up and touched his smooth face. "It hurt me so much to see you like that. My boy. My sweet, sensitive boy. I wanted to protect you from that. I said you were no different, just more beautiful and they were jealous, and so I told you year after year until I believed it myself. I'd protect you still."

"Still?" Patrick pressed her hand to his temple. "I thought I was going mad. I was seeing things, Mother. Avalon brought out things, magnified them until I couldn't ignore them. If only I had some understanding beforehand, I could have dealt with it better."

"I'm sorry." She embraced him. "We live in a Christian world, becoming more Christian with every passing day. No good will come out of clinging to the past. As for this Apparition, this Other you see, I have not heard of such a thing. I could not have prepared you for it. Perhaps it is of your father's heritage."

Patrick shrugged. "I didn't think I clung to the past, but it sure seems to cling to me."

"Then listen to the music," she implored.

"She barely speaks to me now. I've frightened her that much," he responded, casting his gaze to Aimeé who now held Mayana and Maria in a double-armed hug.

"Have you told her you love her?"

Patrick shrugged again. "She knows I do."

His mother's head tilted to one side and a wry smile curled at one corner of her mouth. "Say it like you mean it and the rest will follow."

Patrick tightened the last straps on this saddlebags and kissed his mother on the head.

He paused and he felt his throat tighten before he said, "I love you."

His mother smiled. "I know you do, but it's sure nice to hear you say it every now and again."

After that, Patrick finished with lingering hugs on each and every family member. Sian playfully rubbed at Patrick's chin where he had struck him during his sleepwalking episode. Despite the lightheartedness of the gesture, concern clouded Sian's face as he held his forehead to Patrick's and wished him Godspeed.

They left then, Patrick astride Siegfried and Aimeé on her pony. The good weather they had experienced during their stay turned chilly and turbulent. Dark clouds accosted them with rain as they traveled.

"We picked a fine time to make this journey," Aimeé lamented. Her attempt at making conversation sounded forced.

"All this green comes at a price," Patrick responded, also rather forced.

Silence engulfed them again.

During the long and uneventful journey back, Patrick truly wished bandits or pirates would set upon them once again so he could vent his frustration.

Chapter Three

Dread filled Patrick as he saw the large ship among the two smaller ones moored in the Cornish village harbor. The gloomy weather didn't help his mood.

He chewed on his lower lip as he gazed at the vessel, brightly painted in reds and golds, and flying the flag of the Holy See. Somebody very important from Rome had accompanied this season's Guests, a fact that troubled Patrick. The last time envoys had come from Rome, they had come to perform an inquest into the goblin attack on Greensprings.

"I've never seen a ship so big," Aimeé said, gawking at the fat-bodied Italian boat.

Patrick moved to her side to the railing of their ship. He quickly finished buckling his sword belt after having slipped on his Avangarde surcoat.

"It's called a dromone," he said, eager to make conversation. She had spoken little in the past few weeks. "That's the sort of ship that brought many a crusader to the Holy Land. Though I've never seen one so large myself, certainly not one with fore and aft castles the size of houses."

He continued to point out specifics on the ship; everything from the ship's single mast that would probably require at least four people at its base to encircle with outstretched arms, to the galley oars, as tall as trees and currently standing erect along the gunwales.

Aimeé shrugged indifferently and wandered away.

"It looks like we arrived just in time," Patrick added, trailing behind her, smoothing out the front of his surcoat. "Judging by the activity on the docks, it looks like they're not quite loaded with supplies. I was worried they would have been waiting for us and..."

He stopped his attempt at small talk as she quickened her pace to pull away.

He looked from her to the giant ship, and the gray sky and couldn't decide which caused him more anxiety.

#

Patrick and Aimeé made their way to the local inn that had served as their resting place on their journey to Eire. Upon recognizing them, the innkeeper greeted them warmly at the entrance and led them into the public room.

Normally a quiet place, tonight the inn was full of rollicking strangers. The fire roared almost as loudly as the soldiers in red-and-yellow-striped surcoats. Patrick recognized the hat-and-tassel crest on their surcoats as that of a cardinal, but despite knowing that, he felt a nervousness come over him amid the Italians. One hand instinctively gripped his sword hilt, and the other shot to his temple. For a moment among the cacophony of foreign language and clashing mugs, he thought he heard screams and the clash of steel.

"Sir Patrick!" a familiar face exclaimed, breaking Patrick's thoughts. "We were starting to wonder when you would show up. Have a seat!"

The innkeeper pulled out chairs for them at the man's table.

"Sir Marcus Ionus," Patrick smiled, clasping hands with the Avangarde recruiter. He hadn't seen the man since he first came to Avalon, and seeing him tonight was a surprise. Normally Marcus traveled the kingdoms searching for men to take up the White Swan.

Sir Marcus turned to Aimeé and said, "You must be the mademoiselle I have heard so much about. You've become legend after your... revival."

Aimeé awkwardly allowed the tall knight to take her hand and kiss it.

"Aimeé de la Chasse, Sir Marcus, which surely you must know because I served you often enough at table at Greensprings," Aimeé said, and Patrick didn't know whether to cringe or smile at her boldness.

Marcus smiled the smile that made him famous, lighting up the room with dimples. A smile that had persuaded Patrick to cross a strange sea to a mythical island.

As fair complexioned as Patrick, but with light blue eyes, he responded whimsically, "Apologies, Mademoiselle de la Chasse, but my stays in Greensprings are infrequent and short. When I had heard a maidservant had experienced a miracle, others were at a loss to describe to me which one, when all they had to say was, 'the beautiful one.'"

Aimeé took the seat offered her. With a hint of a smile, she said, "You are redeemed, Sir Knight."

Pleased with himself, Marcus turned to the innkeeper and ordered food. "Your timing is perfect," he said to Patrick. "I was about to eat and did not wish to dine with a bunch of obnoxious Italians."

Marcus spoke true, for the discomfort Patrick had felt when entering the room increased as he noted how the Italian men-at-arms jostled and pushed one another, and not a few locals in the process, while enjoying their drinks. The serving women fared the worst, bounced from one group of revelers to the next.

At his side, Aimeé's shoulders bunched and she pulled her cloak closer about herself. Patrick moved to touch her with a comforting hand, but then his attention snapped back to the crowd. He thought he recognized a face. He could not find it now, but even as he searched he felt eyes upon him.

"Plus, you saved me the trouble of having to find you and deliver a message," Marcus added, drawing Patrick's attention back to their table. "His Eminence, Cardinal Teodorico, wishes to see you before we depart the day after tomorrow."

"Who is this cardinal, and why does he want to see me?" Patrick asked. This news discomfited him even more as he rubbed at his temple, trying to remember something the face in the crowd had triggered.

"I'm sure you saw the rather large boat out on the dock? That is his. He is the papal legate from Rome and the head of the Board of Benefactors for the Greensprings School. You've met him once before when he came to investigate the attack last year. I understand you were one of the knights called to the inquest."

Patrick frowned thoughtfully, trying to remember. Many outsiders came that day, but one did stand out in his mind: a hawk-nosed man with an Italian accent, ruthless in his pursuit of information.

"I believe I know who you speak of," Patrick said uneasily. "Why is he here now? We were told the report we sent over the Loki affair was adequate and another inquest was unnecessary."

"So we were told," Marcus replied, taking dishes the innkeeper brought and helping distribute them about the table, "and I was under the impression when they read it in Rome they did not believe a half of it—which is quite often the case with news coming out of Avalon. Plus, they were truly unconcerned when they learned the only 'death' that occurred turned out to be not a death after all, and even then of a maidservant—no offense, mademoiselle."

Aimeé shrugged and picked at her roast chicken.

"So what changed?" Patrick asked, ladling stew from a small pot into a round of bread. "And why does he need an army?"

"My guess is he was waiting for you," Marcus said, lowering his voice and looking around. "He knew you were gone and so he came with this year's new batch of Guests, knowing you would be here to greet them. My suspicions were confirmed when he asked for you by name—and for the maidservant."

"Me? Why me?" Aimeé asked.

Marcus shrugged, saying, "I'm sure he wishes to lay eyes on the miracle itself. Speaking of cups..."

Marcus poured ale all around.

Patrick did not take his mug up right away. He rubbed his face and groaned. He could guess what the cardinal really wanted. Patrick wished again that he had returned the cup to its guardians immediately. He had not anticipated a papal legate, let alone the head of the Board of Benefactors himself, to show up so soon.

"I'm afraid His Eminence is going to be very disappointed," Patrick said stoically, taking up his mug of ale and sipping. "I made a promise to return the cup. It was a mistake of mine to let Father Hugh talk me into letting him keep the cup to be adored in the church while I was away. I should have returned it right away to the cave from where it came. It needs to go back. I made a promise. No one, not even a cardinal and his army, is going to stop me from fulfilling my oath."

Patrick expected Marcus, a senior Avangardesman, to chastise him for his insubordination. Instead, a shock of a different sort crossed the man's face.

"That's right," Marcus said distantly, as if thinking out loud. "You don't know yet."

Patrick frowned. "Know what?"

"The cup, it won't move."

"What do you mean, 'Won't move.'"

"Just that." Marcus took a drink. "It won't allow itself to be touched. Anyone who tries, their hand passes right through it."

#

The following morning, Patrick stood on the dock beside the cardinal's ship with Marcus. Though not raining, the sky still cast a pallid grayness over the fisherman going about their routines and the workers loading the Avalon-bound boats.

"I will not be joining you," Marcus explained. "I was severely chastised for allowing Loki access to Avalon and ever since have not been welcome in the presence of the head of the Board of Benefactors, or as he put it, 'Get thee from my sight!'"

"You can't be serious," Patrick said, his jaw dropping a fraction in shock at the revelation.

"I'm very serious, and since I was lucky enough not to be expelled from the Order, I'd rather not tempt him into changing his mind."

"Trust me, Loki had a talent for manipulation. Many fell victim to his charms. Perhaps if I could convey that fact to the cardinal..."

Marcus put up a hand, responding, "No need. I take full responsibility for my actions and the consequences. I will wait for a chance to redeem myself through my own efforts."

Patrick wanted to protest but decided to respect the man's wishes.

This news, added to the disturbing revelation of the cup's odd behavior, made his already-spinning head want to fly off his shoulders. He figured he should change the subject and keep his head where it was.

"Sir Corbin is truly Captain of the Guard now?"

"Aye, being the senior Avangarde, he was next in line for succession," Marcus responded, "and it happened rather suddenly when Sir Mark eloped with the Lady Christianne Morneau."

Patrick shook his head, still trying to clear the spinning.

"Speaking of marriages," Marcus added, "and I'm sorry if I'm overstepping here, but after seeing you and the mademoiselle did not share a room last night, may I ask if all is well? Rumor suggested you two would be returning from Eire as a married couple, but that does not seem to be the case."

A tired growl rumbled deep inside Patrick, but he suppressed it and gave Marcus a terse, but polite, explanation of what had happened in Ireland.

"I'm very sorry to hear that," Marcus said as Aimeé approached, making her way through the crowd on the dock. "I hope all works out in the end. She seems like a nice lass."

Patrick nodded silently at Marcus' support.

"My apologies for my lateness," she said as she curtsied. "I came across the Greensprings servants making arrangements for transporting food supplies to the island. I offered my assistance after our audience with the cardinal."

You wouldn't have to work another day in the kitchens if you would just marry me, Patrick thought, but held his tongue.

Sensing some frostiness between Patrick and the maidservant, Marcus cleared his throat and said, "Just up the gangplank here, and to the left, you will find the entrance to the cardinal's cabin. He is expecting you. I'll wait your return here."

Once on board, a short walk on the gently rolling deck brought them to the door of the aft structure that easily could have been a richly decorated house on a merchant street. There, Patrick banged the large iron ring on the door.

"Ah, welcome." A slightly built young man greeted them. His goatee curled into a smile. "His Eminence is expecting you."

Patrick and Aimeé followed the young man through the maze of rooms and doors, finally ending at a room with a plush chair and many traveling chests. Upon the chair sat an older man in a simple red robe, but of rich silk. When seeing his graying hair, only partially covered by a red skullcap, and the hawk nose, Patrick recognized him as the unpleasant inquisitor.

Today, however, the man who had all but dismissed Sir Marcus for the Loki affair now gave warm smiles and came forward with open arms.

"Greetings," the cardinal said putting forth his ring finger with an ornate gold and topaz ring upon it.

Patrick and Aimeé dutifully kissed the symbol of his office as they made their bows and curtsies. Yet Patrick's shoulder blades drew together.

"His Eminence, Cardinal Teodorico," the assistant announced his master, "Archbishop of Albano, member of the Roman Curia, Papal Legate, and Head of the Board of Benefactors for the Greensprings École."

"Well, then, hmm," he said. "I was so eager to meet you two. The discoverer of the cup, and the one who came back to life because of it, hmm, yes? What a wondrous age we live in! The Cup of the Last Supper has returned to us!"

Patrick's stomach tightened and he struggled to maintain eye contact with the cardinal. "Your Eminence, my apologies for my presumptions, but it was made quite clear to me by the guardians of the vessel I was to return it. Its residency in the Greensprings church is only a temporary matter."

"Nonsense," Teodorico said, waving the thought aside with the swipe of his hand. "The cup has revealed itself through your intercession, and more, made manifest its miraculous works for the world to see, hmm?" The cardinal gestured at Aimeé. "It is begging to be shared on a larger scale! Christ told us He would always be with us, in His body and His blood in the holy sacrament of the Eucharist at Mass, hmm? Now that promise has been made more tangible by the revelation of the cup from which He last drank. It is no surprise it happened now, and here on Avalon, hmm, yes?"

"I'm afraid I don't follow," Patrick said, trying not to sound disrespectful.

"Greensprings was tasked with bringing the noble youth of Christendom together to learn peace. Christendom is at war with itself. The Church is in conflict. If ever there was a time for Jesus to be among us in a very real form, it is now, hmm?"

Teodorico left his hands in an open gesture as if to say, *See?*

Patrick's head swam and he resisted the temptation to rub at the pain in his skull. He had walked in with his resolve set, and had even stated his intent. Now, however, he found himself confounded and finding it difficult to argue with the cardinal's reasoning.

Despite the tumult in his mind, he managed to say, "Then why do the guardians insist I bring it back?"

"Yes, yes, the guardians, hmm?" Teodorico said, his tone turning thoughtful. He stood and addressed Patrick closer, his congenial demeanor turning a little intimidating at close proximity. "I read your report about these mystical beings who guard a wondrous treasure in the same cave where you found the cup, hmm, yes? Are you certain they were angels? Was not this same cave, by your own admission in another report, once inhabited by a demon-spawn wolf, hmm, yes?"

"That was different," Patrick said defensively. "That creature was an evil remnant of a bygone era. The guardian spirits were helpless to remove it. I killed it for them, freeing the cave from its evil presence."

"Yes, hmm?" Teodorico said. "But these 'guardian spirits,' hmm? Were they angels, or no?"

Patrick hesitated, then said, "Well, perhaps partially."

Teodorico made a puzzled expression that he shared with his assistant.

"Partially?"

Flustered, Patrick experienced precisely the sort of confrontation he did not wish to have. He much rather cross swords with someone than exchange intellectual barbs.

"They were spirits of the former inhabitants of Avalon. They were creatures of Faerie," Patrick responded. "It is my belief that long ago they were the offspring of angels and men."

Teodorico's smile turned patronizing, though he made an effort to temper any condescension.

"A theologically charming notion, though highly unlikely, hmm?" he said. "We benefactors have long been aware of the ghosts who populate the Misty Isle. We thought them harmless apparitions. Some of us even argued they would serve as good morality lessons to the students. Lessons in avoiding the temptations of devils, and all their glamours."

"But they're not!" Aimeé interjected.

Everyone in the room turned to the maidservant who had spoken out.

She turned sheepish, but added, "My Lord, they are not all bad, the Fair Folk. They sometimes play tricks on us, yes, but they often help, too. Bringing home lost children and such."

Teodorico tsked gently and stroked Aimeé's cheek, saying, "Child, your view is not rare among the common folk, hmm, yes? I imagine you even put out saucers of milk for them on the porch, hmm? You avoid stepping on their fairy rings in the forest? You probably even light a midsummer candle to appease them, hmm, yes?" He crossed himself. "But trust me, I'm a man of God. I know demons when I see them. Since the time of Eden they have manipulated us to do what they wish for their own motives, whether to convince us to eat of the Fruit of Knowledge to cut us off from God, or to simply feed them saucers of milk... or remove a troublesome wolf from their lair, hmm, yes?"

He directed this last at Patrick, and added, "And why do you feel so strongly about them?"

Patrick swallowed hard and his gaze flickered to the flute-crucifix nestled between Aimeé's breasts. In doing so, he noticed Aimeé had grown quiet and her attention was on one of the many travel chests, lined up on the other side of the room. A noise came from that direction and she took a step closer to him.

"I understand your desire to keep your oaths," Teodorico continued, not waiting for a response and drawing Patrick back into the conversation, "but is it not inconceivable the Holy Spirit led you to that cave to liberate the cup from these creatures, hmm? That your true responsibility is to bring the cup into the light of the world, hmm, yes?"

"But they saved me from my injuries after my battle with the wolf," Patrick said, the fog in his mind growing. "I cannot believe they are evil."

Teodorico put up a hand. "All I ask is that you should be open to other possibilities. I would like to see the cup tour the kingdoms, held aloft by the Knight of Cups and the Lazarine Maid, ushering an era of peace. The other benefactors will convene soon on the island and we will discuss the matter, and after they see the moving reaction of the people I have brought with me who wish to adore the relic, they will see the wisdom of releasing it from the island hmm, yes?"

"It may all be a moot point," Patrick said tersely, his fists clenching over the cardinal's dismissive tone. "The cup is not allowing anyone to touch it."

"So I've been told," the cardinal conceded. "It's my belief it is waiting for you, Sir Patrick, hmm, yes?"

"Waiting for me?"

"Yes, you transported it to the church, and there it awaits you to be transported again, and I trust you will make the right choice as to where it will go."

Patrick blinked and opened his mouth to counter with a convincing objection, but nothing appropriate came to mind.

Patrick and Aimeé stayed a little longer, but the cardinal excused them. On their way out, Patrick relented to his desire to massage his throbbing headache, barely noticing Aimeé casting a fearful glance over her shoulder at the trunk in the corner of the room.

#

They made their way down the gangplank, fighting against the flow of porters and servants.

When they reached the crowded dock, Marcus waited for them as promised. They had to stand close to one another to avoid the press of people. Oxcarts also took up space, sitting patiently as their loads were hoisted skyward and into the boats.

All the activity and shouts from the workers made it difficult to concentrate. Patrick ruminated over the cardinal's last words, pondering what on earth he would do when the time came for him to stand over the cup. Eventually, he came to realize through the noise inside and outside his head that Aimeé spoke, trying to tell him something about a chest and a lid.

"Pardon?" he said.

"You didn't see it?" she reiterated, brow creased in exasperation.

"See what?"

Aimeé flailed her hands in frustration. "There was something in the cardinal's trunk, watching us!"

Patrick made a face, trying to process the odd statement.

"Oh, never mind! I am going to help the Greensprings servants. Good day, Sir Patrick." She huffed and departed, pulling her hood over her head. Before striding too far, however, she turned and added, "You know, I find it odd you say you want to talk things out, but every time I try to talk, your mind is elsewhere!"

"Aimeé, wait!" he called after her, but she had stomped out of earshot.

"Women," Sir Marcus said thoughtfully, watching her receding form. "Whether high-born or low-born, they are a beautiful chaos. I often wonder if the world would be better or worse for their absence."

Patrick did not respond—merely ground his teeth helplessly.

"Come, Patrick, let us go drink the universal remedy. Let's get a beer."

Silently, Patrick turned to follow his fellow guardsman, meandering through the crowd. He looked up just in time to glimpse an individual watching him from the crowd on the other side of a passing oxcart. Patrick drew a sharp breath at the face he thought he had only imagined the night before at the inn. A face conjuring memories of battles, hunger, and death. A crusader named Lucan.

"Patrick, what is it?" Marcus asked.

"I saw someone I know," Patrick replied over his shoulder, and plunged into the crowd. He frantically searched for the man, but he had disappeared.

"Not surprising," Marcus said, shrugging when he caught up to Patrick. "The place is full of Greensprings and Aesclinn people."

"No, this person couldn't possibly be here," Patrick whispered, closing his eyes under the attack of a headache and voices in his head. "I saw him die during the Crusade."

#

The moon floated fat and bright in the sky, appearing and disappearing with the clouds.

Gwyndaline waited until late evening to fetch the day's water from the town well to avoid the crowds of Avalon folk. Like the others of the community, she did not mind the extra coin they brought. They paid well to keep the event a secret, but they did cause a God-awful disruption to the daily routine.

She grunted as she worked the winch to bring the bucket from the depths of the well, then when the handle bumped her swollen belly, barked a laugh born somewhere between frustration and absurdity.

"Ah, sorry my darlin'. Only a bit longer and we won't have to worry about that," she said to her stomach, rubbing it tenderly after setting the locking mechanism on the winch. She blew sweaty stray hair out of her eyes. "You're a bit overdue, and you make things a bit difficult, but I'm sure you'll be worth the wait."

Before reaching for the bucket dangling over the well mouth, she hummed to her stomach, wondering not for the first time whether a girl or a boy child heard her voice.

"They say because you hang so low, you must be a boy, but I..."

Her attention suddenly turned to the empty darkness of the cobblestone street. She had heard a scrabbling noise on the stones.

"Who's there?" she called and paused waiting for a response. When none came, she added, "Won't you come out and help a poor pregnant woman carry her water?"

She squinted into the darkness, but only a cat darted across the street.

She huffed and struggled to pour the well bucket into her own. Once finished, she braced a hand against her back and carried the water down the street towards her home.

A cloud moved away from the moon, casting the street in moonlight.

The scrabbling noise came again, this time at a distance behind her.

"I'm not finding this funny!" she called out. Though moonlight may have illuminated much of the village, it also cast long shadows. "Thomas Luther, if that is you trying to scare me I'm going to have harsh words to say to your mother!"

No response came and an unease crept into her gut. She continued on her way.

More scrabbling came, and closer, but this time she did not look back. The unease in her gut turned into a jolt, stabbing at her heart. She picked up her pace.

The scrabbling matched her speed.

She dropped her bucket and broke into a run, her breath coming in hectic gasps.

A shadow passed over her, momentarily blotting out the moonlight around her.

"No!" she cried in a voice strangled by fear. She ran.

Something heavy crushed her, followed by an overpowering flowery smell drawing her into darkness.

#

The following morning, a delay greeted Patrick near the docks. As he had understood it, all the supplies and material had been loaded the previous day and passengers only needed to board. Mass would be held on the deck, as it was the Lord's Day; then they would sail to Avalon.

But when he and Marcus left the inn with a gaggle of young nobles, they found a crowd gathered at the center of the village, blocking the road. Patrick and Marcus pushed their way to the front of the commotion, letting the swan emblem on their surcoats do most of the work.

Near the well they found agitated villagers arguing with an equal number of outsiders.

"It was one of those *people* you brought with ye, that's what it was!" a villager shouted, stabbing a finger at a nun in an all-white habit.

"Don't be ridiculous!" said a clergyman in a green robe, his fuzzy white lamb chop beard bristling in indignation.

"What's the meaning of all this?" Marcus boomed as he approached.

"My lord," the finger-pointing villager addressed the Avangardesman, "one of our people was murdered last night."

A gasp went through the crowd at the accusation. The villager pointed to a prone body on the cobblestones. A man wailed terribly over the woman, holding her body to his breast, rocking back and forth in misery.

"That's a serious accusation," Marcus said, approaching the body. Long hair obscured the face. "What happened to her?"

"That's Gwyndaline, telling by her clothes, but you can hardly tell by her condition," the villager spat. "Something unnatural happened to her. She's all shriveled like a plucked gourd that's been sittin' around fer a month. The only thing else so unnatural are those *people* that nun brought."

Patrick noted the emphasis the accusers placed on the word *people* as he approached Marcus who had dropped to a knee to examine the body.

The villager gently convinced the grieving man to relinquish the body long enough to roll it outwards for examination.

A gasp rippled through the crowd. The color had drained completely out of the poor woman's skin and her flesh had shriveled like a raisin. Hollow depressions formed her cheeks. She looked like someone who had starved to death in a dark dungeon.

"You sure this is Gwyndaline?" Patrick asked, and soon regretted it.

"Don't you think I recognize me own wife!" the grieving man wailed. "She had the most beautiful blue eyes. Look at them!"

They were milked over with cataracts. But they had indeed once been blue.

"The children couldn't have done this," the nun protested.

"That's because they're not children," the accusing villager returned.

"Wait a minute," Marcus interrupted. "Are you referring to the candidati the cardinal brought with him?"

"Yes!" the nun shouted. "Just because they're... special... doesn't mean they're monsters. They are Godly creatures deserving our compassion."

"Bah!" said the fisherman, and the other villagers took up the angry murmur.

"If they are in the cardinal's care, then they are far from evil," Marcus reasoned. "There must be some other explanation."

"Wulfric, what do you make of this?" the clergyman in green asked a colleague. The man, robed in gray with a long white beard, knelt down to the body. When he did, Patrick got a good look at the coat of arms adorning the front of his robe: a cross formed from thorny branches.

"Father Wulfric is an expert on things natural and unnatural," the clergyman in green explained.

"Father," the grieving husband pleaded, now recognizing Wulfric as a priest, "can you please say a prayer for our child? They say the unborn go to limbo, but if you could just... just..." The man broke down again.

"Child?" the long-bearded priest said.

The man weakly gestured to the dead woman's stomach. At first the emaciated condition of the body made it difficult to discern, but closer examination revealed a bump.

Father Wulfric touched the region, and yet another gasp erupted from the crowd when the bump deflated horribly. The husband convulsed in agony.

"Father, what can you tell us?" Marcus asked the priest.

Wulfric examined the body. His bushy white eyebrows bunched over his nose, and he plucked something from the dead woman's clothing.

"What's that?" Marcus asked.

"I'm not sure," the old man replied. "It looks like some sort of skin."

The curious onlookers pressed around Wulfric. Light passed through the parchment-like sheet he held, making it easier to note the fish scale pattern in it. When completely unfolded, it was the size of his chest and had what looked like the spidery trace-work of veins.

"You're not saying Gwyndaline was killed by some animal, do you?" the villager said incredulously.

Wulfric shrugged. "I have no idea, but this was found on the body. Does this look like anything you've ever seen?"

The villager looked the thing over and shrugged inconclusively, his face scrunching up at the sight of it.

Wulfric rose to a crouch and examined the ground, moving away from the well and the docks, towards the forest. Villagers made way for him.

"There seems to be a trail of it, leading to the woods," he said.

"Well, there you have it," the fuzzy bearded clergyman said. "I'd say the poor lass fell afoul of some creature from the wilds."

"Nonsense!" the chief accuser said. "All these people moving about could easily have shifted the trail from the boats to the woods."

"If I may make a suggestion," Marcus said, and all eyes turned to him. "It would appear Gwyndaline ran afoul of *something*. Now, I doubt anyone in Cardinal Teodorico's retinue is responsible, and therefore the whole village could be at risk even after we leave. It is fortunate today we have an abundance of priests and monks on hand who can bless the village and your boats, offering God's protection from further harm."

A favorable murmur passed through the crowd.

"What say you, Abbot Herewinus?" Marcus addressed the clergyman in green. "Is that agreeable?"

Herewinus' face flexed into a contemplative mask. He stroked his great white lamb-chop beard, and finally responded, "Certainly. What do you say, Father Wulfric? Do you think you can coordinate with the Romans to bless the boats and the village in a timely manner?"

"Eh?" Wulfric said, still distracted by the thing he examined in his hands. "Oh, yes, blessing. I'd rather say it would be more expedient if the cardinal would incorporate the blessing into the Mass. He could stand on the upper deck and bless the entire village and harbor from there, especially if the villagers were to gather on the dock beneath the boat."

More favorable murmurs rippled through the crowd.

As Marcus and Herewinus discussed making the suggestion to Teodorico, Patrick noted that Wulfric sniffed at the skin in his hands. When he did so, the thing flaked, fell apart and scattered to the winds.

After that, Patrick and Marcus helped herd the crowd of richly dressed noble youths onto the boats. Perhaps several hundred in all, they came from every kingdom in Christendom, speaking of the morning's commotion in an excited cacophony of languages as they boarded.

Once on board Cardinal Teodorico held Mass on the big Roman ship, turning the upper deck of the ship into a temporary altar and sanctuary. Herewinus did likewise on another ship, as did another priest Patrick had yet to meet on the third boat. Teodorico was happy to agree to the blessing and stood at the ship's railing to bless the village, villagers, and harbor. Eventually, the single giant sail was hoisted, the galley men dropped oars, and the boat got underway.

Patrick stood on the captain's deck near the ship's rudder. There he learned something new about traveling to and from Avalon. Travelers to Avalon could only penetrate the protective mist by invitation—an invitation written only by one of the handful of mystical relics associated with the island, the legendary swan feathers used as quills. Today, however, Patrick watched the cardinal remove a sacred feather from a special box presented to him by his servant Victor. The cardinal then floated the feather on the water in a bowl next to the helmsman. He said a prayer over it and the feather drifted, pointing out to sea. The helmsman noted the subtle changes in the feather's position and adjusted the rudder accordingly. The other two ships followed closely.

Patrick grunted, musing out loud, "I had no idea."

"Aye," Marcus commented next to him. "I didn't know myself until several years after being an Avangarde."

"Did Herewinus tell Teodorico the blessing idea was yours, or did he take all the credit for calming the locals?" Patrick whispered, leaning closer.

Marcus shrugged. "I let him convey the idea."

Patrick shook his head at the politics of it all, and how much he hated it, when he saw Aimeé on the lower deck near the rail.

His eye twitched and his headache returned, a low fire between his temples. He had a sudden desire to throttle Geoffrey and desperately wished the man were present so he could. He still might do just that when he saw him next.

He shook his head.

No, that wouldn't accomplish anything. Wouldn't help. Geoffrey is not the problem.

He looked at his hand that trembled slightly and questioned if his sanity slipped yet again.

Did I not see the face of a dead man in the crowd yesterday? Am I seeing things again?

The pounding in his head escalated and the sound of distant battle rose to a din.

He squeezed his eyes shut and grabbed his head.

God help me, he prayed.

The gentle roll of the deck and the soothing sea breeze calmed him, and a realization came over him.

*The child could be mine. Mine. I could be having a baby...
with Aimeé.*

For the first time, this earth-shattering realization was not
earth-shattering, but remotely calming.

The deck rolled and his hair fluttered in the breeze.

Tell her you love her, his mother's voice echoed in his head.

Patrick excused himself and made his way down the steep
staircase to the lower deck and approached Aimeé.

"Can we talk?" he asked.

She drew a deep breath and crossed her arms. "It is a boat,
and I doubt I can avoid you, so I guess I don't have a choice."

"I just wanted to say..." His throat closed up and he struggled
to swallow. He raised his hand to his throat to rub it, and when he
did he noticed the partially healed wound along his hand. The
hand trembled a bit and he frowned at it. Doubt crept into his
heart as memories of her lying lifeless in a bed of flowers
assaulted his mind.

Wouldn't they truly be better off without me?

"Patrick?" she asked, looking up into his eyes with
anticipation. With expectation.

"I..." Patrick commenced to say, but his attention suddenly
drew to a group gathering near them. His eyes became big as
saucers as he took a sharp breath and stepped back.

Aimeé's brow furrowed in puzzlement as she glanced at the
activity drawing Patrick's attention.

A group of young people in simple clothes milled about,
herded by the nun in the white habit. One of the young people, a
girl, broke away from the group and approached Aimeé, shuffling
along in a lurching manner. When she arrived, Patrick took
another step back.

The young woman before them had very large blue eyes set in
oversized sockets, a plump face, and a slack jaw with mismatched
teeth. She mumbled something.

"What was that, little one?" Aimeé asked, her initial shock
turning into a smiling demeanor, both gentle and kind.

"Pretty," the odd looking girl mumbled again, her slack jaw contorting into a smile. Moisture glistened at the corners of her mouth. She pointed at the maidservant's face. "You're very pretty."

"Aw, bless you," Aimeé said, having no trouble embracing the creature who giggled.

"Candace, come here now," the nun in white sternly called to the girl.

The odd girl shambled away, but before leaving, looked over her shoulder and added, "So is your baby."

Aimeé's jaw dropped.

"Well, I guess news travels fast," Aimeé said, a hint of scorn in her voice as she glared at Patrick.

"What? Me?" he protested, "I haven't told anyone. Well, except Sir Marcus."

Aimeé put her hands on her full hips and glared at the knight.

"Patrick! Will you not respect me in anything regarding this? If we aren't getting married, then I must wait for an appropriate time to tell the staff at Greensprings," she said, her glare far from subsiding.

"Well, if you would just agree to marry me it wouldn't be a concern, and besides, I seriously doubt Sir Marcus confided in a changeling about your condition," he responded.

"How else did she... Wait, what did you call her?"

Patrick stared at the group of odd young people as they moved on, guided by their chaperoning nun. He wiped a nervous brow and said, "Changelings. They're changelings."

"Don't be silly, they're merely simple is all. When I was a child there were several such children in my village. I've never seen so many in one place, though," Aimeé said.

Patrick shook his head. "Where I come from, when a child is born like that, it is suspected an evil fairy has replaced the real child with... that."

Aimeé shook her head, not knowing what to say.

"The villagers accused them of killing that poor woman before we left," Patrick added, understanding dawning on him now he had seen the nun's charges.

Those people.

"That's just ridiculous," Aimeé said.

"I agree," Patrick replied, eyes narrowing in thought. "Changelings are meant to be a burden, dead weight—not malicious."

Aimeé threw up her hands. "That's not what I meant! I think once you get to know them, they're quite lovely."

"'Candidati,'" Patrick said, turning introspective. "That's what Sir Marcus called them. 'The candidati brought by Cardinal Teodorico.' 'Candidati' means 'candidates,' I believe, but candidates for what?"

"You're not listening to me again, are you?" Aimeé slapped Patrick in the chest.

"Hoy, hey," he exclaimed, broken from his introspection.

"I hate it when you do that."

"Do what?"

"Go wherever it is you go when you think deeply," she explained. "You treat me like I'm not here."

Before Patrick could defend himself, another group of youth approached them.

"Sir Patrick Gawain?" they asked, holding their hats in hand.

Three young men in squire tunics stood wide-eyed before the Irishman.

"Yes," Patrick responded, curious.

The two smaller ones pushed the third taller one forward, urging him to say something.

"We just wanted to say what an honor it is to meet you," the elder towheaded boy said.

Patrick's mouth screwed up into a semblance of a smile as he struggled to find the proper response.

He settled on, "Thank you?"

The two younger boys continued to prod the older boy in the back until he angrily turned on them and shooed them away. The older boy then awkwardly took a knee, and the other two followed suit. The display surprised Patrick.

"Our apologies for our presumptions," the blonde said, "but our day of dubbing is fast approaching and as I'm sure you know, we can request whomever we chose to perform the knighting ceremony. Myself, Charles of Flanders, and my companions, Jakob and Josef of Prague, would be greatly honored if you would consider performing the ceremony."

Patrick blinked, all the more shocked.

"Me? Why me?"

One of the dark-haired boys behind the taller boy spoke up, his accent Slavic, but his French impeccable.

"Because you are Sir Patrick Gawain, first over the wall in Jerusalem, Savior of Avalon, and Knight of Cups."

"Ah bloody hell," Patrick grumbled. "First of all lads, I was not the first one over the wall in Jerusalem. Also, I, as well as yourselves, are charged with keeping Avalon and any exploits occurring there secret. The whole point of being dubbed by a knight of celebrity is so you can be associated in some way with their accomplishments. No one will believe, let alone know, what it means to be 'Savior of Avalon.'"

The blonde boy resolutely shook his head, saying, "It matters not if we can tell the world of what you have done in Avalon. It is enough *we* know that you have touched the Cup of the Christ, like a knight of King Arthur. As for Jerusalem, I can swear by my own eyes I have seen you go over the wall. Perhaps not the first individual, but certainly with the first company."

Not for the first time that day, surprise and shock crept into Patrick's chest. He bent over slightly to look into the face of the blonde boy who looked humbly at the ground.

"Charles?" Patrick said. "Charles of Flanders? Do I know you?"

The boy looked up and said, "We met briefly. Though you knew me then as Charles of the Danemark. I was squire to my Uncle Robert, Count of Flanders."

Recognition dawned on Patrick and he said, "Yes, I remember you. I cannot say much for your uncle, I'm sorry to say, but you struck me as a very good lad. My goodness, you've grown much since then."

"Thank you, Sir Patrick," the boy seemed genuinely pleased to receive the praise.

"But you were almost ready to be knighted then," Patrick said, confused. "What happened? You're almost a grown man now and still a squire?"

"Let's just say Uncle Robert picked the wrong side when disputing with Emperor Henry," Charles said sheepishly. "My dubbing was put on hold. When my current master was assigned captain of the Cardinal Guard, he told me Avalon was the 'Island of Second Chances,' and then I saw you and knew it was true."

Patrick couldn't argue.

"Very well," he said. "I would be honored to dub the lot of you."

The boys stood and thanked Patrick excitedly, apologized for disturbing him, and scampered away.

Patrick shook his head in wonderment at their retreating forms in the gathering crowd on the deck. That's when he noticed Aimeé standing by, watching with her arms crossed.

"What?" he asked.

"You're going to let this go to your head aren't you?" she said with a hint of a smile.

Patrick hesitated, then with a hint of his own smile, said, "Perhaps."

With the mood lightened, Patrick allowed the smile to grow and let the warm feeling grow in his chest. He stepped closer to her and reached for her stomach, but people began to crowd the railing, separating them, as word spread the Isle of Avalon neared. Though only a growing wall of mist presented itself on the water, the excited youths jockeyed for position to be the first to see the legendary Isle when it appeared.

Any chance of having a private moment with Aimeé completely extinguished when a seven-year-old girl bumped into Aimeé and dropped her doll in the press of bodies. Aimeé bent to retrieve the doll for the girl, but the child's eyes widened with fear and she disappeared into the crowd.

"Oh the poor dear," Aimeé said, picking up the ragged and dirty item. "I better return this to her."

She slipped into the crowd in pursuit of the little girl.

"Dammit," Patrick grumbled.

"I'm taller than you," a voice said next to him.

Patrick looked down and saw an odd-looking fellow standing next to him.

"I beg your pardon?"

"I'm taller than you," the stranger said again.

Patrick scowled at the man who stood at least a good head shorter. At first glance he seemed to be a child, but his wizened and lined face with receding hairline said otherwise. An idiot's grin stretched from ear to ear. Rail thin and with narrow eyes, he had an oversized head with a mouth full of perfectly straight yet oversized teeth. Though obviously not a changeling, Patrick still felt certain he belonged to Teodorico's candidati.

"I'm taller than you," he continued to insist.

"No, you're not," Patrick replied.

"Yes I am."

"Are not."

"Am too."

Patrick groaned and put his face in his hands.

"You are taller than him," a new voice behind them said, "but you know who is taller than you? The cardinal."

"He is not!" the little man retorted.

"I'm afraid so, you best go take it up with him. You can find him on the captain's deck," the newcomer suggested.

Patrick felt the little man vacate the space next to him in a hurry.

"Thank you..." Patrick started to say, turning to his savior, but froze when he laid eyes on the man.

There stood Lucan, the dead man from his past.

#

Most everyone crowded the sides of the boat to watch for the island's appearance, leaving the deck largely free of people. Aimeé tracked the girl to a pile of crates and watched her disappear among them. She called vainly to the child, telling her she only wanted to return her doll.

She circled the crates until convinced the girl must have somehow climbed inside one of them.

Not knowing what else to do, the French girl got down on her knees and crawled among the crates herself, revealing a warren of narrow pathways. She squeezed along them until she found a hollow space where she could stand. There, sitting on top of the highest crate next to the ship's mast, was the girl.

"No, don't run please," she said gently. "I just want to give you your doll back."

The little girl may have been blonde once, but dirt and grime colored her hair. The rest of her wasn't much cleaner, and her dress was in tatters, like the rag doll.

Aimeé held out the doll and shook it gently, saying, "She's lonely. She wants to go home."

Grave mistrust flickered in the child's eyes and she pulled away at first, but then quick as a viper she reached out and snatched the doll. Then just as quickly she disappeared from Aimeé's sight.

"Well, you're most welcome," Aimeé said, her eyes lingering on the empty space.

She hunkered down and crawled out of the crates. When she emerged, she bumped into a gray robed man, smacking her face into the thorny-cross emblem on his robe.

"Excusez-moi," she apologized to the man.

"That is quite all right, my child," the man with the long white beard said, though his attention was fixed on something in his hand. It looked like the gray paper made by bees in their nests.

"What is that?" she asked.

The old man tried to neatly fold the item and slip it into a pocket, but it disintegrated in the sea breeze.

"I'm not sure," he replied distantly. "I found it on the deck. I wouldn't have seen it if I hadn't seen you follow that little girl. You crawled right over the top of it."

His eyes followed the fluttering remnants blowing out to sea, face drawn into a mask of deep concern.

#

"How is this possible?" Patrick asked, dumbfounded at the sight of the man.

"How is what possible?" Lucan responded, smiling casually against the rail and leveling his eyes at Patrick.

Mist engulfed the ship, limiting vision to only a few feet. The chatter of the crowd around them and the rhythmic splash of the oars one deck below was eerily muffled.

As tall as Patrick, the man wore the red surcoat of the Cardinal Guard, complete with chain mail armor and long sword belted at his hip. A crimson cape trailed down his back.

At first glance, one would have guessed him to be thirty-something years of age, but his weather-lined face and a peppering of gray in his brown hair made his actual age difficult to discern. With his lantern jaw, he was not a bad-looking fellow, but with brown eyes and an unremarkable nose, he could probably disappear in a crowd without trouble. Unless his face had haunted you for years.

"I saw you die at Antioch," Patrick said, scrutinizing the man's face closely, making sure he was not mistaken. He was not.

Patrick fixed his gaze on the man, afraid Lucan might disappear as he had the previous days.

"Ah yes, Antioch," Lucan said, looking out into the mist along with the other spectators who jostled around them. "That was a while ago. When I heard it was a crusader who had discovered the cup, I didn't imagine it would be one I recognized. After all, were there not something like a hundred thousand of us? Well, it sure seemed like it. What are the odds, you think?"

"The same odds as watching a man run through with a half-dozen swords and lances and then be talking to me today. Again, how is that possible?"

"Are you sure of what you saw in Antioch?"

"Yes," Patrick didn't let the man's disarming smile deter him. "You rode next to Count Raymond of Toulouse in the battle freeing us from siege. I was not far behind, mad with hunger and sickness, but I remember well enough."

Patrick's memory wandered to the past, remembering when he and the crusaders found themselves pinned down by a host of Muslims, besieged behind the very walls of Antioch to which they had won access only days before. Already low on food and supplies, their own siege lasted a month, ushering in desperate times when knights had been reduced to eating their horses. Even rats became scarce.

During the siege, Peter the Hermit, a vagabond priest and self-styled leader of the commoners among the crusaders, claimed to have had a vision of Saint Andrew who led him to a Christian church in the city. There, so the story went, the saint beseeched him to dig, telling the priest he would find the tip of the spear that had pierced the side of Christ: a holy object. Peter did as instructed, and with the aid of the noble Count Raymond, they found a fragment of metal.

Even with Raymond's endorsement, and a sliver of hope, Peter met with resistance when he suggested the holy relic would lead them to victory should they charge out the gates to battle. The papal legate, Bishop Adehmar, mocked him and insisted that someone from his own staff—a warrior-scholar, chronicler, and relic expert—authenticate the object as a true relic.

That person was Lucan, and he did authenticate it, giving hope to the beleaguered crusaders.

"You led us out the gates, an army of ragged scarecrows, with that bit of rusty metal tied to a staff, calling it the Holy Lance," Patrick continued, "and when you fell under a swarm of Turks, along with the lance, we fell into a rage. The Turks fled before our fury. When we cleared the bodies, you and the lance were gone. We assumed you trampled to a pulp in the mud."

Lucan leaned forward and his brown eyes peered deeply into Patrick's. "What else did you see that day?"

Patrick hesitated to respond.

"You saw them, didn't you?" Lucan said, not waiting. "The Heavenly Host fighting side-by-side with us to defeat the enemy. I know... Later, others said it was the delirium of hunger, or the tainted rat meat making us see things, but you know the truth. Don't you, Sir Patrick? The Holy Lance flared with a light of its own and the angels and saints fought with us."

Patrick's eye twitched. Images of ghostly warriors danced across his mind, but he questioned his memory. He questioned reality. And something else. Something nagged at his mind, and when he tried to focus on the memory, an ice pick stabbed his brain.

"It's hard to say," Patrick said at last. "It's as you say. We were starving."

Lucan smiled wryly. "Then you easily could have mistaken the gravity of my wounds."

"And the Holy Lance?" Patrick asked.

"Taken into Heaven by the host," Lucan replied with a shrug, "or lost in the mud. I'd rather believe the former." Lucan looked out into the mist again as it swept over them. A gull cried.

"You remember me, then?" Patrick asked, shaking off the memories and the pain in his head.

The man held out his hand and Patrick shook it.

"In truth? I only knew your name from the cardinal's reports. It wasn't until today I recognized your face, though I daresay you look much healthier these days," Lucan said apologetically.

"Let me guess. You are here as part of Cardinal Teodorico's entourage to once again act as relic expert, to validate the cup?" Patrick surmised.

"Precisely. With my credentials, Pope Paschal assigned me as captain of Teodorico's Cardinal Guard and his resident scholar," Lucan said. "Interesting times are ahead of us."

As if to punctuate this, the crowd along the rails gasped in wonder when the mist suddenly broke and Avalon appeared.

Chapter Four

Mooring the boats at the Avalon docks took little time. From the height of the ship Patrick noted the Avangarde's waiting archway of lances. They formed a corridor of strength, inviting the Guests to a new life in the Keep at Greensprings. The two hundred and fifty knights made for an impressive show with silvery helms, mail, and spears polished to a high sheen, glinting in the sun. Black surcoats ruffled in the breeze with contrasting white swan emblems blazing on their chests. Likewise, those same swans adorned their tear-shaped shields.

The previous arrival, he had been one of the mounted knights —though just a Reservist—and he remembered the arrival as a noisy affair with Guests chattering excitedly as they walked down the gangplanks to be greeted by the senior Greensprings staff. Sir Wolfgang von Fiescher, Father Hugh Constant, and Mother Superior each offered their greetings at one of the three respective boats. This time, however, a quiet awe surrounded the crowd, creating a strangely subdued atmosphere.

As a Reservist, he had struggled in all manner of tests; physical, mental, and social. He rarely knew of the tests' existence until after the fact, which infuriated him, and for the longest time the tangible symbol of the office—the swan—remained out of reach. In retrospect, he understood why the Avangarde used such a discerning process: and seeing the mounted knights now in all their glory, he was proud to be one of them.

He made his way down the gangplank from the cardinal's ship to meet Wolfgang's outstretched hand. Patrick clasped it strongly.

"Wilkommen," the German-born Grand Master of the Avangarde Order greeted him. "It is good to see you again Patrick. You look well and I look forward to hearing the tales of your adventures. That is one of the drawbacks of being the leader of the Order—its duties take me away from Avalon too often. To hear about my knights' exploits through correspondence is no substitution for hearing it from themselves over a pint."

"A problem easily remedied tonight," Patrick responded.

Wolfgang grunted a noise of approval through his white beard and mustache. His equally white eyebrows lifted in greeting at Marcus who came up behind Patrick. They too clasped hands and exchanged words.

"After your mounts have been unloaded from the ship, join your brethren," Wolfgang gestured towards the dual columns of mounted knights.

With that, Wolfgang turned back to his greeting duties as he turned to Lucan who came next in line, followed by the nun and her candidati charges.

#

The wagon journey proved long and ponderous, but with plenty of daylight left to reach their destination, the travelers felt no urgency.

The new arrivals drank in the Avalon scenery, which was awash in golden sunlight that brought out the most vibrant colors. Even when traversing the shade-steeped forest, the ferns and mossy stones were luminescent with an emerald glow.

The day's loveliness made Patrick wish he had time to walk in the grass, hand in hand with Aimeé so that they could talk. She had almost warmed up to him on the boat. Now, as his gaze located her among the wagons, he did not know when the next opportunity for a private moment would come.

The long caravan stretched over the landscape. The hundred or so armed Roman contingent mostly clung about the cardinal's colorful wagons at the center of the caravan, though several of their mounted men also roamed as scouts. A third of the Avangarde rode in front of the caravan, a third at the back, and another third were staggered among the wagons. Though attack was highly unlikely, the Avangarde prided themselves on maintaining proper armed escort protocol. The extraordinary did happen, as a year ago when creatures attacked the keep. Therefore, it was best to be prepared.

The formation also allowed some of the Avangarde to start early on the other aspect of their duties: brotherly mentorship. To that end, Patrick inserted himself among those knights riding along the wagons, doing his best to work on his weakest Avangarde skill—conversing with Guests. He wanted to work his way up the column to Aimeé's wagon slowly without being too obvious about it.

"I'm glad you're with us, Sir Knight," said a young man. "If I were to try and find my way from the harbor to the castle by myself, I surely would be lost."

"It is essentially a straight path," Patrick responded. "There is but one path from the harbor to the keep. Only once does the road fork, and that other road follows the coast to Aesclinn. You want the path leading inland."

"Yes, but it seems the path meanders in every which direction, almost as if we were going in circles. Am I mistaken?" The young man looked behind and forward again, eyes squinting, trying to find his bearings.

Freshly returned to Avalon from a long absence, Patrick understood what the young man meant. The island's wonder struck him just as it had the first time. As they plodded down the dirt road through an open field, Avalon enchanted with a surreal quality he found one moment crisp, but then hazy and dreamlike the next.

"No, you're not mistaken," Patrick admitted. "The island has a mind of its own. She is alive and aware of your presence. She will mislead you if she can."

Monolithic standing stones at the bend of the road seemed to lean in and listen to their conversation.

"Really, why?" the young man squeaked in a hushed voice. He looked around and then jumped in his seat, face to face with a gnarled oak tree whose trunk held the semblance of a wizened old man.

Patrick smiled. "Because she wants to send you down difficult paths to test you, to make you a better person. Be vigilant, make the right choices, and you will always find your way home."

The air shimmered as if on a hot day, causing the path to bend and twist. Distant ponds appeared ahead, only to fade as they approached, then reappear behind them as they passed.

"And if I don't?" The young man's already high-pitched voice rose an octave.

Patrick let memories wash over him. "Then you will end up with more time on your hands than you ever wanted. Trust me, you most likely won't need to worry about any of that." He winked. "All the real excitement is in Greensprings. Now, if you'll excuse me—Reinholdt, is it?—I must introduce myself to others."

Patrick squeezed heels to Siegfried, and the big horse dutifully picked up the pace to a gallop. The next wagon held mostly sacks of supplies, but also a couple of Lady Guests in colorful gowns.

"Greetings, ladies," Patrick said with a practiced smile; the other thing he worked on improving. Others often told him he frowned overly much. "I'm Sir Patrick Gawain. I will be one of your guardians and a brother in spirit while you are at Greensprings."

The teenagers introduced themselves as Estelle and Alexia, and did not offer much conversation. They mostly concerned themselves with Estelle's dress, which she had ripped.

"Not much I can do about that," Patrick said, smile straining. "My sewing skills are atrocious."

"That's very disappointing," Estelle said. "We were told the Avangarde were unique in that they would help in all things. They would be our 'big brothers.' My brother back home would be very happy to mend my dress."

I doubt that, Patrick wanted to snort, but instead broadened his smile and said, "I believe the intent is for the Avangarde's interaction with Guests to demonstrate Greensprings's commitment to fostering peace. What better way to show that than to have the peacekeepers capable of doing more than bashing skulls. Swords into plowshares and all that."

"So, you'll mend her dress, Sir Knight?" Alexia asked.

"I can point you in the direction of a good seamstress," Patrick said, then partially drew his sword from its scabbard. "Or, I can I get started right now."

"That won't be necessary, Brother," Estelle giggled.

As they passed an apple orchard, a snow of blossoms cascaded all around them, and Patrick heard familiar music on the wind. He excused himself from the giggling ladies, pressed heels to Siegfried again, and followed the music. He sidled up next to Aimeé's wagon where she practiced on the flute his mother had given her.

"I see you didn't waste any time introducing yourself to the Lady Guests," she said, pausing from her practice and keeping her gaze forward. "And pretty ones at that."

She sat next to the wagon driver, a mere boy who held the oxen's reins.

"I also spent a fair amount of time with the lads," Patrick said, scowling, "and I daresay several of them were prettier than the lasses, but I doubt you noticed that."

A muscle in her jaw angrily worked back and forth even as she blew anew into the instrument. The final note came out with a quack like a wounded duck's.

"Are you ready to listen to some music?" she asked, pausing again, still looking ahead. "I almost have the tune right. I'm very close."

Patrick shifted uneasily in the saddle.

He could see the boy wagon driver watching their exchange with curiosity. "You there." He leaned to look at him. "Have you been informed of the arrival plan?"

"Y-yes, my lord." The boy swallowed, suddenly trying to shrink into his seat. "Wagons with Guests will move to the right after crossing the drawbridge and continue onto the halls for Guests. The Avangarde will unload their belongings and help them move in. Wagons with supplies will remain in the courtyard and will be unloaded by staff. The Roman entourage will peel off before the keep and set up a pavilion encampment outside the walls."

"Very good," Patrick said tersely with a sharp stare, discouraging the boy from further eavesdropping.

Aimeé glared. "My lord, don't you have more Lady Guests to meet and boys to intimidate?"

Patrick prepared to respond angrily, but a wave of scintillating colors washed over them with a feverish buzz. Siegfried reared slightly, and Patrick threw up a hand to protect his eyes. The oxen stopped, and Patrick could hear Aimeé and the nearest Guests gasp in shock. He squinted open an eye and gasped himself as he realized a multitude of dragonflies engulfed them in a swarm of rainbow bodies and gossamer wings. It lasted only a moment, then the migration of insects passed them on their way to the next pond.

"A face!" Aimeé exclaimed. "I saw a face on one of them!"

"A person's face?" the wagon driver asked, skeptically.

"Yes!"

"Don't be silly," Patrick said, watching the glittering storm disappear.

No sooner had he spoke when Estelle and Alexia also exclaimed something about faces.

"You see?" Aimeé scolded him. "You always doubt me. Now, good day, Sir!"

Patrick felt a dagger pierce his heart.

#

When the caravan exited the forest of sentinel evergreens, it proceeded just as the boy driver had said. The cardinal's group quickly set up camp in bright pavilions outside the buttressed walls of Greensprings, and the rest continued onward, to the drawbridge.

The fortress loomed just as Patrick remembered it: a compact affair of gray squares and round towers guarded by a natural crevasse in front, and an army of blossoming apple orchards in the rear. The bleak gray walls acted as a shell guarding the germinating flower inside: a flower of peace meant to bloom across the world. The magnificent long stained-glass dome ran most of the length of the basilica like an elongated raindrop, and offered the only splash of color in the structure. The dome's design was not just an artistic masterpiece, but one of engineering that would be the envy of any cathedral in mainland Christendom. How the stained glass came to Avalon—indeed, the creation of the keep itself—still mystified Patrick, who had only heard rumors and legends.

When the wagons entered the courtyard under the iron teeth of the portcullis, Patrick handed Siegfried over to a servant and made his way to the keep entrance.

"Oi, Patrick, where you going?" one of the Avangarde called out, indignant that Patrick skulked away from the work to come.

"I'm reporting into Corbin," he said truthfully, but thinking of another visit he also wanted to make. Plus, Aimeé's rejection still stung and he didn't feel it was wise to engage the newcomers until he cooled off. "I've been gone all summer. I'm sure he'll want to see me right away. Shouldn't be long. I'll join you soon."

The explanation didn't seem to mollify his fellow Avangardesman, but Patrick ducked through the oaken double doors and was free. A few minutes of navigating the labyrinthine corridors of the main keep led him to the staircase he sought. He climbed to the door he wanted, whereupon he knocked until a shouted invitation urged him inside.

"Patrick!" the stout man at a desk greeted him. Another man, a monk by the look of him, sat next to him behind the desk. They had been looking over a document together.

Patrick found the room different from his memory of it. When Sir Mark had occupied the Keep Steward's room, it had been orderly. Now, Corbin's clothing was thrown over the furniture, reports and ledgers hid most of the desk, and wine goblets and food boards piled in every spare space.

Corbin stood, adjusting the belt about his gut. The gut was deceptive; Patrick knew Corbin only gave the impression of a knight softening into middle age. Corbin's solid build made him a capable fighter, and truth be told, he only had a few years on Patrick. The receding hairline was just bad luck.

Patrick saluted him, something he might as well start getting used to now that Corbin was the right-hand man of Sir Wolfgang von Fiescher.

"No," Corbin said, and beat his breast once and stated in a stern voice. "Fight strong," he said, and then thrust out his arm, adding, "Go on, do it, as I did."

Patrick raised an eyebrow, beat his breast, then stated, "Fight strong," and clasped forearms with Corbin.

"Live stronger," Corbin finished the ritual.

"Fight strong, live stronger?" Patrick asked.

"Our new salute and greeting. Wolfgang and Marcus brought the idea back from the mainland. They say similar rituals are all the rage among orders nowadays," Corbin explained.

"Funny, neither of them used it on me on the trip over from Cornwall."

Corbin shrugged and gestured for Patrick to take a seat, saying, "It's still relatively new and we just instituted it at the end of training—which you missed this year, by the way, you lucky bastard—and before the boys headed out to the harbor for reception duty."

"Which you missed, and are missing placing the Guests in their rooms at this very moment," Patrick added.

Corbin shrugged again and reached for a goblet on the desk.

"Well, I would be there as a dutiful Avangarde, but the presence of his holy eminence dictates all manner of preparations for tonight's reception banquet." He squinted inside the empty cup. Evidently it was clean enough, for he poured a sizable measure of wine into it and handed it to the Irishman.

"Seriously, had I known all the paperwork involved with being Steward I'd run off too," Corbin continued, pouring himself a goblet. "Why they gave the position to me is a mystery. They need to give it someone like you—someone who can read and write. Most of this job is all this confounding paperwork and record keeping and report writing. It's enough to drive a man mad."

He gestured at the pile of paper on the desk with the goblet and spilled wine in the process, staining some of the paper.

"Is that what the monk is for, to help with the reading and writing?" Patrick asked, addressing the quiet young man with shaved pate and dressed in a simple brown robe.

"Aye," Corbin replied, taking a gulp from his cup. "Useless wanker."

"Perhaps the wanker would not be so useless if you'd show up for our appointments more frequently, as well as offered me a cup of wine every now and again," the monk suggested with a hint of a smile.

"Bugger off," Corbin snapped. "You're lazy whether you have wine or not. I was supposed to be down at the harbor this morning with the rest, but no thanks to you tonight's dinner arrangements are still not done."

Despite his pretense of irritation, Corbin poured the man a cup.

"Excuse Sir Corbin's manners. I'm Brother Anton," the monk said, extending a hand to Patrick when he stood to accept his drink.

"I'm perfectly aware of Sir Corbin's manners," Patrick said, taking Anton's hand. "Pleased to meet you. I'm Sir Patrick Gawain."

"So I gathered: Knight of Cups, Savior of Avalon." Anton raised his drink.

Corbin rolled his eyes. "Oh, please! Don't encourage him. The man was lucky, wandering outside the keep while the rest of us were having spells cast upon us. I'd be Savior of Avalon, too, if I'd decided to go on a drunken, naked bender in the woods that day."

"Well, you certainly go on plenty of drunken benders. Maybe your turn will come soon enough!" Patrick laughed.

"Nacht! Watch your language. I'm a respectable man now. Don't go spreading rumors."

Patrick looked at Anton and said in an exaggerated whisper, "We'll talk."

Corbin gave Patrick an obscene gesture with one hand while expertly draining his goblet.

"Speaking of cups," Patrick said, tone turning serious. "I'm sure you realize why the cardinal is here."

Corbin leaned back in his chair and placed his feet on the desk. "Aye. I foresee all manner of drama coming our way."

"What do you plan on doing about it?"

"Do?" Corbin replied with a raised eyebrow. "I'm going to be thankful Wolfgang, Father Hugh, and Mother Superior are here to deal with the matter."

"Corbin, as Keep Steward and Captain of the Guard surely you have some say in the matter. We have a duty to return the cup," Patrick protested.

"We wouldn't have to worry about any of this if you hadn't brought the blasted thing here in the first place." Corbin scowled, but then his demeanor turned soft. "Though I understand why you did. And the girl? Did you give her a happily-ever-after?"

Patrick slumped in his chair as he said, "No, she will not marry me."

"What?" Corbin almost shouted. "The lass is offered the opportunity of a lifetime, and she doesn't take you up on it? Why?"

"There is a complication," Patrick responded, and waved off Corbin's curious look. "I'll explain in good time, but let's just say for now it boils down to the fact the girl has a measure of pride and finds my level of commitment... lacking."

Corbin scoffed and refilled his goblet. "Nonsense, just hit the girl upside the head with the flat of your sword and drag her to the nearest altar. That's what I would do."

"That would probably work for you and the quality of women I've seen by your side." Patrick laughed, and took a drink. "Aimeé has been forced to do many things in her time. I will not be another villain in her life."

"Sir Patrick Gawain," Corbin said whimsically, looking the Irishman up and down. "You've never done anything simply, have you? Uncooperative magic cups, conspiring cardinals, and sassy lasses."

Patrick drained his goblet. "I hate to harp on the issue, but what is the official Greensprings and Avangarde stance on the cup?"

"It appears it is up to the cup," Corbin replied. "It can't be grasped."

"And if someone could suddenly grasp it?" Patrick continued.

Corbin shrugged.

"Or, if it were suddenly to disappear from the altar?" Patrick added.

Corbin smiled. "Then I'd say it was God's will."

Patrick stood, and the Captain of the Avangarde rose, too. "Fight strong," Patrick said, beating his chest.

"Live stronger," Corbin returned, and they clasped forearms.

#

When Patrick entered the double doors of the church, he stopped in surprise when his eyes adjusted to the change in lighting and he saw the scene before him. Under most normal circumstances he felt reverence. But here today, the Greensprings church took on a profound holiness. Sunlight through the clerestory windows pierced the incense-filled air. A rainbow of colors dappled the ceiling, filtered through stained glass.

Patrick knew from Sir Marcus that people had come to pray before the altar and cup as a pilgrimage, but he had no idea of the number. His eyes shifted from the crowd to the cup, and it glinted at him from the marble altar, beckoning.

At the sight of the glimmering gold, even from this distance, Patrick felt his breath catch in his throat as if laying eyes on a friend he hadn't seen in a while. A friend to whom he owed an apology. An irrational mix of feelings to both run and approach the cup warred inside him.

At last he walked forward in the relative silence. His boots clicked noisily on the flagstones, drawing attention. The crowd slowly parted and he heard his name murmured, followed by the occasional "Knight of Cups" and "Savior of Avalon."

When he neared the plinth holding the church's other treasure—a rare and richly illuminated Bible—he paused just outside the communion rail. After a moment's contemplation, he made the exceptional move of opening the little gate and mounting the few steps to the altar, drawing gasps from the crowd.

He stood before the cup, which seemingly emitted a glow of its own. It was as Patrick remembered it, a richly decorated object of highly polished gold, patterned with what looked like trees. Red wine filled it to its brim.

It didn't always look like this. Prior to holding the wine, it had been a simple wooden dinner cup. It had transformed twice: once in a cave while he lay dying of wounds, and again in this church when Aimeé lay dead. Both times it had healed.

Patrick could almost discern a hum or vibration from it, but surely that had to be his imagination. Right? He realized the pain in his head had subsided, overwhelmed by a suffusing warm and comforting presence. But the sensation was also oddly mournful.

With difficulty, Patrick swallowed the breath caught in his throat and he whispered, "I'm sorry. I made a terrible mistake and I plan on remedying that now."

Both the hum and the bittersweet feeling intensified when he reached for the cup.

"Patrick! What are you doing?" a voice called to him from the side of the dais.

Patrick's head snapped in the direction of the voice and there came Father Hugh from a side entrance. His robes swished in a worried beat as he rushed to the altar.

"I made a promise," Patrick explained. "It must go back."

"But you agreed to leave it here," Father Hugh replied, looking around as if someone other than the pilgrims might hear their exchange.

"For a while, for people to adore it, to give praise to God for its miracles... not to become a pawn in a political game." Patrick's voice came in a quiet hiss.

"Things have changed," Father Hugh continued, also in low tones, gesturing to the curious crowd, "and as the head of the Board of Benefactors, the cardinal is my superior. Not only that, my own Archbishop of Canterbury has requested the matter be discussed at this upcoming meeting."

"You see," Patrick said between clenched teeth, "it begins already. People will be fighting over it. It must go back. As I promised."

Father Hugh rubbed his shaved pate. "Then why won't it let anyone touch it?" he reasoned, his pale blue eyes searching Patrick's. His demeanor was not angry, just frustrated. No doubt he felt pressured by his superiors, and now Patrick imagined his own demands made things even more difficult.

Patrick paused at the question, wondering himself.

"Tell me about the cup's behavior," he asked, turning his gaze to it.

"The day after you left, I held Mass as usual," Hugh replied. "I went to use it as the communion cup, but my hand passed right through it. I finished Mass with the usual vessel, consecrating the wine into the blood of Christ, as I have done ever since."

Patrick chewed on his lip for a moment, then asked, "Has anyone else tried?"

"Yes, but all have experienced the same thing," Father Hugh said. "Ironically, its inability to be touched has served as proof of its miraculous nature. People come at all hours to see it."

Patrick contemplated the cup. He felt the priest's eyes on him, expectant.

"I'm sorry, Father, but I must know," Patrick said with an air of conviction.

His hand shot out. He could almost hear the breaths of Father Hugh and the congregation behind him freeze in time.

But his hand passed through it like mist.

Patrick felt a dagger pierce his heart.

Chapter Five

After exiting the church, Patrick braced his back against the wall and leaned on his knees trying to catch his breath. His lungs couldn't seem to decide whether to freeze or panic. When he started to see spots before his eyes, he made an effort to take long controlled breaths, and soon his vision cleared.

"There, sorted out," he said to himself, still shaken.

He stood and while smoothing out the front of his surcoat, he caught sight of Aimeé across the courtyard helping the kitchen staff unload one of the wagons.

He felt his breath freeze up again and he turned on his heel to leave, remembering he had his own duties to attend.

#

He spent the remainder of the day helping the new arrivals settle into the Hall for Guests, the granite building at the far corner of the fortress across the practice field from the main keep —his own former residence while a Reservist. Now a full Avangarde, he would move into the barracks inside the keep.

At first he didn't look forward to the ritual of settling the Guests, as it mostly revolved around the menial labor normally associated with servants. Once the process got underway, however, Patrick remembered the fun one could have with the new arrivals. Also, it distracted from matters weighing on his mind.

The new Guests, wide-eyed at the sight of noble-born knights carrying their luggage, made easy targets for jesting. More than once a young man's mouth hung open in confusion when a knight held out his hand for payment. Some Guests would start to dig into their pouches for coin; others refused indignantly, whereupon the knight would draw a weapon and demand payment. Eventually, of course, the students caught on to the good-natured Greensprings welcoming ritual.

"A silly game," Patrick explained to a student as he handed him his travel bag, "but it is easier for a knight to protect a charge he knows personally. What harm is a little humor?"

"Patrick!" a voice called from down the corridor.

Patrick turned to see a tall, fair knight wading through the milling boys. The man's face beamed a smile from a round, affable face. He struggled to work his way through the crowd that didn't seem to afford his red-and-black surcoat the same respect as the black surcoats with swam emblems.

"Sir Jon!" Patrick returned, making his way over bags, sacks, and trunks to the knight. Jon greeted him with the "Fight strong, live stronger" salute.

"How do you fare these days?" Patrick asked, looking his friend over. "You appear to have put on some weight—the good sort, I mean."

He hadn't, as the Northumbrian maintained his usual, pleasantly soft physique.

Sir Jon waved the compliment off. He was Patrick's closest companion in Greensprings, and spent the rest of the day helping Patrick move the Guests. While doing so, he quickly apprised Patrick of the current gossip. Much of it Patrick already knew: Sir Mark and the Lady Christianne were engaged and gone, most likely to her family's estate in Vichy; Sir Corbin now served as Steward and Captain of the Guard; Sir Jeremiah had been promoted to full Avangarde from Reservist after Sir Hoder left to pursue other opportunities.

"...and as you can see, I am now the lone Reservist. Lucky me," he finished, pointing his thumbs to his red surcoat.

"Don't worry about it too much, Jon. It's just a matter of time."

"Perhaps I should go traipsing off on adventures, and then come back and demand entry into the Order," Jon said with a hint of uncharacteristic resentment.

Patrick didn't know how to respond. He knew firsthand the frustration of waiting for acceptance, and if it not for the events of the previous year, it might never have happened. In fact, he had been on the verge of being asked to leave.

"It will happen, Jon," he said, and then changed the subject, "What else has happened since I left?"

Again uncharacteristically quiet, Jon replied, "Not much."

#

Come nightfall Patrick and Jon stood near their seats in the great hall with growling stomachs, waiting for the formalities to conclude. Squire Charles of Flanders did a fine job: with a booming voice, he announced the arrivals.

As they waited, Patrick admired the banquet hall. Great wagon-wheel chandeliers bore a multitude of candles, their light reflecting from the white walls whose stucco, mixed with crushed quartz, created a scintillating effect. Fresh pine boughs and flower petals adorned the tables, their bright colors and aromas mingling with the smell of cooking foods. Flagons of the local specialty, Aphelon hard cider, waited on the tables.

Maidservants patiently waited to one side, ready to serve. All that was missing were their Roman visitors.

Patrick fought the urge to drink something to get a head start on a mild euphoria that would help him traverse the social landscape. Though he had come a long way with his small talk, he still found it to be his single most uncomfortable duty. Not for the first time Patrick thought how perfect Jon was for the duties of the Avangarde—a born conversationalist, and well-liked. In many ways he deserved the swan more than himself, but for the fact Jon still allowed students to push him around.

The announcement of a pair of familiar names by Squire Charles broke Patrick's pondering and he noted two young men racing for their table.

"William, Trent," he said, smiling and shaking their hands when they arrived. The two boys had almost grown into men since he last saw them.

"It's about bloody time you came back," William, the shorter, dark-haired boy said. "Things were dreadfully boring over the summer."

"Aye," the sandy-haired Trent added. "No goblins, no spells, no thieving nobles. Now you're back, we're wagering the fun will recommence."

"No, not there," Jon almost shouted as he shooed Trent away from the bench seat next to him. "I'm saving that for someone."

"Wanker," Trent shot at Jon with a smile, and a friendly punching match started between them until each felt satisfied they'd left a bruise.

New Guests arrived at their table, and as introductions went around, Squire Charles continued with his booming voice over the chatter of the growing crowd.

"The Lady Antonia Esperanza of Sardinia," he shouted as a dark-haired girl walked elegantly past him. The young man to whom Patrick had spoken on the way to Greensprings appeared in the entrance and whispered in Charles' ear. Charles then turned to the crowd and announced, "Reinholdt von Pufendorf der Munchen."

"Pufendorf?" Trent jibed. "That's a silly name."

"Aye, but did you see the lady who entered before him?" William said, straining over the heads of the growing crowd.

"Willy, you have a one-track mind," Jon said.

William ignored Jon and continued to glance around. Trent grabbed his arm and pointed out the next lady who came into the hall. They spent the remainder of the entrance ceremony commenting on either the odd names or the ladies' beauty or lack thereof. Distracted by their banter, Patrick missed the arrival of the nun in white and her candidati charges. He had hoped their introduction would clear up the reason for their presence at Greensprings.

Soon after that, the students gave way to the benefactors, who made a mixed bag of merchants, nobility, and clergy.

"Abbot Herewinus of Glastonbury, Father Wulfric of Canterbury, Fulk the Fourth, Le Réchin, Count of Anjou, Humphrie de Chaubert, Grand Merchant of Brussels..." Charles cried one after the other.

Then came the cardinal entourage.

"Squires Jakob Vasily and Josef Corvinus of Prague," Charles announced as the young men began the cardinal escort. They wore simple squire tunics, bearing the image of the cardinal mission: a broad-rimmed hat, trimmed with yellow tassels on a field of red. They each carried a banner with the same emblem.

Immediately behind the boys came Lucan, wearing light ceremonial armor.

"Sir Lucan, Captain of the Cardinal Guard, and chief historian and chronicler for the papal legate," Charles cried.

The half-dozen men who followed him, however, came in full mail and padding. Each guard carried a halberd with a wicked hook at its end.

Next came the cardinal himself and his lady companion.

"The Lady Lilliana Vergoza de Aragon," Charles announced, "and His Eminence Cardinal Teodorico, Archbishop of Albano, papal legate to Greensprings, and Headmaster of the Board of Benefactors."

Teodorico wore a cassock and cape of watered silk. The fabric rippled orange-red like a flame. A huge pectoral cross hung from his neck by a thick gold chain, giving the impression the older man bowed under its weight, requiring the need to lean on the crozier with which he walked. On the hand grasping the shepherd's crook glinted the heavy gold Episcopal ring Patrick had dutifully kissed on the boat in Cornwall.

As lovely as the ornate objects he held in his right hand might be, they paled in comparison to that which he held in his left.

Lightly hooked through his left arm was the arm of a tall, beautiful woman who kept stride with him as they approached their seats of honor. Her deep maroon gown shimmered, and its plunging décolletage caused a buzz in the hall, not the least of which came from William and Trent. In whispered tones the stricken young men lamented they could not see more of her bosom beneath the lattice of a garnet necklace.

Patrick turned to admonish the boys for their rudeness, but found his own gaze drawn to the women's neckline. The piece of jewelry, which started out as a choker about her throat, formed a net spreading across her olive-toned chest. A scandalous fashion, but no one seemed to protest, least of all the holy man whose arm she held.

Patrick's voice caught in his throat as the couple passed. William's and Trent's chattering stopped abruptly when the woman shot a playful glance in their direction with luminous amber eyes.

Once on the dais, the cardinal gestured to the assembly and said, "Please, have a seat." Only Teodorico remained standing and motioned for silence. "Please, if you haven't already, pour yourselves a drink."

As the room came alive with activity at the request, Wolfgang poured a cup and handed it to the cardinal, then performed the same task for his other table guests.

When the room quieted down and all watched expectantly in the direction of the standing holy man, Teodorico spoke.

#

Behind the tapestries to the side of the dais, Sir Brian McCabe squeezed a brief note with his instrument, and Lady Katherina mimicked with a hum from deep in her chest.

"Almost," Brian encouraged, blowing the note one more time.

Katherina's brow furrowed in determination and she adjusted her hum.

"Better," Brian said, smiling.

"Better is not enough," Katherina chided herself. "I want very much to do it right."

"Easy, lass. There will be time for that," Brian replied, "but for now it is plenty good and no one will notice the difference save your perfectionist self. Relax. How close to performing are we?"

Katherina moved to the curtain and peeked between the hanging fabric. From her vantage she could see the last of the procession of benefactors entering the great hall.

"Soon," she said, looking back over he shoulder at Brian as he fidgeted with his sprawling bagpipe, then added as she returned her gaze to the hall. "Five minutes maybe? That is if the Headmaster gives his speech—"

Her voice caught in her throat as her eyes came to rest on one of the benefactors who sat near the cardinal. She shook her head, blinked, and gave the mustached older man a long second look.

She backed away from the curtain, letting the fabric fall back into place. She grabbed at her throat as her breath came out in panicked short wheezes.

"What's wrong, Kat?" Brian asked, his bushy red eyebrows knotted in concern.

She looked to the knight and attempted a response, but only a choking gasp came from her mouth.

"Kat, what is going on?" Brian insisted.

Katherina took a deep breath and managed to say, "There is a man out there, a newcomer, a benefactor, who has a striking resemblance to my uncle."

"Welcome," they heard Teodorico say from beyond the curtain. "Your families sent you here as an experiment in hope. Greensprings is not answerable to any one ruler, coin, or bishop. The benefactors, who created this place, are a diverse group whose only goal is to create peace. Your families believe in something greater than the conflicts tearing our Christian family apart. We may come from different lands, speak different languages, but we all believe in Jesus who made it possible to bridge the chasm separating us from God. If God can extend His salvation to us, then we certainly should extend the hand of peace to each other."

Behind the curtain, trepidation crept into Brian's voice as he addressed Katherina, "What of your uncle?"

Katherina took another deep breath. "He is... why I had to leave home. I haven't thought about him in months, but that benefactor reminded me of him and... I..."

She quieted when she realized Brian watched her hands draw protectively to her breasts. His big ruddy features expressed a mix of shock and compassion.

"Look around," Teodorico continued his speech. A rustle of garments filled the air as the crowd complied. "We have Germans from the Empire, French and Normans from the Frankish kingdoms, Italians from the city states, and English from the isle. You should be at each other's throats, correct?" Through the gap in the curtain they saw him make a strangling motion with his hands and twist his face into a parody of fury, drawing ripples of laughter. "You already sit at tables with only your own kind. Before long, you will sit with whom you please and not with whom your upbringing dictated. You will learn, work, and play together. You will learn your neighbor is deserving of friendship. When you leave Greensprings you will take that knowledge with you."

Brian reached out to comfort Katherina, but withdrew his hand just short of touching her. "Look, lass, that man out there is not your uncle. You're safe."

"I know," Katherina agreed, straightening her posture and forcing her face into what she hoped passed for impassiveness. "But my body—my throat—doesn't seem to believe that." Her composure fell apart as she exhaled loudly, realizing she had been holding her breath. Her stomach lurched at memories of a hand clamped firmly over her mouth.

"It won't be easy." Teodorico's went on, his tone turning serious. "The old grudges will rise. Therefore, you will be protected from each other by a band of men dedicated not only to keeping you from harm from outside these walls, but also to keep peace within. They are the Avangarde. They are neutral, answerable only to Greensprings. Do not see them as enforcers, but as big brothers.

"To demonstrate what this miraculous island can accomplish, a student, not unlike yourselves, will sing a hymn for us."

Katherina's head snapped to the voice beyond the curtain and a new round of wheezing came from her.

This time Brian did gently grab her upper arm and looked her in the eye. "Lass, you can do this. Just concentrate on the music. Can you do that?"

Despite the shakiness of the deep breath she drew, she nodded.

Teodorico finished. "She came from a distant land, spoke a different language, and though baptized in the Orthodox Church, we are equally humble before Christ. She will sing in a language previously unknown to her, joined by an Avangarde playing an instrument also foreign to her homeland. You will find their collaboration heavenly.

"First, raise a toast to our coming year! May God continue to bless this place, and you!"

#

When Teodorico finished, a cheer rose from the crowd and all took a drink from their cups.

As maidservants came forward with dishes and students were distracted by their excitement and hunger, the cardinal sat down hard and slumped in his high-backed chair. Sweat rolled down his red face as if from a terrible strain. The Lady Lilliana stroked his arm as she leaned toward him, her lips moving near his ear. The cardinal smiled.

It occurred to Patrick then the cardinal's speech had been almost flawless, without a single bit of stuttering.

The first wheezing notes of a familiar instrument cut through the chatter.

Once, two Scotsmen in the Avangarde had played the bagpipes. One had been the flamboyant Highlander Sir Jason McFowler who had fallen in battle a year ago. The other was the more subdued Sir Brian McCabe—or, as Sir Jason had often referred to him, the "City Boy from Edinburgh." Sir Jason arguably had played better, but Sir Brian played beautifully, capable of anything from a jig to a ballad.

The large man stood on the dais now, squeezing at the bagpipes' leather bladder under one arm. His cheeks puffed out as he blew into a polished wood pipe. It coalesced into a slow and chilling drone that resonated about the hall just as easily as the light reflected from the scintillating walls.

A slender, platinum-haired woman in a white dress joined Sir Brian. Patrick drew an involuntary breath. He shouldn't have been surprised to see her, and had even promised himself he wouldn't react, but that didn't stop his heart from betraying him.

"Katherina," Patrick breathed silently. Memories of her lying next to him in the grass, all smiling eyes, flooded his mind. Just as quickly, however, her final words to him resonated in his skull: *We can still be friends.* The memory of those words stung more than the wounds he had received when rescuing her. At least the physical wounds had healed.

Yet Patrick found himself transfixed by the sight of her.

She clasped her hands before her, opened her mouth wide and issued a long musical note from deep inside that joined the pipes in rhythm, but then cracked in her throat. People in the crowd exchanged glances.

Her alabaster face flushed crimson. She paused, squeezed her eyes shut, and started anew. Soon, an ethereal song came forth, stilling the conversations and rustling movements of the room.

Patrick recognized the Gaelic piece she had been working to perfect with McFowler before his death. Though he could discern her Slavic accent in the lyrics, Patrick still could make out the recurring verse—"Hope belongs." Cardinal Teodorico would have been disappointed to know the song wasn't a hymn as he had proclaimed, but the sort of song sung on the eve of battles.

Perhaps still appropriate, Patrick thought.

Katherina threw herself into the song and as the melody rose and fell in tempo, she turned it into a theatrical performance with grand, expressive gestures.

She finished with her eyes closed, head back—and the bagpipe ended on an upbeat note. At first the audience sat in stunned silence, but then reacted wildly. They stood and clapped with shouts and whistles. Even the notaries at the table on the dais joined the ovation.

Katherina's red face glistened with sweat just as much as Teodorico's had when he had finished his speech.

When the noise died down, Cardinal Teodorico exclaimed, "Ladies and gentlemen, the Lady Katherina and Sir Brian McCabe! Hmm? A splendid performance! Yes?"

After the performers bowed and left, the cardinal led the room in saying grace before the meal and eating got under way.

"Finally," William growled and reached for the food.

Patrick concurred with a grunt and started to reach for the aromatic slices of venison, but stopped in mid-reach when he noticed Sir Jon stand and motion to the Lady Katherina as she descended the dais. She made eye contact with Jon, smiled, and made her way to the table. Sir Jon gestured gallantly for her to take a seat in the spot he had saved for her.

Patrick tried to make eye contact with Jon, silently asking for clarification. Was Jon trying to smooth out the relationship by bringing them together at the same table?

The Lady Katherina slipped into her seat. As she reached for a napkin, she noticed who sat across from her.

"Sir Patrick," she almost shouted, eyes widening. "You're back."

She quickly regained her composure, returned to her usual cool demeanor, and offered no welcoming smile.

"Just came in today with the arrival of the new Guests," Patrick said, "I didn't know you were still at Greensprings. Last I heard, you were considering returning to the mainland. Had I known, I might have found you and paid my respects." He said this last part while looking at Jon, who suddenly found an intense interest in his food.

"No need for that," Katherina replied, accepting a bowl of green beans from William. "We have all year to catch up. And what would your new wife think of that?"

"I'm not married," Patrick said simply, and took the bowl of beans from her.

An odd look crossed her face, but like Jon, she suddenly took a great interest in her food, wrestling with a piece of bread. Jon tenderly took it from her and sliced the tough loaf with his knife.

Patrick then noticed how Jon sat close to her, doted on her every move, and laughed at her every little attempt at humor. He went above the call of knightly duty.

No... Patrick thought with some distress. He shook his head at the possibility. *Poor bastard doesn't even know what he's in for. Serves him right.*

Patrick knew for all her pretenses as a strong-willed woman and loner, she still craved an audience. And as he cut the venison on his plate, Jon's flaunting behavior angered him.

Something heavy dropped on his plate. He looked down to see someone had added a large serving of mashed potatoes to his meal. A beefy arm came into view and dolloped another serving, flinging some on his freshly cleaned surcoat.

"Oi!" Patrick protested. "Watch that, now."

Another beefy arm thrust from his other side and dropped a greasy lamb chop on top of the potatoes, spraying more food.

To either side of him, two of the veteran maidservants went about their work. They moved to throw essentially more food at him, but he waved them off.

"Enough," he growled.

As the two large women served the other Guests at the table, they went out of their way to bump and generally aggravate Patrick with a flurry of linen skirts, food trays, and beefy arms constantly obstructing his attempts at getting comfortable.

"Wait, I understand what you're doing," he hissed quietly to one of them. Certain her name was Clare, which would make the other Anna, both close friends of Aimeé. "It was her choice, not mine. I offered to take care of her."

"She doesn't need 'takin' care of,'" Clare hissed back and snatched the fork out of his hand.

"Aye," Anna hissed in Patrick's other ear and cleared his barely touched plate of food. "She needs 'lovin.'"

They turned to leave with his plate and fork.

"Oi, that's my dinner," he objected. "Punish Sir Geoffrey if you must."

Clare came back just long enough to say, "You should see what we do to his dinner."

Patrick looked across the room to where the handsome knight sat. The man's long dark hair glistened in the candlelight, and was better combed than most of the women's in the room. Currently, he held a fork before him with a velvet-gloved hand, having just put a morsel of food in his mouth. His face contorted as he chewed.

Patrick looked down at the bare spot on the table before him. Jon, Katherina, William, Trent and the others talked and ate merrily.

"Dammit."

#

Patrick did manage to lay hands on scraps of a meal, and Aimeé's guardian angels did not come back to harass him.

The rest of the evening turned into a socializing affair. Trent and William chose to stay close to Jon and Katherina, which compelled Patrick to look elsewhere for conversation. With a drink in hand, he struggled to make clever conversation with newcomers, feeling his soul being slowly sucked from his body.

After several attempts he found himself pretending to see someone he needed to talk to, and then would excuse himself. He moved between groups like this, hoping to find an interesting one. Eventually, however, he found himself cornered by an exasperating young French noble who insisted on talking politics, particularly his desire to know how Patrick felt about dealing with the cup.

The young man's words turned into a drone burrowing into Patrick's ears, rising in pitch to become the familiar ringing assaulting his mind since the night in Eire when bandits had attacked him and Aimeé.

His eye twitched, but he refused to reveal his trembling hand or rub the pain at his temple. Instead, he focused on the young man's mouth, vainly attempting to regain the thread of conversation in the hope of controlling his affliction.

To complicate things, Aimeé passed behind the Frenchman. As he watched her at her duties, he found it easy to forget she was with child; she did not yet show.

With child. My child. Maybe.

He shifted his gaze yet again and it fell to Geoffrey leaning against a wall with one hand, cornering a lady Guest in conversation.

Patrick's hand gripped the stem of his goblet so tightly the vessel shook and liquid sloshed. The ringing in his ears reached a new pitch and he squeezed his eyes shut.

When he opened them again, a chill ran down his spine.

He blinked, not believing the sight of the individual who strolled through the crowd. After such a long absence he had not expected to see him again, but when the figure passed before the dais, he paused long enough to make eye contact.

A mirror image of Patrick raised a gloved finger to its lips, smiled mischievously, then motioned for him to follow. The Other moved towards the back of the hall, passing through people as if made of mist.

Nobody noticed. Except for Patrick, who trembled at the sight.

"I'm sorry? Come again?" Patrick shook his head, returning his attention to the young man who had penetrated his reverie with an insistent question.

"Do you think with all these Germans here from the empire, they'll insist on sending the cup to their antipope?" The young man was perturbed at his distraction.

"Excuse me," Patrick replied distantly, scanning the crowd, "I see... an old friend."

Patrick fought his way through the press of bodies to catch up to the Other.

He looked around, but did not readily see him. After some frantic searching, he caught sight of his twin at the door to the keep gardens, standing between the pillars supporting the arches over the exit.

Patrick pursued. With the light of the hall at his back, his eyes needed to adjust to the dim moon and lantern light illuminating the gardens. Various gravel paths led away from the little cobblestone patio outside the hall.

He saw the Other walking down one of them and gave chase.

At every turn of the path meandering through immaculately landscaped gardens, hedges, and flower beds, he thought he might catch up to him. Instead, he heard laughter and came across a group of people.

The Other had vanished.

He came across the group so suddenly he skidded in the gravel, causing the large men to startle and come forward as if to do battle.

These men, wearing the tunics of the Cardinal Guard, huddled about a figure at their center.

The lead man, a brute with shaved head and broken nose, barked something in Italian at Patrick.

"That's all right, Dragonetti," a feminine, but husky voice said. "Don't you recognize Sir Patrick, Knight of Cups?"

The Lady Lilliana came forward and placed a gentle hand on the wrist of the man she called Dragonetti who looked almost ready to reach for his sword.

Patrick realized he reached for his own sword. Dragonetti growled something in Italian, Lilliana laughed an airy and frivolous laugh and said, "I will be fine, but thank you." She spoke in French so Patrick would understand. "I will be back shortly."

Whether he understood French or not, Dragonetti understood the gist of the statement and her stern look. He grunted, gestured for his men to follow, and departed. He made sure to brush uncomfortably close to the Irishman as he passed.

"Oh, *sergente*," Lilliana sang after him. She then held up a hand covered in a fingerless black lace glove and made a rubbing movement with her fingers. *"Vino, per favore."*

Dragonetti controlled a scowl, reached behind him and pulled a wineskin from his belt and tossed it through the air. He turned on his heel and left with his men, the gravel grinding under his boots.

"Grazie," Lilliana giggled, pulling the stopper off the container.

Patrick looked around, trying to catch sight of the Other, but saw no trace.

"Did you happen to see... someone come this way before my arrival?" he asked.

"I did not, Sir Knight. Is that why you were running?"

"No," he lied. "I just wanted some fresh air."

"And some exercise, evidently. Will you join me in a drink?" She held up the wineskin and took a long, unladylike swig before offering it to Patrick. He accepted it, marveling at the woman who had only hours before been the perfect image of refinement. Now she plopped down on a bench, wiping her mouth with the back of her hand.

"You look surprised," she said as he took a drink.

"I did not expect the cardinal's lady to be so..." He struggled for words.

"Casual?" she suggested.

"As you say, my lady."

"There is a time and a place for protocol," she added, "but there is also a time and place to be free. Wouldn't you agree?"

"Again, as you say, Lady Vergoza."

"Please, you can call me Lilliana. Won't you have a seat?" she said, and made room for him on the bench.

He took the seat, noting how her gold eyes almost glowed in the moonlight.

"You have a lovely island here," she said, stretching her arms above her head and sighing dramatically. "It feels very alive. And the stars! How bright they shine here! I swear I do not recognize the constellations."

"Aye, some of the scholars claim the stars are in an alignment from ages past, frozen here in time."

"And magic? They say there is still magic here, is that true?" she asked, eyes wide. She took the wineskin and drank.

"Aye, there is, but it only reveals itself when it wishes," Patrick conceded. "The whole isle is magical. It is alive and full of mystery, and if you're lucky—or unlucky, depending on how you look at it—she will reveal all manner of things to you."

"Like golden cups that bring people back from the dead?" she said, handing the wine back to him.

"Precisely."

"You know Teodorico is going to take it with him," she stated.

"He can try," Patrick replied just as bluntly, eyes still searching the starry sky.

"If anyone can, it will be he," she said. "Teodorico is a man of singular ambition. What he wants, he gets."

"It appears he certainly got you. No offense, my lady," Patrick said, returning his gaze to the beautiful woman.

"None taken. In any case, perhaps it is I who got him." She flashed a wicked grin. "Ambitious men, regardless of their age, are attractive—and serve their purpose. Teodorico is a rising star I plan to ride to the heavens."

"Is that why you're with him then?" Patrick asked, taking a sip of the wine.

"A girl has to do what a girl has to do to survive," she laughed. "Though my first few husbands were also ambitious men, they expired before they amounted to much. Apparently, I exhausted them. I won't let that happen with Teo. If I have to, I will prop his corpse up to finish the job."

"No doubt." Patrick tried to keep the surprise out of his voice.

"Don't think me villainous," she said forming her lovely lips into a pout. "I merely want what's best for everyone. I want everyone to be happy."

She leaned forward, pressing her body against his as she reached between his legs and firmly grasped the neck of the wineskin he held there. She lingered in the movement just long enough to make him uncomfortable, and to arouse feelings that have stirred men since the dawn of time.

"I like people," she said, sliding the container from his thighs. "I like men, just as men like their swords. Is that so bad?"

She put the skin to her lips and took a sip.

Patrick could feel heat rising in his cheeks and he plucked at his collar to relieve the feeling of constriction. He swallowed hard. "Perhaps we should be returning to the hall," he suggested, standing.

Lilliana laughed, taking the hand he offered and said, "As you wish, my gallant knight."

As she placed her hand in his to rise, Patrick noticed for the first time how her lacy gloves hid her hands. But they didn't conceal her extremely sharpened nails. The gloves ended at the wrists and he could see muscular forearms lined with veins, as if from a lifetime of washing clothes.

He tried not to stare and wondered why he hadn't noticed earlier.

Right, that's why, he thought, his gaze suddenly drawn to her heaving bosom, the garnets glittering even with only the pale moon and starlight.

He could feel heat rising in his face again, and he looked away.

She laughed lightly and slipped her arm into his as they walked down the path back to the hall, following the sound of festivity.

"You have to admit," she said, "the cup is better served in the cardinal's hands. It belongs out in the world, not hidden on a secret island."

"My heart says otherwise," Patrick said. Amid all her distractions, this truth was cleansing in its simplicity, and he hung onto it.

"Ah yes, your heart, your duty, and your honor," she shook her head. "Men and their 'honor.' Consider this: The cardinal is an ordained successor of the Apostles, and it was to Saint Peter Jesus declared, 'Whatsoever you loose upon earth, it shall also be loosed in heaven.' If the cardinal demands the cup leave with him from this place, are you not honor bound to let him? What think you, Sir Knight?"

Patrick rubbed his head with his free hand, saying, "I think I've had too much wine this evening and would rather discuss theology another time."

"You may very well have that opportunity tomorrow morning," Lilliana said. "As I understand it the Board of Benefactors wants to meet in the church just after morning Mass to see if you can grasp the cup."

Patrick only lost part of a step in his stride at the news.

They entered the little courtyard in front of the main hall, and the party had thinned. Patrick froze at the sight of Sir Jon and the Lady Katherina leaving arm-in-arm.

"Is that who you were looking for earlier in the garden?" Lilliana asked, her gaze following Katherina.

"No," Patrick growled.

"She's quite lovely," Lilliana said with a mischievous glint in her eye. "Perhaps you were trying to marry the wrong one."

"Another discussion for another time," Patrick snapped.

Lilliana released the subject gracefully. "Can the cardinal count on your support tomorrow? I'm certain if, as Knight of Cups, you were to have a 'revelation' and openly announce the cup should go with Teodorico, he would find a way to show his gratitude."

After a long pause, Patrick responded, "The cardinal can count on me to show discretion, and keep quiet about your blatant attempt to influence me."

She reached to Patrick's face and stroked his high cheek, probing his hazel eyes with her amber ones. "We're not going to be friends, are we, Sir Patrick?"

Patrick gently took her hand and kissed it, replying, "It's not looking good."

Chapter Six

Despite Cardinal Teodorico's lofty speech the night before about solidarity, the Roman entourage claimed the place of privilege before the altar during morning Mass.

When Mass presided over by Father Hugh had finished, the majority of people filtered out of the church leaving the benefactors and Greensprings leadership to gather about the altar. As people jostled to move in closer, Lucan hung back and turned to Lilliana.

"I saw you with Sir Patrick on a late-night stroll," he whispered. "Making a new friend, are we?"

Lilliana flashed Lucan a mischievous grin. "Jealous?"

Lucan felt his lip start to curl involuntarily, but managed to bend it into a strained grin. "Not for ages."

Lilliana looked as if she might come back with some witticism, but Teodorico approached and also spoke in whisper. "Were you able to convey to the Irishman my wishes for support last night?"

"It would appear his silly honor is getting the better of him," she replied. "I don't think he wants to play our game."

Teodorico scoffed and mumbled, "He'd better if he knows what's good for him, hmm?" He then turned to Lucan. "And you, 'historian?' What say you? You've had opportunity to examine the cup. Is it authentic? Is it the Cup of the Last Supper, hmm, yes?"

Lucan looked over the cardinal's shoulder at the golden chalice on the altar.

"Doubtful," Lucan replied with a shrug. "The actual Cup of the Last Supper was made of plain wood, most likely olive wood."

Teodorico cast a glance over his shoulder. "The Irishman claims the cup was just that—wood—before filling it with wine, hmm? The rest that happened that day, the maidservant coming back to life, was witnessed by many, yes?"

"So they say," Lucan countered. "We will need more than hearsay to convince the rest of the world."

"Your lack of enthusiasm is upsetting, hmm?" Teodorico said, displeasure creeping into his voice.

"I'm a cynical man, Your Eminence," Lucan replied. He met Lilliana's cold stare. "I've had my share of disappointments."

"You had best get over that." Teodorico's whisper dipped to almost a hiss. "You may pretend to work for Pope Paschal while secretly in the service of the emperor, but you tied your fate to mine when you chose the emperor's rebellious son Henry in this endeavor, hmm?" The cardinal looked Lucan up and down and added, "And if you ever want your 'affliction' removed, you will demonstrate a certain level of passion when I ask you to examine the cup before witnesses, authenticating it, hmm, yes?"

Lucan's lip did curl this time. "As you wish, Your Eminence."

Victor cleared his throat to remind Teodorico that the other benefactors awaited their participation.

"But first things first," Teodorico hissed. He put on a warmer face and said loudly to the larger group, "My fellow benefactors, hmm? Thank you for gathering for this informal meeting before the formalities of the council commence. I felt it important for us to see the object of our discussion, and witness its wonder, hmm, yes?"

Murmurs of approval rippled through the group as Cardinal Teodorico motioned to Sir Patrick.

"Sir Patrick, if you would be so kind as to pick up the cup, hmm?" he said. "It was you who could last touch it. Perhaps you can again, hmm, yes?"

The muscles in Sir Patrick's jaw bulged as it moved side to side. He glanced nervously at the cup, the cardinal, the crowd, and Lady Lilliana. Not until after his own leadership's questioning stares weighed on him did he move towards the altar. Lucan thought perhaps he saw sweat beading on the Irishman's brow.

That's right, Sir Patrick, be afraid, Lucan thought. *If you can grasp it, your troubles will be just beginning.*

The cup glinted in the morning rays of sunlight. Sir Patrick took another fretful glance at the crowd and reached for it.

When he did, his hand passed through it.

A collective gasp from the spectators rose, and his shoulders slumped.

Cardinal Teodorico leaned on his crozier, an eyebrow arched.

"What does that mean?" Abbot Herewinus declared. "There is no point in discussing the matter if no one can carry it anywhere."

"Precisely," Father Wulfric added. "It is where it belongs. Greensprings should become a new site of pilgrimage."

More benefactors voiced their concerns, and as the murmurs rose, Cardinal Teodorico pounded his crozier on the flagstones to bring quiet.

"Did you feel anything at the attempt Sir Patrick? Is there anything you wish to add, Knight of Cups, hmm, yes?"

The crowd turned their attention to the Avangardesman, expectant. Lucan saw the Adam's apple in Sir Patrick's throat bob as the man fidgeted.

He glanced at Lilliana, then met the cardinal's gaze and declared simply, "No."

Color rose in the cardinal's face and the knuckles gripping the crozier turned white.

Lucan suppressed a smile.

"We are not even sure if this is the Cup of the Last Supper," one of the merchant benefactors said, drawing attention away from Sir Patrick. "We could be arguing over nothing."

Murmurs in the room rose to full-voiced questions.

"Yes, yes," Teodorico conceded, then motioned to the crowd. "Lucan, come forward, hmm, yes?"

Lucan approached the altar and stood abreast of Sir Patrick, who still hovered near the cup protectively. Lucan noted they shared a similar height and realized for the first time the Irishman's odd eye color when they locked gazes.

"Lucan is the relic expert, yes?" Teodorico said, and a murmur of assent went through the crowd. "What say you, Sir Lucan, hmm?"

Lucan reluctantly tore his gaze from Sir Patrick's unflinching stare and bent over the altar and scrutinized the vessel, noting the surface and the ruby liquid inside. A beautiful object no doubt, but an object made by the hands of man. And not wood. When he felt he had examined it sufficiently, he straightened and addressed the assembly.

"'Tis the Cup of the Last Supper," he announced in a bold voice, and even as he saw the scholars among the other delegates open their mouths to protest, he added just as boldly, "When our Lord Jesus rose from the dead, it was in His glorified form, a form initially unrecognizable to His followers. Mary Magdalene mistook him for the gardener. His disciples mistook Him for a stranger on the road to Emmaus. It was He nevertheless."

Positive murmurs rippled through the crowd. A concerned look crossed Sir Patrick's face even as a triumphant one crossed Teodorico's.

Lucan moved to descend from the dais, but the cardinal stopped him.

"Sir Lucan, you once held a portion of the Spear of Destiny at the Battle of Antioch, the lance that pierced the side of Christ," he said, eyes narrowing at him. "Perhaps you can hold this relic as well, hmm, yes?"

Lucan froze. All eyes came to rest on him.

"Your Eminence, I feel unworthy to even try. I..."

"Nonsense," Teodorico insisted. "How can your examination be complete unless you try holding it, hmm? Any *affliction* of sin is no match for the Blood of Christ. Go on then, hmm? Touch it!"

Lilliana arched an eyebrow.

Lucan at first did not move, but pushed by the weight of stares, particularly Teodorico's, he turned back to the cup. The concerned look on Sir Patrick's face deepened and the Irishman leaned forward as if he might try to intercede.

Lucan reached for the cup anyway. Sir Patrick let him.

His hand paused just before contact, then passed through it.

He drew a breath. A cold tingling crept up his hand to his wrist, and he stared curiously at it. He sniffed audibly at the air, and then put his hand to his nose.

"Roses," he whispered with wide eyes. His knees almost buckled underneath him. He closed his eyes and his senses reeled as an overwhelming sensation of falling came over him.

Even before he opened his eyes, a dustiness replaced the flowery smell in his nostrils and dry heat engulfed him.

When he did open his eyes he stood on a rocky butte in a barren landscape. Sun-bleached stones surrounded him, but this day, the sky was almost dark. What feeble sunlight remained raked the world with a reddish glow.

The dimness oppressed the spirit. It weighed him down with a palpable heaviness, magnifying a pounding in his head. Each heartbeat throbbed painfully.

"Centurion!" a man's harsh voice called to him. "Do your duty!"

Lucan looked down and noted he held a spear in his hand. He looked at the man who had shouted the order.

Armored in an elaborate breastplate and crested helm, the commander struggled to control his mount. His blue cape flowed around him as the skittish animal reacted to the unruly crowd on the hilltop. Men similarly armored shouted commands that barely held the mob in check. The soldiers held their spears horizontally, forming a fence meant to keep the crowd at a distance.

Lucan looked up.

He stood at the base of a crucifix where a man hung naked, nailed to the wood. Blood and bodily waste trailed down the trunk of the cross, pooling at its base. Terrible wounds covered virtually every inch of the man's body. Even the top of his head seeped blood from a score of gouges, wounded by the crown of thorns that had been pressed onto his head to mock him.

The earth moved beneath Lucan's feet.

Again the man mounted on horseback shouted at him.

Again Lucan looked at the spear in his hand. He didn't want to carry out the command. Looking at the condemned man's now-peaceful face told Lucan death had already come. His body sagged under its weight on the cross. The order proved unnecessary, but the crowd surged and the soldiers struggled to control them.

"Lucien!" his companions called to him. They stood by, holding mauls, having just broken the legs of the two other criminals being executed this day. "Do it!"

Lucan hesitated. The man had been innocent. The condemned man had even used much of his last strength to forgive and pray for the people who persecuted him. Lucan did not want to add insult to injury.

The cordon of spears and soldiers started to fragment. A man broke through and a legionnaire beat him with his spear shaft. The mounted man drew his short sword, shouting again to Lucan, this time with desperation in his voice.

With one final look at the spear in his hand, Lucan thrust it into the side of the crucified man. The weapon penetrated the flesh between ribs with a sickening *squelsh*, the metal head and much of the wood shaft swallowed by the chest cavity.

The man did not flinch, proving what Lucan already knew. He was dead. Now the crowd knew it too and started to calm.

The earth also stopped moving, quieting the crowd further. Now, if only the darkness engulfing the land would go away.

With a heavy heart, Lucan withdrew the spear and blood spurted from it, making him shrink to his knees. In his shock, Lucan vaguely understood that it did not ooze like the heavy blood of a dead man, but rather flowed like water.

Between the stunned soldiers, a man rushed forward from the crowd and joined Lucan on his knees before the crucified man. He held out a wooden dinner cup and caught up as much of the liquid he could before the flow subsided.

None of the soldiers moved to stop the man, as it was obvious he was one of the priests. The younger one. The rich one who had vocally disagreed with his elder colleagues over the treatment of the condemned man.

Lucan held up his hands, palms up, noting how the red liquid beaded on his skin like oil.

He sniffed at his hands.

"Roses," he whispered.

"Lucan!" a voice shouted, breaking him out of his reverie.

He looked up, expecting to see the man on horseback, but instead he stood again before the Greensprings altar, Cardinal Teodorico doing the shouting.

"Well, hmm?" Teodorico demanded. "What say you, yes?"

Lucan looked around, dazed. Sir Patrick narrowed his eyes at him.

"It's real," he said in wonder, though more to himself than anyone else.

He absently wiped his dry hand on his surcoat and staggered away from the altar, fighting his way through the crowd toward the exit.

#

The Lady Katherina and Sir Brian McCabe stood alone in the auditorium with pale moonlight illuminating the chamber just enough to serve their purposes.

Katherina bent studiously over a podium at the center of the large room, moving little colored stones on a piece of slate where she had drawn several parallel lines in chalk. After adjusting the black and white stones to strategic locations, she stood erect and sang a note, letting the sound echo throughout the room. Before it faded, they took mental note of how it sounded.

"Almost," Sir Brian said. His baritone Scottish brogue echoed, too. He hefted his bagpipes, put the reed to his lips, and blew a wheezing note. He followed this with a sung note in his baritone. "You hear the difference?"

Katherina struggled to keep from sighing heavily, saying, "Not really."

"You do seem distracted tonight," Sir Brian said coyly. "Perhaps we should try again when your mind is more on it."

He bent to put the instrument in his travel sack.

"Wait," Katherina pleaded. "Just a while longer. I almost have it. I'm not distracted. I promise."

"You mean to tell me you're no longer troubled by the fellow who looks like your uncle?" Brian replied, continuing to stuff his bagpipe into its sack.

Katherina stiffened, her face twitching before she answered. "I've managed to put that behind me. It just caught me off guard."

Sir Brian swung the sack over his shoulder, smiling. "Perhaps you were also caught off guard by the return of a certain Irishman?"

Katherina's faced twitched again, and she couldn't hide it. Seeing Patrick sitting across from her at dinner had surprised her, but that alone she could have managed. It was his scent she found surprisingly difficult to banish from her thoughts. She didn't want to admit the smell of oiled armor, horses, and a man's perspiration—Patrick smells—oddly stirred memories of kisses. They also evoked feelings of safety, which countered the feelings stirred by the man resembling her uncle.

"Don't be silly," she replied, voice catching in her throat. "This piece is difficult."

"Regardless, it is very late and I have Long Patrol tomorrow. I must be off to bed."

"No, please, just a little bit longer," Katherina pleaded.

"That is what you said while the sun was still up," he laughed. "Look at where the moon is in the sky."

"I know, but I want to have the song right before the talent show," she said.

Brian scoffed in a friendly manner. "There is plenty of time for that. I'm available to help next Wodensday. We'll practice again then."

Katherina put on her best pout, but even that could not deter the Avangardesman. He smiled and bid her goodnight. But even before he exited, she set back to moving the stones on the lines and testing the musical notes in the acoustic chamber. None seemed to reflect what Brian had been trying to teach, to her extreme frustration.

She moved the stones one more time, nudging the various colors up and down to correspond to the adjustment in tone she tried to accomplish.

Before she could test the new configuration, however, movement at the corner of her eye caught her attention. She turned and almost jumped, shocked to see a little girl staring at her.

"Well, hello," she said to the dirty little girl who couldn't have been more than seven years old. "What's your name?"

The girl did not respond, but looked shyly down to her hands. In one, she held a tattered rag doll; in the other a bright yellow rose that must have come from the garden, judging by its freshness.

"Is that for me?" Katherina asked, coming forward.

The child backed up, putting both objects behind her back.

"I guess not," Katherina mused out loud. She knelt and came no closer. "I'm Katherina," she said gently. "And you are?"

The little girl drifted over to the podium and looked at the slate and stones. After a moment, she reached up to touch one.

"Please don't," Katherina stood, trying her best not to shout. The little girl jumped back as if stung by a bee, mistrust in her eyes. Katherina didn't mean to frighten the child, but she had worked long and hard to make as much progress on the song as she had, and didn't want to see it erased.

"You mustn't touch people's things," she added both politely and sternly. "Just as you shouldn't pick flowers that aren't yours.

I'm certain Mother Superior would be upset to know you've taken one of her prized roses." Katherina nudged the stone on the slate back into place. "But your secret is safe with me."

She said the last with a wink.

"Her name is Chansonne," a new voice in the room said, "and she is very late for bed."

Katherina turned to see a nun standing in the room, an older woman in an all-white habit; younger than Mother Superior, but older than most of the Greensprings nuns who wore the black and white Benedictine habit.

"Forgive her intrusion," the nun apologized, "but she can be a willful child, and I'd be happy to make any compensation for the flower."

"Oh, that won't be necessary," Katherina returned, smiling. "As I said, it will be our little secret."

Katherina came forward and introduced herself.

Likewise, the nun bowed and said, "I am Sister Abigail, chaperone to the children of Saint Peter's Orphanage."

"You mean she is not one of the students?" Katherina asked.

"No," Sister Abigail responded. "Cardinal Teodorico has a special relationship with Saint Peter's and invited many of the children to see the Cup of the Last Supper as a pilgrimage. We are very grateful for his patronage."

"No doubt," Katherina said and turned to the girl. "I'm very pleased to meet you, Chansonne." Sister Abigail pulled Katherina aside and whispered, "Chansonne does not speak, nor does she associate well with others. She experienced a tragedy in her childhood."

Katherina put one hand to her mouth and another to her breast, squeezing her eyes shut. She breathed, "Oh, my poor dear. I am so sorry to hear that."

Sister Abigail touched Katherina's arm. It made her flinch ever so slightly.

"You needn't worry, child," the nun said. "The good cardinal takes good care of us and we pray daily for all the special children of Saint Peter's."

With that, the nun turned to Chansonne and called her over. The girl reluctantly took the older woman's hand.

"I'll see what I can do to curb her inclination towards picking flowers," Sister Abigail said as they left. "How she loves flowers. Seems everywhere we go she's picking them from one place and leaving them in another."

Katherina bid them goodnight and returned to her slate and stones. She groaned out loud when she saw the stones out of place once again. Evidently she hadn't been vigilant enough to keep the child from moving them, after all.

Katherina bent to readjust the stones, but froze.

Not only did the stones sit in a proper musical configuration, they quite possibly sat in just the position Katherina had been trying so long to find.

#

The inevitable sound of boots came across the floor.

Patrick managed to avoid the Cardinal Guard for most of the day, but they eventually found him in the last place soldiers would look.

The library.

He sat as far away from the entrance as possible, bent over an ancient tome. A single candle illuminated his corner of the library, a nook reached only by traversing the maze of shelves. When the soldiers found him, he sat with his back to them. Even so, judging by the footsteps and their breathing, he counted three of them.

"Sir Patrick," one of them said, the hint of malice in his voice. "It pleases the cardinal you come with us."

"It does not please me," Patrick said tiredly. "If the cardinal wishes to see me, we can have this discussion during the council. Besides, I want to finish this book."

Patrick smiled, feeling the men look at one another in disbelief.

"Irishman." The lead guard said the word as a slur. The sound of swords slithering from leather scabbards filled the air. "You will come with us now."

Patrick breathed heavily out his nose, closed the book, and leaned toward the candle. The thumb on his left hand rubbed the pommel of his sword.

"This isn't going to happen the way you pictured it," he said, and blew out the candle.

#

"The great hall, or the throne room as they call it here, is really the only room large enough to accommodate all the council members and aids," Victor said. "We could use the auditorium, but there is little level space for tables, only the stage, and the seating is primarily for spectators. We do not want to give the other benefactors the impression they are only spectators. Each must be given his seat of honor and made to feel he is a participant."

Teodorico thoughtfully chewed on a nail. He shifted in his plush seat. His sizable pavilion was the largest of the temporary housing in the tent city beyond the Greensprings fortress. He studied the intricate rug that covered the floor of his traveling bishopric. The hours had begun to stretch into the night and he was tired of making preparations for the upcoming council.

"Agreed," he said. "It is always better to leave them feeling the final decision was their idea, though I see the English delegates protesting no matter what, hmm, yes?"

"Their protests would be greatly diminished if the Knight of Cups had only done the simple courtesy of stating the cup 'told him' it belonged in Rome, hmm?" he added with a growl. "Where is that damnable Irishman anyway, hmm!"

"They will find him soon Your Eminence," Victor said, shuffling more papers. "It is an island, after all."

Just then, one of the Cardinal Guard staggered into the tent, his helmet missing, an eye blackened, and his sword scabbard empty. Another guard shot through the tent doorway as if pushed from behind. He lacked his sword and helmet as well, but had gained a split lip.

At last came the largest of the guards, whose face had received the worst of the beatings, with his surcoat pulled down around his elbows, pinning his arms to his sides. Sir Patrick walked behind the angry man, holding the surcoat with a single hand, twisting and bunching the fabric tight.

As they approached Cardinal Teodorico's throne-like chair, Sir Patrick pushed the man into his companions.

A moment's pause hung in the air when no one talked. The Irishman stood by with arms crossed. The three soldiers looked at the ground sheepishly.

"Leave us," Teodorico hissed to the soldiers.

They hesitated at the command, looking unsure.

"His Eminence is in no danger," Victor added. "Leave. You will be dealt with later."

The moment they shambled out of the pavilion, Teodorico shot to his feet.

"What was the meaning of that insolence this morning, hmm!" he shouted, feeling blood rise in his face. "You had a simple duty!"

"I made my stance clear on Your Eminence's boat at Cornwall," the Irishman responded. "The guardians of the cave said it should never have left, and I promised to return it."

"It is the Cup of the Last Supper and belongs to Mother Church!" Teodorico railed. "I've been more than considerate in prodding you towards making the right choice, hmm? Am I not an archbishop? Am I not the representative of the Seat of Peter? Am I not a successor to the Apostles? Are you not obligated to do as I command, yes?"

Sir Patrick glowered silently. Several heartbeats passed while Teodorico felt his eyes might bulge from his head before the Irishman's finally spoke.

"I'm merely pointing out the obvious, Your Eminence," he said at last, some contriteness in his voice. "The cup will not allow itself to be moved. The only 'message' I feel I've received from it is that it has made its own decision. I apologize for my apparent lack of respect, but you did essentially ask me to lie. That I cannot do, and..." The Irishman added injury to insolence when he added with a slight curl of the lip, "I wouldn't want to place a cardinal in a position where other benefactors might ask if I had been coerced by said cardinal to say such untruths."

Teodorico now felt certain his eyes might explode from their sockets. He felt his nostrils momentarily pinch shut when he drew a breath through them.

"Sir Patrick, I did not ask you to lie, hmm? I merely asked you to express an opinion. You could have benefited from having done so, hmm, yes?"

"How do you mean?" Sir Patrick's insolence melted away, replaced by the hint of concern Teodorico hoped the man should feel.

"This is all a test." Teodorico leaned back in his seat and rested his head against the backboard, but maintained a steely gaze on the Avangardesman. "Just as I suggested on my boat. God is testing you. If you fail the test, do you think God will be kind, hmm? He may not 'punish' you, but I would not doubt He would show you the error of your ways in some way, yes? I would hate to be in your boots." The cardinal leaned forward and his tone lowered to almost a whisper. "Or perhaps unfortunate things will happen to those close to you. Sin doesn't always affect the sinner, hmm? I'd hate to see anything happen to that pretty maidservant of yours."

The Irishman narrowed his eyes and said nothing at first. Eventually, his lips slowly curled into a smile and he chuckled.

"Aimeé?" he said with a disaffected shrug. "We've gone our separate ways. It was a foolish romantic notion on my part. A notion that a visit to my family soon remedied. They reminded me I am noble born and can do better."

Teodorico scrutinized Sir Patrick for a moment, gauging the man's impassivity.

"Be that as it may," he said at last, "my point is that God may not be finished with you and those close to you, hmm, yes?"

"I'll take my chances." The Irishman's insolence returned.

Teodorico's eyes flared and he made the sign of the Holy Cross. "Th-th-then may God have mercy on your soul, hmm? Y-y-you are excused."

The Avangarde bowed, pivoted on a heel, and moved towardsthe exit.

"S-S-Sir Patrick, hmm?" Teodorico said before he left, causing the man to pause and look over his shoulder. "I-i-if you are not with me, then do not be against me, hmm? I-I-I am not so forgiving as God, yes?"

"As you say, Your Eminence," he said with a curt nod and left.

Teodorico walked over to the table populated with wine flagons and cups.

"Shame he is not a supporter," Victor said. "His celebrity would have been a great asset."

"Shame, yes?" Teodorico said, reaching for a cup and flagon. "But there is, as they say, more than one way to skin a cat, hmm?"

"Do you believe him? About the maidservant, I mean?" Victor asked.

Teodorico raised his eyebrows. "I'm not certain. It merits keeping our eye on them, yes?"

The flagon shook violently in Teodorico's hand, and the cup in his other hand shook even as he tried to pour the liquid. He bit his lip and returned them to the serving tray, raising the clatter of metal on metal.

"Victor," he said, forcing his voice calm. "I'd like to turn in for the evening. I am not to be disturbed, do you hear me?"

"Yes, Your Eminence," Victor bowed and backed out of the tent.

Once Victor was gone, Teodorico raised his hands before his eyes to note how badly they shook.

He closed his eyes and took a deep breath.

"C-C-C..." he stammered, taking another deep breath. "O-Oh..." Another breath. "Nnn..." And yet another, followed by, "T-R-O-L!"

He thrust his hands down to his sides, forming fists.

"C-O-N-T-R-O-L!" he squeezed the letters between his teeth. "CONTROL!"

He took the deepest breath yet, held it, then said calmly, "Control."

He exhaled, smiled and reached for the flagon and cup. No shaking occurred this time and he had no trouble pouring himself a drink. He returned to his chair, drinking with one hand and rubbing his head with the other.

He sat hard on the cushions and said out loud, "We need to investigate every possibility. We must do whatever it takes to obtain the cup." He took a sip of wine and added, "Oh, and I'm sorry about that 'cat-skinning' analogy. Poor choice of words."

He leaned over to the travel trunk next to his chair and rapped on its surface with his knuckles.

From inside came an answering rap.

#

Silence rendered the church as still as a crypt, though an occasional cough or sniffle escaped from the fifty or so pilgrims who gathered before the altar. Incense thickened the air, giving the candlelight a hazy quality.

At this hour, only one newcomer appeared in the doorway at the back of the church. All others had arrived long ago and taken their place before the cup which was glimmering like a heavenly treasure. Now, they struggled to stay awake to keep their vigil.

But not for much longer.

The newcomer would see to that. She would nudge them into the arms of Morpheus.

The Lady Lilliana stepped to the edge of light and removed her hood, freeing her auburn hair to cascade down her back. Candlelight flickered in her amber eyes, but soon her eyes flared with a light of their own, shining forth from all but her slitted pupils.

She opened her mouth and raised her hands. A mist billowed from her mouth, starting as any mist that might form from breath on a cold day, except no cold touched the inside of the church. Even so, the mist grew thick and dense as a fog engulfing a seashore, then curled along the floor like clouds descending from mountaintops. It spread in all directions from her stationary form, boiling across the flagstones, pooling around the worshippers. It smashed against the communion rail and frothed like ocean waves. The nearest worshipper suddenly rose her head and sniffed, realizing something amiss.

Before slumping forward, the young woman smiled and sighed, "Pretty."

Soon all of them were asleep. Gentle snores replaced the rattle of prayer beads.

Lilliana strode forward, confidently stepping over the slumbering forms, disturbing the pearly mist hovering just above the floor.

As she approached the altar, however, her confident stride slowed until she stood an arm's length away from the cup. Her eyes narrowed and her lips pursed.

She took off one of her lacy gloves and held a claw-like hand near the vessel for a heartbeat, then reached for it.

Her hand grasped it firmly, eyes widening at the achievement, but then widened even more. She screamed as smoke rose from her hand where it touched the cup. She withdrew it, pain searing through her arm. Her skin bubbled as if splashed with acid. She grasped her wrist just below the smoldering hand and raced for a side door, shrieking.

The worshippers twitched in their sleep, troubled by unpleasant dreams.

#

Father Wulfric thought the church bells rang to announce Terce, the late morning prayers sung by the Keep monks, but when the bells continued to ring much longer than usual, and an obvious disturbance erupted around the stables, he knew trouble had risen with the morning sun.

He stopped a running stable boy. "You there, young man—what is happening?"

The boy gasped, "Somebody has died and I have to tell someone."

He ran inside the keep to find someone of authority, but Father Wulfric already spotted several knights in black surcoats jogging towards the building, holding their scabbards steady as they ran.

Father Wulfric followed the crowd toward the stables, where people gathered like bees around a hive. Because of his height he could see over their heads to the two Avangarde knights kneeling next to a body. A third interviewed a stable keeper. He couldn't hear what they said over the buzz of the crowd, but from the crowd itself he heard, "Dried out," "Sucked dry," "Aged," and "Attacked."

"Let me through," he urged as he fought his way through the crowd to the front. "I need to talk to the knights."

Once they saw the cross of thorn branches on his robes, people let him pass.

"Father, thank you for coming," a knight said. "I'm sure this poor soul could use a prayer."

Father Wulfric confirmed his fears. Before him lay a desiccated husk of a corpse like the woman found in Cornwall.

"I won't believe it was the Fair Folk," the stable keeper said to one of the knights, apparently responding to something said.

"They don't kill people. Play tricks on us sure, but not kill. Certainly not like this, my lords."

Wulfric kneeled next to the body to examine it. Like the victim at Cornwall, this older man looked as if he had died days ago, not hours. His clothes hung loosely on his corpse. By the appearance of the body one would expect the smell of decay, but a hint of a flowery aroma wafted on the air. Wulfric leaned forward to make the sign of the Holy Cross. When he did so, he noted something in the man's mouth. He bent closer and extracted something white from the open orifice.

"Only an evil sprite would or could do this," the stable keeper continued to say, "and that just doesn't happen. We've lived peacefully with the Fair Folk for a long time."

"You seem to know much about the Fair Folk," Wulfric said, standing and putting the flaky white object to his nose.

"Aye, Father, I've been in Avalon twenty-two years now," the man replied. "We've had much dealing with the Fair Folk. Mostly peaceable."

"Tell me then," Father Wulfric said, holding out the white flowers. "Have you ever heard of fairies killing people by stuffing baby's breath into their mouths?"

The stablehand squinted at the little flowers.

"No, I have not," he replied.

Wulfric had noted a similar white sprig in the mouth of the woman in Cornwall, but had thought it more of the shed skin found near her body. Now he knew otherwise.

"Did anyone, by chance, see anything suspicious?" Father Wulfric asked, looking around. "Something looking like sheets of thin paper, with a pattern in it? Or, perhaps the skin of a snake, if you know what that looks like?"

The knights and the stable hand exchanged glances and shrugged.

"No, Father, but we've only just arrived," one of the knights answered.

Wulfric started to search the stable, scanning the ground and kicking up hay. He followed the edges of the building to a side entrance. The stable keeper and the knights followed him, curious.

"Look for something unusual," he urged them.

Something between his commanding tone and their curiosity convinced them to comply. As they did, Wulfric noted the crowd at the entrance watched with intense curiosity—all except the child from the boat. The girl turned and left, clutching her dirty doll with one hand and a dead rose in the other.

His eyes followed her as she meandered through the forest of adult legs, but a call from one of the knights drew his attention back.

"Look," the knight said, "I think I found something."

Wulfric hurried over and saw the knight pointing to a wispy, semi-transparent material snagged on the wood of an empty stall.

"What is it?" the stable keeper asked, eyes narrowing. "Cobwebs?"

"No," Wulfric responded, gently picking it up. "It is the skin of some creature. It's as when a spider grows; it bursts out of its skin, leaving an empty shell behind."

When he said this, the substance disintegrated to dust in his hands.

Chapter Seven

"There is a monster among us," Father Wulfric stated, concluding his concerns to the authorities with that simple statement.

"Are you certain it's the same creature from Cornwall?" Sir Wolfgang von Fiescher asked, his voice echoing off the walls of the keep's meeting chamber.

"Are we certain it is a creature at all, hmm?" Cardinal Teodorico added. "Perhaps someone is casting a curse of some sort, hmm, yes?"

"Normally I would agree," Father Wulfric replied, "but the fact that a discarded skin has been found at the scene of every incident —skin which did not come from the victims—tells me it is a creature and not a curse. I believe it came with us hidden on the boats. I should have said something earlier when I thought I found a portion of its skin on the deck."

"You couldn't have known, Father," the cardinal reassured his fellow clergyman.

"But now that we do, we need to take action," Wolfgang said. "Finding a monster should be easier than finding an evil sorcerer disguised among us. We will send the Avangarde to search every corner of the keep. We will find this thing. We have some experience dealing with monsters."

"May I suggest that no one in Greensprings be alone," Sir Marcus Ionus suggested. "Everyone must work and travel in pairs, at least."

"Excellent idea," Wolfgang said.

"Also," Sir Corbin added, "it may not be a bad idea to implement our companion program now."

"Companion program?" Cardinal Teodorico asked, raising his eyebrows.

"Last year, after the goblin attack on the keep," Mother Superior explained, "we had Avangarde pair with a Guest as a 'Brother in Christ' for the Guest's protection. It was originally meant as an added precaution, a way to provide bodyguards without it feeling like they had bodyguards. It worked out rather well, creating a closeness and fondness between the two groups."

"You think this will help, yes, hmm?" Teodorico said.

"Normally we wait a few months until we can match personalities," Marcus added, "but Corbin is right, we may not have that kind of time."

"Make it so," Mother Superior said, turning to Father Hugh and Wolfgang. "Draw up lists."

"The Cardinal Guard can protect the council chamber, hmm," Teodorico suggested. "As well as protect the pavilions outside the keep. That should free up the Avangarde to concentrate on a search, hmm, yes?"

"Very well then," Wolfgang said, "let us all go to our duties."

#

At the sound of a drum beating in the courtyard, knights rushed from their honeycomb of cells in the Avangarde barracks. Word of the monster had reached them, as had the search plan. Patrick paused, however, before joining the parade of pounding boots and jingling spurs. He sat on his bed, staring into the polished surface of his helm, wishing the face peering back at him would say something to put his mind at ease. He had lied to a man of God. He had lied about his relationship with Aimeé.

Many said evil and corruption existed among the clergy as much as anywhere, but Patrick did not want to believe that. His personal experience had not proved that—until yesterday evening, that is, when Teodorico had made veiled threats against Aimeé. The encounter had compelled Patrick to lie. To a priest.

He put on his helmet, and joined the Avangarde heading for the stables. As he exited the barracks, still buckling on his sword belt, he spied Aimeé across the courtyard, paused to watch the commotion with a basket of apples under her arm. His heart fell into his gut and he rushed to talk to her.

As he approached with the obvious intent of talking, her mouth screwed up skeptically and she clutched the little crucifix at her bosom with her free hand. "Ready to listen?"

"No time for that," Patrick said, and looked around fearfully. "Listen, I can't explain right now, but we need to stay away from each other. At least until the benefactors have left the island and..."

"What nonsense is this?" Aimeé almost shouted, her pretty face contorting with disappointment. "I see you're busy now, but why not later?"

Patrick fanned his hands, trying to quiet her. "Shh, I'll explain later, but you could be in terri—"

"Don't 'shoosh' me!" her voice rose to new levels and she struck his shoulder.

Patrick took a step back and clutched at a growing migraine under his helm. All around, people in the courtyard did the exact opposite of what he wanted: stare.

Sir Wolfgang approached, addressing Patrick. "My dear Irishman, your presence is required in council chambers."

"Sir, if I could just have a moment please, I need to—" An apple cut off Patrick's plea when it bounced soundly off his helm. "Aw, son of a—!"

When he looked up, Aimeé stalked away.

"It would appear you have some time after all," Wolfgang said, then added while also watching Aimeé's retreating form, "Nice arm on that girl."

#

A short walk lead him to the great hall currently serving as the council chamber. Just before separating, Wolfgang had informed him the Cardinal Guard would serve as guards to the room, but he still found it disconcerting to see someone other than Avangarde acting as gatekeepers.

"Your business here?" one of the guards said with a heavy Italian accent.

Patrick felt a flash of anger. "I was summoned," he said simply, hoping the brute would send him away. If he did, Patrick wouldn't have to deal with the council and this imbecile of a guard might find himself in trouble.

The man jerked his head toward one of his colleagues who disappeared into the council chamber. While they waited, Patrick quietly judged the stubble climbing the soldier's cheeks. Though the Cardinal Guard obviously meant to appear uniform in appearance, right down to clean-shaven faces, they showed poor discipline in consistently meeting that expectation. It made Patrick wonder where else they showed poor discipline.

The door to the council chamber opened, and a guard motioned for him to enter. The soldier immediately in front of Patrick refused to budge, forcing him to go around.

Patrick rolled his eyes and entered. There he took a seat among several Greensprings folk who had been summoned as well. The smell of fried bacon still hung in the air from breakfast. Now the dining tables formed a square around the edge of the room. A young man with wild, unkempt hair and clothes of a simple fashion, but rich fabric, roamed the open center area with a large open book positioned in the crook of one elbow. With his other hand he gestured as he spoke.

"Furthermore," he said, "these ancient records from the library in Glastonbury Abbey, recognized as one of the oldest in all Christendom, support the oral account that Joseph of Arimathea did indeed bring the Cup of the Last Supper to Glastonbury as its resting place. This text states, 'Arviragus, King of the Britons, gave certain strangers twelve hides of land around

Ynis-witrin in the year 35 of our Lord, whereupon they built a holy place,'" the man paused to explain, "'Ynis-witrin' is the ancient Celtic name of the region about Glastonbury."

"Do the records specifically say it was Joseph of Arimathea?" Teodorico asked, incredulous. "Or are you reading into an ancient document what you want it to say, hmm, yes?"

"Well, no," the man conceded, "but the context of the ancient Latin, '*Quidame advanae,*'—certain strangers—implies foreigners in the sense they weren't merely from another village, but truly alien outsiders. Furthermore, the Christian sect of Culdees, who lay claim as the oldest Christians in the isles, derive their nomenclature from 'refugees,' or more specifically, 'Judean refugees.' Their name and their appearance coincide chronologically with the charter granted by King Arviragus. The point is, there is sufficient tangible documentation to back up the oral account that asserts Joseph of Arimathea, a wealthy Jew and a Roman citizen, had merchant dealings in lead and tin in the British Isles, and came to Glastonbury as a refugee when the persecution of Christians began in Jerusalem. Assuredly, he brought the cup with him."

"Signore William Malmesbury, hmm?" Teodorico said with a condescension-tinted smile. "Your reputation as a historian is well established and admired, despite your youth, but it is irresponsible to read wishful folktales into an ancient document. Nor does it prove ownership of the cup, hmm, yes? It, at best, lends legitimacy to the fact the cup can be found in this part of the world, and not in the Holy Land."

Many of those gathered at the tables murmured their assent. But the young man wagged a finger and approached a table piled high with books and paper.

"This same transaction is referenced in the Domesday Book commissioned by King William of England not more than sixteen years ago," Malmesbury said, exchanging the book in his arm for an even larger, leather-bound volume. "It states, 'The Domus Dei, in the great monastery of Glastonbury, the Secret of the Lord.

This Glastonbury Church possesses, in its own villa, twelve hides of land which have never paid taxes.'

"Now, you may not recognize oral accounts or ancient translations, but you must recognize the royal seal on an official document. And this book is an accounting of all that which belongs to the King of England. If it's mentioned in this book, then it belongs to the king."

"The land, perhaps, hmm?" Teodorico sniffed.

"And all that which resides in that land," Father Wulfric stated, evidently quoting some law.

"Unless the land belongs to the Church, separate from the state, hmm, yes?" the cardinal countered. "In which case what is on or in the land belongs to the Holy See, hmm, yes?"

"Well, it belongs to the diocese of residence, and Saint Joseph obviously meant for the cup to reside in Glastonbury, which is in the Archdiocese of Canterbury... also in England," Father Wulfric said.

"My dearest Wulfric," Teodorico sighed with perhaps a little too much sarcasm in his voice. "We know you're acting as delegate for Abbot Anselm, and you can dutifully go back and tell him you pleaded his case, but *Abbot* Anselm is still not recognized as *Archbishop* Anselm, and has little authority in these matters. England's King Henry cannot invest the good abbot as Archbishop of Canterbury. That is something the pope must do. Another reason the cup should go to Rome. Things are more stable there."

"Nonetheless," Wulfric responded, some anger in his voice, "Canterbury, regardless of the state of its current leadership, is a founding member of the Board of Benefactors and does have a say in the matter. Besides, Pope Paschal allows Anselm to perform archbishop duties. That is why he could not be here today. He is aiding the king in his fight against his brother Robert, who at this moment threatens to invade England. The pope even upholds Anselm's excommunication of Robert."

"The only reason Paschal entertains Anselm's investiture is because Anselm supports the pope's silly notion clergy should not be married, hmm?" Teodorico said, preparing to say more before one of the merchants cut in.

"I believe we are wandering off track," the richly dressed merchant said, having to raise his voice to be heard. "We had an agenda once, I think."

Light laughter rippled through the room.

"Quite right, Signore Humphrie, hmm?" Cardinal Teodorico conceded, and directed his attention back to the young scholar. "Signore Malmesbury, even if it were universally agreed the cup belonged in Glastonbury, it does not change the fact the cup in question today is here in Avalon."

"Excellent point," Malmesbury said with a gleam in his eye. He swept the wild hair from his eyes with the stroke of a hand and continued. "That is an explanation that will require some patience on all your parts while listening."

Cardinal Teodorico motioned for the scholar to continue.

"Consider this," William started. "History tells us King Arthur's last earthly act was to bring the Holy Grail, the Cup of the Last Supper, to Avalon where he is buried after his last battle. If that is so, and this is Avalon," he stomped his foot on the ground for emphasis, "how is it on the grounds of Glastonbury Abbey there is a gravesite with a stone which has inscribed upon it; *Hic jacet sepultus inclytus Rex Arthurius in Insula Avalonia?*" William paused briefly, then translated for the benefit of those who did not know Latin. "Here lies buried in the Isle of Apples, the renowned King Arthur."

The question was obviously rhetorical and because the assembly had been forewarned his explanation required patience, they waited for William to pick up the narrative.

"Avalonia, the Isle of Apples, is obviously Avalon. Yet the grave and inscribed stone are found in Glastonbury in the Summer Country of England," William continued. "The answer is the land about Glastonbury *is* Avalon."

A murmur rippled through the room and Teodorico, losing patience, voiced what everyone thought, "How is that possible? We are on Avalon now."

William held up a finger for patience. He looked to Abbot Herewinus who sat among the Glastonbury delegates. The elderly abbot nodded approvingly.

"Glastonbury lies in the shadow of the Tor of Somerset, the highest point in the area. Before and during the reign of King Arthur this marshy region was underwater, all save the Tor and its immediate surroundings. It was an island. An island called Avalon, and it was to there three fairy sisters took the dying Arthur with his sword Excalibur and the Holy Grail."

"Again, we feel obligated to point out we *are* on Avalon, in the Western Sea," Humphrie said, scowling.

"Yes, we are," Malmesbury said, the gleam in his eye shining brighter than ever.

"Are you implying there are two Avalons?" Lucan asked.

William again wagged a finger and paced with his head down, deep in thought. He drew a breath, evidently winding up for another lengthy explanation.

"Scripture tells us the world we live in is a pale reflection of Heaven," he said, appealing in particular to the clergy in the room. "It is, as Saint Paul says, 'Heaven through a glass darkly.' This is also true about virtually every aspect of our faith. Think about it—baptism by water is a pale reflection of our ultimate baptism by fire and the Holy Spirit. Even Jesus as the man was a mere foreshadowing of Jesus the Savior in his glorified form. The resurrected Jesus appeared to the Apostles in the upper room, even though the room was locked. He passed through walls and locked doors as if he were made of... mist." William paused in his narrative, bringing his theatrical hand movements to rest on Lucan. "Even your relic expert has testified earlier the cup we see in the church is quite possibly the Cup of the Last Supper, but in its glorified form as opposed to its mundane form. Which is why our hands pass through it."

The Board of Benefactors started to agitate in their seats, murmuring and anxious for an answer.

"You see, gentlemen," William said, turning slowly around the chamber, engaging with as many of the members as he could, "there are two aspects to our world. The ordinary and the extraordinary. The natural and the supernatural. The profane and the sacred. Everything has its twin. Even saints in history have been known to bilocate. That is, be in two places at the same time, performing miraculous deeds."

Up to this moment, Patrick had listened with only half interest, mostly shaking his head in wonder at the fact these silly people argued over ownership of something beyond their control. The moment the young historian mentioned twins, however, he had Patrick's full attention.

"People and relics having glorified natures is not so hard to grasp," Humphrie argued, "but places, such as an entire island?"

"Especially places," Malmesbury replied. "As I said earlier, the world is but Heaven through a glass darkly. The Garden of Eden was Heaven on earth, and we are now cut off from it by a cherub wielding a fiery sword. This Avalon we find ourselves on is cut off from the rest of the world by a filtering mist allowing only those with another holy relic, the feather from an Avalon swan, to pass. This Avalon is blanketed by ever-blossoming apple trees, whereas there are few in Glastonbury. A place which nevertheless refers to itself as 'Avalonia.' There is, however, in Glastonbury a thorn tree that blossoms faithfully twice a year: once in the month of May, and again on December 25th, the birthday of our Lord. All other times of the year it bears green leaves, counter to the nature of the species. A species not native to England, but to the Holy Land. That is because this thorn tree sprang from the thorn-wood staff Saint Joseph of Arimathea thrust into the ground upon his arrival at what is now Glastonbury.

"Furthermore, gentleman, there are direct links between that Avalon and this Avalon. It is at Glastonbury, on the River Brue, where the original knights of Greensprings boarded a swan-shaped boat and were carried out to sea until they arrived here to construct this fortress. It was a priest of Glastonbury, Father Dominique Chanceroy, who discovered the gift of the swan feathers creating a passage through the protective mist.

"Lastly, King Arthur's earthly remains are buried in the Avalon of Glastonbury, but his spirit resides on this Avalon." One of William's wildly flailing hands shot a finger at Patrick. "Doesn't it, Sir Patrick Gawain?"

Surprised at the sudden attention, Patrick sat up straight and pointed to himself.

William Malmesbury motioned for the Irishman to come forward, saying, "The Avangardesman who brought us the Grail from a cave on this island also reported seeing slumbering knights in a tomb. That is correct, Sir Patrick?"

Patrick, who dutifully came forward to stand next to the young scholar, awkwardly responded, "Yes, but I was very wounded and quite delirious at the time. I did see what I thought to be knights in repose, but honestly I could not swear they were Arthur and his men."

"I would strongly suspect they were," William said, dismissing Patrick's caveat. He then turned his attention back to the council members. "All this strongly supports that the Glastonbury Avalon is the natural twin of the Greensprings Avalon. Saint Joseph of Arimathea brought the Cup of the Last Supper to Glastonbury to escape persecution in Jerusalem and to evangelize the British Isles, and it was Arthur who ensured that it stayed in Avalon. Therefore in the realm of Avalon it must remain, whether Greensprings, Glastonbury, or Canterbury."

More murmuring echoed in the chamber as the benefactors considered the argument. Patrick, feeling his duty finished, started to move back to his seat, but William gently grabbed his arm and silently bid him stay.

"That is a fine argument, hmm?" Teodorico said, though his demeanor suggested he felt otherwise. "But it's still a—shall we say—'thin' argument, hmm, yes?"

The cardinal nudged Lucan at his side, urging him to say something.

Lucan blinked as if waking from a daydream.

"Yes," he said, clearing his throat. "An interesting theological point, but as you pointed out in your opening argument, the Domesday Book legitimizes the original land grant to the original founders of Glastonbury, but bears no mention to any 'spiritual twin.' Greensprings is not on any map, and technically does not even exist."

"My lords, that is splitting hairs," Abbot Herewinus complained.

"And 'spiritual twins' is not?" Teodorico countered.

More murmuring buzzed the chamber and Humphrie banged on his table with one of his shoes to bring order back to the chamber.

"All this nonsense is giving me a headache," he all but shouted. "Shouldn't we consider if we keep the cup in England the King of England will tax the throngs of pilgrims who wish to see it? And if we keep it here at Greensprings, the sheer logistics of carrying boatloads of pilgrims here is problematic, not to mention it would make it even easier for the King of England to charge exorbitant prices for sea passage?"

"Not any more exorbitant than what the Italian city states currently charge pilgrims to sail to Jerusalem," Father Wulfric said, "and not any less inconvenient a journey. In fact, this journey would be far safer. Besides, Humphrie, you're just concerned you'd be cut out of any revenue from such an endeavor."

"And why not?" Humphrie responded. "The Brussels Merchants Guild is not on the Board of Benefactors just because the Greensprings School for Peace sounds pleasant. There is money to be made in peace, just as there is in war."

More arguments broke out and again Humphrie banged on the table with his shoe.

"All these arguments are moot," Abbot Herewinus sniffed. "As was demonstrated earlier, the cup cannot be moved."

"It may very well be someday," Teodorico replied. "We should be prepared, in writing, when that day comes."

"Speaking of documentation," Humphrie said, "the immediate question is not whether it can be moved or where it should be moved to, but if it's even the Cup of the Last Supper. We still need to declare its authenticity officially."

"Excellent point, hmm?" Teodorico said, and motioned to Lucan. "Sir Lucan, please do the honors, hmm?"

Lucan descended the dais with a leather-bound book and approached Patrick and held out the tome on his palm. Patrick fidgeted. "Sir Patrick Gawain, please place your hand on the Bible and answer the following questions." Patrick tentatively placed his hand on the book. "You are the Avangarde who found the cup and brought it to the church in Greensprings?"

"I am," Patrick replied, relaxing when he realized he was only asked to confirm common knowledge.

"When you originally grasped the cup, it was a simple wood vessel, which turned into the golden chalice we now see on the altar when you poured consecrated wine into it?"

"Aye," Patrick said, again stating common knowledge.

"There were witnesses to this?" Lucan asked, motioning to the bench of people along the wall.

"Aye," Patrick said.

Lucan motioned with his chin and Cardinal Guards herded the witnesses to the center of the room. While they did, Lucan continued with Patrick.

"You witnessed the young woman, Aimeé de la Chasse, dead," Lucan said.

"Aye, and most of Greensprings witnessed that, too."

"With the consecrated wine, the blood of Jesus Christ, in the cup you brought from the cave, you brought her back from the dead?"

"Aye, and there were plenty of witnesses to that as well."

"You swear to this, so help you God?"

"I do, as God is my witness," Patrick said, and crossed himself.

At Teodorico's elbow, Victor's furious scribbling on parchment made Patrick self-conscious. By the time Lucan had performed the same procedure one by one with the witnesses, Patrick forced away the tension building in his shoulders, feeling certain this could be no more sinister than a simple matter of bureaucracy. When Lucan had almost finished with the last witness, however, the loud clank of the chamber doors' locking mechanism drew Patrick's attention to the entrance.

The doors slowly opened to reveal a pair of Cardinal Guard with Aimeé standing between them, hugging herself. Patrick's stomach sank and he cast a glance at the cardinal, noting the cold stare and clear message.

"Mademoiselle de la Chasse," Lucan addressed Aimeé, "please join us."

Aimeé wrung her hands and came forward in slippers that whispered along the flagstones, looking about at the serious faces in the room.

When she stood near Patrick, she crossed her arms and would not look at him. This hurt, but was also a relief. Perhaps now Teodorico would believe Patrick's lie.

"Do you swear that you were, for a period, no longer among the living?" Lucan asked after entreating her to place her hand on the Bible.

Aimeé frowned, not sure how to respond, but nonetheless replied, "As best I can tell, my lord."

Lucan made her swear by God, which she did.

"As the official Historian and Holy Relic Expert," Lucan announced, "and appointed by the Holy See, I declare this cup of Greensprings as the Cup of the Last Supper, the Holy Grail, the Vessel of Christ."

A positive murmur rippled through the room.

Victor held up a writing quill and motioned for Patrick to come forward.

"Sir, I understand you know your letters," Victor said. "Would you be so kind as to perform the honors of witnessing this document?"

Patrick frowned angrily, keenly aware the cardinal leaned forward in his seat to specifically watch his next move.

Resisting the temptation to look at Aimeé, Patrick came forward stiffly, took the quill, and leaned over the parchment. Smugness curled at the corner of Teodorico's mouth.

As he scribbled his signature, the Glastonbury historian William Malmesbury commented, "Sir Patrick, I read your report about the incidents leading you to the cave, and how you eventually brought the chalice to Greensprings. Those were quite the adventures you experienced."

When finished writing, Patrick straightened. "I did my duty."

He turned to leave, but paused when Malmesbury added, "I'm curious about one thing though... In your report you state there were guardians in this cave. Why, exactly, did the cup need protection?"

Patrick froze, conscious of all eyes on him, especially the cardinal's. He struggled to make some mollifying response, but Teodorico cut him off.

"I'm certain the motives of these spirits are beyond an Irishman's reasoning, hmm?" The cardinal sniffed, making a dismissive gesture. "Sir Patrick merely acted as the instrument making the initial transportation of the cup possible. His role in this story is finished and I'm certain he now has *other* concerns to worry about. We should move onto more meaningful matters, such as what we will do with the cup, hmm, yes?"

Patrick balled his hands into fists. His jaw moved back and forth, hurting his teeth, as he stared at Aimeé. She returned his gaze, brow crinkling.

Patrick whirled back towards the dais.

"They were protecting it from us," Patrick declared, almost shouting. Teodorico's head snapped up. Lucan, in the process of returning to his seat, turned with wide eyes. "They told this simple Irishman there would be dire consequences if it weren't returned. It was never meant to be used as a political tool, nor as an object of profit." Patrick paced before the benefactors, addressing them directly. Crimson rose in Teodorico's face and the grip on his crozier slowly strangled the shaft. Despite the grave discomfort it caused, and despite the blinding glint of morning sun reflecting on his pectoral cross, Patrick managed to make eye contact with the holy man. "What is being discussed here today is tantamount to setting up tables of money changers before Solomon's Temple—the sort of tables Jesus overturned before he chased the money changers from the premises with whips." This last portion Patrick addressed to the merchants.

A stunned silence filled the room. Lucan's gaze drifted to the floor, his expression turning introspective.

"Well, then, more evidence the cup should stay on Avalon, at Greensprings," Abbot Herewinus declared.

Patrick moved to correct the abbot, but again the cardinal cut him off.

"The cup has revealed itself for a reason and it will be put to good use. It is not going back to the cave, hmm?" he said, turning to the assembly with a soothing voice that contrasted with his blazing eyes. "It is too important to hide away from the world. It will not be 'exploited' as the good knight suggests, but the miracles it will perform will bring people to the faith, and unite them. Won't it, Sir Lucan, hmm, yes?"

Lucan blinked and tore his gaze from the floor. He cleared his throat. "Yes, that is the role of relics."

Patrick appealed to the assembly. "I do not dispute the role of relics. I am a lover of miracles, and I yearn for peace, but it's just that the guardians warned against the use of *this* relic. Should we not heed them?"

"Sir Patrick," Teodorico said, standing and answering Patrick before any of the benefactors could. The cardinal's voice took on a smoother, even paternal, tone. His eyes, however, were daggers. Both his hands throttled the crozier as he leaned on it. "Your concerns have been duly noted. You have performed a great service, and we thank you for it, hmm? The fact the cup does not allow itself to be touched, let alone returned to the cave, is testament these 'guardians' were merely putting you to a test. I strongly suspect once this esteemed council reaches a resolution, the cup will allow itself to be transported once again, yes? Go in peace, my child."

He made the sign of the holy cross.

The impassive faces of the benefactors offered Patrick no succor.

Reluctantly, Patrick bowed, saying, "As you wish, Your Eminence."

He turned to leave, but paused when William Malmesbury said, "Sir Patrick, why then did you bring the cup to Greensprings?"

Patrick made eye contact with Aimeé who still stood near. His heart broke.

"To save the girl," Patrick almost whispered.

"And why was that so important you would disregard the warning of these guardians?" William continued.

Patrick did not answer right away, watching Aimeé's eyes flare, moisture starting to glisten in her green eyes. For the briefest of moments his vision swam and he thought blood covered her. He rubbed his temple and his vision cleared and she stood there free of blood. Beautiful skin and hair glowing with motherhood.

"Because I..." He swallowed hard. "Because I felt it a shame she should perish after having played her part in saving Greensprings. I wanted to correct that."

The brief shining light in Aimeé's face was snuffed out. She squeezed her eyes shut as if stabbed. Her form bowed slightly, and she clutched her chest as if grasping an actual blade. Lucan stepped closer and offered his arm for her to lean on.

Patrick all but ran from the chamber then, not waiting for any more questions. His boots echoed loudly in the now-quiet room as if mocking the words he refused to say.

#

He burst through the doors of the hall and ran into the backside of one the Cardinal Guards. He pushed the man aside and intended to continue forward, but the guard hurled insults at him.

Patrick turned on the man, ready to fight. Needing to fight.

Instead of accepting the challenge, the man quickly stepped back to his position and snapped to attention.

Patrick turned to see what had changed the man's mind and saw Sir Wolfgang approaching.

"Ah, bloody hell," Patrick mumbled, feeling heat rise in his face.

Judging from the Grand Master's direction of approach, he had been sitting in the balcony above the hall, watching Patrick's rebellious behavior.

"Walk with me, Sir Patrick," he said sternly.

Patrick bowed his head and matched Sir Wolfgang's stride.

"Sir, I'm very sorry, I can—"

"Don't apologize," he said, his bushy white eyebrows bunching above the ridge of his nose. "Though I would never recommend telling an archbishop, let alone a cardinal, his business, I must say it needed to happen in there. His manipulations are obvious. I'm quite proud of you."

"Sir?" Patrick said, shocked.

"You stood up for yourself," Wolfgang replied, slowing his pace and putting his hands behind his back. "You stood up for what you believe. That couldn't have been easy, and more important, you knew just when to back off." Wolfgang's eyebrows lifted halfway up his forehead as he turned and appraised Patrick. "Had you taken it much further, we would be having a very different conversation right now. As it is, you have done the

Avangarde proud. We are charged with neutrality. If we bow too readily to any one authority, we lose our credibility as impartial protectors. After your display in there, no one will accuse the Avangarde of being the cardinal's puppets."

Wolfgang paused, thoughtful, then continued, "I must admit I had my doubts about you. Sir Marcus Ionus obviously saw something in you when he recruited you. Now I see it."

"Thank you, Sir Wolfgang," Patrick said, struggling to keep his voice from cracking.

Wolfgang stopped and turned to Patrick, seriousness in his eyes.

"You are becoming a leader, Sir Patrick, by your deeds if not by your words," he said. "Your fellow knights are watching, and you influence their behavior just as much as they yours. Sir Mark's departure was sudden and his position had to be filled quickly by the next in seniority, Sir Corbin. By his own admission, however, he is not the most effective leader despite his years of experience. A day may come when you will be called upon to do more, Patrick. For now, learn from Corbin, while believing in yourself."

"Yes, sir," was all Patrick could say. He wanted the significance of the conversation to take root, but his mind whirled with the desperate need to find Aimeé and explain his actions.

"Very well. Fight strong," Wolfgang said, beating his chest.

"Live stronger," Patrick replied, beating his own chest.

They clasped forearms.

#

He could not find Aimeé. So while the Avangarde searched for a monster, he searched for a solution.

In the forest, outside a mossy mound of rocks and aspen trees, Patrick reined up Siegfried. He did not see an opening in the mound, and Siegfried struggled through the brush as he circled it, trying to find the cave entrance.

"This has to be the place," Patrick responded to Siegfried's irritable huff. "Though every time I was here I wasn't exactly in my right mind."

Siegfried snorted and bobbed his head.

"You don't have to be so quick to agree, yeah?" Patrick scowled.

"Brother," a feminine voice said, startling him.

He turned to see three female forms standing on the mound, their dark wispy gowns contrasting sharply with the almost luminescent green of the moss. A breeze disturbed their veils, but never revealed their faces.

"Tell me," Patrick said, "how do I return the cup?"

"It is too late," one, or perhaps all of them, said. "Your choice has set in motion actions that cannot be stopped. Before the cup can return, things must happen."

"Buy why?" Patrick protested.

"The answer to that is beyond us," they replied, and the foremost form pointed skyward. "We are only messengers."

"I'm sorry, I should have listened to you, I should never have taken it," Patrick pleaded. "Just tell me what to do."

"If you had a chance, would you really forsake saving the girl?" they asked.

Patrick swallowed hard, but set his chin. "I'd do it again."

"Then there you have it. It is what it is," they said. "Everything must now proceed as it must. Real choices have real consequences. Otherwise, they are not real choices."

"That's it, then?" Patrick said, rubbing his head. For some reason memories of older, jeering children surrounding him and kicking him flooded his mind. "You're just going to abandon me despite my willingness to fix this?"

"You are not alone," they said, "but you have to open your eyes and your heart. Learn to accept. We will be there for you when the time is right and you are ready."

With that, they faded away, leaving him alone with the rustle of leaves in the treetops.

Chapter Eight

When morning crept into her servant's chamber in Greensprings Keep, something other than sunbeams caressed Aimeé's face. An airy hand brushed across her forehead, cheek, and lips, accompanied by a sound like children playing in the distance. When it had happened for the third time, and sleepy attempts at brushing it away failed to make it stop, she woke in earnest.

Her eyes fluttered open to the sound of fading giggles.

She raised her head and looked about the small chamber she shared with Clare and Anna. There was nothing but an empty room. She groaned, realizing the others had already risen for work and given her more time to rest. Though they were kind to think of her pregnancy, tardiness would get her in trouble. So far, she had only confided in her two closest companions, waiting for the right time to break the news to Rosa Maria, the head of the kitchen staff.

She searched again for the playful visitors, this time outside the window, but saw no one. She stared at the ceiling, feeling rotten. She had slept a thousand times in this room and had stared just as many times at the ceiling, noting the swirl patterns in wood, picking out shapes. Here an old man's wizened face, there a puppy, and there a tree. But this morning her brow furrowed in curiosity when she noticed something new on the surface.

Tiny hand and footprints ran the length of the ceiling. The longer she stared at them, the more they faded as if they had never been there.

#

"You're starting to show, lass," Clare said, gritting her teeth as she put extra effort into cinching the laces on the back of Aimeé's corset. "I'm not sure what is best for your figure—to loosen the laces in the back, side, or front. It doesn't matter much, really, as in a few more weeks we won't be able to hide it at all. We need to tell Rosa Maria. She'll reassign your duties, but if you wait until the last minute to inform her, it might anger her. You don't want her to let you go altogether."

Aimeé shifted the corset about her bosom and loosened the strings a bit across her cleavage, but couldn't get satisfied with any configuration. She envied her older friends' wide waists supporting their breasts. Aimeé's narrow waist left her top-heavy, straining her lower back. Perhaps that would change once she had her child.

My child, she thought, rubbing her stomach, still hardly believing. Her world would completely change. A meek pleasure quickly evaporated when her thoughts turned to Patrick. Feelings of confusion and betrayal wriggled through her like serpents as she tried to fathom his behavior; everything from the bandit attack in Eire and his sleepwalking, to his irrational refusal to follow his mother's simple advice. Now, the denial of his love before a crowd.

Had she fooled herself this whole time? Did he ever really love her? He had to have. After all, he took her across the sea to meet his family. Was it simply the not knowing whether the baby was his? No, his odd behavior started even before he knew a baby existed.

She squeezed her eyes shut with the effort of trying to solve the riddle then shook her head, banishing the thoughts before their mounting pressure could burst her skull.

"I know," Aimeé replied, exasperated. "All in good time. First I have things I need to... sort out."

Anna entered the busy kitchen with a tray, set it down on the bench, and started to fill it again with bowls of hot oatmeal.

"The Avangarde lads are all sitting at the same table this morning," she said. "Both Sir Geoffrey and Sir Patrick are at the middle or thereabouts. You can take the far left end, if you like, dear. We'll cover the rest."

"Thanks for the warning, Anna," Aimeé responded.

Clare tsked, "You can't avoid them forever. Someday you will have to face each of them for different reasons."

"All in bloody good time," Aimeé said, brow creasing.

She picked up a tray and left the kitchen for the great hall.

#

Patrick fought his way through the press of bodies filling the great hall while holding a bowl of porridge in one hand and a bowl of raisins in the other. Unapologetic bumps and grumbles from benefactors and their numerous staff clogging up the room had made the simple act of enjoying a meal difficult. The newcomers, it would seem, had abandoned dining in the pavilion city outside the keep for the better food served in Greensprings. Further complicating matters, frequent monster searches—undertaken mostly on false alarms—required night-duty Avangarde to squeeze into limited table space with day-duty Avangarde.

"Oh good, more raisins," Sir Brian said, holding out his hand as Patrick arrived.

Patrick handed the bowl to the large Scotsman who poured a pile of them onto his porridge, prompting his comrades to protest.

"At least I don't destroy them by grinding them into my food," Brian said.

"It's the best way to spread the sweetness," Peredur explained, taking the bowl from him and pulverizing the raisins with a spoon. "Also, it crushes the seeds."

"Sounds like a good idea to me," Sir Geoffrey said, struggling to spit one of the tiny seeds from his mouth. Patrick reluctantly sat across from him in the only open seat and wondered what about the man allowed his fellow Avangarde to tolerate his presence.

The conversation quickly turned from raisins to frustrations over the numerous false alarms.

"I don't know why we're bothering with all this searching," Peredur said, glancing over the heads of those eating in front of him. "The culprit is surely there in that bunch."

Corbin glanced in the direction of Peredur's gaze. There, gathered at their own table and given a wide berth by others, sat the candidati.

"What? Them?" Corbin said incredulously, scowling at Peredur.

"They just *look* harmless," Peredur warned. "I bet at night one of them turns into some sort of strange creature."

"Don't be silly," Corbin said between spoonfuls of porridge. "They're simpletons, like the sort you see in any town."

"Aye," Geoffrey agreed, "just simpletons. I've heard of a 'village idiot' before, but I've never heard of an entire village of idiots in one place."

Laughter buzzed about the table.

"I heard we're starting the companion program already," Peredur said, still watching the candidati. "I hope we won't be expected to work with them."

"Is that true?" Patrick asked, also throwing a fearful glance at the candidati.

"Aye, the companion program will commence ahead of schedule," Corbin replied. "Father Hugh and Sir Wolfgang are drawing up lists as we speak. Assigning knights to Guests may be the best way to protect them from this monster, rather than searching cupboards every day."

"It's a little soon for that, isn't it?" Sir Jon said. "We're going to be awfully mismatched."

"Maybe," Corbin conceded, "but we can make changes later, if necessary."

"But the candidati?" Patrick insisted, not relishing the idea of spending time with changelings. "Will we be expected to chaperone them?"

Corbin shrugged. "I imagine so."

"I know who I'd like to be paired with," Geoffrey snickered, looking among the crowds of young ladies eating at their tables.

"I wager you do," Corbin smirked at the knight. "You lecherous wretch."

A rustle of laughter flittered about the table.

"I do take my 'body-guarding' a little more serious than others," Geoffrey answered smugly.

"I'm glad you take something seriously," a stern feminine voice interjected, bringing the laughter at the table to an abrupt halt.

To the screech of benches pushed along the floor, the knights stood to attention.

"Mother Superior, we didn't..." Corbin stammered.

"See me here. I know." The old nun glowered from behind Geoffrey's seat, her head only at mid-chest level. "I *am* rather small, and easily go unnoticed." She stepped closer with hands behind her back. "I trust you gentlemen are enjoying your meals, and ardently considering how Jesus would approach the day?"

She eyed the bunch with impassive eyes the color of a clear winter sky.

The knights cleared throats and mumbled an acknowledgment.

"Good. Carry on, then." She left, waiting until the last minute to tear her gaze away. Her short legs made quick little steps hardly disrupting her flowing habit, giving the impression she glided across the floor like a ship on water.

The Avangarde released a collective breath, followed by a snort of laughter.

"You tossers knew she was behind me the whole time, didn't you?" Geoffrey growled to his comrades.

"We didn't." Corbin smiled, "but if we did, no, we wouldn't have mentioned it."

The giggling turned to full blown laughter.

"I'm certain to be a candidati chaperone now," Geoffrey lamented as he returned to his seat with the others. "Can't I just be assigned to permanent monster hunting?"

"I wouldn't worry about it too much. Neither candidati nor monsters will be a concern much longer," Brian said. "Both troubles came with the cardinal, and they will leave with him. He will leave with or without his precious cup, but leave he will, taking his spectacle with him. He can't campaign to be the next pope from an isolated island."

"Good," Waylan said, looking down at his porridge while experimenting with the crushed-raisin method. "I've had my fill of debates and holier-than-thou goings-on."

"Hear, hear," Sir Jeremiah agreed. "'I've had enough of, 'My church is better than your church,' or, 'My bishop is the boss of your bishop,' and such nonsense. I'll be happy when they're gone, and all the trouble they brought. Monsters and politics."

"It won't be that easy," Corbin warned, starting the peeling process of a hard boiled egg. "Our very own Father Hugh and Mother Superior and most of our educators here are Glastonbury folk from the English abbey. If the Glastonbury delegates really want to raise a stink about not getting their way with the cup, they could pull their staff out from underneath us. Then what would we do? Teach the children ourselves?"

Sir Jeremiah laughed. "Brian could teach them drinking, I'd wager."

"And you could teach them buggering," Sir Brian called back.

Jeremiah threw a raisin that disappeared into Brian's beard.

Laughter erupted loud enough to draw attention from others in the hall.

After it faded, Sir Geoffrey added, "If the Romans don't get what they want, they're liable to pull their financial support, which fills my purse."

Grumbles of agreement followed.

"I can't tell a Roman from a Glaston from a German," Sir Gregory said, loudly hitting the bottom of his bowl with his spoon. "Who has the last say in the matter of the cup? Because whatever that council decides, somebody is going to be unhappy. What if the Avangarde is called upon to do some head bashing? Do we do as ordered? And who is going to do the ordering?"

"We'll worry about that when the time comes," Corbin said, though by the way his brow furrowed, Gregory's question troubled him. "Sir Wolfgang can sort that out."

"As for who has holy authority, that's simple," Sir Peredur said. "Cardinal Teodorico is the papal legate, a representative of the pope, bishop of bishops. Naturally he should have the final say in holy relics and whatnot."

"You'd think," Patrick blurted. He hadn't planned to speak up —it just came out, and now with all eyes on him he felt obligated to explain himself. "That is, normally I'd agree, but something about this cardinal disturbs me. Something isn't right. He makes veiled threats. What holy man does that?"

Corbin shrugged. "He's a bishop and a cardinal, which essentially means he's a politician. Certain necessary evils are involved with being a politician."

"It's more than that." Patrick tried to articulate his concerns, questioning how much of his gut feeling he could support with facts.

"Why do we need a bishop to tell us about spiritual matters, anyway?" Geoffrey asked, spitting out more seeds despite having crushed his raisins. "Or priests for that matter? Are we not responsible for own souls? Shouldn't we commune directly with God? Too many rules they have, if you ask me."

"We should have spiritual leaders," Waylan countered, "but I think every religious community should have their own. After all, doesn't a community know their own spiritual needs best? What does a bishop in Rome know about my situation in my land?"

An argument broke out concerning the topic.

Corbin turned to Patrick. "Well done, troublemaker. You started this conversation. Should we just hand over control of the cup to whomever the cardinal demands?"

Not bothering to point out Peredur had started this particular conversation, and after careful consideration of the larger story, Patrick responded with the weight of all eyes at the table on him. "I agree with Waylan. I'm all for having leaders in the Church. Someone to guide us in spiritual matters. We have discipline amongst ourselves, do we not? We have a chain of command; otherwise we'd never get anything done. Think about it. What if everybody here just ignored you and Wolfgang and did what they wanted? It would be chaos."

"What do you mean 'if'?" Corbin groused. "You wankers ignore half the things I tell you to do."

Laughter erupted around the table and Corbin's comrades patted his back.

"Precisely." Patrick laughed with the rest, but turned serious. "Eventually we step to it, though, but first a little healthy debate with our spiritual leaders shouldn't hurt. Didn't Abraham argue with God on whether or not to destroy Sodom based on how many righteous people could be found there? I say that is what we do: argue a little first with this cardinal before stepping too quickly to what he demands. God's plan will reveal itself."

Patrick's statement met with murmurs of agreement. Corbin nodded approvingly.

"Still didn't turn out so well for Sodom," Waylan commented sullenly.

Heavy silence followed, punctuated by spoons scraping porridge bowls.

During this lull in the conversation, Patrick spotted Aimeé scolding several young Guests for throwing food at the candidati, only to meet childish resistance from the nobles. His heart leapt, and he rose to assist her, thankful for a reason to talk to her—then Sister Abigail and Victor came to her aid. He thought twice about being seen with her in the presence of the cardinal's people.

Anna and Clare approached to serve the Avangarde table. Patrick sat down hard and covered his bowl with his forearms, glaring at the women. They cast Patrick frivolous smiles as they doted on Geoffrey, making sure the foppish knight's every need was tended to—or at least, so it appeared.

When they departed, Patrick relaxed and uncovered his bowl.

"What was that all about?" Corbin asked.

"They've been disturbing me and my food ever since I returned."

Corbin cocked a quizzical eyebrow. "Because you wouldn't marry the French girl?"

Patrick blew hair out of his eyes. "Aye."

"Yeah, why is that?" Sir Jeremiah asked. "I mean, why didn't you two marry? We were fully expecting it." He shrugged. "You had my support."

Others about the table murmured similar sentiments.

Patrick stared pointedly at Geoffrey and said, "She has a certain—*condition*—she feels would make our relationship difficult."

An uncomfortable silence fell at the table and all eyes shifted between Geoffrey and Patrick. None raised any further questions. For once, Geoffrey's usual cocky facade cracked to reveal something looking like concern.

"By the way, Geoffrey," Patrick said, watching the maidservants' retreating forms. "I don't think those are raisinsseeds you've been spitting out."

#

"Is this seat taken?"

The Lady Katherina looked up at the newcomer to her table, surprised to see the Lady Lilliana.

"Mm, no, not at all, please have a seat," Katherina responded.

"Thank you," Lilliana said, elegantly perching beside her. "I'm so glad to see you eating alone."

"Pardon?"

Lilliana covered the embarrassed smile blooming across her lips. "My apologies. I mean, I'm very happy to see there is someone also alone I could break my fast with."

"Oh," Katherina smiled. "Well, you are very welcome. It is my specialty, being alone, and if my loneliness can make somebody else more comfortable, then all the better."

"Thank you," Lilliana said, addressing both Katherina and the maidservant who filled her cup with apple juice. "Though I find it hard to believe someone as beautiful as yourself ranks loneliness as a gift."

"You're too kind," Katherina responded, a touch of rose growing on her porcelain cheeks. "But I'm certain a woman as strong as yourself understands the isolation of choosing not to play silly games." To punctuate this, Katherina motioned with her eyes over the rim of the cup from which she drank toward a group of noisy, well-dressed women. They frequently pointed at the candidati, followed by a new round of giggling.

"Oh, I don't know," Lilliana said, eyes narrowing at the gaggle of women. "That depends on whether you play the game better. Myself, I rather enjoy stomping on silly little creatures such as they."

"More power to you, Lady Lilliana," Katherina said, raising her cup and touching it to her table companion's. "I don't think the stomping would be worth getting my slippers dirty."

Lilliana touched her cup back, saying, "To each her own, Lady Katherina."

More maidservants arrived and distributed food on the table; the smells of warm oatmeal, bacon, and eggs tantalized the Ladies appetites.

"Two please," Lilliana said when a maidservant held a board full of bacon slices toward her. She turned to Katherina and said, "Still, I normally see you in the company of a knight, and I don't see him this morning."

"What? Sir Jon?" Katherina said, receiving her own slices of bacon and a fried egg. "He is yonder, with the knights. He doesn't break his fast with me every morning. He needs time with his comrades."

Just as she said this, an eruption of laughter came from the table occupied by the men in black surcoats. Jon's red one stuck out.

"No offense," Lilliana said with a smile, spying Jon's moon face among the Avangarde, "but I daresay Jon could use all the time with men he can muster. Were it not for the sword and armor I would not have figured him a knight."

Katherina studied Jon—his affable face framed by his blonde mane of hair.

"No offense taken," she said. "He is a sweet man who is perhaps better suited to being a statesman, but he is determined to prove his father wrong by becoming a capable knight. I support him in his efforts and he has been a pleasant companion."

"'Pleasant?'" Lilliana said, raising an eyebrow. "He certainly seems 'safe' and 'comfortable,' but don't you yearn for something more... fulfilling?"

Katherina directed her ice clear eyes to Lilliana's amber ones, unfazed by their smoldering heat, and said, "I've found many sorts of fulfillment with many sorts of men, and at different times. Who I spend my time with is my business."

"Absolutely." Lilliana's smile was genuinely friendly. "I admire that. I'm quite jealous of your freedom, really. I'm sure you know I'm attached to the cardinal."

Katherina tilted her head to one side, not sure what surprised her more: the beautiful older woman's candidness or her admission of envy.

"Then you can appreciate my not wanting to go into great detail about my relationships, just as you wouldn't want me to pry into yours with the cardinal."

"On the contrary. The nature of mine and Teo's relationship is obvious to all, I'd think," Lilliana said, raising an eyebrow and taking a nibble of bacon. "Standard fare. Your relationships, however, are far more interesting. I mean that in the most respectful way. I've been paying attention to you and your story. Some people may call it 'gossip,' but I prefer to call it 'having a deep fascination with the human experience.' And your 'experience'—dalliances with villainous sorcerers and the handsome knights who rescue you from them—in my eyes, is the only bright light in all this drabness." Lilliana threw out her arms to encompass the hall, but surely meant all of Greensprings. "Your story is one worthy of the bards."

Katherina's covered her mouth to hide a smile creeping across her lips.

"Why, Lady Lilliana, I'm not sure if you're flattering me or accusing me," she said, the small red dots at the center of her cheeks growing.

"Perhaps a little of both," Lilliana replied with a wicked smile and bold gaze.

Katherina scowled, yet her smile continued to grow.

"Tell me," Lilliana continued, and tested a slice of bacon with her perfect teeth. Her smile was as bright as her eyes. "How does one go from yonder Knight of Cups, who rescued you from a dark lord in the land of fairy—a romantic gesture if ever there was—to Sir Comfortable Jon? I must know!"

The question felt intrusive, but Katherina didn't feel like backing down from the noblewoman's challenging stare.

"As I said, I find comfort from different men, in different ways, at different times," she said, regaining her composure in the face of Lilliana's charm assault. "Patrick and I had our moment, and it passed—but through no real fault of his own. He is a good man, an honorable man, who did his best to please me, despite his moodiness and peculiarities. I am greatly indebted to him for what he has done, but the timing was all wrong. We just weren't meant to be."

Lilliana's gaze drifted away as her stare lost focus, deep in thought.

"He was no longer fulfilling, then," she stated, her focus returning.

"I'm afraid not," Katherina confirmed, taking another drink.

"So," Lilliana whispered, leaning forward with her wicked smile returning. "When is the last time Sir Patrick 'filled' you?"

Katherina involuntarily spit apple juice from her cup. "Lady Lilliana!" she protested, coughing.

"Oh, the look on your face!" Lilliana laughed, clutching her chest. "But still, I've met the man. Surely you can share something?"

Dabbing at her mouth with a napkin, Katherina looked across the room to the table of knights. She could see the topic of their conversation in what looked like a serious discussion with his brothers-in-arms. The sunlight filtering from the upper windows cast Patrick's high cheekbones in a glow of polished marble. His face suddenly burst into a rare smile.

"He has a passion of the ages inside him, if he would only allow it out," Katherina admitted, her hand unconsciously drifting to her throat. "Still, he can be romantic and charming when he chooses."

"Do tell me more!" Lilliana pressed.

"Perhaps another time," Katherina teased, returning her attention to her breakfast.

"Done!" Lilliana laughed. "We can exchange stories. Perhaps over another meal? Though the food here in the keep is much better than among the pavilions, I'm already finding it drab."

"We can midday sometime in Aesclinn if you like," Katherina suggested. "The food may not always be better, but it will certainly be different."

"Splendid. Why not today?"

"I have singing practice today, and it's too late to change my schedule, but it is easy enough to change for later," Katherina explained.

Lilliana made an effort to finish quickly what she chewed and said while frowning, "I thought you already practiced today. I've meant to tell you, that piece you sang this morning was beautiful."

"Pardon?" Katherina replied, frowning in confusion. "I didn't sing this morning."

"That wasn't you I heard in the auditorium as I passed by? It sure sounded like you."

Katherina pondered who it possibly could have been, seeing as she knew no one who had a voice quite like hers in the keep. No one liked to practice in the morning, either. Before she could question Lilliana further, the elder noblewoman motioned with her eyes and Katherina turned slightly to see what had grabbed her attention.

Aimeé attended to a commotion about the candidati table.

"And how do you feel about her?" Lilliana asked, surreptitiously regarding the maidservant while nibbling on a piece of bread.

Katherina's face twitched slightly at the corner of her mouth, but she shrugged, turned away, and said, "I was happy for her, but I don't understand what happened. Well, perhaps I do. I guess the poor thing came to realize the depths of Patrick's moods. In any case, it is none of my business."

Katherina noted Lilliana shifted her attention from the French girl back to her.

"Seriously," Katherina added, eyes flaring beneath her straight bangs. "It's none of my business."

Lilliana smiled, "As you say, Lady Katherina."

Aimeé bent down to pick up the bits of food the mean giggly women the next table over had been throwing at the candidati.

"Perhaps she is too good for Patrick," Lilliana continued. "Perhaps our Irish knight needs a bad girl to stimulate his needs."

Aimeé tried to brush food off the shoulder of one of the candidati—a boy who had the peculiar habit of waving his hands in front of his face while moaning—just to receive snarls for her efforts. She snatched her hand back while making a face and gently reached around the boy to take his empty dishes.

"I don't think Patrick knows what Patrick wants," Katherina responded.

#

All but the candidati had finished their meals and left the great hall. Aimeé waited, ready to pounce on their dirty dishes when the hall was empty. Meanwhile, her fellow maidservants cleaned the other tables and arranged them for the council meeting half an hour hence.

Between the pregnancy, the extra number of people who needed serving, and the daily routine of moving the tables for the council, exhaustion was taking its toll.

She leaned back to yawn and stretched her back. When she did, she saw Patrick approaching. Her stomach knotted up, either with excitement or dread.

"We need to talk," he said.

Anna and Clare closed ranks about Aimeé, barring his path while crossing meaty arms across their chests.

"Oh, for heaven's sake," Aimeé said, waving at the messy tables. "Now you want to talk? You couldn't have picked a worse time."

Patrick glared at the other maidservants standing in his way. He reached the nearest table and lifted a pot lid and wooden spoon like a sword and shield. "You two don't frighten me. I've fought mightier monsters than you. I will not let you stop me."

Despite her tiredness and frustration with him, she couldn't help but smile a little.

"It's well," she said to her friends. "I'll only be a moment."

Reluctantly, Anna and Clare stepped aside and continued their duties.

"You don't think they would have seriously fought me?" Patrick whispered, casting an apprehensive glance at the big women.

"Oui, I'm certain," she replied.

Her countenance must have stated she had little time for small talk, because he seemed to sense this and spoke quickly.

"The cardinal made threats if I don't support him. Threats against you. Therefore, I told him we did not marry because you no longer interest me. That is why I said those things in council chambers. I think he believes me, but we need to stay away from each other just in case."

She squinted, scrutinizing him. She crossed her arms. "Is it true?"

"Of course it's true," he replied. "Well, he didn't come right out and say he would directly harm you, but the message was clear."

"Have you lost interest in me?" Her jaw tensed to bite down on the note of heartbreak that escaped with the question.

"Absolutely not!" Patrick almost shouted, but then lowered his voice as he looked around. "I said what was necessary to protect you."

"How convenient." Aimeé scowled at him, her own voice rising, which only seemed to agitate him more.

"What's that supposed to..." he started to say, but a particularly loud outburst from the candidati caused him to jump away.

"It means you've been looking for every excuse imaginable, cardinal or not, to stay away from me," she responded. She noted how he kept his distance from the children he referred to as changelings, and added, "Your lack of enthusiasm for my child, possibly *our* child, has been very disappointing."

Still eying the candidati warily, Patrick said, "I'm sorry, it's just... I've had much to deal with lately." He rubbed his temple with a slightly trembling hand.

"You're going to have to face this," she said, "because life is uncertain. This child might be Geoffrey's. It might be like one of..." She looked at the children who finally started to depart the table "...them. One thing is for certain. It will be mine, and if you're going to be in my life, you will have to accept it."

Patrick's face became impassive with introspection, but he nodded.

Aimeé reached up and took his trembling hand and placed it on the cross on her bosom. "And another thing—no, don't pull away—you must address this. Something troubles your soul. You must follow your mother's counsel and listen to her music to set yourself on the road to healing."

Patrick blinked, and a spark replaced the glazed introspection in his eyes. "I will gladly listen to the music if you will just take me seriously when I say you may be in danger, and we should keep our distance for a time."

For the first time Patrick's sincerity gave her hope, but also cause for concern he might be right about the cardinal.

Nevertheless, she smiled. "Très bien. Meet me in the inner courtyard, among the columns where it is private, in about an hour when I have finished here."

Patrick's shoulders slumped as if a weight had fallen from them. He turned to leave.

"Patrick?" she called to him. "You do love me, right?"

He paused, looking over his shoulder. "Of course."

She wrung her hands. "I wish you'd sound more convincing when saying so."

Patrick smiled wanly and responded before leaving. "Funny, my mother says the same thing. You'll just have to trust me."

Aimeé stared for some time at the door through which he had left, not sure if she felt better or more anxious.

"You can certainly tell we have more children about the keep this year," Clare said loudly and obviously after clearing her throat.

"Oh, how is that?" Aimeé asked, taking the hint she should return to work.

Clare held one of the blown glass goblets from the candidati table to the light.

"You see all the prints?" Clare explained. "Every bit of glass covered as if they couldn't touch it enough. Children do that. Me dear old mum used to call them 'angel prints.'"

#

Patrick decided to put the hour he waited for Aimeé to good use.

It didn't take him long to find Abbot Herewinus in the apple orchard behind the keep, only a few rows outside the gate. He sat on a stump, either dozing or deep in prayer. William Malmesbury and a few monks sat near him with their backs to trees as they read or prayed.

An Avangarde stood nearby in full armor. His dark surcoat contrasted sharply with the white apple blossoms floating in the air and carpeting the ground like snow. Considering the recent attacks, Patrick felt the presence of the Avangarde prudent.

"Sir Edmund, is it?" Patrick asked the Avangarde as he approached.

The Englishman, one of the few knights Patrick did not know well, responded, "Aye, I am, Sir Patrick."

"Is the abbot sleeping or in prayer? I wish to speak to him but don't want to disturb him."

Edmund smiled under his helm. "I think he is doing a little of both. I'm about to nod off myself. I think I'd rather have night guard duty on the wall."

Patrick grunted an agreement and moved towards the group of Glastonbury people, singling William Malmesbury out as he approached.

"Monsieur William Malmesbury?" Patrick said. "They told me you and the abbot could be found in the orchard. I don't mean to intrude, but I was hoping to have a few words with you."

William looked up with curiosity and closed the leather volume from which he read.

"Why, it's the Knight of Cups himself," he said. "How can I help you?"

"I wasn't sure if it were you I should talk to, or the abbot, or both," Patrick said. "Since the abbot is... deep in prayer, I guess I'll ask you."

As if approving his choice, the abbot suddenly snorted loudly, indicating he indeed dozed. His lips fluttered as he exhaled, sending several apple blossoms tumbling through the air.

Smiling at the abbot, William replied, "Ask away, Sir Knight."

"In council, you spoke of 'twinning.' People, places, and objects having spiritual twins. Are such things true?"

"Of course. I thought I stated my case very well in council," William replied. "Though it may be for naught, as obviously the different factions are inclined to believe what they want to believe."

"Certainly," Patrick agreed, "but what can you tell me about people who 'twin?'"

"People? You're not the least interested in my theory of Avalon twinning?" William said, disappointed. "I thought the idea a stroke of genius. I plan on writing an essay on the topic..."

"Monsieur Malmesbury, I'm sure it will be a fine thesis, but I'm interested in the person aspect," Patrick urged.

"Well, Abbot Herewinus here probably could answer that better. Most of the cases of spiritual twins have been due to saints."

"Not 'twins,' good brother William," the abbot said, raising a single eyelid, "but the individual themselves, at different locations at the same time. 'Twin' implies a whole different individual who is the same in appearance."

"Of course you are correct, Father Abbot," William conceded.

The abbot yawned and stretched his arms above his head, his robe sleeves falling about his elbows.

"Saint Ambrose was known to perform Mass at two different places on the same Sunday," he said, "and it was Mother Mary herself, still living in Ephesus, who appeared to the Apostle James the Greater as he evangelized Hispania, encouraging him when he felt he was failing miserably. Though the ability to bilocate has obvious worldly advantages, it is a gift from God meant to be a sign pointing to His glory. A reminder of the Mystery of the Holy Trinity—how God can be three persons, but have one nature."

The abbot stiffly climbed off the tree stump and brushed himself off.

"But that is among saints," Patrick said. "Are there not examples of 'bilocation' occurring among regular folk? You know, less-than-saintly ones, shall we say?"

"Not that I have heard, young sir." Herewinus brushed blossoms collecting in the fuzzy white lamb chops adorning his plump cheeks. "But then again, I have not heard everything. Our young and storied historian here often gives the impression he has heard everything. Perhaps he knows."

"Outside of saints? Not that I am aware of," William said. He narrowed his eyes thoughtfully and chewed his lower lip, adding, "Though something nags at my memory. I'll have to think about it."

Herewinus approached the tall knight and inserted his arm in his, saying, "Walk with us a bit and tell us why you're so curious, won't you?"

Patrick bent his arm at the elbow to accommodate the old man and let him guide him down the rows of apple trees. William and another monk fell in behind them, and at a distance Sir Edmund shadowed them.

"Just curious, I guess," Patrick said. Flashes of the Other and the spectral sisters outside the cave-mound crossed his mind.

"Just curious?" Herewinus said, looking up at Patrick with a kindly face. "You hunted me down in the apple orchard just to ask about one small facet of our argument for bringing the Grail to Glastonbury?"

Patrick cleared his throat and said unconvincingly, "Yes."

The old man chuckled and patted Patrick's wrist, saying, "Are you sure you hadn't come to ask whether or not that really was the spirit of King Arthur and his knights you saw in the cave when you first touched the Grail?"

"Yes," Patrick said, perhaps too quickly, "that was my original meaning."

"I can assure you it was. It would be preposterous at this point to think otherwise, considering all the evidence," Herewinus said, then looked up again to study Patrick's face intently, "but that too is not why you ask."

Patrick felt his Adam's apple catch in his throat and he did not return the abbot's gaze.

An awkward silence passed with only the sound of birds chirping.

How could he ever unravel the mystery of the Other if he didn't investigate? How could he investigate if he didn't trust someone with the knowledge of the thing's existence? Could he trust the abbot and the historian?

"It is very beautiful here, is it not?" Herewinus eventually stated, perhaps sensing Patrick's desire to change the subject. He waved his free hand about. "A truly mystical place, surely only a stone's throw from Heaven. I envy you, Sir Patrick, and the time you spend here, going on adventures and exploring the mysteries of the isle."

"You're the Abbot of Glastonbury, on the Board of Benefactors," Patrick replied, happy to talk about something else. "You can come here anytime."

"My place is in the abbey," Herewinus said, sadly. "We must all do our part, serve our purpose as God sees fit. I enjoy reading the reports coming from here, however, and I must admit living somewhat vicariously through them. Tell me, how many of the Fair Folk do you think you have laid eyes on now?"

"I couldn't say, Father Abbot," Patrick said. "It's quite possibly more than I believe, as they tend to hide in plain sight. I could have looked straight at one and not known it on many occasions."

"But for certain you have seen the Huntsman and his pack, a banshee, a water sprite, and goblins to name a few," Herewinus insisted.

"You have been reading the reports," Patrick said, raising his eyebrows at the little man. "Sir Corbin will be pleased to know all that writing has not been in vain."

"To be fair, I'm probably the only one on the board who reads them in any great detail," Herewinus chuckled. "The other benefactors spend most of their time reading the financial reports and counting profits. Cardinal Teodorico dismisses most of the supernatural reports as fabrication or exaggerations."

"How is that?" Patrick asked, frowning. "How can the cardinal deny the extraordinary nature of the isle?"

"People, even cardinals, have a tendency to see what they only want to see," Herewinus responded. "Just as I tend to focus overmuch on the stories of fairies and dragons, and not enough on the politics swirling about the board, where the true monsters lie in waiting.

"I do know that the isle takes care of herself. Everything that happens here serves her purpose. Nothing happens by accident, however random it seems. Teodorico, Wulfric, and the merchants can play all the games they want. It is they who are being played." The abbot stopped at a tree to pluck an apple, and then held it up. "She plays by her own rules. Why does this tree bear fruit today, yet the others in the orchard are just starting to blossom? Why does the isle, ninety days out of a hundred, have a spring-like climate, but then suddenly cool to frosty evenings? Why does she only allow some people through the mist, but not others?"

"Miracles? Magic?" Patrick suggested with a shrug.

"Perhaps the miracle of magic," Herewinus responded, taking a bite of the apple. "This is God's world and everything in it acts as His agent, whether knowingly or unknowingly. The island is no different. She calls people here to serve a purpose, or people are drawn here to try and fulfill their selfish needs. The island plays them against one another."

"But why? To what end?" Patrick asked.

"I suspect when you removed the Grail from the cave you upset a balance and she is trying to restore that balance," the abbot responded.

"But you are fighting just as hard as anyone in the council chamber to not return it to the cave," Patrick said, brow creasing with confusion.

"Because that is what is expected of me as the Abbot of Glastonbury. I must play my role," Herewinus explained. "I'm certain everything will work out just the way it's supposed to. I put my faith in God. If God and the island choose to let the Grail go out into the world to teach us some sort of lesson, who am I to argue? Obedience is next to godliness."

"Then why don't you just hand it over to the cardinal, since he is papal legate? If Pope Paschal has asked for the cup, why not deliver it to him?" Patrick asked.

"I like Paschal well enough, especially since he shares my views on the celibacy of priests, much as another favorite son of Glastonbury did, Saint Dunstan, who brought our Benedictine Order to the abbey, but we view Paschal's orders more as suggestions than commands."

"You don't believe him to be the absolute leader of the Church?" Patrick asked, surprised.

"Leader, yes," Herewinus said and chuckled, "but 'absolute' leader? He most certainly is the successor to Saint Peter, but if you recall your scripture, the Apostles often argued amongst themselves, not always coming to agreement quickly. Well, that's how we English see it, anyway. Being a layman, it's understandable you don't see the nuances of Church hierarchy. We follow the pope the same way we follow someone we admire from afar. Someone whose decisions we take seriously, but only first after some discussion."

"I never thought of it that way," Patrick said. "Being a soldier, my idea of a leader is more strict. I like very much the idea of order and structure."

"And that would make sense in a military order," Herewinus agreed. "In an organization built on love and cooperation, leaders lead by example. After all, who is more likely to motivate you? The person you respect and want to follow, or the person you fear and must follow? Don't get me wrong—there are and have been plenty of Church leaders who did their best to rule with an iron hand. God allowed them to continue to lead, just as He allowed Peter to continue being an apostle even though Peter could be occasionally obstinate."

"'Get thee behind me, Satan,'" Patrick quoted.

"Exactly," Herewinus said, nodding.

"And Pope Paschal?" Patrick asked. "How would you characterize him?"

"He is no fool," the abbot replied. "I'm certain he is not blind to Teodorico's ambitions. However, he does see the benefit of seeing the Grail in Rome. Also, I believe he is perfectly aware the Holy Spirit often reveals Himself during a lively discussion among the shepherds and therefore was wise enough to allow these proceedings. He could have just sent an army to take the Grail, but didn't. Something is to be said for all that."

A knot he hadn't realized was even there suddenly loosened a little in Patrick's stomach. It didn't disappear altogether, but made breathing easier. The kindly little man in his simple wool robe contrasted sharply with the tall cardinal in silks, and Patrick sighed heavily.

"You give me hope, Father Abbot," he said to Herewinus.

"There, there," the old man said, tossing an apple to Patrick. "Your taking the cup from the cave compares not to Adam eating the apple in Eden. Even that tragedy made it possible for the greatest love to enter the world in the form of Jesus. Who knows what good will come out of all this?"

Patrick smiled, thanked the abbot, and turned to leave while taking a bite of the apple.

"Oh, Sir Patrick," William Malmesbury called after him. "I just remembered an example of 'twinning' outside of saints."

"Oh?" Patrick raised his eyebrows, curious.

"The German folk call it *die doppelgänger*. It is a creature who appears as an exact duplicate of someone, but often is the bearer of disastrous news. The legend also says they destroy the original person, taking over their life and bringing ruin to the lives of loved ones."

#

Aimeé hurried through the keep's inner colonnade, eyes searching as her slippers padded along the flagstones. When she spotted a pair of boots poking from behind a column, a smile spread across her face and her previous anxiety gave way to hope.

As she approached, both her smile and excitement fled like scattering doves when Sir Geoffrey stepped from behind the column.

"So, you have a condition that concerns me?" he said. "Care to share what that is?"

Aimeé backed away, breath catching in her chest. As she felt blood drain from her face, her mind spun while trying to sort out his questions.

"I-I don't know what you mean," she stammered, still backing away as he approached.

"The Irishman says you have a condition I caused," he growled. "What is it I need to worry about?"

Comprehension dawned on her, but she still couldn't fathom Patrick having told him. He loomed over her as she felt stone press into her back. Her lack of timely response intensified his agitation.

"Answer me!" he insisted, his handsome face contorting into a mask of rage.

He grabbed her wrist and shook violently. Flashes of memory of him on top of her grunting like an animal filled her mind and a pitiful wail filled the air. Shock came over her when she realized it came from her. She did not like the sound of it. She wanted to curl into a ball, to shrink into nothing, but Geoffrey's hand brushed harshly against her midsection—and a completely different feeling surfaced.

She shook her arm loose, covered her belly with both arms, and snarled at him through wild strands of hair that had fallen into her eyes.

"Get your hands off me, and never touch me again!"

The blazing anger in his shocked face told her everything that would probably happen next.

"What did you say?" Geoffrey said, voice dropping to a menacing hiss.

Her gaze remained defiant.

Geoffrey raised his hand, but in a blur, he was suddenly on the ground with Patrick on top of him. "Keep your hands off her!" he shouted, standing over Geoffrey.

Geoffrey scampered to his feet, struggling out of the tangle of his crimson cape. "I've had just about enough of the two of you! We're going to finish this now!"

"If you're referring to our last interrupted fight, I agree," Patrick spat. "Let's finish it then."

Patrick tackled him, but Geoffrey caught him in a headlock. Patrick rained blows against his stomach as Geoffrey pounded his back from above.

Aimeé protected her belly and moved away from the mêlée, caught between the need to protect her child and the desire to find something to bash Geoffrey's skull—and half a notion to give Patrick a good whack, as well, for having caused this.

But in an instant, a flurry of black cloaks, capes, and surcoats erupted from the colonnade and tackled the battling knights. Patrick and Geoffrey found themselves subdued in a heartbeat and carried away physically, shouting and squirming in the arms of their comrades.

Sir Marcus Ionus appeared at her side.

"Mademoiselle," he said, sharply making eye contact, "none of this happened. You saw nothing. Understand, Lass?"

She nodded, surprised at the sudden change of events and not knowing what else to do.

He turned on a heel and marched away with his cape flapping.

#

The Avangarde deposited the two battered knights in a secluded classroom.

"Sit! And not a word!" Sir Wolfgang growled at them.

Patrick and Geoffrey obeyed and took seats in the comically little chairs. They waited in silence. Their long limbs cramped as they hunched in the child-sized desks while Sir Wolfgang, Sir Marcus, and Sir Corbin scowled.

At first Patrick thought the silent treatment itself was a form of torture, but when new arrivals walked into the room he realized the senior knights had merely waited for the real torture to begin.

Mother Superior entered with a grim look, followed by Father Hugh, who took a position beside the knights.

"Oh, shit," Geoffrey mumbled and put a hand over his face.

"Good afternoon, gentlemen," Mother Superior said, her demeanor becoming genial. "And how are we today?"

She leaned in close to the troubled Avangarde and leered at them with a frightening smile, waiting for a response.

Patrick and Geoffrey mumbled some words and looked anywhere in the room except at the petite nun.

"What's that?" she asked, cupping a hand to her ear. "I didn't quite catch that."

Patrick mumbled that he'd been better.

"Well, I'll tell you how my day was going!" she shouted suddenly, producing from behind her back a slender rod she banged against an empty seat near Patrick. The end of the rod snapped off and arced across the room.

Patrick and Geoffrey sat erect in their chairs, and even Father Hugh and the knights snapped to attention.

"Here we go," Patrick muttered, squeezing his eyes shut.

"I was having a lovely day," she continued, "playing with children, enjoying peaceful prayer, looking forward to working in my garden. Then I hear this news. News of grown men, Avangarde no less, who are charged with keeping the peace and serving as an example, fighting in public. And this is not the first time, is it?"

"No, Mother," Patrick and Geoffrey said simultaneously.

"What?" she shouted, again cupping her ear.

"No, Mother Superior," they responded, louder this time.

"Pray tell, why?" Her caricature of a smile returned.

"We had a disagreement," Patrick said, crossing his arms and not making eye contact.

"Yes, a disagreement," Geoffrey added, also crossing his arms and looking away, slouching in his seat.

"Over a girl, perhaps?" Mother Superior suggested. "A maidservant? Is that really the reason two shining examples of the Avangarde risk tarnishing the image of the Order and the goal of the Greensprings mission? A common fight over a common girl?"

"No," Patrick almost shouted, "not at all." Then added almost as quickly, "And she is not common to me."

Geoffrey snickered at the statement, but a sharp glance from the nun quieted him.

"Then an 'uncommon' reason for a fight perhaps?" she redirected her gaze to Patrick.

"Geoffrey was attacking her," Patrick explained, "I stopped him."

"I did not attack her," Geoffrey scoffed. "Confront her? Yes. Attack? No."

"Do tell why," Mother Superior asked, shifting her gaze to Geoffrey.

Geoffrey's lip curled as he considered his response.

He finally replied, "I think the maidservant has been spreading lies about me."

"That's itself a lie!" Patrick blurted.

"Then it's you who is spreading the lies!" Geoffrey retorted, rising halfway and stabbing a finger at Patrick. But Mother Superior whacked his finger with her rod, sending him cowering back into his seat.

"And what alleged lie is this?" she demanded, glaring at the two men.

Geoffrey shrugged. "That is precisely what I was trying to find out when interrupted. The Irishman says I gave her something."

All eyes shifted to Patrick. Even Geoffrey's

"Well?" Mother Superior insisted.

Cornered, Patrick saw no option for avoidance. All would know soon enough, and if he continued to keep it a secret they would perceive it as lying, making matters worse.

"She's with child," Patrick finally said, looking her in the eye.

Mother Superior's icy facade cracked briefly, revealing the closest thing to shock Patrick had ever seen in the woman. She straightened from her interrogator's crouch over the two, chewed on a thumbnail when she crossed her arms over her chest and wandered away from the pair, deep in thought.

The other men in the room shifted uncomfortably, clearing their throats.

"And you think it's mine?" Geoffrey scoffed. "That's preposterous."

"You did rape her," Patrick snapped back. "Everybody knows that."

"I raped no one," Geoffrey sniffed. "It was agreeable for both of us. It's not my fault she regretted it later."

"Is that why you beat her bloody?" Patrick replied vehemently, but careful not to instigate another physical confrontation.

"She liked it rough, what of it? Besides, this was a long time ago. You're the one who has been having 'relations' with her since then. If it's anyone's brat, it's yours."

"Enough!" Mother Superior cried with her back to the pair, raising a hand for emphasis. Surprisingly, she did not turn back to them, but to the others in the room.

"So, their first fight, there was more to that business a few months back," she addressed the other knights and Father Hugh with deep scorn in her voice, "and you didn't see fit to inform me?"

"The girl never came forward with accusations. There was nothing to investigate or inform upon," Wolfgang pointed out.

Mother Superior scoffed. "Is that really so surprising? The poor child probably feared retribution from her attacker. Feared upsetting the status quo and losing her employment. Why would she come forward with fine gentlemen like you looking after her?"

Wolfgang and the rest lowered their heads and remained quiet.

"I must say, I'm deeply disappointed. Heartbroken, even. When I agreed to come to Greensprings I was told things would be different here on Avalon. Dawn of a new era and all that. Peace and justice would prevail."

She shifted her attention back to the seated knights, gliding over the stones like an avenging ghost.

"Is it true?" she addressed Patrick. "Are you having 'relations' with the girl?"

"Only once. An occasion I've confessed," Patrick answered.

Mother Superior looked to Father Hugh, Greensprings's Confessor.

Father Hugh confirmed with a curt nod, adding, "As has Sir Geoffrey for his acts and Aimeé for her moment of indiscretion with Patrick."

"Well, thank God for at least that much," Mother Superior huffed.

"Sir Mark, when he was steward, also administered corporal punishment on Sir Geoffrey," Corbin added. "I saw him deliver twenty strikes of the rod to his back. We kept it amongst ourselves, not wishing to demoralize the Order. I'm certain it left some scars. Sir Geoffrey will show you if you like."

Patrick blinked, unaware of this last piece of information. When he looked to Geoffrey the man turned away with red rising in his face.

"That won't be necessary," Mother Superior replied, eyes narrowing at Geoffrey. She then turned to Patrick, leveling a critical stare. "Is that why you didn't marry the girl after all, with the child's parentage in question? Is that why you really attacked Sir Geoffrey?"

Patrick felt as if he'd been stabbed in the gut. "It's not like that," he protested, "there are... other complications."

There came the memory of sunlight reflecting into his face off of Cardinal Teodorico's pectoral cross in council chambers, and the fleeting image of blood covering Aimeé. He wanted to explain the threats the cardinal had made against her, but a glance at the men who had already let her down did not fill him with confidence. He looked to Mother Superior, wondering if she would believe him, but her face said that his word meant nothing to her.

"I can guess," she said. "You don't wish to marry a commoner carrying another man's child." Her look of disdain made Patrick feel worse than any look Aimeé had ever given him.

"It's not like that," Patrick protested again weakly, then added quietly to himself, *Right?*

She shook her head and waved a hand. "No matter. It is not relevant." She slowly scrutinized the men in the room.

"It would appear simple confession and traditional punishment were insufficient. Something more meaningful is in order. More imaginative," she said, turning to the troubled pair. She stared long and thoughtfully and seemed to reach some conclusion. "When the Israelites initially feared to enter the Promised Land, God sent them back into the desert to wander for forty years—not necessarily as a punishment, but to shape them like iron in the forge. Did the Israelites understand this at the time? Perhaps not." She paused, thoughtful again. "The maidservant will be reassigned. Poor Sister Abigail has been struggling with her charges. Even though I've asked the Lady Katherina to direct their energies towards choral music, they still are a handful. Aimeé shall become Sister Abigail's and Lady Katherina's personal assistant..."

"To the candidati?" Patrick interjected.

"Yes." The nun scowled at the interruption.

"May I make a suggestion then?" he asked.

"You may, but I make no guarantees," she replied.

"If I'm not mistaken, lists are being drawn for matching Avangarde with Guests, correct?" Patrick looked at Geoffrey with a wicked surge of pleasure—one he kept to himself. "Perhaps Geoffrey should be matched with one of the candidati."

Geoffrey's head snapped up at the suggestion, a disgusted look on his face.

"What a splendid idea," Mother Superior said, smiling genuinely. "What better way to display true service to God than to aid those who suffer."

Before Patrick's victorious smile could spread very far at seeing Geoffrey's reaction, the nun turned to him and said, "Likewise, you shall do your part as well. You will be assigned yourself to one of the candidati."

"That's not what I meant!" Patrick protested, only to receive a whack to the shoulder.

Geoffrey laughed, but Mother Superior laid a gentle hand on his shoulder, and oddly, this stopped his laughter quicker than the rod.

"You both will report to Sister Abigail in good time," she said quietly and stroked Geoffrey's feathered hair. "She will assign you appropriately. Comply with her every wish. As for you, young man," her caressing hand reached down and viciously grabbed Geoffrey by the ear and twisted. She placed the sharp, splintered end of the broken rod at his throat and said between clenched teeth, "You will never touch a woman again in this keep without her consent, understand?"

The rod moved with the undulation caused by Geoffrey's audible swallow. "Yes, Mother Superior."

With one last withering stare, she left the room, followed closely by Father Hugh.

Patrick and Geoffrey started to rise, but the senior knights approached.

"Gentlemen, that is not all," Sir Wolfgang said. "Both of you have been problematic in your own ways. That must change immediately. It's been my experience Mother Superior's methods are unorthodox, but effective. Therefore, I think I too shall try something unorthodox to teach you responsibility. To that end, Patrick, you will now lead morning reveille and drill."

"What!" Geoffrey objected. "You are elevating him? How is that punishment?"

"This isn't about punishment," Wolfgang said sternly. "This is about learning discipline and responsibility. If Patrick cannot be a proper leader and set a good example, he will no longer be an Avangarde. You will serve day duty under Patrick, as you will be working together with the candidati." Geoffrey did stand this time and kicked a chair. "This too is not about punishment. This is so you can learn discipline and humility, Avangarde attributes you lack. If you cannot learn them, you will no longer be an Avangarde. Make no mistake, this is not an opportunity for Patrick to lord his power over you, nor is this an opportunity for you to antagonize Patrick."

"This isn't fair," Geoffrey said.

"Neither is toying with a village girl's body," Wolfgang said in a low voice, then added while looking at Patrick, "or her heart."

#

This time, finding Aimeé did not prove difficult. One only need follow the sound of crashing dishes and utensils. Evidently Mother Superior had already reached Aimeé and explained her new duties. Patrick had hoped to tell her himself, softening the blow. When he walked into the kitchen, her fury erupted hotter, and with more thrown objects.

"How could you?" she shouted at him.

"I didn't have a choice," Patrick tried to explain in between cups and spoons hurled at him. "They cornered me, wanting to know why Geoffrey and I fought."

"You know what I mean!" she responded, followed by a thrown footstool.

Anna and Clare stood nearby, but for once kept their distance, afraid of their friend's tirade. Concern marked their faces.

"No, I don't," Patrick said, taking a towel to the face.

"Geoffrey attacked me for a reason to begin with. You told him about the child... or told him enough," she growled, pausing to catch her breath.

"Oh, that," Patrick swallowed hard.

"Now I've lost the trust of Rosa Maria and am being sent away from my friends, because I have been reassigned to step and fetch for your snotty *ex-lover!*" Aimeé punctuated the last with a flying dish.

"I'm sorry!" Patrick shouted back, ducking. "I'd take it back if I could. I'd take it all back."

"Everything? You'd take everything back?" she said, her eyes freezing over.

"No, not everything," he replied, catching her meaning. "I do want you in my life. I do want to marry you, but first I have to protect you."

"You can't protect me by keeping your distance," Aimeé retorted, "and you can't protect me by controlling me."

He tried to fathom what she meant.

She made an exasperated sound and stormed towards the door, yelling, "If you want to help me, find me pickles!"

Patrick made a face and looked at Anna and Clare, asking, "Pickles?"

"It's a pregnancy thing," Clare answered, shrugging.

Patrick followed her into the great hall that lay mostly empty this time of day. Several of the candidati sat at empty tables, conversing deeply with a tired-looking Sister Abigail.

"Look, here is one of your new friends now, " she said as Patrick entered.

Patrick held up a finger, not ready to talk with her just yet. "Aimeé!" he called after her. He ran a few strides and lowered his voice. "I may not grab you and hold you against your will like Geoffrey, but I will follow you to the ends of the earth unless you explain yourself."

"Don't you see?" She turned on him with fists on hips. "Every time you try to 'protect' me you make matters worse. Your idea of protection is like trying to hold on to a hand full of sand. The harder you squeeze, the more slips through your fingers... and what you're doing is worse. You are squeezing and releasing." She opened and closed her hand in front of him for emphasis. "Furthermore, it's not I who need help; it is you." She added this last by holding out the cross from her neck.

"Give me a chance to prove otherwise," he pleaded. "I will listen to the damn music!"

"I'm much too angry to play calming music right now!" she snapped, blowing hair out of her eyes. "Besides, that is still just the beginning of my problems with you. You are still so afraid to talk about this." She made a circling gesture around her stomach. "You don't like children, I understand. You especially won't like one possibly not yours, or one who is 'difficult.' How could I possibly let you into my life knowing that? The child is better off having a dozen aunties than a single angry father."

"I can like children just fine. Look..." Patrick said, returned to the table and bent towards Chansonne, arms out. "You there, come, give us a hug."

Chansonne clutched her doll, shook her head vigorously, and slid away.

"You see," Aimeé said.

"I'm taller than you," said the big-headed candidati Patrick had met on the boat.

Patrick wanted to hiss at him like a cat.

"Brother Ambrosius, meet Sir Patrick, your new companion," Sister Abigail said.

"What?" Patrick blurted. "You can't be serious."

"I am," Sister Abigail said, smiling at Aimeé. "Mother Superior just informed me of the pairing."

"I'm taller than you," Ambrosius said, pleased.

"Well, there you go," Aimeé said. "Here is your opportunity to prove to me exactly what you can handle."

"I don't need to be *his* companion to prove that," Patrick growled.

"I'm taller than you," Ambrosius interjected.

"Oh, be quiet already!" Patrick snapped at the odd fellow, who cowed at the verbal assault.

Aimeé cradled her stomach. "If you can show me you can treat him well, then I will consider talking seriously about... us. How can I expect you to be around this child if you can't control your temper? Show me you can by not frightening Brother Ambrosius anymore, and befriending him."

"I don't frighten him," Patrick insisted, then added, confident of the answer. "Just ask him."

"Brother Ambrosius," Aimeé addressed the little man, "does Sir Patrick frighten you?"

"Yes," he replied.

"What the...!" Patrick glowered at Ambrosius.

"Befriend him, Sir Patrick," Aimeé sang, walking away, wagging a finger in the air, "and bring me pickles!"

"I'm taller than you," Ambrosius said again.

Patrick slapped his hand to his forehead.

Chapter Nine

"And then I heard Rosa Maria almost struck this Victor fellow from the cardinal's staff with a rolling pin when he insulted her cooking." Sir Jon droned on, shaking his head in disbelief at his own gossip. "One of the Cardinal Guard had to step in, actually laying hands on her to stop her and... Kat, am I boring you?"

Lady Katherina blinked, realizing Jon had asked a question. "No, not at all. Continue with your morning report."

She slipped her arm into his as they started the long walk to the morning meal. Every morning he escorted her through the garden to the keep, recounting the previous day's gossip.

"You know, we can talk about something else if you like," he said, facing her.

She tried not to sigh, but looked up into his moon face and smiled. "Nonsense, I love how you keep your finger on the pulse of Greensprings. You have a talent and you should use it. Besides, what else would we talk about?"

"Well, *we* don't talk much, it's mostly me going on and on," Jon replied, frowning, but then lit up. "We can talk about the dance they're having during the next banquet."

"They're going to have a dance this year?" Katherina asked, more interested.

"Yes, after your performance, I imagine," Jon explained. "Would you care to be my dancing partner?"

"Well, my candidati must also perform..." Katherina weighed the idea.

"Oh, please say yes, there will be time for you to dance some, right?" Jon took her by the hand and grabbed her about the waist.

He twirled her in his big arms. "See? I've been practicing. I've come a long way since Patrick and I danced that one time."

Katherina's giggles turned to full-blown laughter when he released her; he moved into an exaggerated solo performance, traipsing along the gravel path, waving his arms.

Jon's smile fled like a darting sparrow, however, when he tripped over the path's edging and he fell into a bush.

"Yes, I will be your partner!" she called. "Just stop before you hurt yourself!"

Jon's fist extended from the shrub, pumping in victory.

Laughing, Katherina grabbed his hand and pulled to help extract him from the foliage.

"Do you hear that?" Katherina said, suddenly standing erect and looking towards the keep. When she did, she let go of his hand, letting him slip back into the bush with a muffled cry.

"Hear what?" Jon asked when he managed to stand. He blew a leaf from his lip.

"Somebody is singing in the auditorium," Katherina said.

"Quite so," Jon agreed, cupping his ear in the direction of the sound, "and rather well. Actually, it sounds a lot like you."

Katherina picked up her dress and moved down the path in the direction of the auditorium. "I must find out who she is!"

Jon disentangled his foot from the bush and chased after her, only to have his cape nearly yank him off his feet, strangling him as it remained caught in the shrub.

"Quit fooling around and hurry," Katherina urged, motioning him forward.

He fought free and caught up to her by the time she reached the stairs to the music chamber. They ascended quickly, and outside the door, she paused to listen to the beautiful singing in a language she did not recognize. The singer's voice reverberated, magnifying itself as if an entire choir of angels sang. The sound moved as much as it chilled.

"She's beautiful!" Katherina whispered, awe feeling her face as she pressed her ear to the door. "Whoever she is, I could use her help forming the candidati into a choir."

"Good luck with that," Jon laughed, a little too loud.

The singing stopped abruptly and the sound of startled feet padding away in the opposite direction filtered through the door. Katherina threw the portal open to catch the identity of the singer.

She saw no one, but did see the door on the opposite side of the room slam shut.

#

Though Patrick and Geoffrey had an appointment after morning meal to sit with Sister Abigail, Patrick had decided to make an early start of it by breaking his fast at the candidati table in the great hall: not because he was eager to work with the peculiar people, but because he wished to prove himself to Aimeé.

He sat across from Brother Ambrosius trying to fathom the little man, which did not make for an easy task. The candidati Martin, the "face-waving-boy," constantly bumped him on one side, and Emilie, a changeling if ever there was, mumbled at him on his other.

Patrick tried making small talk with his new charge, but that instantly turned frustrating as Ambrosius' proclivities in conversation proved a challenge. It appeared he only cared to assert his tallness.

"Look, I thought we've established you are not taller than me, yes?" Patrick argued, scowling over his eggs at the man and his grin full of big oversized teeth.

"Yes I am," Ambrosius insisted. "I am taller than you."

Patrick listlessly chased the egg yolk on his plate with a spoon. Emilie mumbled at him like a bumblebee droning over a garden.

"You're very rude," Candace, another changeling, said to him from down the table.

"What?" Patrick replied, his scowl deepening. "*I'm* rude? I can't get a straight answer out of this fellow."

"Emilie has been trying to tell you this whole time how best to talk to Brobrosius," she said simply, "and you're ignoring her."

"Who's Brobrosius?" As far as he knew only six candidati: Chansonne, Candace, Martin, Emilie, Stuart, and Brother Ambrosius.

"Brother Ambrosius—Bro'brosius?" she explained with an exasperated tone.

"Oh, I see," Patrick said. "Still, I haven't heard her 'say' anything."

"That's because you haven't been listening. She's talking right now," Candace said tiredly, as if she found explaining things to Patrick exhausting.

Patrick looked at the chubby, red-faced, girl who might have been as old as fifteen years old. Her watery blue eyes stared at him as her lips moved. Patrick squinted his eyes as he listened intently.

"Just admit it," she finally said. "Admit he's taller and he'll stop."

"Oh, for heaven's sake! Fine then! You're taller than me!" Patrick cried, then stabbed his finger at those about the table. "You're taller than her, her, him, maybe not him, but certainly taller than her. You happy now?"

"Yes." Brobrosius grinned.

From then, the only useful information Patrick learned from him was that he was "Brother Ambrosius" because he was indeed a monk with the Cistercian Order to which Sister Abigail also belonged.

From above, Patrick heard his name called. He turned and craned his neck to see who addressed him.

Sir Corbin leaned over the rail of the mezzanine above the great hall, gesturing with a finger to join him.

Patrick stood and excused himself, glad for a reason to flee.

A few long-legged strides up the stairwell and he stood next to Corbin, who watched the crowd below.

"It's admirable you're taking your new duty seriously," he said, then glanced over at the Avangarde table where Geoffrey sulked. "I wish I could say the same for him."

"I had an extra incentive," Patrick replied, joining him at the rail. "Even so, I don't think this is going to work. I was wrong to suggest Geoffrey should work with the candidati. If the brief interaction I just had is any indication, I'd argue two Avangarde are better placed elsewhere. Perhaps if we—"

"Don't care. It's still happening."

"But Corbin..."

"Don't care."

"Be reasonable now—"

"Shh! Wait, do you hear that?" Corbin said, cupping a hand to his ear and looking around.

Patrick's brow furrowed as he looked around himself trying to detect anything out of the ordinary.

"That's the sound of me not caring," Corbin explained.

Patrick rolled his eyes.

"You will work with the candidati. You will lead morning drill, and you will treat Geoffrey fairly while doing so," Corbin said, "and you will be a good example. It's very disappointing to see you and Geoffrey fight like children, regardless of the reason. Him I understand, but you—I had higher expectations."

Patrick stood silently, cowed by his friend's admonition.

"Don't you understand? The lads look up to you, and even some of us old-timers have been inspired by your actions," Corbin continued. "You have it in you to be a great leader. It's time you realized that and acted on it. No more moping about. No more sleepwalking through your duties. Lord knows, I'm not going to push papers in that office forever and somebody is going to have to replace me."

Patrick blinked, shocked again by what Corbin suggested. Wolfgang had said it, too, and evidently had relayed as much to Corbin since then.

"You know Geoffrey is going to make it as difficult as possible, and what if..."

Corbin put a cupped hand to his ear again, saying, "Wait, do you hear that again?"

Patrick shut his mouth and tried not to roll his eyes.

"Also, I understand several of the lads in Cardinal Teodorico's entourage have requested you for their dubbing at their knighting ceremony. I've invited them and Sir Lucan to drill with us. Try not to disappoint them. I'll be monitoring nearby, but Sir Bisch, Sir Waylan, and Sir Brian will be there to help you out on the nuances if you need it."

Patrick nodded solemnly, adding, "I won't let you down."

"Perfect," Corbin said, pleased. "Those boys need all the help they can get."

Patrick followed his gaze over the crowd and noted the squires Jakob and Josef sitting at a table with the Ladies Katherina and Lilliana. Even from here Patrick could tell the youngsters were trying their best to impress the women. The Lady Katherina covered her mouth with her hand as her shoulders trembled with contained amusement, and the Lady Lilliana shook her head as Jakob leaned towards her with hands over heart. Patrick heard a few snippets of lame poetry.

"Well, you can't say they shy away from a challenge," Corbin said.

"Aye, they went straight for the prize in the room," Patrick agreed, shaking his head at the boys' audacity.

"Were we ever so young and foolish?" Corbin asked, turning to Patrick.

Patrick made a face.

They took another glance at the young men, turned back to each other, and laughed. "Never."

#

Shortly after that, Patrick and Geoffrey grudgingly walked together to the pavilion city outside Greensprings's gates. The bright pinions surmounting each structure flowed in the wind, giving the impression of a school of colorful eels swimming in the air.

Patrick rankled at the man's presence, wanting nothing more than to beat him to death. Aimeé's words, however, echoed in his mind: that everything he did seemed to make matters worse. And Corbin's words kept his temper banked, betrayed only by clenching his hands into fists.

"Let's just get through this, shall we?" Geoffrey said stiffly. "The affair with the council and the cup can't go on much longer. The board will leave and take their band of freaks with them, so let's show a stiff upper lip until we can get on with our lives."

"Agreed," Patrick responded just as stiffly. "That is, if that is your version of a promise of cooperation."

"Bugger off," Geoffrey responded quietly through a smile as he bowed to a pair of Lady Guests walking by.

"Tosser," Patrick returned underneath his breath through his own smile.

When they arrived at Sister Abigail's tent, they were surprised to see the lodging mostly abandoned with some trunks and other luggage in a neat pile. Sister Abigail sat on a campaign chaise, with her back very erect despite her advanced years. She regarded the young men with a maternal air as they approached.

"You're just in time," she said. "I could use a pair of strong arms to carry the last of the children's belongings into the keep."

"Keep?" Patrick asked. "You're moving in?"

"Yes," Sister Abigail replied. "The children are there now with the Lady Katherina and her maidservant in the Hall for Lady Guests. They will remain there for the duration of our stay in Avalon. The Lady Katherina is going to form them into a choir to perform at the next banquet."

"Not that I'm complaining," Geoffrey lied, "but why do they need to move into the Hall for Lady Guests to accomplish that?"

"Because they will be working intensely with the Lady Katherina, and shuttling them back and forth would be problematic, especially in the evenings when it's required all Guests are to have an armed escort."

"Isn't that what we're here for—mainly armed escort?" Patrick said, frowning.

"Partly." The nun smiled, the age lines around her mouth forming a spider's web. "But what I really have in mind for you is something more than an armed escort. Father Hugh and Mother Superior tell me you gentlemen will make fine companions for the children. They could use friends. It is best if we're all in the same vicinity. One grand, happy family."

"Can you counsel us on how we can best accomplish that? The children seem a difficult sort. No offense," Patrick said.

"None taken," she responded. "I know firsthand they are special. Special in more ways than you could possibly know, and each in his or her own way. Each came to Saint Peter's Orphanage with their tale of sorrow. How you treat them will greatly dictate the success you'll have in managing them."

"Yes, about that," Geoffrey stated. "The boy, Martin is it? With the hands? What do we do with him?"

"Ah, Martin," she said with a sad shake of her head. "He was born tragic from the start. He seems to be caught in his own little world, barely aware of this one. We believe by waving his hands in his face like that it helps him focus long enough to feed himself, dress himself, and even use the toilet. Do not try to stop him from waving his hands when he is caught up in it, or he will react violently. Consider him the littlest duckling. He will follow the rest when it is time to move, eat, sleep, and use the facilities. The key is first to manage the other children.

"The trick there is to work with Candace and Brother Ambrosius. They are the de facto leaders of the girls and boys respectively. They are the easiest to communicate with. Work closely with them, befriend them, and the rest will follow, I promise."

"Easier said than done," Patrick scowled. "Brobrosius seems to have a limited vocabulary."

Sister Abigail laughed. "Agree with him, and his vocabulary will increase. He is quite intelligent and capable when he chooses. He also has a fascination with numbers. I would not recommend playing chess with him. He will beat you in three moves, and if you think he thinks he's taller than you now, just wait until he beats you at a game. You'll never hear the end of it."

"And the little girl?" Geoffrey asked. "She does not talk. Can she at least hear?"

"She can hear just fine," she said sadly, "but she does not listen so well. She is a willful child."

"Is it that she can't talk, or won't talk?" Geoffrey continued.

Sister Abigail paused, brow creasing in deep thought before she answered.

"I am certain she cannot speak," she said at last. "I have seen her attacked by other children at the orphanage who pulled mercilessly on her hair, but not a peep came out of her, though tears flowed like rivers. Whether she cannot speak because of a malady of the mind or of the throat, I cannot say."

"Has she always been like that?" Patrick asked.

Sister Abigail averted her gaze when answering. "They say once she was a great chanteuse. The pride of her village's Christmas nativity festival, singing the most angelic of songs, but that all changed when raiders attacked her village and killed her family before her eyes. They say she wailed so loudly, and so long, it destroyed her voice."

"I gather she won't be expected to be a part of this choir Lady Katherina is assembling," Geoffrey stated.

"No," she agreed. "The choir will mostly consist of Ambrosius, Candace, Stuart, and Emilie, if we can tease a little volume out of her. Chansonne still loves to listen to music, however. I have spied her on many occasions sitting outside the auditorium listening to the Guests practice. I've also noticed she's taken a shine to the Lady Katherina, whether Katherina knows it or not."

Patrick and Geoffrey discussed more of their new duties with the nun, and then they gathered the luggage and moved into Greensprings.

#

All knew well that unlike the Hall for Guests, which housed males, the Hall for Lady Guests had a gated courtyard at its entrance with a pair of crenelated alcoves housing a stoic Avangarde in each.

Most, however, did not know the existence of an indoor courtyard at the center of the building. The ground floor acted as the convent for the Benedictine nuns from Glastonbury who served as many of the instructors at Greensprings. The next two floors provided lodging for the lady Guests, mostly as single-room chambers.

The lavish indoor courtyard would be the envy of the boy Guests, if they knew about it. Where the Hall for Guests made for spartan living, the inner courtyard held cushioned couches and a gurgling fountain, and opened to an airy three-story shaft with balconies on every level looking down. The top of the courtyard narrowed to a skylight.

The girls referred to it as the Fairy Room, whereas the boys often referred to their abode as the Dungeon.

Because Aimeé's usual responsibilities mainly involved keep cleaning, kitchen duty, and meal serving, she had only visited the Fairy Room on occasion.

Now, she stood there patiently as Mother Superior held her hand and explained her new duties—and her situation—to the Lady Katherina who sat on one of the couches. The candidati roamed about the room, many of them chasing a butterfly that had somehow fluttered in—all save Chansonne who, upon arrival, immediately hid in a cupboard.

Though Mother Superior had masterfully and compassionately explained the situation, Aimeé still felt incredibly awkward at having her assault paraded in the open as if her greatest trauma was anything more than strictly private. Despite Mother Superior's good intentions, they somehow managed to bring on a twinge of irrational shame. Ripples from the original attack still troubled her, wearing away at her dignity.

She resisted the urge to withdraw her grasp from the old nun's little warm hand to hug herself. Instead, she held her head high as Mother Superior spoke.

Katherina maintained her poise on the edge of the couch, but her face ran through a range of emotions. Her eyes widened at the revelation of Aimeé's pregnancy, followed by an open mouth and gasp of shock and sympathy when told of the rape and Geoffrey's possible paternity. When told Patrick could also be the father, however, her demeanor remained shocked at first, but then turned enigmatic. Aimeé did not shy away from the stare.

When Mother Superior explained her plan for healing all wounds in such a way as to benefit the children, Katherina's face struggled between further shock, confusion, and indignation.

Aimeé let her attention drift to the candidati chasing the butterfly, allowing Mother Superior's voice to fade into a distant drone. She wished to join them in the chase, escaping into a child's carefree world. Her mind also wandered to other possibilities. What if she had just married Patrick, hoping for the best? Could it have been any worse than how she felt at this moment?

Aimeé's eyes wandered to the floor where her gaze picked up the trail of little muddy footprints, sprinkled with tiny pink blossom petals. She followed the trail to the cabinet where Chansonne hid. The little girl's blue eyes glittered from a crack in the cupboard door, watching her intently. When Aimeé made eye contact, the crack slammed shut.

"Isn't that so, Aimeé?" Mother Superior asked.

"I'm sorry?" Aimeé's face heated.

"This is an opportunity for Greensprings to shine in its mission: creating peace and cooperation in the most challenging of circumstances." Mother Superior reiterated.

"Oui, madame."

Mother Superior's tone left no room for argument. What Mother wants, Mother gets. When she had finished, an awkward silence filled the room. Resigned to the nun's steely gaze, Katherina cleared her throat and smiled meekly.

"God does work in mysterious ways."

She cast another enigmatic glance at Aimeé.

#

As the sun set, it cast a red-orange glow behind the keep, turning the gray walls and towers into a dark silhouette.

The Lady Lilliana paused at the edge of the pavilion city long enough to lift the hood of her robe and watch Lucan reach the end of Greensprings's drawbridge. When he had disappeared into the gatehouse, she moved toward the keep.

"Don't forget to find an escort for your return, Signora Lilliana," a Cardinal Guardsman suggested as she passed.

"Certamente," she smiled.

When she reached the gatehouse, the Avangarde there made a similar statement.

"Bien sûr," she said and moved on, following Lucan at a distance as he crossed the cobblestoned church courtyard.

She paused again, allowing him to enter, and then followed again. Inside, she took up a position in the shadow of the Madonna in the narthex, watching Lucan move through the pilgrims. He approached the communion rail in the glow of the votive candles.

He fell to his knees, beat his breast, and then pressed his hands together in prayer before the cup. For some time he rocked to and fro with his head hung low. Even at this distance Lilliana could distinguish his voice in prayer over the other whispered prayers in the building, though she could not make out his words. She did catch the occasional anguished utterance, "Why?"

Eventually, his rocking became more agitated with increased beating of his breast. Something about his prayers must have disturbed, because the pilgrims began to look to one another with frowns. Lucan stood, stepped over the communion rail, and swiped angrily and repeatedly at the cup without success. The pilgrims departed one by one, leaving the distressed man to his passions at the altar.

Lillian's brow creased in confusion. She moved forward, passing through the departing crowd that murmured through coughs as they held their noses.

Then, a tingle pricked the back of her throat and her eyes stung. An overwhelming aroma of roses poured from the altar. When she held up a hand to cover her mouth from the stifling perfume, her skin burned with the sensation of a thousand pinpricks. Smoke drifted off her hands and arms.

She looked up expecting to see the altar embroiled in smoke, but only saw the cup. Lucan exited in haste out a side door.

The burning sensation escalated, causing her to gag and cough. She staggered towards the door where Lucan had disappeared and reached it just in time to see him enter the main keep. She continued her pursuit, gasping for fresh air.

#

After some time, Lilliana reached the top of a staircase and found herself in a long hallway lit by guttering torches. It was the first light she had seen for some time; she had spent most of the journey lost in dark, unfamiliar corridors. She cursed herself for that. She had spent over a month in Greensprings now, and though not the biggest of castles, she still somehow had managed to become lost. Despite the darkness, she felt eyes on her. She had run to shake off the disconcerting feeling, but couldn't escape the echoing footsteps in the corridors had attracted unwanted attention.

She breathed heavily, adjusting her clothes as she half-walked, half-ran, looking over her shoulder. The footsteps whispered behind her. Her heart jumped at the sound and she hurried forward, trying the handle on numerous doors, but found them locked. The footsteps came louder.

Behind her, the silhouette of her pursuer's head appeared in the shadowed stairwell, slowly ascending to reveal the shadow of a man. A gleam of exposed metal in the dim light indicated a drawn sword. Her panic grew as she moved to another door, tried it with no luck, then moved to a set of large double doors and struggled with the large iron mechanism keeping them closed.

Footsteps approached from behind, pausing when the church bells started to ring.

Heart pounding, she turned to face her assailant, but then breathed with relief and leaned heavily against the doors.

"Lady Lilliana?" the fresh-faced Avangarde said. "You shouldn't be alone right now. Someone has caught sight of the monster. The alarm bells are ringing and the guards are being mobilized to hunt it down."

She cried out in surprise when the door behind her suddenly opened, causing her to fall in. Arms caught her.

"The monster has been seen?" the owner of the arms asked with a paternal voice.

Lilliana looked up to see who had caught her and saw Father Wulfric. She stood, catching her balance with the old priest's help.

"Aye, Father Wulfric," the knight said. "One of the guards on the wall caught sight of a giant bat-like creature entering the garden behind the keep."

"*Pfft!*" Father Wulfric said, waving a hand. "That's the third false alarm this week alone. We've heard everything from crocodiles to flying pigs. Now it's a giant bat?"

The knight shrugged sheepishly. "Yes, Father."

"It was an Avangarde that made the sighting, though?" he asked.

"Yes, Father."

"Well, at least that's different," Father Wulfric added.

"Yes, Father. Lady Lilliana? Do you mind waiting here in the library with Father Wulfric until the all clear? I will return for you and escort you back to the pavilions."

"I'd be delighted," Lilliana said, slipping her arm into Father Wulfric's. "I feel safer already."

"Very well, I will return shortly," the young man said, and left in a jangle of armor.

Father Wulfric closed the double doors behind them as they entered the library. He placed a large crossbar across the doors for good measure.

"That should do it. We should be perfectly safe now," the priest said, brushing his hands, then added with a frown, "Then again, this is the very room in which poor Father Benis was murdered the last time the keep was attacked."

"Pardon?" Lillian asked.

"Oh, never mind," Father Wulfric waved the matter aside. "Now is not the time to be frightening you."

Lilliana adjusted her robe about her as she looked around the room: a spacious affair, but crowded with many bookshelves radiating in all directions. A sea of candles lit the shelves, giving the space a reverent glow.

"What are you doing here at this time of night?" she asked.

"I didn't realize it was that late," he explained. "It's very easy for me to get lost in my reading. It's not often I find myself in a library this magnificent. When I'm not in council or hunting monsters, I come here."

"And how goes the monster hunt?" She sauntered among the shelves, letting her hand trail along the book spines. "Any clues on what—or who—it may be?"

She appraised Father Wulfric with a studious eye. Though a bit older than Teodorico, he still stood ramrod straight and had a healthy glow about him. Intelligence gleamed in his eyes as he leaned forward to examine a book's contents, stroking his well-groomed beard. In younger days he must have been quite the handsome man. After a pause in her thinking, she reassessed that thought, concluding he wasn't so bad-looking now.

"Not a clue," he admitted. "I'm starting to wonder if it is a creature after all. I wonder if it is a disease."

"Wouldn't that be a greater concern?" Lilliana inquired. "A disease is far more elusive."

"Yes, but only if it were the sort that traveled by foul vapors," he replied.

"Then it is a disease of the flesh, transmitted by touch?" she suggested, examining an open book on a table. She flipped through the pages.

"Very good, Lady Lilliana," Wulfric said. "I'm pleased to see you are more than just a beautiful face."

Lilliana smiled. "Thank you, Father."

"My pleasure," he responded.

"But what of the flowers?" she continued. "How does a disease account for the flowers stuffed in mouths of victims?"

Wulfric smiled, wagged a finger, and squinted one eye as he replied, "As you say, the disease is transmitted by touch. I suspect the person doing the touching feels remorse, perhaps not intending to kill his or her victims, and leaves flowers as a token of apology."

"But he or she does not come forward to admit the crime, thus preventing further deaths?"

Wulfric shrugged, adding, "The perpetrator has killed, accidentally or not, and would face justice. Plus, there is often a stigma attached to some maladies. Think of leprosy. I suspect this person is very sick, needs help, but will not ask for it. His or her shame prevents it."

Lilliana froze at the assessment, scrutinizing the man's face deeper. When he didn't elaborate and turned back to another book on the table, she released a breath and smiled.

She came forward to see what captured his attention so much. It was an object resting on the page.

"What's this?" she asked, curious.

"Oh, this?" he responded, producing what looked like a silver quill to move the thin material. "It's a portion of the skin I've found at the killing sites."

She stepped away quickly.

"Oh, you needn't worry," he assured. "It's perfectly harmless."

"I'm sure it is, but it was your writing instrument that startled me," she said, eying the metallic replica quill warily. "It's rather sharp. Is it... actual silver?"

He held up the instrument, admiring the craftsmanship. "Why, yes. It was a gift from the Board of Benefactors when I first joined as a member. Naturally it is meant to signify the Avalon swan feather that makes passage to the island possible."

She still kept her distance from it.

"I assure you, it is harmless, too." He laughed, playfully jabbing it in her direction, then his bushy brow furrowed into seriousness. "Unless you're a werewolf, of course."

A silent moment hung in the air. Lilliana blinked and her mouth twitched, but then curled into a smile and she laughed. "Wulfie, you're adorable!"

He laughed too as she bent over to examine the skin.

"What have you discovered about it?" she asked.

"Ah, both much and nothing," he said, turning to another book. "I've been comparing the scale pattern to pictures in a bestiary I found here in the library. I have determined it most resembles that of a great snake. Now, what that could possibly..."

As he rambled on, Lilliana delicately picked up the skin and held it close to a candle. Glancing to ensure Wulfric's back remained turned from her, she let it dip into the flame and catch fire. In a flash it evaporated into smoke.

"Oh my!" she cried.

"What? Oh, dear..." Wulfric said, turning.

"I'm so, so sorry Father." She placed her hands on her chest, eyes turning profoundly sad. "I just meant to have a better look and held it too close to a candle. Barely touched the heat, and... poof! Please forgive me!"

Wulfric stared at the candle with fists on hips and brow furrowed deeply. "That was most unfortunate, but no matter. We've learned something very useful: the skin is highly volatile. That information may come in useful later. I should thank you, really."

"I can see why the Archbishop of Canterbury has sent you to negotiate for the cup on his part," she said, coming forward. She placed her hands on his chest. "You are very clever... and forgiving."

"My gratitude, Lady Lilliana," he replied, taking her hands in his. She liked their friendly warmth.

"Rome could use a man like you," she said, looking into his eyes. "Why do you fight so hard for the cup to go to Canterbury? You must know in your heart it belongs with the Seat of Peter. Imagine the good it could do with a centralized Church."

"I may very well agree it could rest with the Seat of Peter," he admitted, rubbing her hands. "It's just I am concerned who is sitting in the seat."

"You do not care for Paschal?" she asked, brow creasing in curiosity.

Wulfric laughed. "My lady, I like you well enough, but please don't play me for a fool. We all know what Teodorico's ambitions are."

"Apologies, I do not mean to play anyone for a fool," she said, displaying a smile she knew was beautiful. "When Teo's time comes to sit on the seat, would that be so disagreeable?"

"Forgive me, my lady, but his aggressive nature does not sit well with me," he said. "After all, did he not bring an entire army with him? I only brought my wit, charm, and scripture."

"And your good looks," Lilliana added, laughing lightly. "Teodorico has not used his 'army' and prefers dialogue to force. Surely a man of such wisdom is worthy of trust and leadership."

"He hasn't used force *yet*," he responded. "Besides. I am a loyal man. I am loyal to the Archbishop of Canterbury and the King of England, and of course, God."

She kissed his hands. "Loyalty. Truly the rarest and greatest of virtues. I think I'd very much like to see you as a pope someday."

Wulfric laughed with his eyes just as much as his mouth.

"Speaking of loyalty," she continued, "is there a Madame Wulfric back home?"

"No, no," he said, his smile turning bittersweet. "I believe in the virtue of celibacy as well, much like our Pope Paschal. I devote myself to God in soul *and* body. Though I cannot say I begrudge Teodorico for advocating clerical marriage after having met you. Your very presence makes a powerful argument."

Lilliana laughed and hugged the old man.

"You are very sweet," she said. "Regardless of age or vocation, the loss of a handsome man is still a waste."

There came a knock on the door and the Avangarde called the all clear.

"Good night, Father Wulfric," she said and kissed him on the cheek.

"Good night, Lady Lilliana," the priest replied and rubbed his cheek, turning red beneath his snow-white beard.

He took the crossbar down and let her out.

The Avangarde bowed deeply at her appearance, his sword scabbard shooting up and tangling his cloak as he bent over. He struggled to right it as they walked down the hall.

"Lord," Wulfric said, looking heavenward, tingling in a manner he hadn't in a very long time. "You know I love You and would do anything for You, but sometimes it's very, very hard."

He sighed heavily and closed the door.

That night, he dreamt a young man's dreams.

#

Lucan huddled in the cold among the bodies sprawled in the pit, too numerous to count. Cloudy daylight barely penetrated the forest canopy, illuminating the scene with a dim grayness. He rocked back and forth, weeping silently as he cradled the dead woman in his arms. The stench of death and disease filled his nose.

"I warned you." A familiar woman's voice came to him. "They eventually only bring us pain. We are not meant for the likes of them."

He looked up to see Lilliana standing near, pristine in a red dress.

"She loved me. She only left me because death took her," he replied, glaring at Lilliana, and added, "Unlike some people."

"Does that answer comfort you?" Lilliana asked, scornfully.

"No," he admitted. "Why does this go on? How do I make it end? Why did the cup reject me?"

"Because you are cursed," she answered, "but I've met someone. A man. He has a plan, and it just might work. Come with me." She held out a cup. "Drink from *this* cup, and your suffering will end."

When he reached for the cup he saw it filled to the brim with squirming maggots.

#

Lucan startled into wakefulness and looked around in confusion, trying to recognize his surroundings.

He lay among bushes on a bed of mud and pink blossoms, not knowing how he arrived there. Sitting up, he frowned as he looked down, noting his nakedness.

"Dammit, not again," he groaned.

He frantically grabbed at his chest, but relaxed when his hand came to grasp a bit of rusty metal attached to a leather thong hanging from his neck.

Dawn light broke through leaves of the foliage. He stiffly rose, then froze, a vague memory nagging at him. Something about participating in the Avangarde morning drill with his squires. He stumbled from the bushes in the growing light.

#

Patrick stifled a yawn and rubbed his eyes.

He found it difficult enough to rise early in the morning to perform drills before breaking his fast, but even harder to rise earlier and prepare the practice field. It didn't help that he, and all Avangarde, had been up until late the night before on yet another wild monster chase.

Sir Balder's fellow knights would not let him forget it anytime soon, relentlessly teasing him for having raised the alarm.

"I swear I saw something huge, with wings, walk into the garden," he groused under the withering harassment.

"Wings?" Sir Waylan said. "Why was it walking in the garden, then? If it had wings wouldn't it be flying?"

"Well, to be fair," Sir Brian interjected, "a refreshing walk in the garden just isn't the same if you're flying over it."

"Seriously!" Balder protested. "I saw something!"

"Enough," Patrick called. "We have things to do, and we have new trainees among us."

The squires Charles, Jakob, and Josef stood front and center before the fifty or so Avangarde on the practice field. Unlike the veteran Avangarde, the lads had come bright-eyed and eager. They were already dressed in the padded practice armor and had their wooden swords in hand. Their heads looked ridiculously small, poking out the tops of the padded suits.

"New trainees? Is that who they are?" Sir Waylan said. "I thought they got lost on the way to school."

"On the way to the nursery, more like," Sir Brian corrected, approaching the boys and swiping a finger behind Charles' ear. "They're literally still wet behind the ears."

Charles took it well. The young man seemed little perturbed, always having an affable smile. He would have been a handsome lad, too, if he didn't care so much for having a bowl cut.

Sir Waylan approached Josef from the side and plucked at his padded armor.

"Aye, wet, and my God, is that an umbilical cord?"

Sir Brian looked down at the ground about his feet. "Look out for the afterbirth, lest you slip on it."

Sir Bisch, the hulking Teuton among them, laughed. "Good-good!"

All turned to see the large knight approaching late. Children hung from him as he walked. One clinging to each leg, and another on his shoulders.

"Down you go," Corbin said, coming forth from the edge of the practice field to gently pluck the child from Bisch's back. "Uncle Bisch needs to go to work."

"Bad-bad," the child said, mimicking the only other phrase Bisch routinely said.

"Yes, yes, I know," Corbin said, setting the little boy down. "I, too, would rather watch grown men whack each other with sticks than sit in a classroom, but life is not fair." He shooed the children away, who reluctantly waved their goodbyes.

He turned to Bisch, smiling. "I told you not to walk by the classrooms on the way to practice. Children stick to you like burrs on a sheep."

Bisch stuck out his tongue at Corbin as he picked up his wooden sword. Corbin returned the compliment as he took up his position on the edge of the field to monitor the drill.

"Speaking of late," Patrick said, looking to the squires, "where is your master, Lucan? Was he not also to participate?"

The boys looked at each other, shrugging.

"There are enough of us," Sir Edmond said, looking at the squires, "and the good news is we have new practice dummies. Our poor old straw men have had all their stuffing beaten out of them."

"I think you'll find your new practice dummies fight back well enough," Jakob said, proudly.

Unlike Charles, the other two boys did not take the chiding so well.

Laughter and "oooh's" rippled through the assembled men.

"Don't antagonize them," Charles addressed his fellow squires. "They're just friendly in their way. It's a part of the acceptance process."

Josef rolled his eyes and said, "Charles, did you know if you say 'gullible' slowly, it sounds just like 'elephant?'"

"What?" Charles responded, frowning.

Patrick resisted smiling. Rather, he put on his responsible face. Between the Avangarde's teasing of Balder and the various other disruptions, he could see this getting out of hand if he didn't start the day.

"All right, listen up," Patrick called to the group. "Today is a quick ground combat drill, followed by paired matches. Understood?"

Mumbles came from the group of men as they shuffled about, still in varying stages of donning their padded armor. Nobody seemed to have heard him.

Patrick bristled. He wouldn't be ignored on his first day as drillmaster. Naturally, Sir Geoffrey made the worst perpetrator, idly standing by, pretending not to have heard the commands. He'd come fully armored, but leaned lazily on his practice sword.

The anxiety mounted in Patrick as he watched more people jostle Balder and the squires start to exchange harsher and harsher words with the veterans. To make matters worse, Sir Wolfgang arrived and stood next to Corbin on the edge of the practice field to spectate.

"I said listen up!" he finally shouted above the din. "Form a skirmish line! If you do not, this is going to be a very, very long morning and we will miss breakfast. Understood? I can wait all day. Can you?"

To his relief they formed a line as they donned padded helmets, hefted wooden shields, and brought their swords to rest on their shoulders.

Sir Lucan arrived then, strapping on his padded helmet. He apologized profusely and took a place in line. Patrick gritted his teeth and clenched his fists.

"It rained last night," Patrick explained, pacing before the assembled crowd with his hands behind his back. "So today is not the best day to perform a mounted drill. The practice field between here and the gate doesn't need to be muddied up any more than it is. Therefore, we're going to practice close-in combat as a group. There are occasions where you will need to fight on foot, in tight formation, whether because of the press of combatants or because you are in a confined space..."

A quiet voice in the crowd mumbling, "Gul-lee-ble," distracted Patrick.

"Charles! Pay attention!" Patrick shouted, shaking his head.

"Yes, sir!" Charles snapped to attention.

"Where was I? Right. So, I want you to advance as a unit four steps, then on my command perform an over-shield thrust of the sword, followed by a below-shield thrust, then shield buffet, and finally a direct thrust." Patrick demonstrated each maneuver. "We will do that four times. Yeah?"

Collectively, the participants banged their swords against their shields in reply.

"Excellent. Shoulder-to-shoulder now. March! One, two, three, four! Over thrust! Under thrust! Shield! Thrust! March! One, two, three..."

Though rough going at first, especially with the newcomers among their ranks, they had the rhythm down by the fourth reiteration.

"Again!" Patrick shouted when they reached him. "About face, and back to where you started. March! One, two, three, four! Over thrust!"

This went on for the better part of half an hour. Once the ground had become too muddy, and it became obvious the participants had the technique down, Patrick called a halt to the exercise.

"Cheers," he said, pleased to see Wolfgang and Corbin clapping in approval. Seeing the veterans pat the squires on the shoulders for a job well done also pleased him.

"Find a partner," Patrick continued. "Spread out a half-sword-length from each other. On my command, skirmish using the techniques just practiced as a group. Yeah?"

Swords banged against shields.

Bisch approached Josef, the smallest of the squires, and gestured between himself and the boy.

"Wha...?" Josef protested, jaw dropping at the sight of the knight three times his size.

"Good-good!" Bisch said, picking Josef up by the scruff of his armor and walking away with him to their patch of the field to practice on.

"Right, then," Patrick called once everyone had held a sword out and adjusted their distance relative to each other. "Fight!"

The scene quickly turned into a melee of flying swords and shields, the sound of wood almost deafening.

In less than fifteen minutes the men bent over, hands on knees, sweating and muddy. Though they had started out using the technique of the day, the melee quickly devolved to the standard battlefield free-for-all.

Oh well, Patrick thought as he officially called the exercise to a close. *That is why we practice.*

"Cheers," he said, then addressed the squires. "You lads did well enough; you're still standing, I see. Well, almost all of you."

Lucan stretched out a hand to Bisch, who lay flat on his back in the mud. Bisch took the hand and let Lucan pull him up, revealing a wide-eyed Josef who had been squashed flat beneath him.

"Good-good!" Bisch said, clapping Lucan on the back.

Few people could best Bisch in battle, practice or otherwise, but Patrick had watched Lucan do just that in impressive fashion.

"Thank you, sir," Charles said to Patrick. The boy had a large welt on the right side of his face.

Jakob also voiced his appreciation. "Do you think we're ready to slay some villains, then?"

Laughter rippled through the veterans.

Patrick froze and leveled a serious gaze at the boy.

"If you're looking to become a knight just to whack away with your sword, then you're doing it for the wrong reasons," Patrick said. "Vanquishing villains, slaying dragons, and rescuing maidens are all fine and good, especially in stories, but the reality is far more unpleasant. Sometimes, a knight's sole purpose is just to die for what he fights for."

Patrick wanted to rant further, but stopped when noting all listened intently, not just the squires. Even Geoffrey paused in removing his padding. Lucan especially gave him a peculiar look.

The squires nodded solemnly.

"Fight strong," Patrick finished, addressing the crowd, beating his breast.

"Live stronger," came the collective response.

#

After putting away the pads, swords, and shields in the equipment room adjacent to the Avangarde barracks, he made his way to the great hall for morning meal. Before he could arrive, he noted several people walking briskly into the garden. Father Wulfric was among them, a look of concern bunched up in his bushy eyebrows.

Curious, Patrick followed. His boots crunched loudly on the loose gravel of the garden paths as he picked up his pace to catch up. When he did, he found a group of Avangarde, a boy, and Father Wulfric at the fountain at the center of the garden. Normally the site was a frequent location for romantic meetings in the evenings, but today it served as a place of gloom.

"There, you see," the boy exclaimed, pointing to the ground.

Father Wulfric picked up a dark object and examined it.

Patrick approached and saw the priest holding a dead blackbird, though something about it struck him as peculiar. More dead birds littered the ground and bobbed in the fountain.

"I came across it on my way to breaking my fast," the boy continued. "That is what happened to the stablehand, right?"

"Indeed," Father Wulfric replied, sniffing the bird.

What looked like little white flowers boiled out of the creature's eyes and beak.

"I told you I saw something last night," Sir Balder said, vindicated.

"Nobody move!" the priest shouted, freezing all with the sudden force of his voice.

He gingerly walked around the fountain, sandals squishing in the mud, as he inspected the dead birds and the area.

At last he came to a cherry tree whose pink blossoms hung over the scene. He reached up, pulled on a branch, and released it so it swayed.

More dead birds rained down, followed by a wispy white thing drifting lazily in the air. Father Wulfric caught it gently between his outstretched palms.

When he looked at it closely, his face lit up with surprise, but then turned to frustration when the gauzy thing fragmented into tiny pieces in his hands.

"What did you see, Father?" Patrick asked.

"I could have sworn I saw the imprint of a face in it," he responded, frowning deeply. "A human face."

#

"What a lovely place this is," Lilliana said, casting her gaze about the thatched and tiled roofs of Aesclinn. Cottonwood fuzz drifted in the sunlight. "Thank you, Kat, for suggesting we come here for our midday meal. It is a very nice change."

Lilliana belched a very unladylike belch.

"My goodness," Katherina said, stifling a laugh at the reaction of the people around them. "I'm guessing the sausage and beans agreed with you."

"Presently," Lilliana replied, rubbing her stomach. "Soon, I'm afraid, when my wind comes from the other end, it won't be so pleasing. For those around me, in any case."

This time Katherina could not stifle her laugh.

"You're mad. I've never met a woman like you," she said. "How can you be so ladylike one moment, and then so scandalous another?"

"Practice," Lilliana said with a mischievous grin and put her arm around the shorter woman. "With a little work, you too can walk the fine line between good and evil."

They laughed as they entered the town square.

A quick glance around the square testified to the impact of the Roman visitors on the island. Commerce now bustled in the sleepy village. The edges of the square bristled with carts full of goods, and many of the shops opened their windows to the public. Even shops that normally didn't cater directly to the general public, like the silversmith, now had their articles on display.

"A trusting bunch," Lilliana commented, observing commoners examining the glassblower's wares.

"Thieves don't trouble us," Katherina explained. "Oh look, there is the confectionery cart the innkeeper told us about." She took the taller woman by the hand and rushed her over to a cart full of pastries. A ponytailed girl watched over the little mobile store of sweets, and she curtsied with her apron.

"Oh, they all look so delicious. I don't know which to choose," Lilliana lamented, looking over the array of berry filled tarts.

"I'm amazed you still have room in your stomach," Katherina giggled.

"Always room for sweets," Lilliana countered, then addressed the girl. "What would you suggest, signorina?"

The girl, perhaps twelve years old, quickly pointed to a tart filled with raspberries that glittered like clear rubies.

"These are my favorites," she said, "and they are popular, but you might want to take one of the blackberry ones before it's too late."

"Too late for what?" Lilliana asked.

"In a few more weeks, it will be Michaelmas Day, and then after that the Devil claims them and they won't be fit for eating until next year," the girl warned.

"Well, we can't let that happen," Lillian said, making a face. "I'll take one."

"I'll take a gooseberry," Katherina said.

"Ah, I see you like your desserts just as you like your men," Lilliana said, dropping a couple of copper coins into the girl's hands. "A little on the bitter side."

"Jon is not so bitter—quite the contrary," Katherina replied, frowning as she accepted her tart.

The girl curtsied as the ladies moved toward the square's fountain.

"I wasn't speaking of him," Lilliana explained, struggling with her tart after taking a bite out of it. The berries started to run down her fingers. "I was referring to a certain moody Irishman."

Katherina scoffed. "I do not prefer my men moody, nor bitter, and Patrick is but a friend these days." They took a seat on the edge of the fountain and ate their tarts, watching the variety of people in their colorful garments bustle about the square. The water gurgled behind them.

"Then why do you watch him so much when he is not looking?" Lilliana countered, gaining the upper hand on the berries running down her fingers with her tongue.

"I don't think I do," Katherina argued, "and if I do, it is for the same reason I catch you staring at him when he is not looking."

"Touché," Lilliana admitted. "We have a shared appreciation for fine-looking men. Does it bother you I regard your former beau so? If so, I can stop."

"Not at all. He is not mine to claim," Katherina replied, starting to struggle with her own tart. "Though the cardinal may feel differently."

Lilliana laughed. "There is no harm in looking."

They touched tarts and together said, "Cheers."

"How fares the business with him, Geoffrey, the maidservant, and the work with the candidati?" Lilliana asked.

Katherina rolled her eyes as she finished off her tart.

"It will take a miracle to organize the children," she replied. "Geoffrey and Patrick have yet to spend time with us, so I couldn't say what kind of tension that will cause, and the maidservant is useless so far. The little girl, Chansonne? She came into the Hall for Lady Guests covered in mud from the garden yesterday morning. She refused to allow herself to be cleaned. I set the maidservant to the task, but she only managed to chase the girl around the hall, leaving muddy footprints. The poor creature needs a bath. Even though she does not sing, she watches the practices and smells the auditorium up, distracting us all."

"Sounds like you have your hands full," Lilliana said, "but I have no doubt your strong will is up for the task."

Katherina grumbled. "So far my 'strong will' has been best used for resisting what people want me to do, and not for making people do what I want."

"Then why did you agree to the task?" Lilliana asked, genuinely curious.

"I agreed to the challenge of forming the children into a choir —not to all the baggage along with it. I have no idea what I'm going to do when the drama boils over with the knights and the maidservant."

"You will know what to do. You are strong." Lilliana took Katherina's hand and confided, "Men are simple creatures, easily maneuvered. Certainly as women we cannot be expected to fight in the same arenas as they, but we have our weapons: guile, beauty, relationships. All one must do is find what motivates a man, and use it against him. Or, find who his enemies are, and motivate them against him."

"Yes, I understand," Katherina said distantly as she gazed across the square. "Those are time-honored techniques, but there are certain... situations I am not suited for. Certain things that frighten me."

Lilliana followed her gaze to one of the benefactors who stood across the plaza. Count Fulk of Anjou, one of those associated with the Merchant's Guild, watched them.

"What's wrong with him?" Lillian asked, frowning. "What could possibly frighten you about an old man with a silly mustache?"

Katherina shifted her gaze to Lilliana and met the elder woman's eyes. "He reminds me of my uncle. The only man in the world who truly frightens me and makes me feel helpless. The way the Count looks at me is the same way my uncle looks at me. He makes me feel... dirty. Especially when he toys with his belt to loosen it. It reminds me of when he... well..."

Katherina closed her eyes, trying her hardest to not show the tremble coming over her.

Lilliana reached up and stroked Katherina's cheek. "Your uncle is why you are in Avalon, yes? Your mother sent you here in exile when he usurped your father's throne in Kiev."

Katherina nodded.

"Not long ago, a similar man came to Greensprings," Katherina continued. "With him I felt strong, in control, but it was a lie. He manipulated me and caused me to make poor choices."

"Loki," Lilliana said quietly.

Katherina nodded. "I felt ashamed. I've lost confidence in myself ever since then. I've been avoiding Count Fulk since he first came to Avalon and I noticed him watching me. I should march right over there and tell him to stop, but I can't."

Katherina breathed out heavily in an almost shuddering gasp and took Lilliana's hand, despite it feeling like a chicken's foot through the lacy half-glove.

"I've never admitted that to anyone," she finished.

"I feel honored you can share that with me," Lilliana replied, picking up Katherina's hand and kissing it, then added, "and I'm going to repay you for it."

"Oh, how's that?" Katherina asked, squeezing her hand.

"I'm going to show you how to deal with such people, accomplish what you want, and have a bit of fun while you're at it." Lilliana maneuvered behind Katherina, placing her arms around her. She pulled back Katherina's hair with one hand and whispered in her ear. "Take a good look at this silly old man. What does he look like to you?"

Katherina struggled to maintain her gaze on the leering Count Fulk. "A creepy uncle?"

Lilliana snickered and with her hand gently took Katherina by the chin and shifted her gaze in another direction. "You see that next to the farmer's cart? Look familiar?"

Katherina noted the billy goat tied to a farmer's cart. It took her a moment to understand what Lilliana meant, but then it struck her. The white goat's scruffy beard and long face did indeed remind her of Count Fulk and she laughed, especially when the animal chewed. The way its mouth moved reminded her of Fulk at mealtime.

"You see?" Lilliana instructed. "All you need do when dealing with disagreeable people is make an association in your mind with their most harmless feature. Everyone has one. A resemblance to a silly or harmless animal. A lazy eye. A speech impediment. Focus on that. Use it. Then attack! For instance, I have it on good authority the count is attempting to bribe several benefactors to sway their decisions toward the Merchant's Guild's interests. I'm sure, armed with this knowledge, you can get what you want."

To Katherina's horror, Lilliana motioned Count Fulk over with a flirtatious smile.

The lanky old Frenchman sauntered across the cobblestones to the women. A graying blond mustache swam over his lip like a furry eel, mostly hiding his smarmy smile.

"Count Fulk," Lilliana said, back erect, and eyes leveled confidently at him. "I believe the Lady Katherina has something to say to you."

Katherina coughed, her voice catching in her throat.

"Splendid," Fulk answered, turning to Katherina and smiling in anticipation.

From behind, Lilliana nudged her back and quietly bleated like a goat.

An involuntary giggle erupted from Katherina as she pictured a cud-chewing goat before her.

"Count Fulk," she said, regaining her composure and raising her chin. "I do not like it whatsoever how you brazenly leer at me and I want you stop immediately."

The Count groused and his bushy eyebrows closed in around his dark eyes.

"I am not 'leering' at anyone, and what if I were?" he sniffed. "What of it? You obviously like the attention of men. I'm merely providing it."

Katherina imagined the billy goat in her mind with its horns caught in a hedge, struggling and bleating pathetically. She suppressed the desire to laugh again. "I disagree, and in any case, certainly do not wish your attention. As I said, you will stop immediately. I'm certain you are perfectly aware of who my friends are." She gestured with her chin to Lilliana. "And by extension, so is the cardinal. You wouldn't want a full investigation into the rumors of bribery. Leave me in peace, and I needn't insist on one."

Count Fulk's eyes widened and his knees almost buckled.

"Very well, mademoiselle," he said stiffly, smoothing out his mustache in a nervous gesture. He bowed deeply, making it a point to avoid eye contact with Katherina, and then turned on a heel and disappeared into the crowd.

"You see? Picture them as harmless. Lure them in with charm, threaten them with facts, and spell out their certain doom if they don't comply," Lilliana said.

"It worked!" Katherina smiled and let out a guarded breath, but the smile quickly fled from her face. "But this was a stranger. My uncle is a different matter. I can practice this technique until I vanquish a thousand Fulks, but I'm certain once confronted by my uncle, I will cave like a scared little girl."

Lilliana cradled Katherina's face in her hands and looked her in the eyes. "Trust me—you have it in you. Can you imagine? If you support Teodorico's desire to bring the cup to Rome, he would certainly support you in any way he could to return your father's throne back to you. That would put you in the position of strength you would need to face your uncle. You could go home! Then imagine what you could do from there. It has long been a goal of the popes to reunite the Roman Catholic Church with the Orthodox Church. Sitting on the throne in Kiev, you would be in a perfect position to facilitate that. You could be the great unifier! And a woman!"

Katherina's eyes glazed over as her thoughts turned inward to visions of home. Of freedom. Of independence from overbearing men in her life.

While distracted by such thoughts, she felt Lilliana lean in and touch her lips to hers, lingering longer than expected from a friendly gesture.

Katherina pulled away, heat rising in her face.

"I imagine your uncle is the furthest thing from your mind right now," Lilliana laughed.

Katherina cleared her throat and smoothed out the front of her dress. "Yes, now that you mention it."

"Good, then. Mission accomplished," Lilliana said.

In need of another distraction, Katherina noted several children frolicking through the crowd, laughing. Despite the perfectly sunny day, wet hair and clothes clung to their bodies.

"Children," Katherina called to them as they passed near the fountain, "why so wet? It's not raining."

"We were at the swimming hole," an eight-year-old girl replied, lisping through the gap where her two front teeth had fallen out.

"Swimming hole?"

"Yes, ma'am," said a boy who looked to be the girl's brother. "Over yonder, near the hill with the ring of standing stones called the Shrugging Giants."

"Well, imagine that," she said, surprised. "You best go dry off before you catch your death."

"Yes, ma'am!" The children curtsied and bowed, and then scampered off.

"Kat?" Lilliana said, curious at Katherina's thoughtful silence. "Something on your mind?"

Katherina smiled. "I have an idea."

Chapter Ten

"No! No! No!"

Katherina slammed her hands onto the plinth, scattering black and white pebbles in every direction. She addressed the fidgety candidati on the auditorium stadium seats. Her voice echoed in the acoustic chamber, causing others in the room to turn their heads in her direction.

"When Candace finishes, then the rest of you begin on the very next note," she explained, exasperated. "Emilie, I know you can sing louder than that. I've heard you scream when Stuart pulls your hair. Martin, moaning randomly is not singing."

Katherina blew bangs out of her eyes, reminding her she needed a haircut—if she didn't pull it all out in frustration.

Though Sir Geoffrey, Sir Patrick, Aimeé, Mother Superior and Sister Abigail were present, she felt totally alone, as no one else would help. The knights took up opposite ends of the room, ignoring each other. Oddly, Patrick kept his distance from Aimeé as well. The nuns, one in the white-and-black Benedictine habit and the other in the all-white Cistercian habit, chatted merrily over their needlework in the auditorium. Only Aimeé came close to helping by trying to keep Chansonne occupied, but she struggled to keep up with the dirty child. Yet she avoided Geoffrey at all times, which made the room tense whenever Chansonne played near him.

Katherina wanted to scream. Under the best of circumstances, her inability to coax a coherent song from the group would drive her mad, but with the useless adults in the room distracting the children, her head felt as though it would explode.

"One more time," she appealed to the children gathered before her. "Candace starts with the opening note, then the rest follow."

She raised her arms to commence the exercise, and to Candace's credit she sang the first note, but stopped abruptly when she reached up and pinched her nose.

"Candace, what's wrong?" Katherina asked.

Then the smell hit her and she turned to see Chansonne had crept up close to the group.

"Sorry," Aimeé said tiredly. "I tried to keep her away, but she loves listening."

Stuart started moaning and Martin leaped into a furious face-waving spell.

"Chansonne, darling," Katherina said to the girl, "could you please go play... over there?"

The child ignored her, crouching at the base of the plinth to pick up several of the note-stones with one hand while clutching her doll with the other.

"Now, please," Katherina insisted between gritted teeth.

Chansonne looked up and her light eyes locked defiantly with Katherina's. For several long uncomfortable moments their eyes ground on one another like two colliding glaciers. Finally, Chansonne relented and took the stones with her. Katherina sighed heavily, drained.

The children fell into another cycle of fighting. Nothing more could be accomplished this day.

"Very well, then," Katherina all but cried. "Go play."

As they scattered to the four winds, Katherina called the knights over.

"We're going to try something different tomorrow," she announced. "We're going to take a break. We're going to go on picnic."

"Pardon?" Geoffrey raised his eyebrows.

"You gentlemen will escort us tomorrow to the Shrugging Giants for our midday meal."

"How will that help them sing?" Patrick asked.

"I'm thinking several steps ahead," Katherina replied. "First, fix one problem so that the others may be addressed. Just trust me."

"As you wish," Geoffrey shrugged. "Will you have any more need for us today?"

"No, you may go," Katherina said.

When he departed, Aimeé stepped in to gather the note-stones scattered about the plinth.

"I can do that," Katherina said quickly, bending to gather the stones herself.

"'Tis not a problem, my lady," Aimeé said.

Katherina moved to push Aimeé aside gently, but withdrew her hand as if the French girl's skin burned. "No, really, let me gather these. Go see about retrieving the ones Chansonne took."

Aimeé shot her a look bordering on exasperation, but complied and went after the girl. Katherina's eyes followed her for a moment, then she resumed collecting the stones. In the process, a familiar pair of boots stepped into her vision.

"Are you avoiding me?" Patrick asked.

She looked up to see him still standing near, arms crossed.

She stood with her handful of stones. "I just haven't had time."

"You seem to have plenty of time for Sir Jon," Patrick replied, wryly.

"That's different," she protested. "We... Oh, for heaven's sake, can we not argue? My head is splitting already. It's just that... I... I don't know what to say to you right now. To..." Her gaze shifted to Aimeé pursuing Chansonne about the room. "To either of you."

She looked back to Patrick and his probing hazel eyes. His dark hair hung in his face. Again his scent triggered memories of his big hands about her waist as they escaped together down the stairs of a crumbling tower, and those same hands lifting her into a saddle and spiriting her away from a fairy castle sucked into a purple sky.

"Kat?" Patrick asked, face turning quizzical.

She hadn't realized she had closed her eyes and leaned forward, close to his body.

"Why didn't you marry her?" she asked abruptly.

Taken only slightly aback by the suddenness of the question, he grumbled and rubbed his head. "She rejected my proposal. There are complications, old and new. It's a long story."

Katherina stared momentarily at the revelation.

Patrick turned to watch Aimeé finally corner Chansonne and cajole her into surrendering the stones. "It turns out she's just as stubborn as you."

#

The following morning, Patrick reported to the front of the Hall for Lady Guests where Katherina rounded up all those involved with her plan. All, that is, save the two old nuns who declined "to go adventuring in the wilderness," and assured Katherina that she had things well under control. So, the party lost two nuns, but gained one lady.

Patrick eyed Lady Lilliana when she arrived. Though Patrick counted Sister Abigail among one of Cardinal Teodorico's people, he did not view her as a threat. He felt different about the lady, however, and he cast furtive glances at Aimeé to make sure she kept her distance from him, lest word of his lie make it back to Teodorico.

Aimeé did, but it chagrinned him to see how easily she managed without him.

"Thank you for the invite," Lilliana said to Katherina as Sir Patrick helped them up into the front wagon seat. "This should prove much more fun than an outing to the village, and what a lovely day for it!"

"You're very welcome, and thank you for coming. We could use all the help we can find," Katherina replied.

The group loaded the wagon with food, blankets, and squirming children.

"I can take that!" Katherina almost shouted when she intercepted Aimeé as the maidservant lifted a basket. "It's very heavy, and you're, well, you know..."

"Pregnant?" Aimeé said, brow furrowing in agitation. She snatched the basket back. "I can manage just fine, my lady."

Katherina smiled wanly and stepped back. She did, however, pick up a mystery bundle. "Nobody is to open this until the time is right," she announced, hugging the package. "It is a surprise."

Geoffrey helped Katherina up into the front of the wagon from the opposite side. Brobrosius sat between the two ladies, holding the reins of the horses and acting as driver.

Geoffrey eyed the little man suspiciously. "You sure you can handle driving?"

"Of course," Brobrosius replied with his big grin. "Back home I'm the one who drives the abbey cart to market. Besides, I'm taller than you."

"Naturally," Geoffrey said, making a face.

Patrick and Geoffrey mounted their horses, giant cousins to those pulling the wagon, and took the lead. Brobrosius did indeed seem to handle the wagon well enough and soon they exited the back gate of Greensprings, also known as the Back Door.

#

From the keep battlements, a pair watched the departing group.

"I hope you know what you're doing," Sir Wolfgang said, shaking his head.

Mother Superior's normally impassive face cracked with a hint of a smile. "I know nothing, but I'm confident God knows all."

#

The band took the road to Aesclinn, but just past the apple orchards they veered to the left and trundled across fields full of wheat stubble, remnants of the recent harvest.

Patrick turned in his saddle to address Katherina. "What exactly did you have in mind for us today? The Shrugging Giants is a ways to go just for a picnic."

"A picnic is only half my plan," Katherina explained. "After we eat, us womenfolk will go swimming down at the swimming hole while you menfolk and your male eyes will guard us from a distance."

This raised eyebrows from both knights.

"That's right," Geoffrey said, thinking aloud. "There is a swimming hole at the foot of the hill the Giants rest on. The village children go there all the time."

"Which makes it perfectly safe," Katherina added. "No evil water spirits or water monsters. I've thoroughly researched it."

"Is it as safe as Katherina says?" Patrick asked, looking at Geoffrey.

"Aye, safe enough, from monsters and prying eyes," Geoffrey replied. "The swimming hole and the brook feeding them are lined with trees."

"We should still split up when the time comes, each to a side of the swimming hole, patrolling a zone," Patrick cautioned.

"Aye, aye, Sir Patrick," Geoffrey saluted in a manner just short of insubordination.

The flippancy did not go unnoticed, nor entirely unexpected, but Patrick chose not to challenge it. He would save the battle for a more serious occasion.

Shortly after that, they passed from the field into a vale of bright grass neatly clipped close to the earth.

"Sheep," Geoffrey explained. "Though I don't see any about today or their herders. A good day for swimming."

Ahead lay a low hill surmounted by a ring of standing stones—not uncommon in Avalon, though this ring was perhaps the most intact Patrick had seen. All the suspended lintel stones were still aloft on their supports. Several upright stones leaned forward, though, buckling the ring and threatening to cave it in, thus its name: The Shrugging Giants.

At the base of the hill, the land dipped into to a wooded ravine.

"There is the path to the swimming hole, leading downhill," Geoffrey pointed out.

They pulled the wagon onto the level patch of well-manicured grass.

"Good enough, Lady Katherina?" Patrick asked.

"Excellent," she responded.

As they unloaded the wagon, Candace stared up at the stone ring. "The little people used to dance there."

"What's that?" Patrick asked. Candace did not respond. When he nudged her, she startled as if waking from sleep. "Tell me about the little people," he urged.

"What little people?" she replied, her eyes focusing.

"You spoke of little people dancing up there."

"Did I?" she shrugged and moved to help unload the wagon.

"Now, how could you possibly know that?" Geoffrey said, frowning at the girl.

"She has a habit of just knowing things," Patrick explained, glancing at Aimeé, who didn't seem to take the hint regarding the episode on the boat to Avalon.

"I know things," Brobrosius said.

"What, like you're taller than everyone?" Patrick laughed, shoving a picnic basket in the little man's hands.

"Like the wagon horses took seventeen thousand and sixty-six steps from Greensprings to here, and the big horses only took eleven thousand and ninety-four steps, and I'm taller than you."

"Really?" Patrick said, impressed. "What else do you know?"

"Sir Geoffrey's breathing almost doubles when he looks at the Lady Lilliana."

Patrick laughed heartily at the statement.

"Almost as much as yours does," Brobrosius added.

Patrick's laughter suddenly choked off. "That will be quite enough now." He punctuated this by draping a blanket over the little man's head.

They quickly set to spreading blankets and preparing boards of honey-roasted ham, cheese, crisp peas, butter, cracked bread, roasted hazelnuts, and goblets of wine.

They ate mostly in silence. Even Martin took a break from his usual moaning and outbursts to indulge in the sumptuous food, though he made a mess of it. Katherina and Lilliana tried to start a lighthearted conversation, but it never really took. Only Siegfried managed to break the ice by nuzzling the women and children as he grazed.

While the gentle giant distracted the rest, Aimeé leaned nearer to Patrick. "Have you made any progress in befriending Brother Ambrosius?"

Patrick shot her a reproachful look. "Shh. The lady's ears may as well be the cardinal's."

Aimeé scrunched up her nose at him. "Don't shush me! I'm tired of being afraid. And stop using any excuse to run from your promises!"

Patrick sighed and nodded a concession. He let his fingers crawl along the blanket behind a picnic basket and took her hand in his. "I'm sorry. No, I haven't yet, but I will soon."

Aimeé sighed in return. "I suppose you forgot to pack the pickles as well."

Patrick's eyes widened. "Oh..."

Aimeé scrunched her nose again and squeezed his hand painfully.

Before anyone could notice his cry of discomfort, Brobrosius roused the excitement of the children by suggesting they go explore the stone circle.

"Sir Patrick?" Brobrosius asked. "Can we?"

Patrick looked in the same direction as the little man. The ring of dark gray stones sat invitingly on the green hill. Wispy clouds floated behind them in a sea of cobalt.

"I see no harm," he replied. "Let us go exploring, then."

They mounted the grassy hill, and though a short walk, it made for a steep trek that winded everyone. Even long-legged

Patrick had a tough time of it in his heavy armor. But the stones evoked fascination, making the effort worth it. Once recovered, the children started chasing a dragonfly among the stones.

Aimeé gasped. "What a marvelous view," she exclaimed, taking in the vista. "You can almost see the ocean from here, and Greensprings, too."

"The island is much bigger than I thought," Katherina added. "You can't see the far side from here."

"I've seen few ring-stones so grand," Patrick added.

"Is that a sacrificial altar?" Katherina asked, approaching a waist-high block of stone. Weather and time had rounded and smoothed its edges.

"An altar, certainly," Patrick replied. "Whether used for sacrifice, human or otherwise, I couldn't say."

"Places like these are from your people, your ancestors, yes?" Aimeé asked. "Who or what did they worship?"

"You'd have to ask my mother if you see her again."

Aimeé smiled sadly, toying with the cross on her chest. "I hope to see your mother again."

The memory of her made Patrick sad. He cast a guarded glance at Lilliana who walked ahead of them. He began to answer Aimeé, but a pain stabbed him behind his eyes. Not again. He pinched the bridge of his nose and squeezed his eyes shut, afraid to open them again. He feared to see Aimeé covered in blood. He feared to see the Other. Cries echoed in his mind.

"Patrick, please do something," she pleaded. It wasn't until her voice broke through that he realized the cries weren't just inside his head.

He opened his eyes and saw her gesturing towards little Stuart sitting in the grass, wailing. Patrick grumbled and approached the boy. He was maybe six years of age.

"Did you fall? Are you hurt?"

Only wails answered him, which magnified the pain in Patrick's head. He gritted his teeth as he became conscious of the others watching.

Brobrosius approached, red-faced and catching his breath from chasing the dragonfly.

"Is he in any pain? Should we do something?" Patrick asked.

"No pain," Brobrosius explained, "he's just upset he can't keep up with the older children. His legs are short and can't run so fast."

Patrick chewed his lip, studied the boy a bit longer, then asked, "How do we make him stop?"

"Talk to him, I suppose. Cheer him up." Brobrosius shrugged.

"I was afraid you might say that." Patrick placed his hands on his hips.

Brobrosius took the initiative and addressed the crying boy.

Placing his hands on his hips he announced loudly, "Guess what, Stuart?" He then gestured to himself with his thumbs. "*You're* taller than *me!*"

Stuart stopped and looked up with his chubby face. His dark eyes blinked, then scrunched up into a smile. His cries turned to giggles.

"Not so hard, see?" Brobrosius said to the knight.

Patrick had to admit Brobrosius both surprised and impressed him.

"That wasn't easy for you, though, was it?" Patrick asked. "Allowing someone else to be taller than you, just to make them happy. You care very much for your friends, don't you?"

Brobrosius flashed his usual big-toothed grin.

"I'm still taller than you," he pointed out.

"I'm not so sure about that," Patrick returned with a smile, "but you just might be the better man."

Patrick noted Aimeé still stood by with arms crossed, watching him.

"Stuart?" Patrick turned to the boy, an idea forming. "How would you like to run faster than everyone else?"

Stuart's giggles stopped abruptly and his big eyes grew even bigger, staring at Patrick. He nodded vigorously.

Patrick bent over and lifted the child onto his shoulders, which brought squeals of delight.

"Ready?" Patrick asked, bouncing slightly.

Stuart grunted in the affirmative. Patrick spotted the bobbing dragonfly and took off at a run after it. The other candidati joined in the chase, darting through the stone circle. In his heavy chain mail Patrick didn't quite manage to keep his promise to run ahead of everyone, but Stuart didn't seem to notice. He laughed and laughed.

Just before Patrick's stamina wore out, he tripped on a tuft of grass and stumbled a few steps. Patrick sat down hard, and joined Stuart in his laughter. The sound echoed off the stones.

"Did you hear that?" Katherina asked, then turned to the candidati. "Children! Come here, please."

They obeyed and approached as she leaned against the altar stone.

"Hush now for a moment," she said, then belted out several notes.

They echoed among the stones, magnifying in intensity. Pleased with the results, she improvised a hymn. The echoing stones created a natural harmony, making it sound as if two or three voices sang.

When she finished, the children clapped with glee. Chansonne's normally impassive face regarded the princess with wide-eyed wonder.

"It's like a cathedral," Katherina said, "designed for singing."

"Much truth in that, I think," Patrick said, brushing himself off. "It's a place of worship, a sort of church. Though I believe the echo effect was for drums, if I'm not mistaken. The magnification was to communicate better with the Otherworld."

"I imagine even Emilie's voice could be heard without a problem here," Katherina suggested, eyeing the girl. "Would you care to try? I know your voice is beautiful. It just needs a little help."

Emilie timidly came forward.

"Now, listen to me, then repeat it," Katherina said, smiling. "Pretend you're casting your voice out against the stones as if throwing a pebble."

Katherina sang a note, and urged Emilie to do the same.

The round-faced girl squeaked out the note, physically projecting her body as if ejecting a pebble from her throat.

Katherina suppressed a smile. "Very good! Now, turn that pebble into a rock, then into a boulder!"

Katherina sang a series of escalating notes.

Emilie did the same, and as each note echoed louder among the stones, her eyes grew larger as did her confidence. Soon she sang the entire song Katherina had tried teaching them the day before.

"Excellent!" Katherina cried when finished.

The candidati clapped again in glee and Emilie grunted with wide-eyed joy.

"Does it work as well for music, I wonder?" Aimeé inquired at Katherina.

"I imagine so," she replied.

Aimeé held the little cross/flute in her hand and looked at Patrick.

Patrick almost raised a hand to stop her, but nodded his consent.

Aimeé smiled and put the little instrument to her lips. A shrill sound came, forming into a stumbling melody. It did echo among the stone like the singing, but rather than magnify into a symphony, it turned into a discordant clanging of dropped metal instruments. The children put their hands to their ears, the adults grimaced, and this time Patrick did rub his temple.

"Oh, bother!" Aimeé said, lowering the flute in disappointment.

"You're getting better," Patrick said through a strained smile.

Aimeé scowled at him. "Perhaps I'd do better if I weren't distracted by a pickle craving."

"Pickles?" Geoffrey said, grimacing.

Aimeé scowled at Geoffrey and wandered away.

"She has cravings. It's a pregnancy thing..." Patrick began to explain, but stopped and narrowed his eyes at Geoffrey. "Why am I telling you this?"

"Oh!" Aimeé exclaimed, staggering back. A hummingbird with a shiny emerald breast and sun-yellow head buzzed in her face.

Next, a storm of dragonflies, hummingbirds, and thrushes flew through the stone ring, drawing a sharp breeze across the grass. They were gone in a blink.

"What was that all about?" Katherina said, watching the flock disappear over the ravine next to the hill.

"I guess they liked Aimeé's music." Patrick laughed, but stopped when he noticed Aimeé's blank stare. "Not funny?"

"It's just..." Aimeé blinked. "I thought, for just a moment, there was a little person riding the back of the bird."

Patrick took a turn blinking and he gazed at the little flute in her hand.

"Well, this day is full of wonders, and just getting started," Katherina declared, drawing everyone's attention. "Now us womenfolk will go for a swim!" She held up the mystery bundle of cloth and motioned for the women to follow her.

Emilie mumbled something in protest.

"Emilie doesn't want to go," Candace translated for her. "She says it is only for the pretty girls."

"Nonsense," Katherina insisted. "It's for all of us girls, regardless of what we look like."

Emilie's face screwed up into tears.

"Oh, no, no!" Katherina said in a panic, coming forward to embrace the girl. "That is not what I meant at all!"

Emilie ran from Katherina, hid behind Candace, and could not be convinced to go swimming.

"I better stay with her," Candace said as she held the sobbing girl. "Once she gets like this, she will cry for hours." And under her breath, "She's very sensitive about her appearance. Go on."

Katherina tried to protest, but Lilliana pulled her away. "One battle at a time. Wait until the storm has passed on that one."

Reluctantly, Katherina did as the elder woman suggested.

"You ladies sure you don't want me to come watch over you?" Geoffrey called after them, leering.

The four pairs of glittering daggers that glared back at him suggested his services would not be needed.

"You can, however," Patrick said, "cross the brook and guard them from the other side of the tree line. Patrol a zone."

"My pleasure," Geoffrey stated, and turned to leave.

"Take Candace and Emilie with you," Patrick added, crossing his arms.

Geoffrey frowned. "Why?"

"Because we need to share the guarding duties," Patrick explained, "and you're not leaving me alone with all the children so you can take a nap."

Geoffrey shrugged. "Very well. The more the merrier."

When they reached the bottom of the hill, Geoffrey mounted his chestnut destrier. The horse had a flowing white mane that prompted many people to comment that it was "almost as pretty as Sir Geoffrey." Patrick lifted the children onto the saddle.

"Whistle when the ladies return from their swim," Geoffrey said. "I'll return then."

Patrick nodded, and waved goodbye to Candace and Emilie.

#

On the opposite side of the brook, another swath of green grass separated the wooded ravine and the harvested fields. This grass, however, had not been grazed down by sheep, and its long blades rippled in the breeze.

"This should do. Now off you go," Geoffrey said, letting the children down.

He dismounted, removed his sword belt, and lay down in the grass, letting his horse roam freely.

"Aren't you supposed to 'patrol a zone' or something?" Candace said, standing over the prone knight with a scowl.

"That is precisely what I'm doing," Geoffrey said simply with a smile, eyes closed.

"Doesn't look that way to me," Candace said, sitting beside him. Emilie flopped down next to her and buried her face against Candace's shoulder, still sobbing.

"Au contraire, *ma cherie*," Geoffrey responded. "The 'zone' is not that large. I can see it quite well from this central position and will act accordingly if need arises."

"But your eyes are closed. You can't see anything," Candace returned.

"I can hear just fine, and so can Samson there."

"Samson?"

"My horse. He is very capable. Have you not noticed he is free to leave, yet faithfully stays near?" Geoffrey's voice became irritated. After a moment he sat up. "I could hear much better, though, if she would stop with that damnable sobbing."

The girl's sobs had turned to hiccups.

"She is sensitive to what people think of her," Candace explained.

Geoffrey scoffed. "I don't give one fart in the wind what people think of me, nor should she."

"That is not true," Candace replied distantly, looking off into the distance as she rocked gently back and forth with Emilie. The gesture slowly soothed the girl to quietness. "You care very much what people think of you. It's why you act so arrogant. You're trying to make up for how you feel on the inside."

"Pardon me?" Geoffrey said, scowling at the girl. "I am no such way. If other people confuse my confidence for arrogance, then that says more about them than about myself, I would think."

Candace's eyes glazed over even more as her rocking became rhythmic.

"You're hurting inside," she said quietly. "For a very long time now. Your father was an angry man, and your mother liked her drink too much. He used to hit her in front of you when you were little."

Geoffrey's eyes widened.

"You were so little and helpless to do anything. Your father was a big man, a powerful man, respected by all. You wanted to be just like him, but he hurt your mom."

"Now listen here!" Geoffrey tried to growl, but it came out more like a mewling calf. "You stop this nonsense immediately!"

Candace flinched some, but continued with her sibylline discourse.

"Your father would tell you it was necessary and she deserved it, and to make matters worse, her drinking and behavior made you think he was right."

Geoffrey rose to his knees and shook the girl by the shoulders. Emilie got scared and let out a screaming cry.

"I said stop! Do you hear me?" he cried, tears blurring his eyes. His hand was gripped around a brooch on Candace's cloak, and the pin sank into his palm.

"You've been hurting ever since," she continued. "You hurt so much on the inside and are... conflicted. You loved your mother so much. Now, you don't know how to act like a proper man, or how to treat women. You make up for it by acting tougher, cleverer than others."

Geoffrey threw her down, causing her and Emilie to fall as one. Yet the revelation seemed to sap the knight of strength, and he sagged onto his knees.

"Shut up! Shut up! Shut up!" His demands turned to requests, then to pleading.

"It's not your fault," Candace said after a pause. Her focus started to return, and she sat up. "You were so little. There was nothing you could do."

Geoffrey slumped to one side, his own eyes glazing over.

"It wasn't your father's fault, either. His father hurt him, too. He loved you very much, and so did your mother. They just had a very difficult time showing it."

A long pause followed, filled only by a breeze whispering through the grass.

"I ran away from home. I abandoned her," Geoffrey said quietly. "There isn't a day that goes by I don't regret that." Then after a long pause, he added, "I've never told anyone that." His look implored her to keep it a secret.

"It wasn't your fault. She made her choices too," Candace said gently. "It wasn't your fault."

Geoffrey felt something tugging at his hand and he looked down to see Emilie pulling it toward her. The brooch had left a long jagged cut on his hand and she bent forward to kiss it.

When her lips left his skin, only smooth skin remained. The wound was healed.

#

During her time on Avalon, Aimeé had never visited this swimming hole. Now that she did, she saw it was lovely; a pool with a rocky shelf, surrounded by overhanging ancient oak trees draped with bright green moss. The pool itself was roughly round, just large enough for proper swimming. A gurgling brook coming from the left fed the pool, feeding first into a mossy punch bowl before spilling into the larger body of water. A slow current rippled over a gravel bank before coalescing into a ribbon of water that wound into the forest.

"Very nice," Katherina said, surveying the area. She dropped the bundle on the rock. "Well, let's not waste any time shall we?" she said, kicking off her slippers.

"I haven't done this in such a long time!" Lilliana said, laughing and kicking off her slippers.

Katherina turned her back to the older woman for help with her dress strings, and then returned the favor when her dress started to slip from her shoulders.

Aimeé bent to do likewise for Chansonne, but the little girl shook her head and moved to where the shelf met the path to play at stacking rocks.

"Well, we anticipated that," Katherina whispered to Aimeé as she started to unlace the maidservant's corset and dress strings. "All in good time. Come to the water with us for now."

Once Katherina reached a point in Aimeé's unlacing that the French girl could manage herself, she approached the water's edge and dipped in a toe.

"It's perfect," she announced.

With that, she let her white gown slip from her shoulders and slid into the water.

"Oh, my eyes!" Lilliana exclaimed melodramatically next to her, shielding her eyes. "Surely sunlight never reflected so whitely off a bank of Ukranian snow!"

Katherina giggled and reached for Aimeé. "Come on then, don't be shy."

Even before her belly had started to show her pregnancy, Aimeé had already been conscientious of her form, especially beside Lady Katherina. Now, Aimeé's discomfort became all the more palpable as Katherina stood before her in all her lithe, naked grace. Minstrels sang ballads about princesses like her. And Lady Lilliana, who walked like a lioness, made her feel no better. With every step toward the water, and she exuded a supreme confidence in her nakedness, as if it were her natural state.

Aimeé ran her calloused hands over her belly and considered staying with Chansonne on the water's edge, making mud pies. Katherina had other plans and called to her, reminding her she had agreed to help.

As the noblewomen jumped into the water with squeals, she let her corset and dress drop to her big ankles.

She, too, jumped in—plunging into the clear coolness before the women could resurface.

"My, what fun this is!" Katherina said loudly, coming up for air. She directed it at Chansonne, who was at play on the shore. The child did not look her way.

"Yes, how wonderful the water is!" Lilliana added.

Still no response.

Lilliana nudged Aimeé, encouraging her.

"It is splendid," Aimeé said, unconvincing at first, but then added with more conviction, "I'm so glad I did not miss this! It feels so good!"

Chansonne looked over with only mild curiosity, then returned to making mud pies, most of which splattered over her dress and body more than anything.

Katherina's lips formed into a determined line. "Time to raise the stakes."

With her feet just barely touching the bottom of the pool, she swam-hopped back to the shore and undid the bundle she had brought. She removed a white palm-sized item and rejoined the women.

Katherina rubbed the white object against Lilliana's collarbone, creating a foamy lather. Once a sufficient amount covered the woman's chest, she turned to Aimeé with the bar of soap and did likewise, then lathered herself up.

At the sound of coordinated shrieks of delight, Chansonne looked over to see the trio of women gleefully splashing in the water, rubbing suds on each other, and chasing chromatic bubbles in the air. The bubbles finally won her full attention.

She dropped her current batch of mud and came to the water's edge, swiping at the colorful globes. They teased her, floating just out of reach. Though she did not form words, her excited eyes spoke volumes.

When the bubbles winked out of existence against the water's surface, she jumped up and down in frustration.

Lilliana blew a handful of suds in the opposite direction, further out into the pool, creating more bubbles bobbing in the air.

"Come on," Katherina urged, waving her forward. "Jump in. The water is wonderful, and we won't let you drown. The bubbles are waiting for you."

Chansonne paced on the shore like a caged animal. Aimeé came forward and offered her hand. The girl eyed it skeptically at first, but then took it. Aimeé guided her into the water; dress, doll, and all. Clutching tightly to the French woman's arm, her eyes grew wide and her grunts more frantic as the pool grew deeper toward the center. Her feet kicked out, but Aimeé cooed to her, promising safety and bubbles. By the time the trio of water nymphs encircled her, the rabbit's heart in her chest had calmed and her attention turned to the soap.

The women took turns while one would blow bubbles, and then the other two would lather and massage the child with suds. Chansonne's smile grew from ear to ear.

"Thank you, Sweetie," Katherina said. "Do you mind if we do the same for your doll?"

Chansonne smiled her approval and rubbed suds on the doll, too.

Aimeé gasped as she held up a filthy strip of cloth.

"*Mon dieu,*" she said, eyes wide. "Her dress has just plain fallen apart."

"I suspected it might," Katherina said without concern. "You needn't worry. All a part of the plan."

Fortunately, the doll fared better and survived the cleaning.

Chansonne, now as naked as the women, didn't seem to mind one bit. She jumped through the water, chasing bubbles and splash-fighting with a giant smile.

Next Katherina managed to wash Chansonne's hair, revealing a head of golden silk. "What a treasure you've been hiding," she breathed, tilting her head to one side as she inspected the girl's mane.

Chansonne had a surprise of her own when she reached up and worked her hands in Aimeé's hair. She wove the strands into a delicate, complex plait.

"Ah," Katherina exclaimed, "she can braid, I see."

Aimeé returned the favor and when finished, Chansonne and she could have been sisters with shoulder-length golden plaits. Aimeé stood straighter, took a step back and admired her handiwork in Chansonne's hair.

Katherina's eyes came to rest on Aimeé's midriff. "Why, Aimeé!" Katherina exclaimed. "You're showing. I hadn't noticed. You look so beautiful!"

Aimeé's body glistened with moisture in the sunlight. Aside from a peppering of freckles and moles, her skin glowed just as young and vibrant as any other woman present, but with honey tones.

"Pardon?" Aimeé asked, covering her belly.

"Yes, it suits you," Katherina continued. "You are absolutely glowing."

She took Aimeé's hands and spread them to expose her stomach. The maidservant awkwardly let Katherina give her a good looking-over.

"Yes, very beautiful," Katherina declared, "and I'm extremely jealous of your breasts."

"Wha—?"

"Durable, I'm sure they are," Katherina explained. "I'm certain when my time comes to have children, my breasts will require yards of cloth to keep them from sagging. I'll look like my mother. You, on the other hand, have the sort of breasts that defy age, no matter how many children you have. I'm very jealous."

Aimeé smiled meekly at the unexpected confession.

"Speaking of children," Lilliana said, rising from the water like Venus ascending from the ocean. "I mean no disrespect—quite the contrary really—but I'm surprised you chose to keep the child, considering the circumstances. You could have privately done away with it, like so many women do."

"There was no choice in my mind, really," Aimeé said, protectively covering her belly again. "Even if I knew for certain it was Geoffrey's, even despite the manner it came about, it is a child, and I intend on honoring it."

"That is courageous of you," Lilliana walked her way towards the women, the water splashing at waist level. "I've heard children born of trauma are often born... like them." She gestured with her chin in the direction of the path leading to the picnic site where the candidati wait.

"If it is God's will, I accept it." Aimeé shrugged. "Is that what happened to you, Lady Lilliana? Did there come a time when you had to 'do away' with a child, and the process left you barren? Despite your maturity, your stomach bears no markings. I can only assume you cannot have them."

"Aimeé..." Katherina cautioned, scandalized, though not necessarily angry, for she too had felt Lilliana's words were harsher than necessary.

"No, it is quite all right," Lilliana reassured them. She seemed impressed with Aimeé's boldness. "No, there were no herbal concoctions for me. It would appear it is a simple matter of God the Father seeing fit that I am not ever a mother."

"Did you even want children?" Aimeé asked.

A pause hung between the question and the answer where the corner of Lilliana's mouth twitched imperceptibly. The awkwardness was leaden, broken only by Chansonne's ripples in the water as she approached Aimeé. Lilliana's eyes followed the girl, and a strange look came over her face as if emotions warred inside, alternating between longing, anger, and pride.

"Certainly, but it's as you say—God's will."

"It's probably just as well," Aimeé said quickly, trying to fill the awkward silence. "You're quite beautiful as it is, and a baby might ruin that."

Lilliana's lip began to curl, but she tempered it. "Perhaps, but then I'll never experience your 'glow,' either."

"Oh my," Aimeé exclaimed as Chansonne reached up, grasped Aimeé's belly with both hands, and kissed it. The distraction broke the awkwardness, and all three women were relieved.

"Ah, how sweet," Katherina said, stroking the child's newly braided hair.

Chansonne gasped and pulled her hands away momentarily, just to put them back and look up with big blue eyes at Aimeé and Katherina, grunting excitedly.

"Yes, he does that," Aimeé said, also stroking Chansonne's hair.

"*Who* does *what?*" Katherina asked, confused.

"She felt the baby kick; he is quite lively already," Aimeé explained.

She took Katherina's hand and placed it on her belly.

Katherina and Chansonne moved their hands over her stomach like wizards scrying over a crystal ball.

"I felt it!" Katherina cried in wonder. "Lilly, come feel this!"

Lilliana hesitated, but at further urging she reluctantly came forward and extended a hand. But at the sight of her vein-covered hand and extremely sharp nails, Aimeé instinctively covered her stomach. Even Chansonne shied away.

"Oh, I'm very sorry, please... go ahead," Aimeé apologized, exposing her belly again.

"No," Lilliana said quietly, a hurt look in her eye slowly turning to disaffected coldness. "Perhaps another time."

An awkward silence hung in the air, filled only with the brook's murmur.

"We should be going," Katherina announced. "It will be getting late soon."

They splashed their way to the edge and climbed out. As they donned their clothes, Chansonne looked around, forgetting her dress had disintegrated in the pool. Katherina came forward with the bundle she had brought and shook out its contents.

"What do we have here?" she said, unfolding the white cloth garment.

Chansonne watched with mild curiosity. It was a white gown sized to fit the eight year old, in a color and fashion similar to Katherina's wardrobe.

"What do you think?" she asked, holding it up to Chansonne. "It's yours."

At first the girl eyed it, but then lifted her arms, allowing Katherina to pull it over her head and lace her up.

"My goodness," Aimeé whispered. "All this time, there was a truly beautiful girl underneath there."

She squirmed under their stares, not used to the attention. Rays of sunlight caught in her gold hair, creating a halo around her face. She had aquiline, regal features. Her eyes, washed of the grime that had given the impression of sleepless rings, now shone like captured bits of winter sky.

"Beautiful, yes," Katherina whispered back, "and someday, that kind of beauty is bound to break many hearts."

#

The next several hours passed uneventfully as Patrick waited for the women to return, but eventually he spied their heads bobbing up the trail. He took off a gauntlet, placed a couple fingers in his mouth and whistled to signal Geoffrey.

As the women approached the wagon, he did a double take, especially on the girl Chansonne who ran by him, now streaming white silk and golden tresses.

But then his attention snapped back to Aimeé. His jaw dropped. "Aimeé, I've never seen your hair like this before," he said, clearing his throat. "It suits you very well."

"Thank you, Sir Knight," Aimeé replied, smiling. "Have you been playing well with the children?"

"They're still alive, aren't they?"

Aimeé chuckled, but then looked around with a concerned expression. "Where are Candace and Emilie?"

Patrick motioned with his chin. "There, they return now."

Geoffrey pulled up Samson after arriving at a gentle gallop. Even before he came to a full stop, Aimeé turned to Patrick angrily.

"Are you mad!" she snapped, and rushed towards Candace and Emilie as Geoffrey let them down.

"What's wrong?" Patrick asked, puzzled.

"How could you leave them alone with him!" she growled over her shoulder. She hugged the girls and turned them away from Geoffrey.

Geoffrey, oddly quiet and subdued, looked wounded.

"Aimeé... I'd very much like to talk to you..." he said.

Aimeé didn't hear. She merely stabbed at him with her eyes and she marched the children away. As she passed, she shot Patrick a look no less unkind, stinging his heart.

Katherina joined him and placed a sympathetic hand on his forearm. "It seems we've accomplished just as much harm as good today."

Patrick followed her gaze to Lady Lilliana, who sat on the wagon with a sullen expression. Before he could inquire about what had darkened the woman's mood, Katherina patted his forearm again and said, "Two steps forward, one step back."

#

They arrived at the Hall for Lady Guests just as the sun set. Patrick and Geoffrey dismounted and helped the sleepy women descend from the wagon. Aimeé came last, and with his hands still on her waist, Patrick steadied her on the ground, keeping the wagon between them and Lilliana. He looked deeply into her eyes.

"I'm sorry about leaving the girls with Geoffrey," he whispered. "It was thoughtless of me."

Aimeé looked up into his face and accepted the apology with a curt nod.

His hands lingered on her hips. "When next we have the chance, I'll be happy to listen to your flute... and I'll bring all the pickles I can find."

Aimeé smiled and her hands squeezed his arms. Her green eyes stirred butterflies in his stomach and he found himself leaning towards her lips.

A scuffing noise to his right broke the moment. When he looked, his heart skipped a beat when at first he thought the Other stepped into the gate's torchlight, but then froze as the individual removed his hood.

"Sir Lucan," Patrick said as he and Aimeé clumsily disentangled from each other. "What brings you here this evening?"

"Good evening," he said impassively. His eyes clung to Aimeé. "I am to escort the Lady Lilliana back to the pavilions."

"That won't be necessary," Lilliana announced cheerfully from the far side of the wagon. "The Lady Katherina has graciously invited me to stay the night, and fulfilled my wish to sleep in a real bed. But thank you for your diligence."

"As you wish, my lady," Lucan replied, still studying Aimeé strangely.

"I best be going and help the others," she said, trying to sound normal, but her voice shook. "Goodnight, Sir Patrick. Thank you for your assistance today."

Patrick cleared his throat. "Of course, mademoiselle, good evening."

Not liking how Lucan's eyes followed her to the hall entrance, Patrick stepped in front of the man, arms crossed.

"You needn't worry," Lucan said. "Your secret is safe with me, but if you truly care for her, you'll let her go." His eyes shifted to Lilliana as she disappeared into the hall. "They only hurt you in the end."

#

When they had extinguished the candle and Mother Superior had bid them goodnight, Lilliana rolled towards Katherina on the bed.

"This is wonderful," she said. "A real mattress. Thank you, Kat."

"You're very welcome," Katherina said. "It's the least I can do. The day didn't seem to sit well with you, in the end."

Lilliana sniffed, rolling to her back. "I care not what a scullery maid thinks."

Despite the elder woman's pretenses, Katherina sensed smoldering anger. She also felt the emptiness in the bed when Lilliana rolled away. "I think you're beautiful whether you can have children or not."

Lilliana's imperious sniff turned to a strained scoff. "The nitwit of a French girl thinks I'm some freak, just because..."

Her voice caught short when Katherina fumbled in the darkness and found the bony roughness of one of Lilliana's hands.

"Shh," Katherina said, squeezing, "talk to me of something else. Tell me about your husbands and your adventures with them."

In the darkness, Katherina could hear Lilliana's lips part as if nonplussed. After a moment, Lilliana rolled back and strongly returned the squeeze. As strong as a man.

"Well, first came Clay. A beautiful man, but very gullible. He only wanted to tend his silly garden. His father did not approve of me, and so banished me from Clay and the garden. Then came Cain, a real man's man. Hair all over..."

As Lilliana's voice whispered into the night, Katherina snuggled closer, the fresh scent of soap on Lilliana's skin caressing her nose. For the first time in a long time, she felt comfortable.

#

The following morning, Lilliana heard voices as she approached the entrance to Cardinal Teodorico's pavilion, and judging by their repetition and the respectable distance the guards kept from the door flap, she knew what the cardinal was doing. Indeed, even before moving the flap aside, she could hear him spell out, "C-O-N-T..."

She entered just the same, and moved to a table and poured herself a flagon of wine. Then she settled herself on one of the couches near the cardinal's throne-like chaise.

"...R-O-L," Teodorico finished and took a deep breath.

"Now hold it," Sister Abigail said, standing before him. "Sit straight, expand your torso, and picture tossing a ball into the air. When in your mind's eye you see the ball start to come back to earth, slowly release your breath... good... and let it all out when you have pictured the ball resting in your hand again."

She emphasized with her hands as she gave instruction.

"C-O-N-T..." Teodorico began again.

"Good, slow, controlled," the nun encouraged.

"...R-O-L. CONTROL," the cardinal finished with conviction.

His smile indicated he felt quite pleased with his progress.

"Now, close your eyes and imagine the ball going gently into the air. Draw in a breath as it climbs upward. As it stops momentarily at its height, begin to release your breath slowly, and finish exhaling as it lands back in your hand. Good." Sister Abigail, too, seemed pleased with the cardinal's performance.

"Control," Teodorico said evenly, and with a smile as he opened his eyes.

"Very good!" The nun clapped her hands.

"Thank you, Sister," Teodorico responded, without the slightest hint of a stutter. "Your skills have been a tremendous asset during these negotiations. Indeed, they have been a tremendous asset to my career. Without your guidance, I'd be nothing more than a stammering fool."

"Now you're just a fool," Lilliana laughed, rising from the couch and coming forward.

"Now, now. Let that be our secret," he laughed with her, taking the cup from her hand and taking a drink.

Lilliana leaned forward and kissed his cheek.

"Your career is due solely to your strength of will," Sister Abigail said. "Any lesser man would have let his disability hold him back. You, on the other hand, sought me out and humbled yourself before God, and He has seen fit to help you overcome your affliction."

The cardinal said, "You must give yourself some credit, too, Sister. You have transformed my life, as well as the lives of many others who suffer from a number of maladies for which society would have condemned them."

"And you have made that work possible," Abigail returned. "Your contributions to Saint Peter's Orphanage and our work there have been invaluable."

"Greensprings. Saint Peter's. I do my best to carry out Christ's lessons. Or, perhaps it's just that I know what it means to be a misfit," Teodorico said, then added, "Would you care for a drink, Sister?"

"No, thank you, Your Eminence," Abigail replied, "but may I be candid about something?"

"Of course," Teodorico said, blinking at the sudden change in tone.

Sister Abigail wrung her hands, obviously struggling for right words.

"It's the children," she said at last. "Taking them out of their accustomed environment and transporting them vast distances alone has been stressful. They are disoriented and agitated. Despite that, they still have discerned what your intentions are for them. They may come across as simpletons, and in a sense they are, but even they know what you have planned for them and it weighs heavily."

The muscle in Teodorico's jaw moved visibly and a tinge of red rose in his cheeks. Rather than make eye contact with the nun as she spoke, he turned his attention to the trunk next to his chair and ran his finger across the gold filigree designs. He then cracked the lid and began to move it up and down with an annoying squeaking sound.

"The stress of all this has caused the children's afflictions to become pronounced," she continued, despite the distraction, "and under any more stress, they could truly become unstable. Especially with Chansonne. You know perfectly well what she is capable of. Such passions race around the cup as it is. It can only become worse if the children become involved. Who knows what would happen. I must protest their involvement. For their sake, and everyone else's."

"Is that why you moved them to the keep?" the cardinal said coldly, lifting the trunk's lid completely to reveal an empty space. He let the lid drop with a loud bang and turned his attention back to the nun. "So they could be 'safe' from me and my villainous influence?"

He said this last part with a smile, but it shown strained and contrived.

"I moved them into the keep so they could be closer to the chanteuse Katherina as you suggested," Sister Abigail responded, back stiffening, "and so I could have some help managing them in their agitated state."

"But of course," Teodorico said with just a hint of flippancy.

"Not that I'm not appreciative of what you have done for us," she added, "and not that I don't believe in what you're trying to accomplish—it's just that I don't think you need the children to do it. By pushing them, the results could be... tragic."

Victor entered the pavilion.

"Duly noted, Sister," Teodorico replied coolly. "Perhaps you're right and we won't need them, but I like to have options. Now, if you'll excuse us, we have some business to discuss. Go in peace."

He made the sign of the cross, and his tone suggested the matter closed.

Sister Abigail hesitated as if to muster courage to continue her argument, but decided to bow and leave.

"Is she going to be a problem, my love?" Lilliana asked when the nun had left.

"I sincerely hope not," Teodorico responded, frowning at the tent flap through which she had left, "because despite what I just told her, the children are our best chance for success. Victor, how stands the council on the matter of the cup?"

"Divided, with a compromise as the best solution to date," Victor replied. "With the cup presently untouchable, the suggestion made by the Merchant's Guild has gained traction: to divide logistical control for shuttling pilgrims—and the profits gained from such an activity—among the various factions on a rotating basis."

"And if the cup can suddenly be held?" Teodorico asked, taking a drink of wine.

Victor smiled. "Why, then I'd imagine the faction holding it takes ownership. Winner takes all."

"Excellent," Teodorico purred. He turned to Lilliana. "What is the status of the 'gift' from our good patron, the young King Henry? When will it arrive?"

Lilliana made a pouty face. "Not soon, I'm afraid. His Highness wanted certain 'favors'..." The tip of her tongue glided across her upper lip. "Only then will he lend the artifact to our cause. This delays its delivery, but it will arrive."

Teodorico grunted. "I'm amazed it is coming at all, thanks to your skills and his...'proclivities.'"

Lilliana laughed lightly.

"Even if we had the artifact today, are we certain Lucan will eventually have success holding the cup?" Victor asked, stroking his goatee. "It surprises me, of all people, he can't touch the cup now."

The cardinal grunted again. "I'm surprised as well, but with Henry's gift I believe he'll be able to do much more than perfume a room."

"Perhaps, but we do not have the artifact just yet," Victor pointed out, "and our stall tactics are wearing thin. We must do something soon."

"Agreed." Teodorico leaned back in his chair. "It's time to make a move. First a soft move, then a harder one later if necessary."

"The children?" Victor stated, smiling.

The cardinal nodded.

"What pretext shall we use to test them?" Lilliana asked, taking her cup back from the cardinal and finishing it off.

Teodorico remained silent for a moment, plots running through his mind, but he finally stated, "Those squires. Their knighting ceremony is fast approaching and they have requested Patrick to perform the ceremony. A special occasion calls for special events. We will have the children try then."

"And if they fail? What do we do with them?" Victor asked. "If they no long serve a purpose, then they still pose a liability, as Sister Abigail reminded us."

Teodorico pondered quietly again. "God allowed both Nero and Herod to slaughter thousands of children so destiny could be fulfilled. What's a few more?"

Chapter Eleven

Aimeé could not believe her eyes when she entered the great hall. The usually pleasant dining experience had become a mob scene. Twice the ordinary number of people crammed into the room for dinner, raising a din that could rival that of a battle. Just then, a stranger bumped into William of Monmouth while he reached across to rip off the last drumstick on a roasted duck. The stranger neither apologized nor offered an explanation.

She took a seat next to him. "These board folk are becoming insufferable," Willy confided in a whisper. "When are they ever going to leave?"

Trent grunted from across the table. "Soon, I hope. It seems the longer they stay the more they feel entitled to act as they please. Look at that duck—there's hardly anything left of it, and I've hardly eaten."

In the beginning, the Board of Benefactors, their ladies, and their innumerable servants stayed within their pavilion city, but as the weeks wore on and it became apparent the council debates over the cup would not end anytime soon, they began to filter into the keep for its comforts. They filled the dining hall to capacity, overflowed the privies, and made bolder and bolder demands of the staff.

"Come to join us for dinner, Aimeé?" Willy asked, changing the subject. "I thought you had become too good for us since working in the Hall for Lady Guests."

Aimeé smiled with a wink. "Never too good for you boys, but no, I didn't come to eat. I'm looking for Sir Patrick. I heard he might have something for me. Have you seen him?"

Willy and Trent looked to one another, shrugging. "Not since he's become drill-captain," Willy lamented. "Now *he's* become too good for us with all his new responsibilities."

"Aye, he's no fun anymore. Up at the crack of dawn, and goes to bed exhausted," Trent added. "He's already in bed tonight, I think."

Aimeé frowned, clouds darkening her mood. When she had heard someone had raided the store of pickles, she had assumed Patrick had finally made good on his promise. Disappointment and more cravings fought for her attention, but a disturbance from across the room drew her eye.

"More wine, wench!" one of the Cardinal Guard shouted from his table, hoisting a goblet into the air.

The offending off-duty guard, the Sergeant Dragonetti, looked no less threatening with his mail hood pulled back. If anything, he looked more brutish with his squashed nose and exposed hair, cropped to pig-hair length.

"We are not 'wenches,'" the nearest maidservant, Anna, explained patiently. "A 'wench's' duties involve the sort you will never see from us."

Dragonetti's eyes bulged in disbelief. He slurred, "Don't get saucy with me, wench. You're a servant, so act like one!"

"As are you," Anna scowled at the big man. "You are neither knight nor nobleman, but a hired hand... and a drunk one, at that."

Sensing trouble, Aimeé rose from Willy and Trent's table and went to Anna's aid. Before she could cross the floor, however, Sir Geoffrey intercepted her with a cloth-covered dish. Aimeé backed away as if confronted by a snake.

"Aimeé, please, I need to speak to you," he said with imploring eyes.

She side-stepped him like a pool of urine on the floor.

"Aye, a hired hand," Dragonetti was saying, wavering comically when he stood, "but a hand sufficient to smack you upside your insolent head."

He staggered forward to the sound of gasps in the room and Anna backed away, clutching the pitcher of wine to her chest.

Aimeé inserted herself between Anna and the guard. "That will be quite enough, Sergeant. If you would please take a seat, we will provide you with all the wine you will need."

At first agitated by the interloper, Dragonetti's scowl turned to a malicious smile. "Well, hello, pretty. I have a better idea. How about we take us some wine and have our own private party?"

He reached for Aimeé, but before he could make contact, a crimson-cloaked figure swooped in from one side, grabbing the belligerent Italian's arm.

"Sergeant, I think you've had a little too much to drink," Sir Geoffrey said sternly. He shoved the covered plate into Aimeé's hands, moving her aside in the process. "You can't possibly mean the things you're saying. I'm sure once you've gone for a walk your mind will clear and you'll be your good self again."

Dragonetti shook off Geoffrey's grasp. "Bugger off," he sneered. "I answer only to the cardinal, and to Sir Lucan if it pleases me."

"You're drunk," Geoffrey insisted. "Nothing good will come of this."

Dragonetti ripped the pitcher of wine away from Anna. He splashed fluid into his cup, and again as much onto his red and yellow surcoat. "There is so much good drink to be had here, and nothing else to do but drink."

"Nothing else to do?" Geoffrey frowned at the brute. "Last I heard, a monster is running about. Why don't you put yourself to good use and go hunt it down?"

"Hunt it down?" Dragonetti shouted, addressing the crowded dining hall. "There is no need. We all know exactly where the monster is."

He gestured with his wine cup towards the table of candidati, spilling more in the process. Some in the room murmured in agreement.

Dragonetti approached the candidati table and grabbed Emilie by the collar of her dress and pulled her up. She squealed in protest and began to wail horribly, disturbing the other candidati to wails in the process.

"I say it's this little ugly one," Dragonetti leered at the girl and made a show of dusting off his hands. "Always touching things, she is. She..."

Before he could finish, Geoffrey grabbed him and tossed him across the room, sending him crashing into a table of his fellow Cardinal Guards. Geoffrey stood between them and the candidati, gloved hands balled into fists, ready for action.

The candidati clung to one another, sobbing, as the cardinal's men struggled to set Dragonetti back onto his feet. When he achieved solid footing, he shook free of his companions and reached for his sword.

Geoffrey partially drew his and shouted, "Please, I beg you, give me sufficient cause!"

The other Cardinal Guard had started to reach for their weapons as well, but when every black surcoat with swan emblem rose in the room, they stood down.

"Listen up!" Geoffrey addressed the room that had fallen deathly quiet at the drama. "I have spent a great deal of time with these children, the candidati as they are known, and I can tell you they are no monsters. Different from you and me, certainly, but not foul creatures. All harassment of them will end now!"

He leveled a serious gaze about the room, eyes coming to rest on the worst perpetrators.

"Or you will have to deal with me. Is that understood?"

The room murmured, and the disgruntled Cardinal Guard filed out the door, casting angry looks over their shoulders.

All the children save Emilie calmed. She continued to sob in Candace's arms.

"What's wrong with her?" Geoffrey glowered, still hot under the collar.

"He called her ugly," Candace said. "It would have been better if he had just called her a monster."

"Ah, bloody hell," Geoffrey rolled his eyes. He kneeled on the floor next to the child on her bench and grabbed her by the shoulders. "Look at me," he said, making a stabbing gesture at his eyes with a pair of fingers for emphasis. "You're not ugly, you hear me? There are all kinds of beautiful in the world and you're one kind, see? By that reckoning you're the most beautiful girl in all the world, no questions asked." Geoffrey stood and announced the next loudly to the room, gripping his sword again. "And if anyone has a problem with that, they can talk to me."

Emilie's sobbing transformed to giggling.

"You won't hurt anyone just because they call me ugly," she said.

"Like hell I won't," Geoffrey insisted, scowling.

"You won't kill anyone, though," Emilie laughed.

"Well, perhaps not," Geoffrey conceded, but addressed the room again loudly, "but I'll certainly pull some ears!"

This elicited more giggles from the girl.

Aimeé stood by throughout the episode, brow creased with conflicting emotions.

Sister Abigail arrived just about when the room started to settle down. Even when the nun gathered the children to take them to bed, Aimeé still found herself frozen, especially when Emilie and Candace each clung to one of Geoffrey's hands, and he helped lead them from the hall.

After they had left and Aimeé had shaken her head to clear her mind, she realized for the first time she still held the plate Geoffrey had shoved in her hands. Curious, she removed the cloth.

A pile of pickles stared back her.

#

Despite an evening nap, Patrick still found himself yawning during his shift of night watch. His was indoors, on the mezzanine above the great hall and out of public view, so at least he did not have to stand at rigid attention. He could relax while monitoring the floor below for monsters.

Unfortunately, the late quiet hours offered too much time for reflection. His mind drifted to dark places in just the sort of manner Corbin had recently chastised him for.

Soft footsteps made their way up the stairs toward his position. By their sound, Patrick could tell even in the darkness they belonged to a woman, so it came as no surprise when a woman leaned against the pillar opposite him.

"Smile," Katherina said to his gloomy countenance.

"I am." He glowered, not quite able to stifle his surprise at which particular woman was paying him a visit.

Katherina's breath of a laugh echoed in the empty chamber. In the low light, Patrick could just make out her smile crinkling the skin around her beautiful icy eyes. They almost luminesced in the darkness. In fact, in her white gown she could have been a ghost come to visit him. A lovely ghost of lovers past.

"If that is what passes for a smile, I fear your frown."

"You've seen my frowns and my smiles. You've seen it all," Patrick replied, a real, but tired, smile creasing the corner of his lips. "This shouldn't surprise you."

"It surprises me now," she said. "Recently, you were a changed man. You were no longer 'Sir Silence.' Now, you have slipped into your old ways. Why is that?"

"The burden of leadership, perhaps," Patrick said, shrugging. "Much more is expected of me these days. And I feel responsible for all Greensprings's troubles because I brought the cup here."

"I sympathize about the responsibilities," Katherina replied. "I did not expect to be in the position I am now, doing the things I am doing..."

"You are doing very well," Patrick interjected. "What you did at the Shrugging Giants, that was nothing short of miraculous. Even Sister Abigail says she has not seen the children open up so much."

"Thank you," Katherina said, smiling, "but do not change the subject. When you left Greensprings for your home, you were a hero with a beautiful future bride. Now, look at you. No, it is not the burden of leadership or even the cup that troubles you so much. It is something else. What happened?"

Patrick rubbed at the thin scar running the length of his palm. "It's like an old wound opened inside me and bleeds, but I can't find where, and I can't stop the bleeding. Aimeé says I don't try hard enough. She seems to find fault with everything lately. She hates me... and it hurts."

Katherina came closer, leaning against the rail next to him.

"She does not hate you. Have you told her you love her?" she asked.

He had no trouble making out her face now. She looked up at him earnestly.

"Well, not in so many words, but why should I? Why must we play games?"

"There's your problem," she said. "Just tell her, and all will be better, I promise."

"I don't believe you," Patrick scowled, consternation rising in his voice. "It seems once upon a time I told another person I loved her and she threw it back in my face. *That* didn't go so well."

Katherina placed her hands on his chest, her eyes drilling into him. "That's because it was painfully obvious you didn't love me." And louder, when he tried to protest, "There is a difference between love and... excessive fascination."

Patrick took a deep breath, closed his eyes, and let it out slowly.

"You are quite right," he conceded, relaxing and taking her hands in his. "I know that now, and I won't argue it. I was a bit... obsessive."

"A bit?" She laughed, though not maliciously. She let him knead her fingers.

"Very well, perhaps a bit more than a bit," he replied, and they both laughed.

"Patrick, please don't let our experience ruin it for you two. Tell her how you feel."

"Maybe I shouldn't," Patrick said, swallowing hard and looking askance. "Maybe I don't love her. If I did, wouldn't I rush to admit it? Perhaps I'm doing her a favor by keeping my distance."

"You are not," Katherina persisted. "Just say the words."

"That's just it." Patrick's frown deepened. "What is love, after all? I thought I loved you, but that turned out to be an obsession. I love my comrades, but that is a different kind of love. Am I even capable of real romantic love? Am I such a bad person that I can't?"

"You are not a bad person," Katherina replied. "You will never know if you can love unless you try."

"I'm afraid." Patrick shook his head. "She has been treated so badly in the past, and no less by me, that if I told her I loved her and it turns out I was wrong... It just wouldn't be fair."

"Well, I've told you everything I know," Katherina breathed out, not so much in exasperation, but in mutual frustration. "Love is a complicated matter."

Patrick blinked, returning from deep thoughts. "Why did you come here tonight to talk about this, all of a sudden?"

Katherina shrugged with a mischievous smile. "Let's just say someone recently reminded me of the importance of companionship."

"Jon?" Patrick said incredulously, smiling wryly.

"Stop changing the subject," Katherina replied, mischievous smile turning enigmatic, then added, "You have a good thing with Aimeé. I wouldn't let her get away."

Patrick's smile wavered. "I'm not sure who I'm having more of a difficulty convincing: her or myself."

"You are having a baby," Katherina replied. "That should motivate you."

Patrick sighed, not for the first time that day. "It shouldn't matter whether it's mine, right? Again, if I truly loved her, I would do the courageous thing and accept it as my own, regardless. Yet I tried, and she didn't believe me."

"Perhaps you will yet," she said, running her fingers along the scar on his hand. "You are not a bad person, Sir Patrick. When I find love someday, I hope that person has many of your qualities. I will not settle for less. For now, I am content to wait, and I am happy for both of you."

"Thank you, Lady Katherina," Patrick said, stroking her hair out of her eyes.

They lingered there for a moment, sharing a gaze. Patrick hovered over her while her hands, resting now on his chest, rose and fell with his every breath.

When she leaned forward to inhale deeply, he leaned forward as well. Her mouth fell open slightly, and his lips came to rest on her forehead.

"It is getting late," he whispered.

She smiled. "Of course it is. I should be going. Goodnight, Sir Patrick."

"Goodnight, Lady Katherina," he returned.

She pulled away, letting her hand trail across the front of his surcoat as she departed.

#

When relieved of his guard duty later that evening, he made his way across the great hall towards the exit. When doing so, a brief heavy breeze moved his hair across his scalp. He looked up to see what could have possibly caused the breeze, but only saw the chandeliers swaying.

#

Before the midnight hour, Patrick performed his final duty of the day.

He attended on the squires Jakob, Josef, and Charles as they prepared for their vigil. Their knighting ceremony was set for the following day.

"The white gown signifies your purity of mind, heart, and body," Patrick explained to the freshly scrubbed boys. The monks of Greensprings lowered the white garments over the squires. "You are freshly bathed, and confessed, and now commences your all-night fasting. You will keep vigil here in the church before the altar, praying until Mass starts tomorrow. After you receive communion, your dubbing will take place. Understood lads?"

The boys nodded solemnly.

"Very well then," Patrick said, looking them over, finding it hard to believe the trio of ruddy faces old enough for knighthood. "We'll see you soon."

The squires sank to their knees before the altar and cup. They held their unsheathed swords point-down before them so that the hilt and crossguard formed a cross. Watching them settle into this pose, Patrick's back and knees ached in sympathy as he recalled his own ceremony. He knew the position would become very, very taxing over the next many hours.

He left then, casting one final glance at the boys before withdrawing an object hidden in an alcove. He thrust this into his surcoat, exited the building, then bore right and followed the side of the church hidden from most people's view. There, he climbed one of the flying buttresses and clambered along the thin stone arch until he reached the roof.

Once on top, he paused near the stained glass that ran the length of the basilica. He looked in and could barely make out the shapes of people below gathered around the altar's candles. The thick glass made them appear warped and squiggly.

He moved away and found a familiar corner bathed in moonlight. He sat and took out the skin of wine he had secreted in his surcoat. As he drank in the moon and stars above with his eyes, he took deep pulls on the wine.

With an effort, he let anxiety drain out of him and he took a moment from moon-gazing to close his eyes and rest. Despite his efforts, everything just continued to churn and froth inside him.

A strong breeze swept across him, brushing the hair from his brow.

"May I join you?" a voice asked.

Shocked, Patrick stumbled to his feet and looked at the intruder with wide eyes.

"Lady Lilliana," he gasped. "How did you get up here?"

"Surely you don't think that only boys are capable of climbing trees and rocks?"

"You saw me come up then?" Patrick asked, biting his lip.

"Yes," she replied, coming forward and taking the skin of wine. She took a sip. "I believe this is how we first met; over a flask of wine."

"Aye," Patrick agreed.

"Is this your sanctuary? Above the sanctuary?" she asked, looking down through the stained glass. "I don't mean to intrude, but you looked as if you could use some company."

Patrick shrugged as he took the skin back and took a sip. Lilliana took a step forward, and when she did the moonlight struck her amber eyes in such a way they almost glowed yellow in the dark.

Patrick leaned back in surprise.

"What's wrong, Sir Knight?" she asked, reaching to take a turn at the flask.

"Your eyes—for a moment they seemed to move about the center," he said, squinting at her.

"A trick of the light," she explained, taking a drink. "It often happens in moonlight. I'm afraid it has been known to disturb people. My apologies."

"No need," Patrick said, retaking his seat against the wall. "They're quite beautiful. I have to admit they're the best part of my day."

"Ah, there you go again," she said, taking a seat beside him.

"What does that mean?"

"You tease and you flirt. Through brief poetry you make romantic gestures that go unfulfilled," she explained.

"I do no such thing," Patrick protested, taking a drink. The flask sloshed.

"You do," Lilliana argued. "How else should a woman take a compliment on her eyes, delivered in such a way?"

"I only meant to apologize for my reaction to them, by way of compliment," he clarified.

"Yes, without giving mind to how a woman hears such a compliment. You say the most intimate of things, innocently perhaps, but intimate just the same. When they are an obvious attempt to seduce, they can be laughed off. But when said innocently, they sound like truths—and teases."

"You certainly speak as a woman: confusing." Patrick frowned and took another drink.

"Then there is the touching," she added.

Patrick gagged on the wine, a good portion of which came out his nose.

"'Oh, hello, how are you?'" Lilliana said, deepening her voice in an imitation of his own. She also held up one hand and moved it like a talking sock puppet. "'My name is Sir Patrick. Let me stroke your hair or touch your wrist as I talk to you. Isn't that lovely?'"

She then reached up and petted his head with hard exaggerated strokes.

"I do not," Patrick said skeptically. "Do I?"

Lilliana laughed a deep throaty laugh and took the skin. She leaned heavily into him as she drank. "And you don't even know it! Which makes it charming."

Patrick propped his elbow on a raised knee and leaned his cheek on his fist.

"I suppose I should stop that," he grumbled.

"Oh, no you won't. And it will be even more amusing to watch your behavior now that you're aware of it." She was still laughing.

Patrick grumbled something not meant for her ears and yanked the flask away from her, which only elicited more hysterics.

"I like it," she admitted, leaning into him more. She looked up into his face. "Women like attention and affection, and physical contact is the most tangible of them. I like receiving it... and giving it."

To accentuate this, she stroked his cheek, whispering, "See how it feels to be on the receiving end?"

With his eyes closed, he turned to her and leaned his forehead against hers. He took a deep breath and inhaled the scent of perfume and red wine. He let his breath out in one long exhale, at the end of which he opened his eyes and met her amber gaze. His lust stirred beyond doubt, but his heart weighed heavily in his chest.

"I would kiss you," he said, "but it would be for all the wrong reasons. Recently I did much for the wrong reasons and made a mess of things. I will not do that to you."

"Perhaps you should do it for the right reasons," she said, tugging at his long dark tresses, "like because I want you to."

He shook his head slowly, adding an apologetic smile to his gaze.

"It's the maidservant, isn't it?" she said, disappointed, pulling away and leaning her head against the wall.

"Partly," Patrick confessed, "but she is certainly the most obvious of my errors, and by that I mean my treatment of her, not that I got her with child. Possibly got her with child. Maybe. Whatever."

He shook his head, frowning, trying to sort it out in his mind.

"Or is it Katherina?" Lilliana asked, turning her head back in his direction. "Would you rather be with her, but your honor prevents you because of the maidservant?"

Patrick ground his teeth back and forth, recalling his encounter with the princess. Somewhere, in the back of his heart, the suggestion enticed.

"You know, either way, the cardinal can help you with this matter," Lilliana added.

"Oh, how is that?" Patrick asked, out of nothing but idle curiosity.

"If it is the Lady Katherina you wish to have," Lilliana explained, "I'm sure she could be convinced to accept your hand in marriage in exchange for the cardinal's support in reclaiming her father's kingdom. First, you would have to use your influence as Knight of Cups to champion the cardinal's right to possess the cup, and then of course, travel Christendom extolling its powers."

Patrick scoffed. "I doubt Katherina would agree to such a thing."

"You never know until such an offer is made," Lilliana pointed out, "but if it is the maidservant you prefer, it would be a simple matter of the cardinal leaning on the girl to marry you. After all, it was the cardinal's original plan to marry you to the maidservant, then parade the two of you throughout Christendom as the Knight of Cups and the Lazarine Maid; living proof of the power of the cup. He reconsidered, however, when he discovered she was pregnant out of wedlock."

"And what would make him reconsider?" Patrick asked incredulous, shaking his head at the blatant politics of the matter.

"Everyone loves a story of redemption," Lilliana said, then elaborated in a storyteller's voice, complete with grand hand gestures. "It could be heralded as a story of two young lovers, a knight and a commoner, swept away by their passions that led to sin, until the power of the Cup of the Last Supper entered their lives and rescued them from death and damnation. After a proper confession, the two lovers wed to great fanfare, and they lived happily ever after. A fairy tale with universal appeal to commoners and nobility alike." She paused in the telling. "Actually, one might argue such a redemptive story is the preferable scenario, inspiring the masses to come forward and confess their own sins before the cup."

"Naturally with Cardinal Teodorico acting as confessor, building his image as a great redeemer, which would go a long way to solidifying his position as successor to the pope." Patrick wasn't sure she heard the wry note in his voice.

"Naturally," Lilliana replied, leaning in and kissing his cheek. "That will not work for me for one simple reason."

"Oh?"

"This plan is based on coercing a woman to marry me," he explained. "Especially Aimeé. I will not force anything from her. I want to marry for love, not for my selfish desires or because it is convenient or expedient. Who wants to spend the rest of their life in a purely contractual arrangement? I know that is necessary under many circumstances, but if I can have love, I will gladly wait for it."

"You are a fool," she said sadly, stroking his hair, "a beautiful, romantic fool."

"Perhaps so, but I've been spoiled by my mother and father's true love. That is what I wait for."

"Who's to say it won't come eventually in an arranged marriage?" Lilliana argued. "First comes obedience, then love. Even God demands obedience from those who love Him."

"True," Patrick admitted, "but it seems those who love God gladly give their obedience, not the other way around. And you, Lady Lilliana? You argue obedience and love, but don't seem to have much of either in your life, no offense."

"No offense taken, but I confess I am personally not a believer in either love or obedience," she said, frowning thoughtfully. "Such notions are best left for romantic fools such as yourself... no offense."

Patrick smiled. "None taken. Perhaps if you showed a little obedience, as you say, you might experience love. And then you'd understand my position."

She scowled. "What? Obedience to Teodorico or any number of halfwit husbands I've had in the past?"

"Well, to God for starters," Patrick clarified. "The rest would follow in due time."

Lilliana scoffed loudly. "I do not believe that."

"What do you believe in?"

Lilliana's demeanor changed as a smile bloomed across her face. She leaned her face into his, lips hovering over his so her warm breath caressed his skin in the cool night air. Her eyes answered his question. Patrick tensed under the gaze and the hands she pressed against his chest. She all but sat in his lap now, and surely felt his arousal.

He closed his eyes and sucked in a deep breath, holding it.

"What's wrong, Patrick?" she implored. "Do you not want pleasures of the here and now? There is no one to see, and your secret is safe with me. Am I not beautiful enough?"

"Yes, you are beautiful," he admitted. He let out his breath and opened his eyes. He grabbed her by the wrists and gently pushed her away. "You are proof that God exists. Someone as beautiful as you couldn't possibly be an accident. You were created as assuredly as a statue was crafted by a sculptor. You are poetry walking through this world."

A heavy silence hung in the air between them. Her eyes seemed to dim as she tried to reconcile the sincerity of the statement mixed with the rejection. Eventually, her alluring smile vanished.

"Don't speak to me of God when I am speaking of pleasure!" she hissed, grasping his throat with her claw-like fingers. Patrick froze. It seemed to him through the haze of wine and the tension of the moment that Lilliana's eyes flared yellow and her pupils expanded and contracted. He gave one long squeeze of his eyes to clear his vision. When they opened, she appeared to be just a woman again. A very angry woman.

"What does God know of pleasure?" she continued. "What does He know of a woman's needs? Her desires? His record with women throughout time has been less than admirable! He has consistently regulated women to second-rate creatures! He has condoned all manner of violence and injustices against them by men!"

"Not true," he managed to whisper. "God did not force Mary to bear His child. He asked her permission, and despite criticisms from the Jews who felt it unlawful, Jesus kept company with women. Even allowed a prostitute to bathe his feet with her tears."

Lilliana screamed as she suddenly released her grasp and rose to a standing position over him as if pulled there by a string. A blast of wind swirled their corner, stirring leaves, hair, and their garments.

"Is that supposed to make me feel better?" she cried, stabbing a finger at him. "That Jesus deigned to let a woman, forced into her profession by other men, wash his feet?"

Patrick grasped his throat, certain she had drawn blood, but his hand came back clean.

"Mary Magdalene?" Patrick coughed, continuing to rub his throat. "Who was it that came to her aid when she was about to be stoned? Who defended her? It was Jesus."

Lilliana paused in her seething, eyes narrowed.

"Yes, Jesus saved her," she acknowledged. "She was grateful and fell in love with Him for it, and how did He return that love? He showered her with chaste kisses and nothing else! Which reminds me of yet another man."

She glared at him.

"How could you know how the Magdalene felt?" Patrick asked, surprised by her ferocious sincerity.

"Because I was th—" she started to shout, but caught herself and instead growled. "Don't change the subject! You're a bad man, Patrick Gawain. You are the worst sort of man. The sort of man who makes women fall in love with him, and then denies them the fulfillment of that love. You are a fool!"

In the blink of an eye she turned on a heel and disappeared around the corner of the stained-glass dome.

Patrick rose to his feet and pursued her. Another blast of wind whipped his hair and surcoat.

"Lilliana, wait!" he shouted, but when he turned the corner she had disappeared. He ran to the edge of the building to catch her as she descended the flying buttress, but did not find her there, either.

He looked at the wineskin he still held and wondered at its potency.

#

The church bells tolled in the late morning, calling all to worship. More people than usual streamed into the basilica, as this Sunday's Mass promised an adoubement—a knighting ceremony—as well as the fact a cardinal from Rome would act as the presiding priest. People from Aesclinn abandoned the village church for a day to fill Greensprings's entire basilica floor as well as its upper balcony. When these filled, the faithful and the curious milled about the entrance and windows whose shutters were thrown wide for the occasion.

"You are certain our Irishman will not support our cause, hmm?" the cardinal asked Lilliana before Mass. He greeted parishioners as they filed through the entrance. His smile and his friendly gaze did not waver as he carried on the conversation with the beautiful woman at his side.

"No, he will not jump up and shout from the rooftops that you have the sole right to take the cup away from Avalon," Lilliana replied, also smiling and greeting the arrivals. "However, he will not interfere in your attempts to do so. He takes rather seriously his Christian and knightly sense of duty that you are God's representative on Earth, and therefore His will be done, however you choose to go about it."

"Well, at least we have that going for us, hmm?" Teodorico said. "Perhaps his example alone will be enough to help persuade people, hmm, yes? What do you think, my dearest? Lilly?"

Teodorico paused in his greeting to turn and determine what had caused his consort to fall silent. He watched her maintain a steady gaze upon the statue of the Madonna in the entrance as people flowed around it, on their way into the nave. Her eyes narrowed and her mouth twitched, turning to a scowl when her eyes fell upon the child held in the arms of the statue.

"Lilly, hmm?" Teodorico persisted.

"Sorry?" she said, shaking herself out of her reverie.

Teodorico tsked and touched her arm, "Never mind, my love. We mustn't be distracted, as we are so close to our prize. We must stay focused."

Teodorico missed the glare she shot him; he had turned to greet the Lady Katherina, who herded the candidati before her with the aid of the maidservant and Sister Abigail.

"Lady Katherina," he called to her, "please, let my man Victor escort you and your group to a place of honor."

Katherina paused, surprised at the consideration. She bowed slightly, and Victor stepped from the cardinal's side towards her. "Thank you, Your Eminence."

Victor led the group into the growing crowd. The church bells stopped ringing, and despite the ethereal choir music, it seemed as if the air had emptied suddenly.

"You really think this will work?" Lilliana whispered, eyes following the band of misfits.

"I believe it is very, very likely, hmm, yes?" he replied. "Let us now go find out."

He adjusted his white vestments. Father Hugh handed him his crozier and Fathers Wulfric and Herewinus lined up in front of him with candles atop tall holders.

Lilliana worked her way into the crowd, but paused again to stare at the statue.

#

Memories flooded her. First came those of lying face down on the ground with dust and blood filling her nostrils. Her face ached from a beating. Whimpers filled her ears from the other two women on the ground with her. She wished they would meet their end with more dignity, for none of them had done anything wrong. They had only danced with men other than their husbands. Nothing else involved or intended. Just danced.

Even though Lilliana knew she would survive the impending stoning, even if she had to pretend death, she knew her crying companions were the lucky ones. Their pain would end.

The excitement of the growing crowd reached new heights as the first stones flew. One struck Mary next to Lilliana. When the sickening thud cut off her cries, Lilliana at first thought it had knocked the pretty girl unconscious, but when she glanced over she saw a steely look on Mary's face even as blood ran down her forehead. Martha continued to wail.

Good, Mary, be strong.

The crowd suddenly went quiet.

When they dared to look up they saw the visiting holy man, the Nazarene. He wrote in the dust at the feet of the mob of angry men. He wrote women's names; the names of the men's mistresses.

"Let he who is without sin, cast the next stone," he said, voice quiet but cutting clearly across the square.

When the angry men finally left in disgust, the Nazarene left flowers before the three women on the ground.

The next memories flooding Lilliana replaced the smells of blood and dust with expensive perfume.

"Don't be a fool," she lectured Mary, tugging on the alabaster jar of ointment. "Don't waste your life savings on gifts for this man. He cares only for children and the birds!"

Mary pulled the jar back, her serene face momentarily agitated. "You only say that because he won't marry you and give you children of your own. His concerns are not of this world."

"Exactly!" Lilliana retorted. "First he says he loves you, then ignores you!"

"You're just jealous." Mary shook her head sadly, and stalked away through the market crowd.

Lilliana stood still, eyes following Mary, as she pondered how such a strong woman could be so naive.

"Tired, aren't you?" an icy voice said from a nearby darkened alley.

Lilliana looked to the shadows where a pale man was hunched over.

"What business is it of yours?" she said angrily, approaching the stranger, ready to cast a few stones of her own.

The man raised his head to reveal a beautiful face, but she froze when he opened his mouth to speak again, displaying a rotten ruin in the place of teeth. She covered her nose and mouth when the smell of death engulfed her.

"You've been ignored or pushed around for a long time now." His voice rattled like an icy breeze scattering bones littered on the ground. "How would you like to have the power to push back?"

#

Excitement filled the basilica, accompanying the tolling bells and the harmonized chanting of the clergy. It swirled above the heads of the growing crowd like a circulating flock of doves.

Katherina drank in the music with her ears, savoring the sounds she loved. She especially loved High Mass—this morning's special occasion—when all the prayers were songs.

When the children had proven difficult to rouse that morning, Katherina worried they would miss the chance for a good spot to hear the choir and view the knighting ceremony. Sure enough, they entered the church almost last, but Cardinal Teodorico's generous offer lifted her spirits.

She had no idea, however, just how generous the offer until Victor led them directly to the front of the congregation, right to the communion rail—a place normally reserved for the most important benefactors. Patrick already waited for them there. He exchanged greetings as she, the candidati, Aimeé, and Sister Abigail all pressed around him.

He and Aimeé kept their distance, though he did glance at her long enough to send her a pained look. When he looked away,

Aimeé did the same. Katherina felt a twinge of sadness for them both.

They stood so close to the sanctuary she could see the trails of sweat pouring down the faces of the poor squires who had been kneeling since last night. The altar loomed impressively, and every item on the long marble table stood out larger than life, especially the shimmering vessel that had caused so much controversy. It sat out of place, askew from the conventional objects of the Mass; candles, flowers, the Bible, a crucifix, wine, and bread wafers on an ornate platter.

Her eyes lingered on the cup. How odd that others could almost disregard this miraculous object—this assumed true Cup of the Last Supper—while a worldly imitation took its place underneath a cloth at the center of the marble.

Patrick glanced at Aimeé again, sadness darkening his face.

Katherina tugged on his surcoat. "I'm told you have an understanding of Latin and the Mass."

"Oh really," Patrick replied quietly, cocking an eyebrow. "Now how would you know that?"

"A little bird told me," Katherina said, smiling as she cast a glance at Aimeé.

Patrick's eyelids fluttered as if he struggled to keep from rolling his eyes, but he smiled. "I have some idea, yes."

"Can you explain to me all that happens?" she implored. "Though my language has improved this last year, I still feel I'm missing much. I want to understand all the differences between the Orthodox liturgy and Catholic Mass."

Again Patrick's eyelids fluttered. "I can do my best."

She smiled her thanks just as the bells stopped ringing and the choir quieted.

A hush fell over the murmuring crowd and people bunched up against them, signaling the entrance procession at the back of the church had begun.

The choir began anew as Father Hugh led the column, parting the crowd with a swinging thurible, sending up fragrant white smoke that chased away the musky odor of the pressed bodies. Fathers Herewinus and Wulfric followed, walking side-by-side carrying candles on tall holders. Lastly came Cardinal Teodorico, poised and erect, with the crowd closing behind him like the wake of a boat passing through water.

They arrived at the altar and Mass progressed normally. Katherina watched with a new fascination as Patrick whispered explanations and translated the Latin prayers though it garnered them the occasional hushing and disapproving looks from their neighbors. The beautifully complex ritual played out like a performance, with the cardinal at the center and the attending priests coming and going as needed like actors performing their parts. Periodically, the congregation played their parts as well, as if in a dance, by frequently standing, crossing themselves, and kneeling again. Katherina especially enjoyed it when they sang with the choir.

When the time came for the day's Bible readings, Teodorico stood before Greensprings's massive Bible on its lectern. Father Hugh turned the heavy pages for him as he read. Though he spoke in the common French used at Greensprings, his thick Italian accent, and occasional stutter, made it difficult for Katherina to understand. She nudged Patrick one more time and asked him to summarize.

"He's reading from the Book of Samuel," he explained, "about how King David coveted Bathsheba, the wife of one of his men and got her with child..." His brow crinkled and his description trailed off as he seemed to turn introspective. She nudged him again and he snapped back to attention "The baby became ill and died. The prophet Nathan told David it was because sin still has its price, even though David had repented..." Patrick trailed off again with a far away look in his eyes, muttering, "The baby died..."

Teodorico went into a long, animated sermon. An occasional grumble came from the crowd, making Katherina curious.

"Patrick!" she hissed. "What's he saying now?"

Patrick shook himself, listened, then frowned, this time a bit angrily. "I think he's making a connection between today's Bible reading and the council business with the cup—something about coveting that which belongs to God."

When finished, Teodorico moved to the altar and began the consecration portion of Mass, changing bread and wine into the body and blood of Jesus through prayer.

He faced east toward the rising sun, with his back to the crowd, as priests did in all churches. From behind, his frequent signing of the Holy Cross in the air above the altar and instruments of consecration gave the impression of a baker kneading dough. Ultimately, he held a piece of bread high, announcing, "*Hoc est enim corpus meum.*"

"For this is my body..." Patrick translated, but Katherina cut him off with an elbow to the ribs.

"I know this part," she said, leaning forward to have a better look at the transformed bread.

Teodorico held the body high for a long while. Though no one uttered a word at this moment, a rustle rippled through the basilica as one thousand people likewise leaned forward.

Teodorico set it down and reached for the miracle cup. His hand passed through it, and without so much as a pause, he moved to the imitator cup, picked it up with both hands, then went through the ritual again with the wine, converting it to the blood of Jesus.

Katherina tugged on Patrick's surcoat.

"Now I have a question," she whispered.

"Of course you do."

"Why did he try grabbing the miracle cup first?"

"Because in addition to being a revisitation of the sacrifice on the Cross, the Mass is a revisitation of the Last Supper, and ideally you'd want to use the cup from that event."

"Certainly, but if a priest can make any old wine in any old cup into the blood of Jesus," Katherina continued, chewing her lower lip, "then what is the fuss with the miracle cup?"

"Because even though Jesus' blood works miracles on our souls from inside us, the Cup of the Last Supper works miracles for all the world to see, which is a very powerful thing—especially for men with political ambitions."

He shook his head, whether at her exasperating questions or at the troubling reality of what he had just said, she did not know.

"Why can't the cardinal grab the miracle cup?" Katherina asked.

Patrick leaned in closer than usual to respond. "For the same reason none of us can."

"Which is?"

"That is the question many people would pay a wagon full of gold to find out. Perhaps God simply has a sense of humor."

When ready, Teodorico ate and drank a portion of the transformed bread and wine and shared it with the attending priests and the squires in the act of communion. Next, he cleansed the cup and platter with water and returned them to the altar underneath a cloth.

"Squires, if you would?" Teodorico said, and gestured to the floor at the foot of the dais.

The boys came forward and knelt again as Teodorico motioned for Patrick.

The choir went silent.

"Charles," Patrick said, approaching the tallest of the boys. Whether by accident or design, the lads had arranged themselves from tallest to shortest: Charles, Jakob, and Josef. Patrick spoke loud enough to reach the far reaches of the church. "Do you accept the responsibilities I'm about to administer?"

"I do," Charles said loudly, yet solemnly.

"Very well," Patrick replied. "Do you promise to live without fear of your enemies? To be brave and upright so that God may love thee? To speak always the truth, even though it may lead to your death? To safeguard the weak and helpless and to do no wrong? To defend all women? To be loyal to your lord? And above all, be devoted to the Church?"

Charles nodded curtly, stating, "I do!"

"That is your oath," Patrick said, and suddenly and violently slapped Charles across the face. His head snapped to one side, but otherwise he stood stock-still. "And that is so you do not forget it."

Patrick drew his sword, extending the blade to Charles' head.

"In the name of God, Saint Michael, and Saint George I give you the right to bear arms and to mete out justice," he said, touching the blade to each of Charles' shoulders every time he invoked one of the holy names. "I dub thee *Sir* Charles. Rise a knight."

Charles rose with a smile and a light in his eyes. Patrick moved to Jakob.

In rapid succession, he performed the same ritual on him and Josef. As the serving priests assisted the young men in donning surcoats with their family heraldry, Patrick affixed riding spurs to their heels.

When finished, the new knights turned to the people and a roar of approval filled the basilica. Patrick shook hands with the beaming men and returned to his spot. The knights returned to their former places as well. When the clamor had died down, all expected Cardinal Teodorico to start closing prayers.

Instead, he stated, "On this special occasion, I invite any who feel worthy to try and grasp the Cup of the Last Supper, starting with those most loved by God, the young afflicted by infirmities."

He gestured to Sister Abigail, who escorted the candidati.

"Did you know about this?" Patrick asked Katherina.

She shook her head, as surprised as anyone.

A murmur rose from the crowd and Fathers Hugh, Wulfric, and Herewinus scowled. Wulfric leaned towards Teodorico and muttered something, only to have the cardinal wave him off.

The nun aligned the children in single file and led them up the dais stairs to the altar. Teodorico greeted them and urged them to grasp the cup.

First Candace tried and failed, her hand passing through it. She shrugged. Next came Martin, who also failed and happily returned to his face-waving. Only Emilie and Stuart seemed disappointed at their subsequent failures, sulking near the altar.

"Teodorico!" a voice boomed from the balcony. Count Fulk, glowering among the Merchant's Guild members, leaned against the rail. "It's very obvious what you are attempting and I must say it's in poor taste!"

"Hear, hear!" another merchant said.

"Candidati, indeed!" another man cried scornfully. "We see now why you call them that. Candidates to hold the cup for you, because you cannot. Manipulating innocents! Poor taste indeed!"

"Gentlemen, hold thy tongues. You are disrupting the Holy Mass!" Teodorico called back to the balcony, taking several angry steps toward them.

"Except this is not a part of the Mass!" Fulk countered.

"I have not dismissed the congregation." Teodorico sniffed.

"A small detail that—" Fulk's voice caught in his throat and his gaze turned in shock toward the altar as a collective gasp went through the church.

Teodorico turned.

Chansonne held the cup, looking at it as if not sure what to do now.

"Don't let go!" the cardinal cried, lurching forward.

Chansonne balked at the sudden command and staggered back in a panic, trying to determine what she had done wrong. She looked again at the cup and quickly replaced it on the altar.

"No!" Teodorico shouted, hovering over her. "Take it back up!"

Chansonne backed away, more frightened than ever.

The cardinal railed at her violently. "I said take it again!"

Sister Abigail inserted herself between them, crying, "Stop it! You're frightening her!"

An outraged uproar came from the congregation. Katherina tensed and felt Patrick quivering with anger next to her. He crouched as if ready to pounce over the rail.

Seething, Teodorico collected his composure and addressed the crowd. Throughout the Mass his stutter had been almost non-existent, but now his voice shook as he said, "T-t-t-this Mass is ended, g-g-go in peace."

#

"How dare you question my authority like that, hmm?" Cardinal Teodorico shouted.

His peculiar speech impediment did not diminish the anger in his voice. His dark eyes bulged, his neck strained into cords, and spittle flew from his mouth.

"You frightened the child," Sister Abigail protested, wringing her hands. "You know what she is capable of when panicked. I just couldn't risk it with all those people present."

They were in the Fairy Room. Teodorico had wanted to sequester the children in general, and Chansonne in particular, from the other board members as soon as possible. He found the children's current residence—the Hall for Lady Guests—near and easily guarded, and therefore a convenient place to regroup. Not to mention vent his anger.

"It is not your place to make that judgment, hmm?" the cardinal shouted, making a chopping gesture with his hand. "I had things well under control, hmm, yes?"

"So much so the girl set the cup aside and wouldn't touch it again!"

"S-s-silence!" Teodorico's rage reached a new height. "You forget yourself, Woman, hmm? I-I-I have accomplished precisely what I hoped and I-I-I could have been on my way back to Rome right now with the girl holding the cup if you hadn't interfered, hmm, yes?"

Sister Abigail cowed away from the tall man, shrinking away as if he might strike her. Despite her terror, she still dared to ask,

"Do you really think when it comes time you will be able to control her?"

Unexpectedly, Teodorico drew a calming breath as he drew himself to his full height, becoming the very image of composure and control.

"Yes, I do," he replied without stutter. "She is no longer the feral child I brought to this island. Look at the transformation."

"Thanks to the compassionate touch of a woman," she acknowledged, "but I doubt she will respond now to an angry old man. Especially if she were to find out just how much that angry old man had manipulated her."

Teodorico leaned into the nun with a calm that disconcerted her as much as his rage had. "Then it would serve everyone well she not ever find that out. Especially from you. I imagine her anger would be far greater toward someone who has given the impression of caring deeply for her this whole time."

The cardinal turned and retrieved his crozier leaning against a pillar. By the time he straightened out his cape, Sister Abigail was trying to hide the tears that sprang to her eyes.

"Now, if you will excuse me, hmm?" he said. "I have matters to attend. Make no mistake, Sister Abigail. The cup will be mine and I will do whatever I must to make that girl carry it out of this place for me, hmm? If you won't help with that, then the least you can do is stay out of the way."

He turned in a flourish of his cape and flew from the room like an angry bird.

High above, Chansonne sat watching from the balcony. Her mouth twitched in her impassive face for some time after the cardinal had left.

Then she, too, flew like a darting sparrow.

#

Despite the drama of Mass, it hadn't dampened the spirits of the freshly minted knights and the parade of men who accompanied them to Aesclinn for their first drinks as "real men."

None, that is, save Patrick's. He hadn't wanted to go. He did not feel very festive after the revelation that Chansonne could grasp the cup and all its implications; but it would be in poor taste to miss for the boys' celebration, as he was their sponsor.

"Well, if it isn't Moody McGee," the innkeeper greeted him. "It's been forever and more since I've seen you at my bar."

"Hello Frederique," Patrick greeted the slight man with a smile, "I'm just here to support the lads. It's not every day we have an adoubement at the keep."

"Fresh knights, eh?" Frederique glanced in the direction Patrick had jerked his head. The boys already had tall mugs filled for them down the bar, surrounded by an army of well-wishing Avangarde. "God bless them, and may they drink as much as you, because Lord knows my business has fallen since you stopped visiting. If it weren't for all these board people abouts, I might be a poor man."

"Nonsense," Patrick scoffed with a friendly scowl as Frederique poured him a mug of ale, "you'll never go out of business. How are your brother and little Freddie?"

"They are well," Frederique replied, "and little Freddie is not so little anymore. Growing like a weed he is, and always asking after you. Wants to know when you will be coming by for a visit."

"Perhaps after all this nonsense with the board has passed," Patrick said, waving his mug about the room full of non-islanders. "I'll be happy to make a visit. And I've been told I need to spend more time with children." He gave Frederique an unhappy smile, but didn't explain.

Dragonetti and several other off-duty Cardinal Guard shuffled through the door.

"If any other knight said so, I wouldn't have believed it, but you are a man of your word," Frederique said, touching his cup to Patrick's.

Soon the crowd turned to Patrick with the three former squires leading the bunch in demanding, "Speech! Speech!"

Patrick smiled and raised his mug, which quieted the crowd.

"To knighthood's newest and finest members!" he proclaimed. "Much of what I am about to say was said in the knighting ceremony, but it can never be said too much; may you serve your lords nobly, rescue many damsels, slay many dragons, never run from a challenge..."

Dragonetti and his companions rudely called for drinks, disrupting Patrick's address.

"Oy, do you mind?" the new Sir Jakob scowled.

Dragonetti raised his eyebrows. "Apologies, my young lord, I did not see you among all these grownups."

Jakob looked as if he wanted to rebuke the man, but the congenial Sir Charles put a hand on his companion's shoulder and turned to Patrick. "Carry on, Sir Patrick. Those are fine words."

Dragonetti and his men quieted, but they continued to harass the women servants for food and ale.

"And know when to choose your battles," Patrick continued, "for a good knight fights with more than his sword and lance; he fights with his mind, wit, and heart. As for your heart, follow it when all your other senses fail you, especially when your eyes deceive..." Patrick paused momentarily, turning introspective at his own words "And remember above all else, you are a servant of God. The strength and abilities you have are blessings from Him. Use them wisely. Champion the weak. Fight the strong. Do what is right. Serve the Lord in all these ways and your rewards will be great." Patrick raised his mug higher into the air and finished with, "Fight strong!"

"Live stronger!" came back the roaring response and a dozen mugs hoisted into the air.

After all had taken a drink, Patrick added with a broad smile, "Now, if you'll excuse me, I think I will go out back to the privy and fight a turd out of my arse."

A roar of laughter followed him out the back door.

When the laughter had subsided in the room, plaintive protests replaced it. The women servers were still at the mercy of hungry and thirsty Cardinal Guardsmen. One of the prettier servers struggled to escape Dragonetti's grasp, who laughed as he tried to pull her into his lap by her wrist. She escaped long enough to break a mug across the brute's head.

Dragonetti rose angrily, hands balling into fists as ale ran down his face.

Sir Josef turned to his companions Sir Jakob and Sir Charles. "Fight the strong, yes?"

His companions raised their eyebrows and smiled.

#

Even before Patrick reached the back door, returning from the privy, he could hear the muffled sounds of a commotion coming from inside. Then a chair busted through the shutters of a window, and the noise turned into the unmistakable roar of a full-fledged brawl.

"Was I gone that long?" he wondered aloud, and rushed in.

To his dismay he found the room in complete disarray with the Avangarde and the Cardinal Guard locked in combat. So far, the only weapons were fists and ale mugs.

He ducked one such item and hurried to Frederique, who cowered behind the bar. "Sir Patrick!" he pleaded. "Do something!"

"Listen up!" Patrick shouted. "Stand down now! Do you hear me?"

His only response came as a whole cooked chicken thrown at his head.

"Ah, bloody hell," Patrick cursed, and changed tactics.

He approached Josef and a Cardinal Guardsman entwined in battle. The guard had pulled Josef's cape over the young knight's head and held the garment firmly in place to avoid Josef's furiously windmilling arms.

"You there," Patrick shouted at the guard, giving him a shove. "I said stand down!"

The man punched Patrick in the face, which allowed Josef to escape. Suddenly thrown into a rage of his own, the next thing Patrick realized, he had both men in a headlock.

How long this went on, he didn't know, but it seemed quite awhile before a new voice entered the fray.

"What the bloody hell is all this?" a voice accustomed to commands boomed.

A piercing whistle followed the question.

Both brought the fracas in the inn to a standstill. Avangarde, Cardinal Guard, and the occasional Aeschlinner held each other in pairs like bloodied dancers. All looked towards the entrance where Sir Wolfgang von Fiescher stood with a deep scowl. Next to him stood Sir Lucan just now removing fingers from his mouth after having delivered the ear-piercing whistle.

"Patrick!" Wolfgang shouted after his eyes came to rest on the Irishman. "What is the meaning of all this? I should have known you would be involved."

"No, sir," Patrick protested, still clutching Josef and the guard about the necks, "I wasn't even here when it started. I tried to stop it."

"It's true," Sir Charles added. "Certain members of the Cardinal Guard were harassing the women. Myself, Jakob, and Josef stepped in to stop them."

"It's true," said a swollen-lipped Jakob. "We started it. Sir Patrick wasn't here."

From Patrick's armpit Josef gave a muffled agreement while waving an arm.

"None of this really matters for now," Wolfgang growled, "for we have a more important matter to address; the girl candidati, Chansonne, is missing and feared a runaway. We must form search parties to find her, so to your horses!"

The Avangarde moved towards the door. The Cardinal Guard lingered, slow to gather themselves.

Lucan addressed his men angrily. "Find the girl, you fools. The sooner you do, the sooner we can go home."

"Not if we find her first," Patrick admonished. "The matter hasn't been settled by the council."

Though not threatening, Lucan's response still suggested trouble. "Do you really think that now someone under the cardinal's patronage can hold the cup, he's going to continue debating the matter?"

Both the Avangarde and Cardinal Guard paused in their movement, looking to one another, pondering the implication. Hands drifted subconsciously to sword hilts.

"Do you hear that, gentlemen?" Wolfgang interjected, turning an ear towards the open door. In the distance, they could hear Greensprings's church bells sounding an alarm. "No one will get what they want if the monster gets her first."

The men recommenced their exodus of the inn, picking up the pace. Patrick and Lucan tarried a moment longer, letting the hurrying men pass between them.

"Sir Lucan, you strike me as an honorable sort," Patrick said, "so surely you can see your master does not have the child's best interest in mind."

Lucan shrugged, replying with what might have been a hint of sadness. "What would you have me do? I am bound by duty, as are you. Or did none of those words you said matter tonight?"

Josef, Jakob, and Charles exited last, but first they paused before the two older knights as if conflicted, looking for guidance.

Patrick chewed his lip, then nodded to the boys. "Go on lads, do your duty."

#

"Sister Abigail, please," Katherina pleaded, pulling on one limp arm of the old nun. "We need help putting the children to bed. They're more difficult than usual."

"We can't do it without you," Aimeé added, pulling on the woman's other arm. "They're very upset with Chansonne's absence, and the bells ringing nonstop."

After a few more attempts, Aimeé smelled the strong scent of a hot herbal tea still lingering in the room, and realized the old nun had medicated herself to sleep. Apparently, the harsh questioning from the cardinal and other officials had proved too much.

Though limp as a bag of bones, Abigail momentarily stirred closer to consciousness.

"Danger," the woman mumbled, eyes vacant and head lolling from side to side. "So much danger. My fault. I shouldn't have let any of it happen."

"It's not your fault," Aimeé insisted, "Chansonne is prone to hiding, and we didn't see her slip away either."

"And we don't believe for one instant you hid her on purpose, as that mean old cardinal accused you," Katherina added. "If anything, one of those other board people is hiding her. The knights and guards will find her."

"I don't know which I am more frightened of..." Sister Abigail said with some measure of lucidity and suddenly looking around as if realizing for the first time where she lay, "That they'll find her, or not find her."

"Why would you say such a thing?" Aimeé said, sniffing at the empty tea cup. She wrinkled her nose.

Sister Abigail's eyes glazed again. "My fault. I let the cardinal use her. Now she is in danger. We're all in danger. It's best if they don't find her."

"Don't say that," Katherina said, brow creasing.

"The cardinal is her protector. He wouldn't put her in danger, especially now she can hold the cup." Aimeé wanted to reassure the nun, but her words seemed to do the opposite.

"That is why." Sister Abigail half rose, agitated. "She will become a target. Attacked by those who would possess the cup for themselves, or want to destroy it as a fraud. She will be under great stress. She will be forced to defend herself, like a cornered animal, and may heaven help us all when that happens. Oh God, forgive me! Chansonne, forgive me!"

The nun broke down into sobbing.

"Sister Abigail, you're not making any sense," Aimeé said. "It is this tea you drank making you say such things. She is just a child—harmless."

Katherina eased the nun back down.

Sister Abigail had briefly closed her eyes and looked on the verge of calm as she allowed herself reclined, but her eyes suddenly snapped open and she grabbed Katherina's wrist with such a desperate strength it caused Katherina to gasp.

"She is a threat!" the nun hissed, her frenzied eyes speaking more than her whispered words. "She has a frightening power. Raw. Undisciplined. Unfocused. It comes out when she feels most threatened."

Aimeé and Katherina shared a concerned glance as the maidservant helped remove the nun's grip from Katherina's wrist.

Once her grip eased, her eyes flickered shut.

"Sister Abigail," Katherina gently shook the nun, "what do you mean? How?"

The nun's eyes flickered open again and she looked around, momentarily confused, then focused on Katherina.

"Her voice," she explained. "It has power like an angel's voice, capable of destroying like a heavenly battle trumpet. The sort that brought down the walls of Jericho. The sort used by the Archangel Michael that destroyed the Assyrian army as it marched on Jerusalem."

"Come now..." Katherina said incredulously.

"It's how she came to us at Saint Peter's Orphanage," Sister Abigail continued. "She was orphaned, everyone knows that, but they do not know how. Once she had a family." She reached up and stroked Katherina's cheek, then did the same to Aimeé. "Two older fair-haired sisters. They were all famous chanteuses in their village though Chansonne was just beginning to learn how to control her voice. That is when brigands broke into their home. Chansonne reacted in the only way she knew how: she screamed. Her voice caused blood to flow from their eyes. Killed them."

Katherina and Aimeé drew breaths.

"But she was too late to save her family?" Aimeé asked.

Tears welled up in Sister Abigail's eyes. "No, the poor child accidentally killed them, along with the soldiers." Again the younger women gasped. "She has not spoken since. That is, until recently." Again the nun touched their cheeks. "You two have managed to bring her back, but I'm afraid it may play into Teodorico's evil plans."

"How is that?" Katherina asked.

"The cardinal insisted I place Chansonne with Katherina so she may learn to control her voice, focus it. I agreed because I felt discipline and structure would be good for her. Now I see Teodorico only hoped to amplify her gift to better her chances of grasping the cup. I'm afraid he will also use her as a sort of weapon. Can you imagine? Power like that at your disposal, *and* the Holy Grail for the kingdoms to rally around?"

"Why would you help the cardinal use Chansonne at all?" Aimeé asked, her brow creased in confusion and disbelief.

"Because I believed the cardinal when he said he wanted to unite Christianity, to bring peace to the warring kingdoms. He does, but now I realize it is for his own ambitions, not for God. He will destroy anyone who stands in his way, and the girl and the cup will be his means of making that happen." Sister Abigail tried to sit up, staring heavenward and cried, "God forgive me! Chansonne forgive me!"

They struggled to comfort her until she eventually relaxed, closing her eyes for good.

"We must find Chansonne," Katherina whispered.

Aimeé nodded in agreement. "But then what?"

"The cardinal can't have her," Katherina explained. "Even if we hadn't heard what we just did, you saw how he treated her when she held the cup."

Aimeé nodded again. "We'll find and hide her, but who else can we trust?"

"We'll worry about that later," Katherina replied. "She is alone and scared, and if it's true what Sister Abigail says, she could be very dangerous. It must be us who find her, but I'm not sure how."

They both paused long in thought.

"Candace," Aimeé exclaimed quietly, "She 'knows' things. She will know where Chansonne has gone."

Katherina's eyes flared in shared enthusiasm. And just like that, they had a plan.

#

Some time after they had left, as Sister Abigail mumbled in her sleep, a mist flowed from underneath her door and carpeted the flagstone floor.

As it crept towards the nun's bed, it coalesced into a solid form with four tiny padding feet. The form's misty translucence darkened into sleek black cat fur.

The feline paused at the edge of the bed, crouched, and leaped onto the covers, making its way to the chest of the old woman.

There, it settled peacefully before her snoozing face and inhaled.

Wispy tendrils floated from Sister Abigail's nose and mouth and floated into the cat's nostrils. With each subsequent breath from the nun the tendrils solidified, turning from pale mist to a white ribbon.

Sister Abigail's eyes opened suddenly, and she gagged as she tried to sit up. The cat's forepaws flared open, digging claws into the nun's habit. She could not rise, pinned down as if the weight on her chest was not a cat but a giant beast. She struggled to call for help, but no sound other than a weak cough came from her, disrupting the ribbon flow into a nebulous puff of smoke. The ribbon quickly re-established itself when the cat drew in a new breath. Some of the free-floating vapor gently fell like ashes about the corners of her mouth and nose, frosting into little florets of baby's breath.

Sister Abigail's feeble flailing eventually subsided.

Chapter Twelve

Katherina and Aimeé crept to Candace's bed and sat on either side of her. Moonlight bathed the sleeping girl in a pastel glow. Apparently, once the church bells had stopped their incessant monster alarm, Mother Superior had managed to calm the children long enough for them to surrender for the night.

"Candace," Katherina whispered.

Candace rolled over and looked at the concerned pair. She hadn't been sleeping, after all.

Aimeé said, "You know things. Where did Chansonne go?"

"That's easy." Even in the moonlight they could see her eyes glazing over with that far-away look. "She went to her happy place."

"What, the auditorium?" Katherina frowned. "We already looked there. That was one of the first places we looked."

"No," Candace replied distantly, tiredly. "She went to the flowers."

"Where is that?" Aimeé asked, exchanging a glance with Katherina.

Candace shrugged, though her vacant gaze did not waver. "Flowers. Pink. That is what I see."

She rolled over and her breath deepened. Now she really did sleep.

"Pink..." Aimeé murmured, then looked up excitedly. "I think I know where she is!"

"Where?" Katherina asked.

"The garden, near the fountain," Aimeé answered, rising from Candace's bedside. "There is a cherry grove. They've been blooming since the council started."

"Then what are we waiting for?" Katherina rose as well and they hurried from the dormitory. A quick descent of the stairs led them to the Fairy Room and the exit.

When they opened the door, however, they met a rude surprise.

"Back to bed!" A guard in yellow and crimson surcoat barked at them.

"What are you doing here? Where are the Avangarde?" Katherina asked, indignant.

He barked again in bad French, thickly laced with an Italian accent. "Back to bed! Monster on loose!"

"I beg your pardon, do you know who I am?" Katherina glared at the man.

"Do you know who cardinal is?" the brute responded, reaching in to grab the door handle and slam it shut.

"What is going on?" Aimeé said, staring at the closed door.

"I don't know," Katherina responded, almost kicking the door. She crossed her arms hard, thinking better of bruising her foot. "But we have to get to the garden and find Chansonne before anyone else does... or the monster."

"I have an idea," Aimeé said and raced off down a corridor.

Katherina followed the maidservant to a room filled with baskets and bed linens.

"I didn't even know this room was here."

"Why would you, princess?" Aimeé said, bending to retrieve several sheets. "This is where we collect the bedding."

Katherina made a face, not sure if Aimeé was being sarcastic. She watched the French girl knot several sheets together and then tie one end to a brazier. After that, Aimeé mounted the sill and pushed open the shutters on the room's sole window.

"It is only a short drop from here, then we can cross the practice field and sneak into the garden." Aimeé moved to squeeze through the window.

"Aimeé," Katherina almost cried, touching her hand to her mouth. "The baby."

Aimeé placed her hands on her hips and narrowed her eyes at the princess. "Look, I'm not a delicate flower. I'm far enough along that things are 'well anchored.'" She palmed either side of her stomach for emphasis. "We must hurry."

Aimeé threw a leg over the sill and slipped down the makeshift rope.

Katherina fumbled her way down the knotted sheets, finding it difficult to do in her dress, but the distance to the ground proved only a long jump at most. The only difficulty occurred when she landed on Aimeé's shoulders, causing a moment of comical confusion.

#

Once disentangled and with feet firmly on the ground on the outside of the Hall for Lady Guests, they prepared to run straight for the garden, but the clank of arms and armor alerted them to approaching soldiers.

Despite the late hour and a low-lying mist, the moonlight shown from a clear night sky. They gasped and ducked, thinking themselves already discovered. But the clanking continued at an unhurried pace, and they relaxed. From their position they watched a large group of Cardinal Guard march through the shifting mist. They filed from the main keep, splitting into two groups, one entering the Hall for Lady Guests and the other continuing into the darkness towards the Hall for Guests.

"I'm not liking the look of this," Aimeé whispered. "They must mean to turn every room inside out."

Katherina wondered in a concerned tone. "Where are all the Avangarde?"

Aimeé shook her head silently, and once the last soldier disappeared, urged the princess to follow her. She took them by a route that would avoid the soldiers, though she would have to enter the garden from still another direction if more soldiers should appear. To that end, Aimeé led them to a servant's entrance and a dark little room smelling of herbs and spices.

"We're not far from the great hall, and from there we can enter the garden from within without notice," Aimeé explained.

She peeked through a door on the far side of the room, and satisfied, she opened it. They darted down a corridor to the kitchen. Normally alive with activity, the large room now struck her as strange and ominous in the quiet darkness. She and Katherina made their way across the flagstones to a pair of double doors that would lead them to the great hall. Before they could reach them, however, Aimeé tensed. Before she knew what she was doing, she tackled Katherina to the floor and held her prone under a workbench.

She started to protest angrily, especially when Aimeé roughly put her hand over her mouth, but Katherina froze when the double doors burst open and a half-dozen men entered.

From their vantage they could only see their legs, but the women recognized the voices. "We're wasting our time here," Dragonetti growled, "the kitchen is obviously empty."

"Search it, anyway," Victor's voice responded smooth as silk. "Leave no pot or pan unturned. She's a clever child and could be hiding anywhere and we haven't much time. The Avangarde will return when they realize the reports of the monster chasing Chansonne through the countryside are fabricated."

"But some of the men say they've actually seen something huge flying above the garden," Dragonetti admitted.

Katherina felt Aimeé tense at the words. An odd pause hung in the air after the statement, and Katherina wished she could see Victor's face to help explain it.

"Well then, all the more reason to hurry," he said cooly. "Any news from the units searching the Guest residences?"

"The Guests are annoyed, but no little girl yet," Dragonetti replied.

"Very well, carry on. Once done here, move into the classrooms." Victor's slippered feet turned and exited. The boots of the Cardinal Guard moved deeper into the kitchen, followed by the clamor of utensils and pots emptied from cupboards in an angry cacophony.

Katherina squirmed under Aimeé's grip and she urged them to move on. Aimeé relinquished her hold and led them in a crawl along the floor away from the noise. They exited a small side door, entering the great hall at one corner. The arches to the garden opened only a few feet away. Patches of moonlight bathed the patio stones like shimmering, fallen leaves.

"I'm not so sure this is such a good idea now," Aimeé whispered, wringing her hands. She cast a furtive glance towardsthe forest of bushes, trees, and tall reedy plants that seethed with menacing shadows in the moonlight. "If it's true what that guard said about the monster flying about, perhaps we should wait for the Avangarde. Maybe if we find Patrick, we can still find Chansonne first and keep it a secret..."

"Under any other circumstance I would have agreed with you," Katherina replied, surprised at Aimeé's sudden change in demeanor. Aimeé had pushed her along until now, almost to the point of annoyance. "But you can't forget: Even if Patrick removed that 'stick-of-duty' from his backside and agreed to keep this all a secret, there is no time. Chansonne needs us now."

As if to punctuate this, the crash of pots and pans thrown about the kitchen rang nearer and now they could hear a ruckus coming from the upper windows of the keep. Voices of complaint floated down to them, as well as a pillow and some bedding thrown from a window.

Aimeé managed to chuckle. "I dare say your description of a stick up Patrick's arse is rather accurate. I had no idea you had a sense of humor."

Katherina grinned and headed for the garden, but paused and turned to Aimeé.

"Aimeé," she said, "I feel I must apologize."

"Oh?"

"Yes. I've treated you poorly," Katherina confessed. "You're right, you're not a delicate flower. You're not a victim. I've been treating you like one and I'm sorry. And I must admit I'm..." She searched for proper words as her expression slid along a range of emotions. "I'm conflicted... over the possibility the child might be Patrick's. Though he and I are truly just friends, I still wonder about lost possibilities, and I think I've been secretly blaming you for that. I am wrong to do so. You are a strong woman and I admire you for that and I wish you and Patrick the best."

Aimeé stood with mouth agape. "Well," she stammered, "thank you. As for Patrick, that remains very much to be seen."

"I wish you would give him a chance. He is a good man," Katherina implored.

"You mean he is the best I'll ever do," Aimeé returned, an angry line creasing her brow.

"Not what I meant." Katherina wrung her hands into knots.

Aimeé came forward and took Katherina by the hand and led her toward the garden. She kissed her gently on the cheek and embraced her. "I know what you meant. I guess I've reacted poorly to your treatment, and therefore it's my turn to apologize. Let us not talk of such things any more, and instead find us our lost child. Monsters, cardinals, and the stick in Patrick's arse all be damned!"

#

It did not take them long to reach the fountain and the blooming cherry trees, but they found no Chansonne.

"If she's hiding, it only makes sense she wouldn't be out in the open," Aimeé reasoned. Katherina agreed and they poked around the bushes nearest the circular path about the fountain.

"Wait, do you hear that?" Aimeé asked, straightening.

Just barely over the gurgling water, there was the faint sound of sobs.

They followed the sound, ducking underneath the branches of the trees, causing blossoms to fall like snow. In the small grove they found no one, but near the center of the expansive garden, they found her small form curled up on the manicured sward.

She must have heard them coming, for her sobs abruptly stopped and she looked up, ready to bolt like a frightened animal.

Katherina put a finger to her lips. "Shh," she cooed to the girl, "you're safe."

Chansonne's tense form relaxed, and she allowed the women to join her on the grass.

"Chansonne, you must come with us," Katherina reasoned. She thought of Sister Abigail's fears of Chansonne's voice and of her impulsive nature.

Chansonne shook her head violently and her eyes grew to giant proportions.

"We won't let that bad old man take you," Aimeé added. "We'll hide you, but Katherina is right, you can't stay here. It is only a matter of time before they look here."

Again Chansonne shook her head.

From their current position, the keep walls peeked over the tops of the garden's trees and hedges. If someone were to walk the top of the battlements and look down, Chansonne was in plain view.

Worse, voices from the keep floated through the air. Katherina caught a few words; the Cardinal Guard's search was making its way through the building. Soon they would move to the garden.

Chansonne must have intuited this, for she clung to Katherina.

"Please, Chansonne..." she started to say, but a cooking pot clanged inside the great hall. Apparently the Cardinal Guard had finished their search in the kitchen.

Chansonne's hands dug painfully into Katherina's arms and her eyes grew bigger than ever. Her usual nondescript grunts of distress turned to an escalating keening. A pain like a pinprick attacked Katherina's inner ear and she saw Aimeé grimace. Katherina gently tried to soothe Chansonne, but her voice betrayed her rising concern.

"Chansonne, remember when we sing in the auditorium? Songs are most beautiful when sung correctly, yes? We control our voices. We don't let our voices control us."

The keening intensified and the pinprick in Katherina's ear turned to a jabbing knife. Chansonne's eyes scanned the foliage separating them from the keep.

"Remember the Shrugging Giants?" Katherina asserted. "Remember how Emilie controlled her voice? She made it do what she wanted. You can do that right now."

Katherina desperately wanted to cover her ears, but Chansonne's iron grip pinned her arms down. Instead, she squeezed her eyes shut. The pain in her ears and the out-of-control pounding of Chansonne's heart against her bosom were overwhelming.

Just when she didn't think she could take the pain anymore, a gentle music interrupted the keening and Chansonne stopped.

Katherina opened her eyes and saw Aimeé holding her crucifix to her mouth, fingers fumbling along the tiny holes as she blew in one end. The little flute played the tune from the Shrugging Giants. Chansonne listened, fascinated by the sound.

Then a wondrous thing happened.

The stars themselves seemed to descend upon the sward, bobbing among the blades of grass, the trees, and shrubs. Ten thousand motes of light surrounded them, shimmering with every hue of color. A hum filled the air, roughly mimicking the flute music. The lights swirled and danced to the tune.

"What are they?" Katherina asked in wonder, holding a graceful arm out so the little creatures would alight there.

A group of them danced around Aimeé's stomach, their hum turning into a happy squeal. Another group formed a tiara around Chansonne's head.

One of them fluttered to Aimeé's face, growing when it did.

It turned into a little winged girl, held aloft by a pair of furiously beating gossamer dragonfly wings. A dimpled smile beamed from a sharp-featured face and a tiny mop of yellow hair brushed the girl's long lashes.

"Fairies," Aimeé gasped.

The spindly creature swooped over to Aimeé's ear and hummed loudly.

"What's that?" Aimeé asked, frowning and tilting her head to one side to hear better. "Call for help? I suppose so, but I was just trying to make the peaceful music. The healing music."

The little fairy girl put hands to her mouth and made a laugh like tiny chimes.

Aimeé still held the flute suspended before her mouth and the fairy swooped down and danced along the holes. She did this repeatedly, tiny feet stepping in the same rhythmic pattern.

"Oh!" Aimeé cried and put the flute to her lips.

She blew and her fingers moved among the holes. The new tune was sweeter and more melodic than before. The fairy girl grinned hugely, but then her attention snapped to one side. The field of lights shifted in the same direction and the collective hum stopped.

"Over here!" a man's voice called. "I heard the sound this way!"

Aimeé stopped playing and Chansonne gasped, renewing her iron grip on Katherina. The sea of lights coalesced around the trio, making an obscuring mist of living lights.

At the edge of the little glade a man stumbled from the cherry grove, swatting at the multitude of lights like a man walking into a bee swarm. He stumbled towards the girls, and Chansonne tensed, a noise coming from her throat. The fairy who had talked to Aimeé, however, buzzed before Chansonne's face and put a finger to her lips with a mischievous grin. Chansonne calmed and the fairy shot off, turning back into a little mote of light.

She attacked the man's head, causing him to swat even more furiously. Other fairies joined in, turning into a swarm of fireflies. The man stumbled within feet of the women, revealing himself to be Dragonetti, but his eyes remained squeezed shut and within moments he had stumbled completely out of the glade.

"Over here!" another voice called. "I hear something over here!"

The outline of lights that clung to Dragonetti made it possible for them to see him run in the direction of the other voice.

"Good," Dragonetti grumbled. "Nothing but bugs over here!"

He faded from view.

The girls let out a breath they hadn't realized they had been holding.

A miniature shooting star shot from the trees and came to Aimeé, growing back into the helpful fairy. She buzzed about Aimeé's ear.

"Yes, thank you Talia!" Aimeé cried.

The fairy girl kissed Aimeé on the cheek, then gave one to Chansonne and Katherina before darting off into the darkness, trailing a comet's tail of fellow lights.

"Well, I never," Katherina breathed.

"We should go," Aimeé said, "The fairy, Talia, says they drew the soldiers away with their own singing, but she doesn't know how long they will fall for it."

Chansonne shook her head furiously, curling up next to Katherina in the grass.

"What is that business with the flute?" Katherina asked, brow crinkling at the instrument. "I daresay it averted disaster."

"Patrick's mother said the music soothes people," Aimeé explained, looking at the flute as if for the first time. "It puts people into a peaceful state, making it possible for them to heal wounds of the mind and spirit." She squeezed her hand around the instrument. "But only when you use the correct tune. No wonder it hasn't helped Patrick. The tune I've been using is a call for help, and that's exactly what he's been doing: trying to save me—even if means pushing me away."

Katherina stroked Chansonne's hair. "Chansonne could use some healing of the spirit. How long has she been carrying her guilt around, I wonder?"

Aimeé's eyes brightened and she put the flute to her lips and played.

The melody surrounded and comforted them as if the cloud of fairies were still there. Chansonne's head turned in Katherina's lap, all her attention bent toward the music. After some minutes, her pounding heart softened and an icy fist behind her eyes slowly released, allowing peace to slowly cross her face. Her eyes closed halfway.

Aimeé stopped and smiled when she felt she had done all she could and whispered, "We should go."

Chansonne startled at the suggestion and reached up and pulled Aimeé down to the grass with her. She did the same to Katherina and pulled their arms across her like a protective web.

"In a bit," Katherina suggested, "just a bit."

Katherina sang then, to the tune Aimeé had played.

> *Hush little sister don't you cry,*
> *because in the morning we're going bye-bye,*
> *But first we're going to close our eyes*
> *In the morning the sun will rise*
> *We'll be home when it's high in the sky*
> *But first we have to close our eyes*
> *So hush little sister, don't you cry.*

Chansonne's eyes went from half to completely closed, and her little chest rose and fell steadily. A light snore came from Aimeé.

"Just a bit longer," Katherina murmured, and her eyes closed, too.

When morning came, and a dozen Avangarde arrived on the scene, the women were still entwined in each other's arms.

#

"How did you find us?" Katherina asked, sipping at a mug of hot cider.

"When I heard reports of flute music from the garden, I knew it had to be you," Patrick responded, regarding Aimeé next to her.

The pair sat on a bench in the kitchen surrounded by Avangarde. Chansonne slept in her room under guard. Anna and Clare placed the women's feet in pans of hot water. Though the weather had not been severe, sleeping outdoors all night still made for a chilly morning. Katherina accepted a blanket thrown over her shoulders, as did Aimeé.

Patrick was cross. "That was very foolish. There's no telling what the cardinal's men would have done if they'd found Chansonne with you and you had tried to run."

"We did the right thing finding her," Katherina insisted, "and lucky for you. Otherwise she'd be on a boat to Rome right now with that evil man."

"That 'evil man' is the head of the Board of Benefactors and a papal legate," Patrick snapped, "and he is the girl's patron."

"You can't be still seriously considering handing her over. Not after how he treated her," Aimeé said.

Patrick shifted uncomfortably. "He merely was stern during Mass and frightened her."

"Patrick!" Aimeé cried. "You can't be serious!"

"We can hold onto her a little longer until the matter is sorted out," Geoffrey said, placating. "No one will hurt her, I promise."

Aimeé's head swiveled between Geoffrey and Patrick as if confused by who had said what.

"Er, right, we're not handing her over just yet," Patrick added, also eyeing Geoffrey. "There are questions about the Cardinal Guard's conduct during the search of the keep while we were gone. They damaged property, hurt some people, and most of all,

332

it's apparent someone from the cardinal's staff lied to us into leaving Greensprings. All these things raise concerns with the board. They will decide soon what to do."

"That's all?" Katherina protested.

"We are the Avangarde," Corbin explained. "We keep the peace between the factions and do not choose sides. If the board decides to hand her over to the cardinal, we have to oblige."

"Now that she can hold the cup, he will take advantage of her," Aimeé said.

"She has a power he will abuse, and her along with it," Katherina almost shouted, slamming her mug on the table.

"So you say," Corbin said.

"Just ask Sister Abigail," Aimeé pleaded, "she will tell you."

"Yes! She will tell you the whole story."

The Avangarde exchanged glances.

"Why, what's happened?" Katherina asked.

#

"Don't disturb anything," Father Wulfric said upon entering the room.

"We know, Father," the Avangarde inside the room said. "We haven't touched anything. Nor has anyone since the body was discovered, just as you always advise."

"Excellent, lads," Father Wulfric responded, approaching the body.

The pair of Avangarde bowed at the waist and left him alone. He shook his head sadly at the gentle old woman he had come to know during the board meeting at Greensprings. Of all the people to be the next victim, why her?

He sank to his knees, inspected her corpse, found nothing new, and so turned his investigation to the room.

It didn't take him long to find what he sought. On the floor beneath the window was the wispy spider's web of skin. Rather than pick it up, he crawled up close and manipulated it with his silver quill he had brought just for the occasion. He teased it open it until it revealed what he had hoped for: a face. A portion of the skin touching the silver, however, turned to smoke.

Before the rest of it smoldered away, he stood up in shock, recognizing the murderer.

Chapter Thirteen

The church bells jangled as if a corpse bobbed from the ringing rope.

The sound made it difficult for Father Wulfric to concentrate on his writing, but he managed to finish the letter. Once done, he set the silver quill down on his desk, rubbed the bridge of his nose, and contemplated the words he had put to parchment. He did not cherish what had to come next, but he saw no alternative.

Drawing a deep breath, he folded the letter to a meticulous square and inserted it into a pocket in his robe sleeve.

The clamor of the bells continued to assault his mind as he scrutinized the silver quill suspended between his index fingers.

A knock came at the door and he bid the visitor enter.

"Sorry to disturb you, Father," an Avangarde said, poking his head inside his chamber, "but I've been told to inform you the bells signify a call for a meeting in the church among the board members."

"Of course they do," Father Wulfric replied sourly. He tempered his tone. "But thank you, young sir. I'll be there shortly."

The knight left, leaving Wulfric to stare at the quill a moment longer.

"Soon, it will be over," he said. "No more flower-covered bodies."

His hands shook and a bead of crimson pooled where the sharp tip of the quill met his finger, forming a drop that fell to the desk.

#

Father Wulfric took up a position on the steps near the doors of the church and scanned the crowd as they filed past him to enter. He slid each hand up the opposite sleeve of his robe and fingered the letter up one sleeve, and the quill up the other. He searched among the faces, waiting for the one he sought.

When he saw the girl Chansonne approach with her gaggle of governesses and Avangarde protectors, he made his way towards her, going against the flow of bodies. The clanging bells reached a new level of dissonance, matching the pounding in his head, as he neared. Standing before her and barring her path, he gripped the quill tightly. The bells stopped abruptly.

"Father?" Sir Patrick said. "May we help you?"

The other Avangarde—was his name Sir Geoffrey?—shifted uneasily.

Father Wulfric smiled, withdrew his hand, and stroked the child's hair. "I just wanted to assure the young lady all will be well. That she is among friends and she will not be forced to do anything against her wishes."

"Thank you, Father. We appreciate your support," the Lady Katherina said.

She and the maidservant placed protective hands on Chansonne and Wulfric let the group continue on their way.

Sir Lucan was approaching with a group of crimson-clad guards. Wulfric stood in place, waiting as he fingered the quill and letter. Sweat beaded on his forehead. He almost wished the bells continued, for he found the click of their boots and the jangle of their spurs menacing.

Gathering his nerve, he stepped in their path. "Sir Lucan, if I could have a moment?"

Sir Lucan slowed to a stop, raising an eyebrow. "Only a moment, Father. As you can imagine I'm very busy."

"Of course," Wulfric responded, removing a hand from his robe sleeve to hold forth the letter. "If you would be so kind as to deliver this to the Lady Lilliana? I fear tensions are rather high right now and receiving this from a friendly face would be wiser."

Lucan eyed the paper, shrugged, and stuffed it in his sword belt. "Consider it done, Father."

#

Cardinal Teodorico and the Romans took up a position in front of the communion rail, forming a wall of reds and yellows. In his black cassock, Victor was the sole exception. All others in the church formed a semicircle around them, leaving an open space, keeping their distance as if the Romans carried a sickness. More than the usual crowd of benefactors gathered today. All in Greensprings sensed an endgame and were eager to witness it.

Patrick was watching Lady Lilliana, wondering what passed through her mind since their last encounter, which was why he noticed the message from Sir Lucan and her hasty departure. After a quick exchange of words, Cardinal Teodorico appeared unfazed by her withdrawal and commenced with the proceedings.

"Gentlemen," he addressed the board, "we have been deadlocked in council chambers for a long time now with no resolution. We have, essentially, been waiting for a sign from God, hmm? That sign came yesterday in the form of a small child taking up the cup, hmm, yes?"

"And naturally, she happens to be someone under your control," Count Fulk interjected from the crowd.

"Naturally?" Teodorico sniffed. "You act as if I had something to do with it. Providence is the domain of God. Who am I to question His choices?"

Angry murmurs rippled through the building.

"Let us recognize that now, hmm?" Teodorico shouted, banging his crozier on the flagstones. "The sooner we can share the cup with the world, the better, hmm, yes?"

"You mean so *you* can show the world the cup," Abbot Herewinus said.

Teodorico shrugged. "God has spoken. It is time to move on. I thank the Avangarde for finding my charge, but she must now now returned to me."

He gestured officiously to Chansonne, beckoning her forward.

Katherina and Aimeé placed hands on her shoulders and Patrick and Geoffrey took up positions in front of her.

Abbot Herewinus announced, "Cardinal, no disrespect, but we are not in agreement with your assessment. We feel more discussions are in order, especially now that someone can grasp the cup."

"And you must answer for the conduct of your people during the search for Chansonne," Mother Superior added bluntly. "Many people were unfairly put upon, and we feel deceived."

"Nonsense," Teodorico replied, face wrinkling in irritation. "There is a monster on the loose, hmm? Time was of the essence in finding the child. I'm sorry if a few feathers were ruffled. There is nothing left to talk about. Now hand her over, hmm, yes?"

Silence filled the church.

Cardinal Teodorico looked from one side of the crowd to the other. Color rose in his face as the color drained from the hand gripping his crozier.

"It is obvious you are all lovers of politics and not lovers of God! I see it is necessary for me to step in and make the right decision for all of us, hmm, yes?"

"You can't do that!" someone cried from the balcony.

Teodorico sniffed. "No, hmm?"

"This is Greensprings, under the auspices of the Board of Benefactors. The entire board must make a decision, not just any one member," Herewinus pointed out.

"*I* am the Director of the Board of Benefactors, hmm?" Teodorico countered. "*I* am in the College of Cardinals. *I* am the legate from Rome. My primacy as an archbishop alone gives me the right to make a decision in all matters holy and profane unilaterally, hmm, yes?"

"This is not your jurisdiction as an archbishop!" Abbot Herewinus challenged. "The closest thing to jurisdiction in that regard is Father Wulfric, who is the legate from Canterbury, and I'm certain he wishes for more talks. Right, Father Wulfric? Father Wulfric...?"

All turned their heads to search the crowd for the priest.

#

It didn't take long for the Lady Lilliana to find him. He sat on the edge of the fountain in the courtyard.

Many people moved around the large fountain—not everyone had wanted to crowd into the church, preferring to go about their daily chores of fetching water or washing linens. The location was very public, yet noisy enough that private conversations could go unheard under the sound of the gurgling water.

Lilliana flowed onto the fountain edge, coming to rest next to the priest like a silk scarf poured from a vase.

"You wished to see me, Father?" she purred with a smile.

"Do you know what a humidor is, Lady Lilliana?" Wulfric asked without preamble, looking straight ahead and making a point not to look her in the face.

Lilliana blinked and shook her head, surprised at the odd question.

"A humidor—do you know what it is?"

She cleared her throat, sensing an unpleasant conversation. "I do not, but I imagine you're about to tell me, aren't you?"

"It is a box," Wulfric explained, "having the ability to maintain a certain temperature and moisture inside. It is often used by scholars in certain climates to condition ancient documents slowly so they can be safely and easily handled. William Malmesbury had such a box and he was kind enough to lend it to me."

"Dearest Father Wulfric, wherever is this going?" Lilliana said, raising a beautiful eyebrow.

"Up to this point," he continued, "I have been thwarted in my investigation into the deaths caused by the creature that leaves its skin behind. That is, until now."

"Creature? You said you believed it was a disease."

"So I did, until Sister Abigail's murder. But I found something."

"Which was?"

"I was correct in my original supposition that the creature sheds its skin like a snake or an insect," Wulfric continued, "leaving an impression of its owner's image in the skin. Until now the skin was so fragile it disintegrated. I could not make out the image in time, let alone keep it as evidence for all the world to see before it fell apart." He turned slowly towards her, this time making full eye contact. "But with a humidor, I was able to coax a face out of the skin. And do you know whose face I saw there, peering back at me?"

Lilliana held his gaze, but bit down on her nail, making a crunching sound.

"That's right, Lady Lilliana, or whatever your name is," Wulfric finished with a tone of satisfaction, looking straight ahead again. "Your face is still there for all to see. I do not know what manner of creature you are, or how you came to consort with an Archbishop of the Holy Church, but your game is over."

Lilliana smiled, casting a glance around the courtyard and at the people walking through it.

"If so, then why are we having this conversation? Why not go straight to the Avangarde?" she asked, maintaining the pretenses of a pleasant chat.

"Because I wish to avoid more deaths," he said simply.

"More likely so you can maneuver to possess the girl and cup yourself."

Wulfric shrugged. "I admit I may benefit by not revealing your identity, but I do wish to avoid more death, as I doubt you wouldn't be taken captive easily—not without loss of life. This way, you and Teodorico can slither back to Rome, and the cup can fall into friendlier hands."

"You would just let us go quietly, just to avoid bloodshed?" Lilliana said, incredulous.

"Yes, after you have convinced the cardinal to give up his quest for the cup and to publicly advocate putting Chansonne under my protection," Wulfric responded.

Lilliana tittered. "Playing with fire, Wulfie? Besides, you're a little late. Teo is in there right now making his final push to keep the girl and take the cup."

Wulfric shifted uneasily, but replied with confidence. "I'm sure he is, but we both know after recent events no one is going to return the girl to him. I realize he won't let that stop him. That is where you and my message come in. Once Teodorico meets rejection in there, let that be the end of it. Let him declare his desire for the girl to be put under my protection, and then leave."

"And once you have the girl? What is to keep you from informing on us?" Lilliana asked, plucking at her dark lacy gloves, removing little bits of lint.

"Only my desire to avoid tragedy," Wulfric said, nodding and smiling at a passer-by. "Besides, what choice do you have? Some chance of leaving here alive is better than none, don't you think? Oh, and before you think I might meet an unfortunate 'accident' before day's end, keep in mind I've instructed certain individuals to open the humidor should anything 'unnatural' happen to me."

The jaw muscle in Lilliana's face worked back and forth for a while.

"I will pass your demands on to Teo," Lilliana said. "Should things not go his way in the meeting, I'm sure he will have an answer for you before nightfall." She turned to him and placed her hand on his lap, gently rubbing his thigh with her harsh fingers. "You know it doesn't have to be like this, though. Regardless of whoever possesses the cup, you have to admit a new world order is about to come, and Teodorico is in an excellent position to make the most of it. In this order, he will need men like you. You can profit from this."

Wulfric gently but firmly took her hand and removed it from his thigh. "No need to seduce me. My resolve is firm."

"Don't be so sure, dearest Wulfie," she said, leaning towards him and sniffing like a predator. "All men have their weaknesses, and I think I know yours."

#

Patrick plucked at his collar, adjusting the weight of the chainmail coif hanging from his neck. Heat rose along with the rising tension in the room. Shouts from the crowd drowned out the individual arguments each benefactor tried to interject into the chaos. Though the exchange was no more severe than the most heated of past council meetings, Patrick squeezed the hilt of his sword, watching the Cardinal Guard across the room. It just now occurred to him the men in red surcoats outnumbered the Avangarde five to one in the church. When he noted Sir Wolfgang and Sir Corbin unperturbed by this, he relaxed some.

Some.

"Dismiss this mob," Count Fulk shouted above the din, "and convene a more seemly council meeting. We still have much to discuss."

Those siding with Cardinal Teodorico shouted Count Fulk down, creating a new round of heated exchanges. Teodorico's livid face shifted about the mouth as he readied to join the arguments, but then his eyes suddenly cut away. Patrick followed his gaze and saw Lilliana enter the church. She made eye contact with the cardinal and her index finger nonchalantly moved across her throat before continuing to pluck at her tresses. The gesture happened so quickly and subtly Patrick almost questioned if he had seen it, but when he turned his gaze back to Teodorico, the acknowledgement in the older man's eyes proved some sort of communication had indeed happened.

"C-C-CONTROL!" Teodorico shouted, raising his arms. The crowd quieted. He briefly closed his eyes and shook his head. "ENOUGH! The time has come to put this matter to rest. I have the authority to take what I please in all jurisdictions."

Confused murmurs echoed in the church, sprinkled with some nervous laughter.

"How so?" Abbot Herewinus asked skeptically.

Teodorico turned to Victor and nodded, sending his aide into a flurry of activity behind the group of Romans as he and some other courtiers gathered items.

Teodorico turned back to the crowd. "I must apologize for my subterfuge these past few months. Difficult times call for difficult choices. I did not wish to distract or unfairly influence the council proceedings with my newly elected office, so I kept it secret. I had hoped the council would peaceably arrive at the logical conclusion by now. I see now I have no choice but to force matters to break this deadlock that continues to keep the Cup of the Last Supper hidden from the world."

"New office?" Count Fulk said, frowning.

Teodorico extended his arms, allowing his courtiers to remove his crimson garment and replace it with a white one. A tall white mitre replaced his red skullcap and an even larger ring replaced the one on his hand. "I am *Papa in Pectore*—the pope in hiding."

Victor stepped forward and dramatically held before him a large scroll.

He read, "It pleases the Holy Roman Emperor Henry, the fourth Salian to the throne, to announce Teodorico, formally Archbishop of Albano, as Pope Theodoric of the Opposition, the Antipope, in opposition to the false Pope Paschal in Rome." The crowd gasped. As Victor continued reading the article, angry murmurs escalated. "All matters spiritual are invested in Pope Theodoric by divine right through his Grace Emperor Henry..."

Victor continued for some time with cryptic legalese until his superior cut him off.

"That will suffice, hmm?" Teodorico said. "I believe they grasp the situation, hmm, yes?"

Victor stopped and turned the document so the crowd could see its dense text and many and various wax seals. Even from a distance all could see a large sweeping signature at the bottom of the document.

"You lying snake!" Abbot Herewinus' normally gentle face contorted into a mask of rage. "We do not recognize you as any kind of pope!"

The angry buzz in the church erupted. A pounding started in Patrick's head and he rubbed his head. The Cardinal Guard looked agitated. Only Sir Lucan remained calm, watching the drama with calculating eyes.

"E-Enough!" Teodorico shouted, pounding his crozier on the flagstones.

The crowd quieted once again and Teodorico stepped out into the open space of the church. He slowly turned, thrusting out his fist so all could see the giant glittering ring of his office.

"I am the only pope that matters, hmm? The pope backed by an Emperor. Let me remind you what world you live in, yes? A world in which your safety, your commerce, and your livelihoods all depend on living peacefully with a giant. And as God's true recognized representative on Earth, I hold your souls in my hand!" Teodorico made a point to look every noble and benefactor in the eye as he slowly made a circuit about the semicircle, turning his fist into a claw, held up cup-like. When he came to a stop a good distance before the Greensprings group gathered about Chansonne, he addressed them. "If you don't believe in the power of God, then you very well believe in the power of the emperor and his armies, hmm, yes?"

The nervous rustling of bodies almost drowned out the murmurs.

Teodorico said his next words without stutter and stabbed a finger to the floor to emphasize each word. "So bring me the child now!"

Sir Wolfgang, Mother Superior, and Father Hugh exchanged concerned glances. When they looked to the other benefactors and saw them hang their heads and look away, the Greensprings trio slowly nodded to one another.

"No!" Katherina and Aimeé cried together, holding Chansonne tight.

"I'm sorry, but this is a different matter," Sir Wolfgang explained. "We have to think of the greater good here. This man can bring an army down upon us. Sir Patrick, please, take the girl to Teodorico."

Aimeé turned a shocked look to him.

"Sir?" Patrick hemmed at Wolfgang.

"Being a leader means making difficult choices and carrying them out. You know what can happen if we don't do this. Do your duty."

With thoughts of Greensprings burning, Patrick turned to Aimeé and held his hand out.

"Patrick!" Aimeé cried, pulling Chansonne closer. "You can't be serious!"

"We can appeal to Pope Paschal, the real pope, and win her back, but Wolfgang and the others are right. We must do this for now."

"In the meantime he will visit all manner of crimes upon her!" Katherina shouted.

"You can't!" Aimeé added, giving him an accusing look more hurtful than any look she had given him yet. The sensation of having betrayed her wound its way through his intestines. A sharp pain stabbed Patrick behind his eyes and a white light temporarily blinded his vision. His hands shot to his head and he rubbed his temples. Words like 'duty,' 'love,' 'righteousness,' and 'danger' bounced inside his skull like a trapped sparrow.

"Must I do everything myself, hmm?" Teodorico shouted and strode forward, his fresh white robes making a whisking noise.

He snatched Chansonne by the wrist and dragged her from the crowd. "Come, girl, take up the cup as is your destiny!"

Shocked with disbelief at the maneuver, no one initially moved to intervene, and the few who did froze when the Cardinal Guard took a step forward.

"Patrick!" Aimeé pleaded. "Do something! This can't be right!"

Patrick's heartbeat pounded in his head, crowding out the words. Events slowed to a crawl: Chansonne's frantic struggle to escape the old man's grasp, Aimeé's face contorting into a mask of horror and anger, the guards and knights fingering their hilts.

Patrick squeezed his eyes shut to clear his vision, but when he opened them, things had only become more surreal. Events slowed down even more. Voices were distorted, as if coming from underwater. Aimeé's green eyes turned blue and blood covered her from head to foot. Blood also covered Chansonne.

The pounding in his head suddenly ceased, as did his breathing when he saw the Other walking through the crowd behind Teodorico, looking at him expectantly.

Patrick rolled his eyes skyward, and whether voiced the words or merely thought them, he said, "God in Heaven, please give me the strength to do the right thing."

The cup on the altar hummed.

"Stop fighting me!" Teodorico shouted at the girl, and events returned to a normal pace. They had almost arrived at the steps of the altar. "Go up there and take the cup, now!"

Chansonne struggled so much the old man dropped his crozier with a loud wooden clack and commenced to drag her with both his hands.

She bent over and bit his hand.

"D-d-damn you!" he shouted, eyes bulging.

He released his hand, only to draw it back with the intention of striking her. She cowered under his shadow.

Before he could vent his fury, however, Patrick's hand grabbed him by the wrist and swung him around.

Patrick punched him in the face, sending him sprawling.

The only thing more profound than the initial gasp from the crowd was the following shocked silence filling the church.

That is, until Teodorico regained his bearings and sat up from the floor in a pile of white robes, shouting through a spray of blood, "S-s-seize him!"

As a unit, the Cardinal Guard came forward.

"And bring the girl to me, hmm?" Teodorico added, dabbing at his lips.

Patrick drew his sword with one hand and Chansonne grabbed the other, hiding behind him.

"What do you think you are doing, Sir Patrick?" Teodorico hissed. "Do you really think you can change the natural order of things, hmm? Who do you think you are? This is going to happen. The only difference now is I will see you hanged!"

The Cardinal Guards gathered about him in a half-circle. Though they outnumbered him by a dozen, they still looked to one another with trepidation, not in a hurry to make a move on the Knight of Cups, Savior of Avalon.

"Patrick, what are you doing?" Wolfgang demanded.

"I'm very sorry, sir, but I've listened to my heart," Patrick explained, blinking sweat out of his eyes. "I've prayed and asked for guidance."

"And this is what you came up with?" Wolfgang said, either exasperated or angry.

Teodorico struggled to his feet, wiping the last of the blood from his mouth.

"So be it," Teodorico sneered. "If you wish to die alone, then we shall dispense with the trial and simply cut you down where you stand, hmm, yes? Guards!"

The red garbed men-at-arms drew their weapons.

"He won't be alone," a voice behind Patrick said, along with the sound of a sword rasping from its scabbard.

Though Patrick knew the voice, it still came as a surprise when Geoffrey stood next to him with a naked weapon. The Cardinal Guard hesitated, divided over who posed the bigger threat.

"Geoff," Patrick said. "You may want to sit this out. Play by the rules now and you may still escape any stain my actions have caused."

"Paddy, my boy," Geoffrey smiled, taking a swordsman's stance. "When have I ever played by the rules?"

Patrick shrugged. "Excellent point."

"Sir Wolfgang, hmm?" Teodorico called. "Tell your men to stand down and take responsibility for their actions, hmm, yes?"

"Patrick, look at me," Wolfgang said.

Patrick chanced a glance over his shoulder. Wolfgang, Father Hugh, and Mother Superior watched him with grave concern. His stomach bunched into serpentine knots.

"Is this truly the answer God has given you?" Wolfgang asked with deadly earnestness.

"Aye, it is," Patrick said, and another bead of sweat dripped from his forehead.

His attention snapped back to the soldiers before him.

More swords slithered out of their sheaths and boots struck the stone floor as Sir Wolfgang, Sir Corbin, and a handful of other Avangarde joined them, shoulder to shoulder.

"God has spoken," Mother Superior declared. "It is obvious now why the cup came to Greensprings. We are to protect it."

Teodorico's eyes bulged. "A-a-arrest them! A-a-all of them!"

Though they currently outnumbered the Avangarde, the Cardinal Guard fidgeted.

Teodorico shouted, "Sir Lucan, motivate your men, hmm?"

Lucan calmly came forward, drawing his sword blithely as he meandered through the bodies of Cardinal Guard until he stood before Patrick.

Patrick gripped his sword, bracing himself.

Lucan appraised him, smiling. "You Avangarde say, 'Fight strong, live stronger.' Honestly, I did not understand what that meant. Until today. You showed me the strength of living, as opposed to the strength of fighting. This could not have been an easy decision. I commend you, and..." He turned and took a step backward, now standing next to Patrick, facing the Cardinal Guard "I feel inspired."

The church buzzed anew and a weight partially lifted from Patrick's shoulders.

Jakob, Josef, and Charles started to cross the floor to join Lucan.

"Lads, you might want to stand back," Lucan admonished. "There's no telling where this wind blows."

Jakob puffed out his chest. "Sir, I'm sure you've noticed we are no longer squires and can make up our own minds." The other two nodded to Lucan.

"Very well, have it your way, bo... Gentlemen."

Oddly, Teodorico's rage did the opposite of what Patrick expected, turning into a mask of contained calm. Perhaps it was the reassuring river of new Cardinal Guards entering the church. But just then, an equal number of black and white surcoats filed through another church door, backing Patrick and his group. Teodorico's calm was short-lived.

Civilians scattered to the sides, clearing a space between the two regiments.

"Teodorico," Mother Superior reasoned, "you do realize you're outnumbered? Outside this church, if not already inside. This is ill-advised."

"I say we arrest him, and find out what the emperor is willing to do to get him back," Count Fulk suggested.

Favorable murmurs rippled through the crowd.

"N-n-no one is being arrested, least of all the pope, hmm?" Teodorico scoffed, then addressed the crowd at large with a booming voice. "And I *am* the pope."

"I'm taller than you!" Brobrosius' voice came from somewhere within the crowd.

Laughter erupted in the church and Teodorico's face turned livid.

"Quiet!" Sir Wolfgang called, quelling the crowd, though some snickering lingered. "We will not detain him. He is not worth shedding blood in this church, nor the bloodshed that would follow." He turned towards the angry pontiff. "Just leave, Teodorico, and take your politics with you."

Teodorico assessed the crowd with a cold eye.

"This isn't the end of this," he said frostily, and without stutter. "I will bring brimstone and hellfire down upon this place."

No one laughed.

#

Lucan mounted the stairs and followed the battlements toward the tower doorway. Before he reached it, however, he noted Sir Patrick in the courtyard conversing with the maidservant. He could not hear their words, but the French girl's smile and the glint in her eyes spoke volumes. Patrick kept his usual guarded demeanor, but even he had a hint of a smile as he embraced her.

Painful fingers constricted Lucan's heart. Instinctively, he clutched the object dangling at his chest beneath his garments.

"Sir Lucan," a voice said, startling him.

Sir Corbin stood in his path. Lucan held his breath.

"Lucky you moved into the keep earlier this month," Corbin said smiling, jerking his head toward the other side of the battlement, where servants had begun dismantling the pavilion city for departure. "Otherwise you would have a very awkward move right now."

Lucan cleared his throat and also smiled. "Yes, lucky indeed."

Corbin held out his hand. "Thank you for your support. There will be a meeting with the Greensprings leadership tomorrow. We'd like to see you there."

Lucan took his hand. "My pleasure."

Corbin beat his breast as he departed, stating, "Fight strong."

"Live stronger," Lucan replied, and continued on his way.

Inside the tower, he mounted another set of stairs and entered the apartment he had come to occupy. In the dying daylight, he immediately went to the table where he kept his wine.

He drew himself up just short of the table.

No, I shouldn't, he told himself. *Bad things happen when I drink. I lose control.*

After a moment he growled and reached for his goblet after all, but found it missing.

Before he could contemplate what had become of it, the sound of methodical clapping came from behind him. He whirled and drew his sword.

"Calm thyself, Sir Ferocious." Lilliana laughed, sitting on a strange trunk in the middle of his room.

"What are you doing here?" he demanded.

"I've come to congratulate you on a performance well done," she said. She stopped her clapping and picked up his goblet, which rested on top of the trunk. "I think you missed your calling. You should have been a thespian." She took a drink as she stood and approached. Her eyes narrowed at him. "You were acting, right?"

"Of course," he said, sheathing his sword. "They have invited me to their war council. They are convinced I have switched sides."

"Excellent," Lilliana purred. "You will be in the perfect position when the relic arrives."

Lucan scoffed. "I do not believe for one instant it will come. Even the young King Henry would not be so foolish as to give up such a treasure."

Lilliana tsked. "It is coming, I assure you. I can be very convincing. Besides, never underestimate the efforts of a young man struggling to get out from his father's shadow."

"I'll believe it when I see it," Lucan said.

"Have faith. It is worth the try, anyway." She shrugged. "And if it doesn't work, you will still be inside Greensprings to eliminate at least one key person, preferably Sir Patrick, making it easier to take the girl and cup by force."

Lucan's back stiffened. "So, not just a spy, but an assassin, as well."

She gave him a coy smile and sipped her wine.

"And what if," he growled, "I refuse to be a killer—an honorless murderer?"

Lilliana approached him from the side and whispered in his ear. "Then we will tell the emperor it was you who took the relic, and not his son. With your unique nature—" She trailed one of her talon-like fingernails across his cheek. Blood trickled from the thin red line her nail left behind, finally causing him to wince. "I'm certain the emperor will find an imaginative way to torment you for a hundred years... or more."

The wound on his cheek closed up almost as quickly as her nail created it, and the fresh blood dried up and flaked away.

"But it needn't be like that," she finished, her demeanor turning more cheerful as she tossed the empty wine goblet at him. He caught it from the air. "Do what is asked of you and you will get what you want: an end to your suffering."

Lucan contemplated the cup, wishing to fill and drain it repeatedly.

"What's in the trunk?" he asked, changing the subject.

"Open it," she said.

He did and peered down at the contents. His chest rose with a suppressed laugh.

"Is this a joke?" he asked, twisting his mouth thoughtfully as he looked at the breastplate and crested helm. Both rested on a neatly folded blue cloak.

"It represents what is to come if you accomplish your mission," she explained, "*Pope* Theodoric will need men like you in positions of power. It is a promise."

"I don't want a position of power," Lucan said, frowning. "I want an end."

"And you will have it," Lilliana replied, "but the end will not come quickly. You are a man of action. You will not want to sit idly by, waiting patiently to die. Between now and then you will want a hand in the biggest show of power on Earth."

Lilliana turned to leave, but Lucan caught her arm. "Stay a while."

"I cannot. I have several more visits this evening." She hesitated in his grasp, then kissed his unblemished cheek before leaving.

#

Katherina answered the knock at her door. "Lilly!"
The women embraced.

"I would have thought you would have gone to the ships while the pavilions are being taken down," she said as Lilliana stroked her hair and face.

"It would appear that of all the Romans, I'm the only one still tolerated in Greensprings. And someone needs to coordinate the evacuation of benefactors loyal to Teo. Which is why I'm here—we haven't much time."

The tall woman set about removing articles of clothing from Katherina's armoire and throwing them on the bed.

"Lilly, what are you doing?"

"The ships will be leaving soon, and we must pack your things. Do you have a trunk or some such?" Lilliana replied, looking around.

Katherina stopped Lilliana's frantic arranging of her clothes. "I'm staying," she explained. "Chansonne needs me."

Lilliana froze and stared with disbelief in her eyes. "You're mad. Did you not hear what Teo said in the church? He means it."

Katherina drew herself up, resolute. "This is my home now. I've run enough in my lifetime. This is where I belong."

Lilliana's eyes were full of a pleading hurt, but Katherina did not waver despite the tears gathering in her own vision. Lilliana dropped the dress she held to the bed in defeat. She removed a scarab-shaped lapis lazuli brooch from her dress and pressed it into Katherina's hand.

"To remember me by," she said. She kissed Katherina and left.

#

"Good night, young sir," Father Wulfric said to the Avangarde standing in the corridor outside his room. The young man saluted him.

Sighing in relief, Wulfric closed and barred the door behind him.

Though he doubted Teodorico would be so foolish as to have him attacked in the open, Wulfric had made it a point to stay in heavily trafficked public places for the rest of the day. When night came, he made certain to commandeer an Avangarde to stand watch near his room, knowing full well a locked door had made little difference in stopping the creature from killing Sister Abigail.

Creature? He shook his head, still finding it hard to believe the lovely Lady Lilliana was a monster. Even when he had confronted her, he had hoped for a reasonable explanation, but she did not deny it.

"What is she?" he mused out loud, but judged that detail unimportant for now. Currently, he needed to stay alive and wait for Teodorico to make his announcement, hoping the man was wise enough to know when to quit. If he didn't, Wulfric didn't know what to do for his next move. The humidor did not exist, nor did a preserved face in a box. Only a ruse. Wulfric hoped it was enough, because pleading his case to the other benefactors would only gain him raised eyebrows, at best.

He shook his head again as drowsiness stalked him. "Awake. Stay awake. All the victims were attacked in their sleep. Stay awake and you will live."

He paced the room, noting he had chosen wisely by picking a room with no windows. One entrance, guarded by a knight.

And he would not sleep.

He paused to rub his eyes. When he opened them, he stood in a field under a blue sky.

"I know this place," he mumbled, "I haven't been here in years."

He stood in a field near the monastery where he had undergone training for the priesthood, long ago. He had loved this field and visited often to clear his mind of doubts about committing his life to God.

"Yes," he said, "and there was a..." He turned and sure enough, a beautiful white horse approached him. He loved that horse, too. He had often brought it carrots or turnips to eat. He would lie in the grass, admiring the beautiful animal's snowy coat.

"But not alone," a feminine voice said. "I was here, too."

A beautiful blond stopped from behind the horse and stroked his mane.

Wulfric joined her in stroking the beast. "Yes, the farmer's daughter who taught me so much about horses."

"Not just horses." She winked.

Wulfric sat up in bed, startled. He didn't remember lying down on the bed.

"Dreaming," he breathed, "I was dreaming. I mustn't sleep. Must stay awake. All the victims were asleep."

He looked to the door as he repeated this mantra, noting the crossbar in place. Movement from the side caught his attention. When he looked, the white horse stood in his room.

"I'm still dreaming," he muttered. "I have to wake."

"Are you in such a hurry to forget me?" the farmer's daughter said, making a pouty face.

"Oh, I'll never forget you," Wulfric replied, smiling and touching her face. He stood again in the sunlight. "If not for you I would have always wondered what worldly pleasures were like. That curiosity would have always been a distraction. You saved me from that."

"Aye, you told me all your worries and doubts. You told me all your secrets," she said, joining his hand against the horse's muzzle. She squeezed his fingers. "Tell me another secret. Did you really see her face in the skin?"

"What? Lilliana? Yes, of course. Just long enough to..." Wulfric said, but caught himself.

"Just 'long enough?'" the farmer's daughter said, and she laughed.

Her face shifted, her hair turned dark, and she grew in stature. Lilliana stood in her place.

"No, I must wake," Wulfric said, shaking his head.

"You will, but for now, enjoy the moment." Lilliana shrugged her robe off, revealing her nude glory. "For in a dream, you can do all manner of things your worldly vows will not allow. You cannot be held accountable for what happens in a dream."

He lay in his bed again, but now paralyzed. A mist filled the room.

She came forward and rolled up his robe past his thighs. His arms lay weakly at his sides. He wanted to move, to sit up, but couldn't.

He made the mistake of looking at her directly, for when he did, his body grew hot at the sight of her. Her skin so smooth. Her smell intoxicating.

"Just relax, Wulfie, you've earned this. You've been lonely for so long, with no one to appreciate your sacrifices, but now you will be rewarded."

She climbed on top of him, straddling him with her warm body, moving rhythmically. He became lost in the pleasure of the moment. Even when bat-like wings extended behind her, spanning the room, and her eyes turned to feline slits, he did not want her to stop.

"I will resist... in a moment," he told himself. He turned his head and reached for the silver writing quill on the desk near his bed. His hand faltered just short of it. "I will resist in a moment. In a moment."

The white horse hung its head, turned, and faded away.

When they found him the next day, baby's breath filled his cold mouth.

#

"You're late," Teodorico snipped at Lilliana as she boarded the ship.

"Somebody had to organize those who wished to depart with us," she replied, stepping aside for the porters. They brought luggage, crates, and boxes up the gangplank, hurrying to depart. "Besides, I wanted to make one more attempt with Katherina."

"And she said no, didn't she?" Teodorico smirked.

Lilliana's disappointed look was all the answer he needed.

"The sooner we leave, the sooner we can come back. I cannot believe it has come down to this. I gave them every chance, every reason to do the right thing. Victor, are the preparations in place?"

Victor nodded, "They are, Your Holiness."

"Good," Teodorico responded, shaking his head at the all-but-useless Cardinal Guard he had brought with him. "It is time we try a different quality of soldiery to get what I want."

"Yes, Your Holiness," Victor replied, "those waiting for you come highly recommended."

Teodorico gazed long in the direction of Greensprings.

"A pity it comes to this, and at such an expense! I've been more than generous, don't you think, Lilly? Lilly?"

Lilliana herself stared thoughtfully back towardsGreensprings.

He touched her face and looked sympathetically into her amber eyes.

"I hope you haven't become too attached," he said, "because they're all going to die soon."

Chapter Fourteen

Though the sun crested at midday, a darkness filled the woods. Siegfried's hooves thudded on the mossy forest floor. Patrick reined him in and looked frantically about.

"I thought you said you could find the cave?" Aimeé said from behind him, struggling for comfort on Siegfried's back.

Patrick grumbled and gave up scanning the trees, which all started to look alike. "When last I did, I could not enter. The guardians met me outside. Now it would appear they do not want me to visit at all."

Aimeé shifted positions. "Can we at least take a break? My arse hurts from sitting on Siegfried's arse."

Patrick smiled and let her down onto a fallen log.

Aimeé looked around, rubbing her rump. "Plenty of aspens, hillocks, and rocks just as you described, but nothing big enough for a cave."

Patrick grunted in agreement. He climbed down from Siegfried's saddle and took Aimeé's hand. "Even if we found it, I'm afraid Chansonne is scared to death to touch the cup, let alone carry it here for us. Still, I wanted to ask the guardians if she was the key to returning it."

"Well, I'd say their absence is answer enough," Aimeé replied sadly.

"Perhaps not," Patrick said with a spark of hope. "You said when you played that tune on the flute it brought the Fair Folk to the garden that night. Maybe if you played it now they will come."

Aimeé scrunched up her nose at him. "I thought you brought me so we could we spend some time together now that His Evilness is gone."

Patrick grinned and kissed her. "I'm killing two birds with one stone."

After a few more kisses and a pinch on her rump, she conceded to playing the tune.

After they waited many minutes, still nothing happened.

"Drat, just when I get the right tune, I've forgotten how to play the wrong one," Aimeé lamented, frowning at the tiny combination flute and crucifix. Her eyes brightened and she addressed Patrick. "You know, we have time now. Would you be willing to listen to your mother's music?"

Patrick stiffened slightly, but sat down hard on the log. He gripped his knees. "Why not? Ready when you are."

Aimeé frowned. "A little less sarcasm in your compliance, if you don't mind?"

"Still ready," Patrick said through a strained smile.

"Fine," Aimeé replied, and set to playing the music.

He had to admit that the music did soothe. His eyes drooped and he felt his chin come to rest on his chest. His mind, which had roiled with anxieties from Teodorico to the cup to the baby to his guard duties, suddenly calmed and became a blank canvas.

That is until one image assaulted him like an arrow shot from the darkness. An image of a blond woman with blue eyes. She was covered in blood.

"Patrick! Stop!" Aimeé's voice broke through the fog.

He startled into wakefulness, not even realizing he had fallen asleep, and saw he now stood and had forced Aimeé to her knees by a harsh grip he had on her wrists.

"I-I'm sorry," he choked out. He helped her up. "I'm so sorry. What happened?"

Aimeé rubbed her wrists. "You fell into a... trance. You were peaceful at first, but then resisted. You shouted names."

Patrick hugged her and apologized profusely.

"Patrick," Aimeé said, looking deeply into his eyes, "who is Philip?"

Patrick froze, rigid with the memory of that name and the barbarian it belonged to. "I don't know."

Her accusing look told him she did not believe him, and that he wouldn't be able to lie. "Patrick..." But her eyes grew wide as her attention turned to the forest.

He followed her gaze. The rocks and trees moved, rising and taking a step forward on the likeness of legs. They bobbed and weaved, and seemed to stare curiously at the two strangers in their midst.

A mote of light darted from the trees and buzzed near their faces.

"Talia!" Aimeé cried, holding her hand out for the fairy to land on her palm.

Patrick squinted at the tiny girl who lit on Aimeé's palm. "It's like my mother's name."

Talia smiled and made a trilling sound at the declaration.

Aimeé nudged Patrick. "Go on, ask."

"Right," Patrick said, clearing his throat. "Talia, there is a cave about here where three Fey abide. They are tall like me. Three sisters, perhaps. They once guarded a cup, which I'd like to return. Can you show us the way?"

Talia's smile faded and her trilling turned to what sounded almost like a whine. Her bright almond eyes were heavy with regret. "No need. They sent me to deliver a message: 'The cup is of your world, not ours, and we were only caretakers of it for a while. If it wants to return to us, it will have to make that decision for itself.'"

She shrugged sadly, turned into a mote of light, and shot off into the woods.

The trees and rocks returned to normal, and Patrick's wonderment faded.

"That wasn't very helpful," Aimeé said, scowling into the woods. "They didn't even let us ask about Chansonne. How do we know when the cup wants to come back?"

"I shouldn't be surprised," Patrick said, only hearing an echo of Aimeé's words. "When I was a child, the other children tormented me because of my mother's origins. I prayed the Fair Folk would make them stop, protecting me as one of their own. But they didn't help me then, either."

#

"He did not confide in me directly what his next move would be, but I'm certain he has one and it will involve much pain and suffering," Lucan confessed at a council of the Greensprings hierarchy. He had been generous with the information he had, which affected little—Teodorico had been private with his plans, and Lucan knew little. Nothing save that which Lillian had conveyed to him in his quarters.

"You should have killed him when you had the chance," he added vehemently. They seemed to believe him.

"Avalon may weather one errant holy man," Father Hugh replied nervously to Lucan's suggestion, "but perhaps not so the wrath of an emperor if we should kill his appointed pope."

Wolfgang nodded. "We have a modicum of protection here with the wall of mist, King Henry of England, and Pope Paschal as our patrons. Killing Teodorico would have nullified much of that."

"You have simply delayed the inevitable," Lucan replied, "or have you forgotten Teodorico has a swan feather that will help him lead a fleet of warships here?"

"No doubt he will come with an army," Corbin said, "but the question is: how large of one?"

"Hopefully not so large we can't hold out long enough to get word to the King of England. Regardless of the politics, he will not tolerate a foreign army in his backyard. We have a swan feather, too," Abbot Herewinus pointed out.

"That is problematic," Lucan replied. "Even before we left Rome, Robert of Normandy was moving his army against his brother in England. London is going to be very busy and will not have the time or resources to help us."

"I don't doubt Teodorico had his hand in that, as well," the Abbot responded. "The timing is too convenient for him."

Grumbles of agreement.

"If nothing else, we need to evacuate the Guests to a safer place," Mother Superior said.

Herewinus agreed. "I am happy to house them at Glastonbury. From there we can send them to their homes. Also, we can send messengers on to London for aid."

"Better to send the messengers to Rome," Lucan urged. "Pope Paschal is your best chance for aid. I'm sure he will be eager to punish his traitorous cardinal."

"But that will take weeks longer, perhaps months," Wolfgang mused, his bushy eyebrows furrowing in concern over his nose.

Lucan suppressed a nod, *Exactly*, then added out loud. "Then let us pray God loves Greensprings. May I suggest our newest knights be our messengers?"

This suggestion upset his former squires, who lined the wall behind his chair.

"But, sir," Sir Jakob protested, "Greensprings will need all the help they can get if this place should fall under siege."

"Yes, I would like to volunteer to protect the cup," Sir Josef added.

"We could use their help," Corbin admitted. "Evacuating Guests will require an Avangarde escort, leaving us shorthanded here. We can only spare one of them."

Lucan nodded solemnly. "Then let it be Charles, and just as well. His Uncle Robert, Count of Flanders, and especially his mother, the Lady Adele, would have my head if I let anything happen to him. I'm sorry, Charles, but we all must do our duty."

Charles hung his head in disappointment, but obeyed.

"Very well, then," Wolfgang finished, "let's get to it. We have much to do."

#

As they filed out the door, Patrick leaned over to Corbin and whispered, "I don't see why you insisted I sit in on this council. I didn't have much to offer."

"I wanted you informed of all decisions made today so when I assign you to incorporating the villagers into the defense of Greensprings, I won't have to repeat myself."

"But Sir Waylan and Sir Brian outrank me," Patrick objected, finding it hard to believe only a few weeks ago he had sat in a little chair while chastised by Mother Superior and threatened with expulsion from the Order.

"Perhaps," Corbin explained, "but we call Sir Waylan a 'warrior hermit' for a reason—he's even less personable than you —and Sir Brian would be a great leader if we were organizing a barroom brawl. You are a former crusader and have experience with sieges. Besides," he added, leveling a serious gaze at the Irishman, "they aren't the Knight of Cups. You brought the troublesome thing to Greensprings, so it is only fitting you have a hand in its defense. Also, you're essentially the one who told Teodorico to take the cup and stick it up his arse when you laid him out in the church. You're in deep and will see it through to the end, from every angle."

Patrick swallowed his tongue and his pride in one gulp.

#

A controlled chaos reigned in Greensprings.

The biggest challenge proved to be dividing the keep's wagons and ox teams between evacuating Guests and moving villagers and their supplies inside Greensprings's walls. This continuous traffic created a permanent cloud of dust hanging over the practice field.

Most Guests chose to leave Avalon, not wishing to be caught between the hammer and anvil of fate. There were Guests, however, who either stubbornly chose to remain, such as Trent, William, and a handful of others, or those who could not leave—the candidati. Teodorico had abandoned them when he could not gain control of Chansonne, not even caring to inquire about their well being. Just as well, for the children refused to leave Chansonne. And Chansonne refused to leave Katherina and Aimeé.

Nobody, not even the acerbic Count Fulk, had attempted to make Chansonne take up the cup again—thus rendering the argument as to where it should reside moot.

"God has spoken," Abbot Herewinus had declared, "and if He wills it to be elsewhere, He will let us know. As for me, I relinquish any claim to it. If peaceful times ever return to fair Avalon, then I will not contest this place as a holy site, a place of pilgrimage."

"There will be a need for ships to ferry pilgrims, and at a price," Count Fulk had advised.

"A discussion for another time," the Abbot countered.

Count Fulk must have agreed, because his vessel was counted among the first to leave Avalon.

Patrick worked with Sir Jakob, Sir Josef, and Sir Jon to prepare the keep's defenses with the villagers. Sir Geoffrey would have joined, but the children insisted he stay close to them and Chansonne.

Despite his recent experience as drill instructor, Patrick found Corbin's and Wolfgang's faith in his leadership questionable. Delegating tasks to others? The mere thought frightened him. And it specifically burdened his mind when he met representatives from the village at the Back Door gate. Though peasants, they were freemen, and like the serving staff at the keep, they served voluntarily. If you pushed them too much or unreasonably, they would become uncooperative. Which went a long way in explaining Aimeé's stubborn streak.

"When traffic through the gate has calmed down, I'd like to create an entrenchment here," Patrick explained to the lead representative, a willowy, towheaded man named Fletcher. His weathered face and keen light eyes followed Patrick as he paced out the dimensions of the earthworks he had in mind. "It needs to have sheer walls, and be at least twice as tall as you, with no more than a foot's distance from the gate, extending another body length to either side of the gate."

"All well and good, my lord," Fletcher agreed, "and I understand the need to create such a murder hole, but I was to understand you wanted to apply us to tasks more in line with our specific skill sets."

"Aye, they will, I promise," Patrick replied, matching Fletcher's bold gaze. "I can't begin to tell you how pleased I was to learn virtually every man in Aesclinn is an accomplished archer, but when it comes to siege preparations, I can tell you that everyone, high and—" he almost said "low," but at the last moment, altered it to, "—higher, must do their share of labor. Or you can watch your loved ones die horribly. First the hard work of labor, then the joy of slaying evil. Agreed?" Fletcher and his men smiled. "And to prove my point, I'll throw in two knights to help you dig."

With that he pushed Sir Jakob and Sir Josef forward.

"Wha—?" The young knights groused.

"Welcome to Greensprings, my noble volunteers." Patrick winked.

This seemed to truly mollify Fletcher and the others who nodded and chuckled. The knot of worry tying up Patrick's guts finally loosened.

"Oh, and this won't be a murder hole in the usual sense," Patrick pointed out.

"You don't want us to line the bottom with sharpened stakes?" Fletcher asked.

"No," Patrick replied. "When William of Normandy first gained control of his Duchy before moving to England to become

William the Conqueror, he would defeat a town, round up the surviving men, gouge out their eyes, cut off their hands and feet, and send them crawling to the next town as a warning as to what was to come." Fletcher grimaced at the image. "Which is an effective strategy if you're conquering a series of towns, but I have a more practical plan in mind—not to mention a less gruesome one."

"If you say so, my lord." Fletcher looked skeptical.

"It will make sense when the—" Patrick started to reply, but something in the practice field caught his attention. "If you'll excuse me, Mister Fletcher."

Patrick walked in a daze towards the luggage-laden wagon train. The vehicles sat before the gate, waiting for a herd of sheep to pass inside. He stopped at a distance and watched as Sir Wolfgang and several other Avangarde gave orders to the drivers. Sir Marcus Ionus stood by his horse, having conversation with Aimeé. Patrick could not hear their words, but both smiled and laughed lightly, and when Marcus reached out to touch Aimeé's wrist, an irrational flash of jealousy rose in Patrick's chest. He clenched his fists. Though innocent enough, Aimeé enjoyed it.

He squeezed his eyes shut against the image of a bloody woman. He'd hurt Aimeé because of it twice—in the forest and back in Eire. He ground his teeth.

Chansonne crept up on him and took his free hand. She looked into his face, not exactly smiling, but she did not squint at him suspiciously anymore.

And all I had to do to finally win her trust was punch a pope in the face.

A peaceful feeling came over him, chasing away his selfish anxieties. She led him towards Aimeé. Marcus stepped away to give orders to the wagon crews, and Chansonne transferred herself to Aimeé's skirts.

"I see you finally made a friend," Aimeé said.

"And I think motherhood will suit you very well," Patrick replied as Aimeé stroked the child's hair. He closed the distance between them and looked long into her green eyes, then towards Marcus' retreating form.

"You know, I'm certain a suggestion from me alone would be enough to convince Marcus to take you with him. It will be safer with the Guests."

"Patrick, you will not be rid of me that easily," Aimeé replied.

Patrick struggled around the knot in his throat. "I'd rather see you safe and happy than trapped here with me."

Aimeé smiled sweetly. "Greensprings and Aesclinn are my home, and there are those here who need my protection, as well."

Patrick smiled and nodded.

"And I will do everything in my power to protect you. All of you. God is my witness."

#

Once the Guests, board members, and their Avangarde escort set sail into the Avalon mist, the transport wagons shifted to hauling as much grain and vegetables as possible to the storage silos. The practice field turned into a giant barnyard of sheep, cattle, and goats. A wall of hay rested against the eastern battlement, and next to it a wall of firewood. The courtyard squawked and clucked nonstop with chickens, geese, and ducks. The same army of women who fashioned buckets for firefighting and stacked them next to the courtyard fountain also worked diligently to keep the waterfowl out of the water to keep the drinking supply clean.

The Hall for Guests and Hall for Lady Guests, now mostly empty of students, filled with the elderly, children, and families, and when those rooms filled, the rest of the villagers built a shantytown of leaning boards and canvas against the walls. The kitchen staff worked day and night preserving food. Their cooking cauldrons prepared large quantities of oil to dump on besiegers. Larders were filled to capacity. The battlement catwalks were armed with piles of stones. As many able-bodied villagers as possible received weapons and armor. They ripped every scrap of spare linen into strips to bind wounds. The great hall transformed into a hospital with fire and hot irons at the ready for staunching wounds.

When these things were done, Greensprings settled into a tense, waiting stillness.

#

One late afternoon, Patrick and Corbin inspected the bushels of arrows fashioned by the village archers. Corbin ticked off the number of arrows in each bushel as Patrick noted it down on parchment with a piece of charcoal.

"For someone who doesn't read or write, you know your numbers well enough," Patrick said.

"Sixteen, seventeen, eighteen... Counting is easy," Corbin grunted. "Numbers make sense. All those letters just float every which way on paper."

From the corner of their eyes, a light shot into the sky, seizing their attention with an icy grip.

"It can't be," Corbin murmured as another light shot up to the far left of the first.

"Both harbors?" Patrick mused out loud, almost dropping his bit of charcoal.

Even before the first pair of flaming arrows started to fall back to earth, a second pair shot into the sky.

"That's confirmation," Corbin breathed. "The enemy is here."

"So soon? How can that be?" Patrick shook his head in disbelief. Barely two weeks had passed. The last of the supply wagons from Aesclinn had yet to return to the keep.

The bottom of his stomach fell out like the last sands in an hourglass.

"Evidently Teodorico had an army waiting all along," Corbin realized.

They ran for the front keep walls as the church bells started to sound. The courtyard buzzed with activity.

When Patrick and Corbin gained the top, they could see a lone Avangarde galloping from the tree line towards the gate. When he crossed the drawbridge and passed through the gatehouse, Corbin called down to the knight, "Well, what did you see?"

"Eight ships and large ones," the knight answered, "and floating low in the water as if filled to the gills with men and supplies."

Corbin sucked in air as he turned back to the road between Greensprings and the harbor. "What of the last supply wagon?"

"I didn't know another wagon was out there," the knight responded, eyes widening. "I should go back, as I'm certain the lead ship unloaded scouts."

A small warning bell in a corner tower rang frantically. The Avangarde manning it pointed to the tree line.

A lone figure ran on foot. Even from this distance the man's clothing identified him as a villager, and most likely the missing wagoner. Patrick imagined the man had come under attack and abandoned his lumbering ox cart to escape.

As if to confirm this, and to Patrick's horror, a group of unknown riders in dark armor burst from the forest road, riding the villager down. The lead horseman made a swirling gesture and the villager jerked to one side, his neck snared by a whip. The villager fell, but the rider dragged him a good distance before stopping.

"I'm going out there!" the knight in the courtyard called, his horse rearing.

"Stand down!" Corbin called. "He is too far and it is too late."

The knight opened his mouth to protest, but then saw through the gate what Corbin already saw from the wall—a river of more cavalry pouring from the forest road, surrounding the handful of riders who surrounded the villager.

"Dammit!" Corbin cursed, pounding his fist on the wall.

They watched helplessly as the lead rider dismounted and approached the villager, who was trying to crawl away. The rider snatched him up by the hair, pulled back his head, and looked to the keep walls. Distance and a visored helm could not stop Patrick from imagining an evil face grinning behind it. The brute produced a dagger and dragged it across the villager's throat.

Red blossomed long enough for all to see, and then the assailant pushed the limp body forward.

"Raise the bridge and drop the portcullis," Corbin growled.

As Patrick's stomach turned with anger, and the battlements vibrated with the gate mechanism, Corbin drew his own dagger and carved a notch in his glove.

#

Over the next few hours as the sun set, all their visitors appeared.

First came the flocks of carrion birds swirling like a noisy black cloud against the setting sun. Then came the drummers; a long line of footmen beating methodically at their instruments, who moved aside to let the seemingly endless procession of mounted men and infantry pass. They carried banners with a simple insignia: a field of half black and half white. In the fading light the men looked more like black ants, regimented into neat squares. The drums tapped away as the field grew thick with them.

The villager's killer leisurely rode forward and took up a position on a hillock to regard Greensprings.

Patrick squinted at the figure, trying to make out his features, but the distance and fading light made it impossible. Yet, something about him seemed familiar.

"God, how many are there?" Corbin whistled. "The sooner we can take an accurate count, the sooner we can distribute our defenders."

Agitating to do something other than watch, Patrick considered an idea.

"Brobrosius!" he called to the little man.

"Yes," Brobrosius answered, looking from under a cooking pot on his head. He stopped waving the stick around he used as a sword. "I'm taller than you."

"Right, quite so." Patrick no longer bothered to contest the point. "Would you be so good as to come up here and help us with something?"

Without hesitation Brobrosius broke into a run and mounted the stairs. The other candidati followed close on his heels. Patrick shook his head, not expecting the whole lot to come.

Brobrosius stood next to him, breathless, and saluted.

"Brother, can you tell us how many people are out there?"

Brobrosius took a glance, looked back to Patrick, and said, "Two thousand four-hundred and thirty-eight, plus one thousand sixty-two horses. So how can I help?"

Corbin coughed and his eyes bulged for a moment.

"You just did, Brobrosius, thank you," Patrick patted the man on the shoulder, "and by the way, you're taller than me."

A huge smile spread across Brobrosius' face and he saluted.

Candace, however, moaned as she looked out on the field of gathering darkness.

"What's wrong, child?" Corbin asked.

Her head snapped in their direction and she put a finger to her lips. "Shh," she whispered in a frightened raspy voice. "The bad man is coming."

"Well, that is not exactly news," Corbin said, frowning, "we know Teodorico is out there."

Candace returned her gaze to the field and continued to moan.

"Looks like they're settling in, despite all that drumming," Corbin said squinting out into the darkness. "We'll double the watch and see what the morning brings. Probably best to be prepared for something at dawn."

"Agreed," Patrick said. "I'll go inform the Back Door to double the watch."

Patrick turned to leave and had descended partway down the stairs when he heard the horns, stopping him in his tracks. Though far away, they shook the walls and rattled his nerves. The gravelly sound washed over him like a rockslide.

The swirling carrion birds scattered, disrupted by the blast. The note came from an instrument sounding more primal than anything produced by a mere brass trumpet made by the hands of men. In the darkness, one could imagine a dragon belching wind from horns on its head, or perhaps the ghost of Hannibal had descended upon the keep with his trumpeting elephants.

As the second barrage of long sonorous notes shook their bones, Corbin cursed. "I've never heard such a thing, have you Patrick? Patrick?"

He turned to see the Irishman sitting on the first flight of stairs with his knees pulled up against his chest, hugging them and rocking back and forth, mumbling in a fashion similar to Candace.

"Patrick, what's wrong?" Corbin asked, a chill running up his spine. "You're frightening me."

"No," Patrick mumbled, eyes staring vacantly. "It can't be. It just can't be."

Chapter Fifteen

"They're *routiers*. Mercenaries," Patrick explained to the Greensprings leadership in council chambers. "German folk mostly, who took up crusade and attached themselves to the crusader armies that came out of Flanders. They, like many companies of mercenaries, paid their way by acting as foragers and suppliers for the main army. They did this by pillaging the countryside, and were not above rape and murder in the process. They are made up mostly of bandits, criminals, and heathens. Their leadership is a posse of landless nobles who are not much more than criminals themselves. Most of the atrocities associated with the crusaders, even long before they reached the Holy Land, were at the hands of mercenaries. The leaders of the Crusade, the princes of Christendom, turned a blind eye to their actions so long as their own men and horses were fed and supplied."

Patrick paused, frowning and feeling anger boil in his veins.

"I figured Teodorico would be ambitious and ruthless in obtaining what he wants, but employing such people to obtain something holy is... grotesque. Throughout the journey to Jerusalem, this particular army has been called the Company of Bad Men, which became, as jest, the Company of Bad Boys. They have been more accurately called, the Company of Lost Souls. Last I heard, they have been called a combination of all these: the Company of Lost Boys. There is no doubt in my mind they will burn down Greensprings, murder every man inside, and rape every woman.

"They are led by a..." Patrick paused, his vision blurring a moment as he searched for the right words, "...a particularly brutal man by the name of Philip der Rhinelander. He is a disgraced knight who had been excommunicated until he successfully participated in the siege of Jerusalem."

The room fell quiet. When he had nothing more to add, the knights cleared their throats and pondered the news.

"Well, we knew we were in for a rough time," Corbin said at last. "We should count ourselves fortunate. The more we know about them, the better off we are."

"How is it you know so much about this particular band of mercenaries?" Mother Superior asked Patrick.

Patrick took his time, swallowing hard before looking into her eyes.

"Because I was one of them."

The collective gasp that rose in the chamber reflected the shock in Mother Superior's face.

"I don't believe it," Father Hugh said.

"Nor do I. Surely you mean you had to associate with them as a crusader is all," Sir Corbin added.

Patrick shook his head as he hung it.

"I was not always the man you see before you today," he said, "and though I was not the worst of them, I was one of them. I was lost for a time. A lost soul. A Lost Boy."

"But how? How is that possible?" Mother Superior asked.

"Getting lost is easy," Patrick explained. "All a boy needs to head down the wrong path is to go on crusade because a girl hurt him. Then, because you are a foreigner who doesn't speak any of the languages very well, the leaders of the Crusade throw you into a crowd of ruffians and scoundrels because they don't know what else to do with you. After a while, those ruffians and scoundrels are the only ones who treat you well. The only ones to accept you. They become your brothers. That's how."

Despite the shame and bitterness in Patrick's voice, Mother Superior's gaze turned kind and compassionate. She reached over to touch his forearm.

"You won't have to worry about associating with them now," Corbin assured Patrick. "We have enough men and supplies to defend the keep. We only need to wait them out before help comes from either England or the pope. I am of half a mind to take the battle to the field, if what you say is true they are mostly bandits and criminals—I'd put any Avangarde against any two average knights, and against any five common scoundrels."

Patrick shook his head gravely. "According to Brother Ambrosius they number well over two thousand, and even their common foot soldiers were uncommonly vicious. Their core cavalrymen are capable knights. After all, I was one of them. As for waiting them out, we had better pray that help does arrive because this Philip understands siege warfare. He played crucial roles in the fall of Antioch and Jerusalem, and those were tougher nuts to crack than Greensprings."

"Then we are indeed fortunate," Corbin said, smiling and clapping Patrick on the back, "because we have you to tell us every move this Philip will make."

"Yes," Patrick conceded tiredly, "and Philip knows it."

#

The enemy advanced on Greensprings the following morning. Patrick went to command Fletcher to assemble the archers on the walls, but Corbin stopped him.

"No need—they come under a white flag," he said. "They are not rushing the keep, and there appears to be a group in front coming for a parley."

Skeptical, Patrick mounted the walls with Corbin and what seemed like half of Greensprings. Indeed, the enemy had assembled a fair distance from the walls, but Corbin spoke true: no ladders or any other siege equipment. In front waited several mounted men, one bearing a white strip of cloth dangling from a lance.

Even at this distance he could see their armor. Allowed to oxidize to a black color, it consisted of a mixture of chain mail, leather, scale, and the occasional plate. Helmets and shields had no standard shape or size. Though the arms and armament did not match, they were quality: the best pickings of the battlefield. Their outer garb carried no visible emblems or heraldry, the absence of which served just as well as any coat of arms to mark their allegiance.

They were armed: swords, maces, pikes, halberds, spears, cudgels, hooked bec-de-corbins, and every type of axe imaginable. They carried something else, too. Something small in their hands. These they raised to the keep walls and shook violently, creating a discordant jangling that sounded like Hell's orchestra tuning its instruments.

"What are those?" Sir Jakob said, eyes squinting at the little objects.

"Spurs," Corbin replied simply.

"Spurs?" Jakob said, making a face, "why on earth would they shake spurs at us?"

"It's a taunt. It's their way of saying they know Greensprings is full of knights and they don't care. They're still going to kill us," Patrick answered.

"How does shaking spurs tell us that?"

"Where do you think they got all those spurs from in the first place?" Patrick pointed out, raising his eyebrows.

"Quiet, someone is coming forward to talk," Corbin hushed. "I'm certain it's the man who killed the wagoner."

One of the mounted men, the larger one not holding the white flag, approached the gate. Chain mail wrapped his meaty forearms, which were exposed from under a great cloak similar to the sort Patrick wore. Though just as dark as his men's, his mail had a certain sheen to it, as did his visored helmet. The sun caught a wide mouth and strawberry-blond goatee as he looked up to his gatehouse audience.

He studied them long and quietly before removing his helmet and hanging it on the pommel of his huge broadsword. On his other hip coiled a whip.

"What a fool," Sir Josef murmured. "Who removes their armor on the battlefield?"

"He's showing he's not afraid," Patrick murmured back, eyes fixated on the man on horseback.

Corbin hushed them again as the man peeled back the coif of his armor to reveal blond hair fashioned into a bowl cut. Peering up at them was a round, weathered face with a scarred right cheek.

"Greensprings!" he called in a booming voice heavily accented in German. "I am Sir Philip der Rhinelander. I know there is one among you who knows my company. You must know by now what we are capable of. His Holiness Pope Theodoric urges you to reconsider your position and enter into negotiations to surrender the girl and the cup."

"We have no doubt Teodorico will take the girl and the cup and still turn you loose on us," Corbin called down, refusing to refer to Teodorico as a pope. "So the answer is no. You can take that message back to him."

"And you are, good sir?" Philip asked, raising his hand to his eyes to shield them from the morning sun.

"Sir Corbin, Steward of Greensprings," Corbin replied.

"You are not the one I was hoping to talk to," Philip said, searching among the row of faces lining the walls. "Patrick! My brother! Where are you? Show yourself!"

Patrick leaned heavily into Corbin and grabbed his arm to steady himself. Once steadied, he leaned forward and responded to the mercenary.

"I'm here, Philip," he said in an almost whisper, but his voice reached its target just the same.

"Greetings, brother." Philip smiled, though no warmth filled his voice. "I see you've filled out nicely. Good. You are going to need your strength."

"Corbin is the one you need to talk to," Patrick responded flatly. "He is the one who makes the decisions."

"There will be plenty of time for all of us to talk," Philip returned, locking eyes with the Irishman, "unless you insist on refusing the pope's offer. Personally, I hope you reject his offer as that would give me the opportunity to exercise my talents."

Corbin was still preparing a retort when Patrick leaned into his ear and whispered, "Take the offer to negotiate. It will buy us time, plus we may learn something new. It is as you say—the more we know, the better off we are."

Corbin nodded curtly and called down to Philip, "Tell Teodorico we will meet him for talks."

"Very well," Philip replied. "I will tell His Holiness to bring his silly little tent and you can discuss matters with him within walking distance of your gate. However, His Holiness insisted on one condition for any discussions."

"Oh, what might that be?" Corbin asked, incredulous.

"His Holiness feels there is only one among you worthy of having dialogue with a pope," Philip explained "He will only negotiate with her."

"Her?" Corbin asked.

"The Lady Katherina is *bona fide* royalty," Philip continued, "and Pope Theodoric feels she is not so tainted by recent events as the rest of you. His Holiness will not waste his time with excommunicants and followers of false popes."

Corbin shrugged. "As he wishes. Bring forth his tent."

Philip bowed slightly in acknowledgment and turned his giant horse. Before leaving, however, he looked over his shoulder and addressed Patrick.

"I always said you looked good in black."

#

Katherina fidgeted with the lapis lazuli brooch on her white dress, taking deep breaths without trying to look obvious about it.

"Are you sure you're up for this?" Patrick asked her while they waited for the gate to open. Katherina's throat contracted as she swallowed hard, but she held her head high and smoothed out the front of her dress.

"I'm quite ready, thank you," she replied.

"You're perfectly safe."

The iron portcullis rattled upward, and it made Katherina jump.

"You will have six Avangarde with you, and you will be within bow-shot of a hundred Aesclinn archers. They don't miss."

Katherina nodded. The drawbridge descended. Beyond was a white cupola tent with fluttering pennants. Teodorico sat in his throne-like chair, surrounded by soldiers in a mixture of red and black garb. Her stomach knotted at the sight of the old man. Powerful old men made her uncomfortable, and the pressure of her mission to draw out negotiations as long as possible made her sick.

"Thank you for this, my lady," Corbin added. "Every hour we can delay an attack on the keep is one more hour for a rescuing army to come closer."

Katherina nodded again and set off across the bridge of the rocky chasm that separated Greensprings from the plain.

A lifetime of protocol and palace life had taught her the importance of projecting confidence. Therefore, she made every effort to walk with chin up, back erect, and hands held gently together in front of her as she strode forward with an entourage of six Avangarde: six knights whom she had requested for their height. To that end, Sir Corbin, Sir Patrick, and the hulking Sir Bisch walked on one side of her and Sir Brian, Sir Waylan, and Sir Edmund on the other. Their silvery mail and helmets glinted in the sun. They carried only their sheathed swords as weapons.

Before they reached the canopy, the Lady Lilliana approached them. Sir Edmund moved to bar her path, but Katherina admonished him. "It's quite all right, Sir Edmund. She is my friend."

"As you say, my lady," Edmund replied, and stepped back into his position at her side.

The women embraced and kissed and continued to the meeting spot arm-in-arm.

"I'm so sorry it has come to this," Lilliana said.

"I know," Katherina responded, patting Lilliana's arm, "but the world is a big place and things beyond our control often happen in it."

"You still can take control," Lilliana whispered, looking side to side. "All you need do is agree to hand the girl and the cup over to Teo. If it is her safety you are concerned about, know that she will be with me as much as with him, and I will protect her. Or, if it pleases you, she can stay in your charge and you can be her protector. Teo would not dare harm her, especially if you become his liaison to the Orthodox Church. Not only can you save your friends here, but you can make the world a more peaceful place."

Katherina's back stiffened and a whirlwind of doubt stormed behind her eyes. Uncertainty nagged at her. Would Teodorico just go away if he got what he wanted? Would Greensprings, with Father Hugh, Mother Superior, Jon, Willy, Trent, Patrick, and all the rest be allowed to live? Could she save them if she decided to agree? What would really become of Chansonne then?

They neared the canopy where Teodorico sat.

Lilliana added, "I know you'll do the right thing." She squeezed Katherina's arm and slipped away, taking a place among the entourage.

Among them, Philip der Rhinelander was holding a staring match with Patrick. The sheer fierceness of the display of bravado unnerved her, but she tried not to let it distract from her duties.

"Your Eminence," Katherina said, bowing.

"His *Holiness,*" Victor corrected, scowling.

The antipope tsked. "Now, now, we are all friends here, hmm? We are just having a friendly chat, and she is about to tell me what Greensprings has to say after they've had time to think about... recent changes, hmm, yes?"

Katherina drew herself up, preparing to respond, but paused when Lilliana caught her eye. The woman's amber eyes silently urged her to consider her next words.

She did.

"I'm afraid those in Greensprings—we in Greensprings—are compelled to keep the girl and the cup," she said, looking Teodorico directly in the eyes. "The cup will only allow itself to be held by the girl, and the girl has made it perfectly clear she does not want to leave Greensprings."

Teodorico's eyes flared and his lips formed a hard line. He glanced to Lilliana, whose expression fell to one of profound disappointment.

"Young lady," Teodorico addressed Katherina, "I want you to consider very carefully what you are saying, hmm? This is not a game. Many people are going to die unless you do as I say, hmm, yes? Now, be a good little girl, run along, and GET ME THE GIRL AND CUP."

Katherina stiffened at the condescension. Heat rose in her as she realized Teodorico had never intended any real negotiations. She took her time responding, using the technique Lilliana had taught her. She pictured Teodorico as a rat with a twitching nose. A grin spread across her lips.

"No," she said pointedly, "I made myself very clear. Surely, someone who prides himself on having control of a situation should see I am not about to repeat myself."

"Y-y-you petulant child!" he raged. "I-I-I should put you over my knee and spank you for your insolence!"

"We can make that happen, Your Holiness," Dragonetti said, taking a step forward. "I say we take her now."

In a flash, the Avangarde closed ranks about the princess with swords drawn, forming a black pincushion about a white spindle.

Katherina did not move; instead, her fingers calmly formed a steeple as she pointed them downward, creating what looked like a dove held in her pale hands. She regarded Teodorico, who labored to control a fit coming over him. A spasm rendered him speechless and breathless.

Meanwhile, like a stubborn and ignorant dog, Dragonetti did not take the hint to stay away from Katherina, even after Patrick tapped the Italian's chest with the tip of his sword.

"Sir Patrick, I'm going to enjoy—" Dragonetti started to say, but Philip grabbed a handful of the guard's cape and yanked him back.

Dragonetti turned to strike whoever had dared to touch him, but backed down when he saw who had done the deed.

"Why are you stopping me?" he growled.

Philip didn't bother to face the guard, but kept an unwavering glance on Patrick. "I'm saving your life."

"E-e-enough!" Teodorico cried, finally managing to gain a measure of control over his paroxysm. "I am a man of my word, hmm? I said no harm will come to them, and so none shall for now, but as God is my witness, I will burn Greensprings to the ground! So go back to your death trap. See if I care, hmm, yes?"

"Are you certain of that, my lord?" Katherina asked, tempting him back into dialogue.

"Yes, quite certain, hmm?" Teodorico snapped. "May God have mercy on your soul, hmm, yes?"

Katherina bowed and turned to leave.

"However, consider this, hmm?" Teodorico called to her back. "Lady Katherina, your mother still resides in Rome, hmm, yes? When I am through here, it will only be a matter of time before I'm recognized as the only pope, and I will run Paschal out of Rome and his protection of your mother will come to an end, hmm? Your uncle will pay handsomely to have her returned to him, where he will give her his own kind of justice, hmm, yes?"

Katherina stopped cold in her tracks. After a brief moment, she turned back towards the gloating old man, the confidence in her face wavering.

Teodorico stood. "You remember your uncle, hmm, yes?" He took a step forward, reaching the rope that held his robes in place, toying with it. "He would like to see you too, I'm sure, hmm?" he said. "Perhaps I'll instruct Philip here to save you from destruction, just so I can send you back to your uncle and his loving embrace, hmm, yes?"

His wrinkled hands toyed again with the belt about his waist as he subtly thrust his hips. Her heart skipped. She wanted to respond confidently, cleverly, but found herself strangled by fear. Her uncle's touch spread like a spider crawling along her spine—the memory of it was the same as the real thing.

Only Lilliana had known. It was she who had told Teodorico her secret.

Anger rose in Katherina and the confidence that had evaporated slammed back into her frame with righteous indignation.

"My lord Teodorico," Katherina addressed him icily, "my mother has survived better men than you, as have I. Your threats ring hollow with me. As for your success here at Greensprings? It is gravely premature and before all is done and said, it may very well be your head that will rest on a stake. Now, good day."

She turned to leave again with the Avangarde close behind her, but Philip spoke up. "If I may make a suggestion." He spoke gruffly but formally. "I would like to invite Sir Patrick, Sir Corbin, and another man of their choosing over for... dinner. Naturally we can make an exchange of men so no harm will come to you."

"Don't be ridiculous, hmm?" Teodorico growled. "They gave us their response. You will attack them in the morning as I command, hmm, yes?"

"And so I shall," Philip responded without looking at his employer, "but you have given all tactical control of the siege to me, ja? It serves my purposes to hold my own dialogue with them. Plus, it pleases me to do so."

"Bah!" Teodorico scowled, waving a hand. "If it pleases you to toy with your meat before you devour it, so be it, so long as you clean the plate."

"What say you, men of Greensprings?" Philip asked.

Corbin exchanged a look with Patrick. *Time.* Patrick shrugged.

"Very well, though I promise you will not gain anything by it," Corbin responded.

"Perhaps," Philip smiled. "I will send three men over to your gate at dusk for exchange, and then you can be my guests."

"I will pick the three men," Patrick warned, "for three men of little value just won't do. Is Jon de Lorraine still with you?"

"Ja, he is."

"And Jeremie Le Beau?"

"Ja, he is, as well as Diego from the old days. Are those the three you wish to exchange?"

Patrick barked a laugh. "You can keep Diego. I'd wager you'd be happy if we were to kill him for you. Honestly, I'm surprised that little sodomite is still alive."

Philip laughed a genuine laugh.

"Very well then," he said, "Jon and Jeremie, and one of my lieutenants."

Patrick and Corbin nodded and left.

At the edge of the tent as they passed, Lilliana spoke to Katherina.

"You've broken my heart," she said.

"You've broken my trust," Katherina responded, and tossed the scarab brooch at her feet.

#

As promised, at dusk three unarmed figures approached the gate.

Before Patrick, Corbin, and Bisch went out to meet them, Corbin had reassuring words for Katherina.

"You did well," he said, "as well as can be expected. I fully expected him not to entertain any real discussion, yet you still managed to buy us some time. Plus, you managed to enrage him, and an enraged enemy is an unbalanced enemy. Unbalanced enemies make mistakes. So, all in all, it went well. Fret not."

Katherina thanked him, wished the knights a safe return and saw them out the gate.

On the grass, Patrick dismounted Siegfried and approached two of the Lost Boys who also had dismounted. They embraced strongly to the clink of gear and the creak of leather.

"Well met Patrick!" the taller man cried. He had eyes as cold as marble, but his greeting was genuine. "How long has it been? Two, three years?"

The smaller man had curly hair and a lantern jaw, and he complained, "You just had to insist on us. How are we supposed to catch up if we are locked up in yonder keep while you drink our ale?"

"You'll be treated well enough, I promise," Patrick responded, smiling, "and God willing there will be other opportunities to talk old times."

"I truly hope we don't encounter each other on the battlefield," the tall man said. "I'd hate to kill you."

"I'd hate to be killed by you," Patrick returned, "God, what an embarrassment!"

They laughed and talked some more before Corbin cut them off.

"Gentlemen, we best be going our separate ways," he said, then added with a frown, "before you start kissing each other."

They laughed some more and they mounted their respective horses. The Lost Boys disappeared into the mouth of Greensprings's gate and the Avangarde rode the short distance to the enemy encampment. There, someone took their horses and another led them through the sprawling camp.

The smells of campfire smoke and cooking meat engulfed them, making Corbin pat his hungry belly. But to Patrick, the odor of camp was unmistakable. Along with the smoke and food were the musky smells of body odor, urine and excrement—human and animal alike.

Even though the sun had barely set, the camp was already in full festival mode. Men carried mugs and cups of ale, running hither and thither among the tents, chasing women of dubious occupation who had come with the mercenaries. Brash music filled the air, some of which came from the outlandish horns that had announced the arrival of the Lost Boys on their first day.

Conversations paused as the strangers passed the mercenaries. The hostile gazes made Corbin profoundly nervous. He grasped at empty air where his sword normally hung. He shot Patrick a glance laden with meaning; that he hoped these miscreants showed enough discipline to follow Philip's orders, and not attack.

Eventually, their guide brought them to a roaring bonfire.

"Wilkommen!" Philip der Rhinelander called from its edge. With a foot on a log, he leaned casually on his knee with mug in hand. "Come, have a drink!"

Urged to the side of the fire, they accepted mugs thrust into their hands. Waves of heat and smoke stirred around them as they took seats on logs destined for the flames.

"This is aphelon," Corbin said, sniffing at the drink in his hand.

"Is that what it's called?" Philip asked, taking a drink. "We found the village full of it. I'm surprised you left it all behind."

The Lost Boys gathered around the Avangarde, watching their visitors with the curiosity of children studying insects.

"Well, we did piss in it," Corbin pointed out.

They made faces and looked at their drinks.

"I jest," Corbin laughed and took a drink.

Laughter erupted around the fire.

"I like these people!" Philip guffawed, slapping Corbin hard on the back, causing the knight to cough up his mouthful of drink. "Bring them some dinner!"

A rotund man with an eyepatch and leather apron came forward with boards heaped with sausage and cooked apples, and he thrust them at Corbin and Bisch.

"I appreciate the hospitality," Corbin said, taking a long sniff, "but I don't see what you hope to gain by having us here tonight."

"Nothing to do with strategy," Philip admitted, "not strictly speaking, in any case. I merely wanted to satisfy my curiosity, to see who it is I am fighting. Also, to agitate the holy man. He pays well, but I like him not."

The fat cook returned with a board for Patrick.

"Your curiosity?" Corbin said, biting into a sausage. He made a favorable face. "Certainly Dragonetti and Victor or any number of others have given you all the intelligence you need to attack us. They were guests inside our walls long enough."

"He means me," Patrick spoke up for the first time. Until now he had only silently watched Philip.

"Ja, that is it," Philip said, putting his mug down and taking a bucket from the cook. He came forward and personally ladled a pale, stringy substance from the bucket onto the plates of his guests. "I asked myself, 'What kind of people would defy a pope and face certain death? What kind of people would our brother Patrick join? More curiously, what kind of people would accept him, a Lost Boy, among them?' These things I had to learn before I kill you all. Not secondhand, but from you directly."

"Former Lost Boy," Patrick said coolly, taking a bite of cooked apple.

"Once a Lost Boy, always a Lost Boy." Philip tsked, waving the ladle at Patrick. He then continued around the fire, ladling the substance onto waiting plates.

"It is simple, we protect the cup. God has spoken. The cup chooses to remain at Greensprings and not be exploited by a pretender pope," Corbin explained, turning up his nose at the steaming pile deposited on his board. It smelled rancid. "As for Patrick, he has been nothing but a fine Avangarde, despite his former associates. What on earth did you put in front of me?"

"Former associates!" Philip laughed, then added, "That is sauerkraut. Das ist gut!"

"Gut-gut!" Bisch agreed, eating the stuff up. Strands of it hung in his beard.

"Ah, aus bayerischen?" Philip asked Bisch.

Bisch replied in the affirmative and the two exchanged amicable words in German.

"Be careful what you say around this one," Philip called to the crowd with a smile. "He speaks the tongue and we don't want too many of our secrets slipping out."

Laughter came from a smallish, dark-complexioned man with a manicured goatee. He approached Bisch and put a friendly arm around him.

"No worries," he said with a laughing Spanish accent. He produced a dagger and held it to Bisch's throat. "I will cut that tongue out before any secrets escape."

More laughter filled the air. Bisch found none of it amusing and shoved the little man away. He went sprawling, but popped back to his feet and rushed Bisch who rose to meet the attack.

A mix of laughter and concerned agitation erupted in the crowd. Corbin stood, and not for the first time reached for his missing sword.

Philip, however, stepped in and grabbed the little Spaniard by the wrist and violently twisted it, taking the dagger away. He pushed him aside and glowered at him.

"Diego, listen up!" Philip yelled at his comrade, pointing the dagger at him. "These people are under my protection." Philip then turned round and addressed all the Lost Boys, gesturing with the blade to make his point. Corbin realized for the first time Philip's eyes shone brilliant green and they blazed in the firelight. "No harm will come to them while they are here! This is my word! Tonight, we feast! Tomorrow, we kill each other like civilized men!"

A roar of approval rose around the bonfire along with mugs hoisted to the heavens.

Satisfied, Philip tossed the dagger back to Diego who slid it into its sheath.

"I only make jest," Diego said, approaching Bisch with his hand held out. "No hard feelings."

Bisch reached to take the hand, but Diego withdrew it at the last moment and danced away, laughing. Bisch bared his teeth and glowered at the capering little man, then muttered, "Bad-bad."

"So you fight for God?" Philip asked, leaning again on his knee and taking up his position on the log with a fresh mug. "I've heard such words before—even fought for God myself on crusade, as I'm sure Patrick told you. But this is a relic. A simple cup. Really, who cares if this pope or that pope has it? We are simple men, are we not? We are fighting men. Let men in robes and fancy jewels decide what to do with relics."

"Normally, I might be inclined to agree with you, especially if these things happened in a distant land," Corbin admitted, finishing off his board, except for the sauerkraut. "Yet these things happened before my eyes. I saw the cup raise the dead. This tells me it is the Cup of the Last Supper. I also saw Teodorico attack a child to possess it. This tells me it doesn't belong with him. You say you went on crusade, so surely you must understand what it means to fight for something bigger than yourself."

"Bah," Philip said, waving the notion off. "I went on crusade just long enough to have the excommunication removed from me."

"What do you fight for now?" Corbin asked, and glanced at Patrick as if wondering why the Irishman held his silence. Patrick knew the look. Corbin was wondering if he'd be honest. If he had, shouldn't Patrick have more to say? But Patrick only regarded Philip with narrowed eyes over the rim of his mug every time he took a sip. Philip, too, went out of his way to not address his former comrade.

"Treasure, of course," Philip responded, "and to regain my father's kingdom. To have an excommunication removed is one thing, but to regain the kingdom my family lost before the excommunication is quite another. If I put the cup in yonder irritable holy man's hands, I regain my family honor."

"Then I guess you can say we fight for a kingdom, too. A Kingdom of Heaven," Corbin replied, giving a pleading glance to Patrick. The Irish knight held his silence.

Philip scoffed and took a drink from his mug. "Good luck with that."

Most everyone finished their meals, but the cook set roast fowl and pork on tables. The tables were fashioned from doors from Aesclinn cottages. New barrels of ale and aphelon appeared next to the fire as well. The Lost Boys lost no time relieving the village and countryside of its wealth.

"So Patrick has been a fine example of an Avangarde, you say," Philip asked.

Patrick stiffened between Corbin and Bisch.

"Yes, quite so," Corbin replied, "an inspiration in knighthood, though I have to admit he has been the occasional hothead."

Patrick's eyes narrowed.

Philip guffawed at this. "Yes, our Patrick has always been a nonconformist. It took a very long time to tame him. Why, when he first came among us he ran up a tree to avoid our little rite of initiation. The nerve! And he never submitted to the final test."

"The nerve?" Patrick growled angrily, breaking his silence. "Because I did not want to have my arse branded with a hot iron? Forgive me for wanting to keep my hide intact."

Laughter erupted from the crowd as the cook opened the barrels and passed fresh mugs around.

"All you had to do was say no," Diego laughed taking a swig of his drink.

More laughter.

"What?" a smallish voice from the crowd said. A young man with wide eyes looked about with shock and indignation. "You mean I didn't have to be branded?"

The laughter rose to a new height as the boy's comrades slapped him on the back and rubbed his curly head. Diego tackled the boy and threw him over one shoulder and Lost Boys pulled his trousers down to reveal a scar on his lily-white backside in the shape of a square with a line through it.

"Enough, enough," Philip laughed, and they put the hapless young man back on his feet. The young man, despite the revelation and ribbing, smiled good-naturedly. As he pulled up his trousers, Philip put an arm around him. "This is Jean-Jean. I like to call him my Little Patrick, because he reminds me of a certain someone. He too knows his letters and likes to put on airs. We rescued him from a boring life in a monastery. He's turning out to be quite the little warrior, though he has yet to become the ferocious fighter or ravisher of virgins as his namesake."

"Ravisher of virgins?" Corbin scoffed at the description. "Surely you're mistaken."

"What?" Philip said, raising his eyebrows. "Why, you didn't know your virtuous, holy knight was a rapist?"

Patrick's back went ramrod straight and his mouth twitched between a firm line and baring his teeth. Philip matched his baleful stare.

Corbin and Bisch looked to the Irishman in disbelief.

"That's right," Philip continued, "our favorite son, our favorite brother, who came to us lecturing us on the virtues of knighthood, turned out to be far worse a villain than any of us. Certainly, we were murderers and scoundrels, one and all." Philip moved about the fire, addressing the crowd, telling his tale with a malicious grin. This, perhaps, was the true reason for inviting Patrick to the camp with his closest comrades: to shame him. To sow doubt. "But none of us dared to commit the sacrileges perpetrated by this fellow. Why, you might say he was an inspiration of sorts to us. He showed us there were no bounds, no bottom to the depths of depravity. Our adversaries shrank from us in horror. What more could a band of mercenaries hope for?"

Philip made the full circle of the bonfire and again stood near Patrick and his companions.

"Yes," he said, making eye contact with Patrick, "we're all rapists, no doubt there, but a *nun?* Who among us would rape a nun?"

Patrick leaned forward with clenched fists, a murderous look in his eyes.

Corbin and Bisch still stared at him in disbelief. Philip threw back his head and laughed.

"What was her name?" Philip said, wiping a tear from his eye in his laughter. "Oh, that's right, Yvette, Yvette La Petite."

To punctuate the story, Philip gyrated his hips in a lewd manner drawing more laughter from the crowd.

Patrick rose suddenly and struck Philip across his huge jaw. The Rhinelander flew back into the dirt. The crowd went deadly silent, leaving only the crackle of flames as an immediate comment on the incident. A few men reached for weapons, but otherwise made no move.

Corbin and Bisch rose slowly to stand next to Patrick, not sure what would happen next.

Chuckling rose from the dirt as the mercenary leader rubbed his jaw.

"Das ist gut!" he cried, his chuckle escalating to a full-throated chortle and the crowd laughed nervously with him. "That is the brother I remember!"

Philip brushed himself off and threw up his hands, crying, "Now it is a party!"

The Lost Boys roared with approval and more drink flowed.

"I didn't rape her," Patrick shouted to Philip over the clamor of people moving about the fire to dance and play musical instruments.

"You still de-flowered a nun, whether you used the silver of your tongue rather than the iron of your sword," Philip shouted back. "Details, details." He gathered Patrick up in a bear hug and shook him merrily.

#

For the next few hours the party escalated to a fevered pitch, proportional to the quantity of drink poured. Bisch, who had spent years in near silence, now chatted non-stop with the Lost Boys, learning news from Germania and singing their songs. Corbin loosened up as well, competing in feats of drinking and strength.

At one point in the night, from across the fire, Philip made eye contact with Patrick, jerked his head in one direction, and disappeared into the darkness.

Patrick caught up to Philip who looked up at the brilliant starry Avalon sky.

"Is it true?" he asked. "Is this place truly Avalon? The place of König Arthur?"

"Aye," Patrick replied.

"I believe it," Philip whispered, chewing his lip and squinting into the dark forest. "I sent men into the forest to fell trees. Only half of them came back, and those babbled of goblins and trolls and lights leading them astray. The other half... I won't see them again, will I?"

"No, you won't," Patrick said, "Avalon protects herself. You will not have an easy time here."

Philip either grunted in agreement, or scoffed at the notion. Patrick couldn't tell which. "I have to admit, I won't have an easy time breaking the walls of Greensprings either," he said. "What a tough little fortress you have. It seems a combination of the old Roman forts and the castles the Normans are just now starting to build. Reinforced buttresses. High walls. Stone merlons. I'll wager even that gatehouse has hidden traps and murder holes Dragonetti never saw."

Philip looked Patrick square in the face, hoping his expression would betray information.

Patrick shrugged with a mischievous grin. "Maybe."

Philip laughed and clapped Patrick on the back.

"Come, I like this aphelon," he said, belching, "but let us have some good red wine from the Rhine Valley, shall we?"

He led Patrick to a large, well-lit tent on a hillock. Inside rested all the trappings of a knight on campaign: cots, chests, armoires, lamps, bits and pieces of horse tack and harness, weapons, and pieces of armor. The place smelled of leather, oil, and wood.

As Philip rummaged through a cabinet, Patrick steadied himself against a table as the ground moved. The night's drinking was already catching up with him.

"I see you're still carving," Patrick said, picking up a little horse's head from among a pile of shavings on the table. He admired it, noting it already resembled a chessman. "I've also been carving, but I've never matched your skill. Did you ever complete a whole set?"

"Several," Philip replied, shaking a bottle, then throwing it over his shoulder when he found it lacking. "Do you still play?"

"Aye, but I've never managed to match your skill there, either," Patrick replied, noticing for the first time a tarped object occupying most of the table. He picked up an edge of the cloth, but only managed to see a portion of a model before Philip appeared at his side, put a goblet in his hand, and led him away.

"From my father's estate," he explained, gesturing at the goblet. "Outside?"

Patrick took a sip as he stepped out under the stars. The wine indeed tasted very good. "I would have thought you would have reclaimed your father's land by now," he said, recalling the conversation between Philip and Corbin.

Philip heaved a sigh and drank. "It is as I said; removing the excommunication was the first step. Now I must win the land back through politics and intrigues." Philip spat. "The Rhineland has become too civilized. I just can't walk up to the bastards who stole my family's name and property and kill them. Both Emperor Henry and King Henry will not tolerate such things. Therefore, I must be Pope Theodoric's lapdog for a while to obtain this cup. That would be greatly expedited if you would stop being so stubborn and just hand the damned thing over."

"Corbin is right," Patrick replied, swirling the cup around in his goblet. "We fight for something greater than ourselves. It is not by choice, but by destiny. Besides, everybody knows that even if we hand it over, Teodorico will kill us all and level Greensprings to make an example of us."

"True," Philip admitted, and Patrick felt a chill go down his spine when he heard him say it so nonchalantly. "But at least I could offer you a quick death."

"Thanks, but no thanks," Patrick returned, frowning.

"You should take me up on my offer," Philip said, true anger creeping into his voice. "It is the best offer you will get. You are doomed, you know that? And you owe me."

"Oh, how is that?" Patrick asked.

"You damned well know how!" Philip responded, draining his wine and flinging the cup against a nearby tree. "Karl died for you! You are only here to have this stupid argument because my brother died rescuing you from the Muslims. If not for him, they would have burned you at the stake as they did that nun you chased after. She did not come back alive, and neither did my brother! But you did! Why?"

Patrick's stomach bunched up into knots. He had known this conversation would come, but that knowledge did not make it any easier.

"I don't know why. I did not ask him to come after me," Patrick explained. He kept his voice level, lest he run the risk of antagonizing the already-agitated man. "I did everything I could to slip out of camp and not make my quest a burden on the rest of you. Honestly, I don't even know why he did."

"Because he loved you like a brother," Philip retorted, "a *real* brother."

"Oh?" Patrick snapped. It was his turn to shout. "He had a funny way of showing it! It was he who chased me around camp with that hot iron. It was he who beat the hell out of me for months to 'train me proper.' It was he who terrorized me daily during my duties."

"Bah!" Philip cried, waving his arms. "Of course he did. Sure, his manner was hard, but he loved you well enough. He made you tough! He made you hard! If he hadn't done those things, do you think you would have survived the journey? How many people survived the journey from Flanders to Jerusalem? Not many. You were one of them. Karl was not! Yes, Karl was hard on you, but if he hadn't loved you he would have ignored you and let you die straightaway. Yes, he was hard, but it was he who also put his cloak on you when you were cold, and, God knows why, he was the only one who approved of your forbidden liaison with the girl."

Philip finished his rant and silence engulfed them temporarily before being replaced by the distant sounds of the camp. Patrick swallowed hard.

"I'm sorry," Patrick said at last. "I can't change the past. All I can say is I truly did not want him to come after me. I often wish I had died in the desert, tied to that stake."

"You know what bothers me?" Philip grumbled. "That stupid girl didn't even want you. After her little fall from grace with you, she still chose to go off with her band of holy idiots to certain death. What made them think they could convert the enemy?"

Patrick had no words.

"In a way, I'm glad you stubbornly wish to defend this cup," Philip said, "for it gives me the opportunity to do what I've always wanted."

"Which is?"

"Kill you."

Patrick nodded solemnly and they regarded the stars for a time in silence.

After a while, Philip took the goblet from Patrick's hand, took a sip and asked, "Did you ever get a chance to see your family again? Did you ever make it back to your Green Isle?"

"Aye, I did," Patrick replied, taking the cup back and taking a sip himself.

"Das gut," Philip said, nodding.

Thinking of family, Patrick blinked and scanned the camp, listening to the raucous sounds of the party. "Is... is Brutus out there, somewhere?" he asked.

"Oh, good Lord no," Philip said, scowling and taking the goblet back. "As God is my witness, that boy will not know this life. He will not lead the life his brothers Philip and Karl have had. I have higher expectations of him. I want him to be more like... you." He took a drink. "He is with our sister."

"And how is Sigirid?"

Philip snorted.

"She is safely married to some lady-pants nobleman in Landshut," he said, shaking his head with a look of genuine sympathy. "The poor bastard doesn't even know what he's in for."

Patrick snorted as well. He had only met Philip's sister briefly, but knew Philip's words rang true: she was a handful. He took the cup back and drank. They watched the stars and listened to the party for a while longer.

"Well, we best get back," Philip said, taking the cup a final time and turning it upside-down to demonstrate its emptiness. "We're out of drink."

"Good idea."

"Patrick," Philip said, smiling, "I'm going to kill you."

Patrick returned the smile, shrugged, and said, "You'll try."

#

The next morning, Teodorico and Victor picked their way through what looked like the aftermath of a battle. Bodies lay sprawled in every direction, and though plenty of fluid wet the dirt, very little of it was blood. Deep snores and a low-lying miasma of flatulence greeted the pontiff.

He found the body he sought: a large man wrapped in his cloak, snoring heavily in the grass. Teodorico poked the slumbering giant with his crozier.

"Excuse me, Sir Philip, hmm?" he said. "But aren't you supposed to be attacking the keep? It is well on its way to midday, hmm, yes?"

"Eh?" Philip grumbled, sleepily looking up at the holy man with bloodshot eyes. "Oh, yes, that. Tomorrow."

He covered his head again with his cloak.

"What!" Teodorico bellowed, poking the man again with his crozier.

Philip lashed out with one of his legs only to have it tangled in his cloak. Teodorico jumped out of the way, shocked and enraged.

"Piss off, vicar," Philip groused. "The battle will be tomorrow."

#

A similarly bloodshot-eyed Corbin wavered where he stood on the walls of Greensprings, watching a man leaning to one side in his saddle as he approached the gate. His white flag sagged.

When the messenger came within shouting distance, he called up with a hoarse voice, "My lord Sir Philip der Rhinelander wishes to inform you the battle has been delayed until tomorrow, due to... inclement weather."

Corbin blinked, trying to focus long enough to answer.

"Suits me," he finally replied.

The messenger turned and wandered off.

"Is he gone?" Corbin asked Patrick at his side.

"Yes," Patrick replied, "and he's not looking in any case."

"Good," Corbin said, and became violently ill over the side of the wall.

Patrick laughed and started to admonish him, but caught wind of the smell of Corbin's vomit and joined him.

Chapter Sixteen

The first rays of morning illuminated the host as Father Hugh held it aloft. A special Mass took place in the courtyard, which was crowded with four hundred kneeling knights, archers, and villager men-at-arms. When the time came, Father Hugh and his acolytes administered communion to those wishing to receive it. Many had gone to confession the day before in anticipation of this perhaps being their last day on earth. Patrick had done so, too. Not only did he confess to Father Hugh, but to Corbin as well.

"I did not rape a nun," he said. "It is a long story, but I did have a brief relationship with a girl who was conflicted about her vocation."

He rubbed his temple, finding it hard to believe how much he had stifled the memories of Yvette. He marveled at the mind's ability to conceal spiritual wounds; it was not unlike the flesh's ability to envelop bits of iron from battle. Both, apparently, could cause the wound to fester.

"I know you didn't rape anyone," Corbin said as if it were obvious. "I believe you were lost for a while, and I know you were a Lost Boy, but you are Patrick, and Patrick is a good man. Now, go fight like one."

Patrick wanted to find Aimeé and talk to her, explain things to her. Maybe then she would understand his behavior lately.

Then again, did *he* really understand his behavior?

Before he could ponder this, the church bells began to ring and a lookout on the wall called, "They're coming!"

Patrick and Corbin jogged to the staircase leading up to the catwalk, moving as fast as their full armor would allow.

"I guess this is the real reason for the battle's delay," Corbin said, looking out onto the field to see large contraptions rumbling towards them. A mass of black-garbed bodies marched behind the siege engines.

"Aye, they assembled them quick enough," Patrick agreed. "Philip must have held a group of men in reserve who did not join in the festivities, keeping them fresh to build those engines yesterday. By the look of that pile of lumber next to their camp, they have plenty more left to build."

Corbin watched the first siege engine trundling forward on large wooden wheels. The mobile wooden tower stood as tall as the castle walls and had multiple doors and ports, especially at the bottom front, from which poked a battering ram. The top opened to the sky, and several dark dots bobbed back and forth— a contingent of soldiers manning the upper portion. What looked like a drawbridge rested at the top as well, ready to drop down to the wall, should they somehow get close enough. A mob of men pushed the device from the back, protected on all sides by other men bearing shields.

"I don't understand. They have to know the chasm is too wide for them to use the towers and gangplanks. Even the gate is out of reach of a battering ram," Corbin said, chewing his lip.

"Aye, this is not like Philip," Patrick conceded. "Either way, we will find out—they're almost in range."

The contraptions, which wobbled almost comically in their movements, seemed absurd on such a quiet and lovely day. Patrick struggled to believe blood would finally spill. So hard to believe in fact, the day felt... empty.

Despite the odd feeling, Patrick turned to Fletcher and gave the order. Fletcher smiled. One of the engines, a catapult, pulled ahead of the tower, passing a landmark that marked his archers' range. Fletcher yelled a command, and the bow chorus struck its first notes: feathered whistles and twanging string. Patrick watched a score of arrows arc into the sky, pause at their zenith, and then fall gently back to earth. The silence and peace of their descent contrasted with their purpose. Patrick's stomach tensed.

Screams erupted. Arrowpoints rained on the catapult crew. Fully half the enemy collapsed. A few arrows decorated the wood of the device.

A thousand strong infantry now rushed forward to the roar of a battle cry joined by drums and the blaring of those unnerving horns. They carried shields and portable plank walls with little windows.

Strangely, Patrick's tension eased. *So it begins.*

The catapult crew survivors scrambled to the front of the engine and pushed it back out of the archers' range.

"No, again! Before they're out of range!" Patrick called to the archers, who had paused to celebrate.

A few men complied, but not enough to kill any more enemy soldiers before they pushed out of reach.

"Now, the tower," Patrick called.

As the catapults pulled up short, and the crews began to prepare them for action, the taller siege engine continued to teeter forward, squeaking and rattling. The archers released another barrage on the mobile tower, but their arrows only feathered its walls. The mob of men behind the engine stayed mostly hidden, except for only a few who stumbled back with a quill sticking out of them.

"Time to light the arrows," Patrick ordered, even though the tower was covered with cowhides, glistening in the sunlight and undoubtedly soaked with water. The archers selected tar-and-pitch-coated missiles and touched them to the burning censers situated every few paces along the catwalk.

Fire rushed from the sky and collected on the side of the tower like a swarm of yellow hornets. Just as Patrick had feared, the tower's hides were saturated. Worse, several upper portals flipped open, and hands emerged to pour buckets of water over the flames.

"Shoot straight up, then," Patrick commanded, "and let the arrows fall directly down on the top."

The archers adjusted their tactic. The enemy crew on top of the tower popped up and fired their own bows. And with a series of *ker-thunks*, the catapults launched their first wave of projectiles. The larger rocks bounced harmlessly into the chasm, and the smaller ones were dashed to pieces at the base of the walls.

"A victory for the archers," Corbin said, hefting a shield to ward off the attack from the top tower crew. "They've rendered the catapults mostly useless."

"I'll be sure to tell Fletcher and credit his men," Patrick said, catching an arrow with his own shield.

Crossbows protruded from the little windows in the infantry's barricades. Bolts shattered against the wall, whizzed among the stone merlons, or struck shields. At least one man cried in pain and fell from the catwalk into the courtyard with a shaft sticking out of his chest. The Aesclinn archers exchanged barbs, both physical and verbal, with the tower archers.

The tower came as close as it dared to the chasm before the main gate. The battling ram slid forward like the tongue sticking from a serpent's mouth, but only reached halfway across the natural rocky moat. Likewise, the drawbridge on the engine fell, but spanned just a portion of the distance. Both as Corbin predicted.

The enemy's arrows and bolts were the only threat, frequently pinning the defenders down.

"The main body of men is not advancing," Patrick said, sneaking a glance over his shield, "nor do I see any scaling ladders or ropes among them."

Indeed, the enemy seemed intent on their drums, horns, and weapon rattling.

"Aye, and that tower is doing nothing but acting as an arrow sponge..." Corbin responded and then the expression on his face fell. Suddenly, Patrick felt as if someone pulled a sheet out from underneath him. The day was not empty, but full of peril.

Together, he and Corbin cried, "It's a diversion!"

#

Morning sunlight kissed the white and pink apple blossoms, creating a canopy of flowers undulating in the chill morning breeze. On the Back Door gate catwalk, Sir Brian kicked rocks from the battlements, bored and impatient as the men around him. Though he had just explained to Sir Edmund the importance of their orders, he felt the urge to rush off to join the fight at the main gate.

"He is right though," Sir Waylan said as he continued his watch over the orchard behind the keep. "I'm about to die of boredom while everyone else has all the fun."

"It is as you say—patience," Brian replied, then squinted into the trees. "Do you see something out there?"

"Just wishful thinking," Waylan responded.

"Look! There!" Sir Peredur cried.

Tension knotted their stomachs as a hundred and fifty eyes followed Peredur's pointing finger, searching the tree line for movement.

The knots in their stomachs unclenched when a deer bounded from the trees.

"Damn animal..." Brian started to mumble, but stopped when another deer appeared, then another, followed by rabbits, and all manner of birds.

"What the..." Waylan said, then the arrows came.

A half-dozen men to their left and right sprouted feathered shafts. One fell from the catwalk into the practice field, an arrow protruding from his face. Volley after volley whizzed from the apple orchard like a swarm of deadly thrushes, followed by the collective cry of men as they poured from underneath the tree canopy. What seemed like a thousand men in black armor and clothing rushed up against the keep walls like oil. These men carried ladders.

"Sound the horn!" Brian called. "Shields! Prepare for scaling!"

No sooner had he said this than the attackers raised ladders against the walls and quickly set to ascending them.

"Archers!" Waylan cried. "Rocks! Spears! Poles!"

The majority of archers were engaged at the front of the keep, but the fifty or so at the Back Door went to work, plucking the strings of their instrument to the tune of death. Defenders placed poles with prongs on them against the ladders and heaved as hard as they could to send them falling back onto the attackers. Spears poked at the enemy who dared to reach the top of the remaining ladders. Other defenders hurled rocks at the climbers. The morning filled with the deafening roar of battle and death cries.

"Edmund!" Brian called down to the Avangarde on the practice field. "Send a messenger! A thousand attackers scaling the wall!"

Edmund turned to a boy next to him, nodded and sent the lad off at a sprint.

Before long, enough attackers reached the top of the walls that true hand-to-hand combat began. For the time being, no Lost Boys gained a foothold for long before being cast back onto their brethren.

As Brian pounded away at one such assailant, he noticed a group of men that charged out of the orchard carrying a sizable log with hand bars fashioned into it. This device and its handlers struggled through the crowd of attackers to the gate.

Brian punched his immediate opponent with his shield and sent him flying backward, then shouted back to the practice field, "Here it comes! Get ready!"

Edmund nodded and motioned to his men-at-arms. Peredur and Waylan took up positions on either side of Brian, shielding him from arrows as he leaned over the wall to mark the progress of the battering ram.

"One!" he shouted to Edmund, who in turn shouted to his men.

"Two!" Brian called again, then held out his hand in Edmund's direction as he snuck one last peek over the wall.

"Now!" he yelled, gesturing with his outstretched hand for emphasis.

Edmund relayed the command to the groups of men who manned the ropes on either side of the gate doors. The ropes went taught, pulling on the door's giant iron rings.

The battering ram, which had just been pulled back to gain maximum momentum, now shot forward to strike at empty air as the doors opened. The momentum that had been meant to smash the portal now carried the attackers forward, tumbling them into an open pit dug before the gate.

The defenders cheered as dozens more attackers followed the battering ram crew into the pit.

The battering ram struck bottom and tilted forward with a half-dozen enemy combatants still clinging to it. The log came to rest on the far side of the pit, sticking out at an angle: an impromptu ladder for those in the pit. The Avangarde's cheers went silent.

"Oh damn!" Edmund shouted, drawing his sword and coming forward to hack at the survivors.

Likewise, Brian cursed. "Close the gate!"

He and the others pelted the enemy with rocks, trying to push them back from the thin strip of earth between the gate and the pit. Edmund's archers fired into the crowd before the gate, creating enough space for another group of defenders to shut the gate.

"Edmund!" Brian shouted, realizing as many as twenty Lost Boys remained inside the castle walls.

Five or six surrounded Edmund while the rest quickly dispatched his men-at-arms. When the last villager fell, his throat spraying blood, the enemy latched onto the gate, intent on opening it from the inside.

"The gate!" Waylan shouted and jumped from the catwalk onto a group of Lost Boys.

Brian and Sir Peredur joined him. They made short work of the mercenaries and ran to the log and stood over it.

"Don't even think about it!" Brian shouted down to the dirty faces trying to climb out next.

"Edmund, get over here," he said, though he didn't dare to look away from the pit, "and watch here while we get back to the wall."

A moment of silence, and Peredur said, "He's gone."

"Wha—" Brian said, and dared to look.

Sir Edmund lay in a bloody pool on the practice field. His one good eye stared sightlessly, a dagger jammed through his other. One of his arms laid a few paces away.

Fury rose in Brian and he braced himself to vent it on the enemy, who was just beginning to swarm over the wall.

#

"What's happening?" Jon called to Patrick, who raced across the catwalk. He brought with him many Avangarde from the front line.

Sweaty faced and heaving for air, Patrick bent over on his knees. "We think the attack at the front gate is a diversion, what news here?"

"All quiet, except the occasional scout roaming the trees," Jon answered, jerking a thumb beyond the wall. A steep rocky cliff separated Greensprings from a forest of evergreens.

Just then, a horn blared from the Back Gate.

"The real attack," Patrick said, then departed at a run.

"We'll come help then," Jon said, starting to draw his sword and motioning to his fellow guards.

"No," Patrick replied, "they want to divide us. Stay here and watch the wall."

"But nobody is going to climb that," Jon said, pointing to the cliff with his chin. "I can do more than just stand guard with five men."

"I know you can," Patrick yelled over his shoulder, "but we can't take the chance!"

The front line Avangarde filed past Jon, disappearing behind Greensprings.

Red faced, Jon pounded a gauntleted fist on a stone merlon of the wall.

#

When Patrick arrived with his men he saw Brian, Peredur, and Waylan fighting on the practice field, back-to-back among a mob of Lost Boys. Many more threatened to climb out of the pit on a log. The defenders on the wall were struggling to keep more attackers from swarming up ladders. Corbin arrived just then from the opposite catwalk with a score of Avangarde, evidently finding no attack on the far side of the keep, just as Patrick hadn't found any at Jon's position.

"Reinforce the wall!" Patrick called to Corbin, and he and his group jumped to the practice field.

Once on the ground among the enemy, Patrick swung viciously and let months of pent-up rage and frustration explode with each swing. Blood sprayed, taking him full in the face, making his world red. He saw images of a bloody Yvette, and his swings and cries redoubled as he realized the possibility that the next dead woman in his life might be Aimeé.

The battle rage engulfed him, and Aimeé's face flashed again and again across his mind. He did not stop hacking at a prone body until Waylan seized his arm.

"We've turned them!" he cried.

Patrick staggered back, wheezing and blinking blood from his eyes.

Perhaps only ten minutes had passed since his arrival, but it felt like an eternity. The attackers who had managed to penetrate

Greensprings's walls lay dead, leaving the besiegers outside the walls stymied. An enemy horn sounded and the mercenaries pulled away, melting away under the canopy of apple blossoms. A similar horn sounded from the front gate.

The scene calmed and retreat was confirmed. The enemy was streaming en masse back to their camp, pulling their siege tower with them. At last, Patrick took a knee over Sir Edmund and crossed himself.

"I'm sorry, Edmund," he whispered, clutching his breast. "It was my plan and it failed miserably. I'm sorry."

"Don't be so hard on yourself," Corbin said, taking a knee beside him and closing Edmund's staring eye with a finger. "Your plan probably saved the gate from being smashed, and we took many prisoners. Ultimately, the responsibility was mine for approving the plan. Like you, I should have anticipated the problem with the battering ram and had insisted the pit be dug deeper."

Not for the first time Patrick noticed Corbin cutting lines into the leather of his gauntlet with his dagger.

"Why do you do that?" Patrick asked, frowning in puzzlement.

"Every time we lose someone, it's my fault," Corbin grumbled. "This is so I don't forget them. It helps remind me to make wiser decisions next time."

Patrick nodded, looking down at Edmund and the villagers, many of whom he recognized. He didn't need to cut into his glove to remember this, however, as he felt each groove automatically cut into his heart.

A commotion rose near the pit as Brian snatched a bow from a villager and approached the edge of the hole, fumbling an arrow to the string.

"Brian, wait," Corbin called, rising and leaving Edmund's body.

"No way are we letting them live," Brian snarled, bow shaking in his anger as he pointed an arrow at the men in the pit. They cried out and cowered from the weapon.

"No!" Corbin commanded. "We stick to the original plan."

"The original plan?" Brian shouted incredulously. "The original plan got Edmund killed!"

Patrick winced at the accusation.

Corbin put his hand on the bow and arrow and pushed them down.

"That's an order. Besides," Corbin said, bending over to pick up a large wooden mallet from the ground and handing it to his comrade, "you can administer the next portion of the plan."

Brian exchanged the bow and arrow for the mallet and smiled wickedly.

#

An hour later, twenty-two Lost Boys limped heavily over the drawbridge of the main gate. They did their best to help one another, which proved difficult to do with two smashed hands and one smashed foot each.

"I don't like this plan," Brian grumbled, watching the maimed enemy shuffle towards their camp, "as much as I enjoyed taking the hammer to them. I still don't see how it helps us."

"Because those men are now a burden to their comrades," Corbin explained, "and each has to be cared for, fed, and housed. They cannot so much as sew or whittle. They'll just take up space, eating food and drinking ale and generally being in the way."

Brian snorted, "I hope so."

#

Patrick meandered through the bodies in the great hall transformed into a hospital.

Once a place of joy and festivity, it now became a place of anguish and suffering. Cries of pain replaced laughter. People writhed on cots or the floor, amid the smells of blood, urine, and excrement. Apron-wearing monks, nuns, and maidservants drifted among the wounded like blood-splattered ghosts, tending to their needs.

One of these phantoms ran to Patrick.

"Patrick!" Aimeé called. "Are you well?"

She patted down his blood soaked surcoat, searching for wounds.

"I am well," Patrick said distantly and cupped Aimeé's clean, smooth cheeks. "You're alive," Patrick breathed, staring at her as if seeing her for the first time. He reached a hand down to her bulging stomach and touched the apron covered in blood. "And this is my baby. No matter what. My baby."

Aimeé struggled to say something and moisture gathered in her eyes.

"I..." Patrick also struggled so speak, but Mother Superior called Aimeé from across the room with urgency in her voice.

"Aimeé, we need you over here," she said.

"I have to get back to the wall," Patrick said, "but I will come here after."

Aimeé nodded and turned to leave, but before she did, Patrick noticed a small form wandering among the wounded.

"Is that Emilie? This is no place for a child," he said, concern in his voice.

"She is special," Aimeé explained, her eyes following the girl as she stopped by suffering individuals to lay a hand on them. Each person she touched calmed. "She heals people—and they love her for it."

#

Back in the courtyard he regrouped with Corbin and Brian.

"I don't understand," Brian said. "There is plenty of daylight. Why aren't they attacking again?"

"That was only a probing attack," Corbin explained, "to find what adjustments they need to make on their engines."

"And to find our weaknesses," Patrick added.

A wailing sound filled the air, growing in intensity, followed by a wet "thump" as something hit the cobblestones of the courtyard. Another and another hit the ground as they fell from the sky, preceded by a *ker-thunk!* from beyond the wall. They bounced with flailing and broken limbs. People approached the objects, just to turn away.

The trio of knights approached one.

The body of a Lost Boy lay there, and despite the mangled condition, its hands had obviously already been smashed as was one foot.

"It would appear Philip does not have any weaknesses," Brian said coldly, "nor does he tolerate them."

#

"Two hundred?" Teodorico scoffed. "That's how many men Philip lost in that attack, hmm, yes? Are you serious? At that rate he won't have any men left."

"Around two hundred—the number is uncertain," Victor replied. "He did not bother to retrieve their bodies. However, he does insist it is all a part of his plan."

"Plan?" Teodorico said, scoffing again. "So far I don't see a plan. I'm starting to question seriously your judgment in soldiers, hmm?"

"He came—"

"Highly recommended, yes, I know," Teodorico cut him off, and poured a drink, "but forgive me if I don't try a plan of my own."

"As you wish, Your Holiness," Victor responded, bowing slightly.

Teodorico handed the drink to Lilliana. "You may not be able to hold the cup, hmm? But I wager you can hold the girl and twist her little arm, hmm, yes?"

Lilliana's eyes turned to slitted cat eyes as she smiled and took a sip.

#

Though the sun had just set, weariness weighed Patrick down and his bed called to him. First, he needed quiet time to reflect.

To that end, he entered the church, dipped his fingertips in the basin at the door, crossed himself, and approached the altar. Refugees adoring the cup cleared a path for the Knight of Cups.

As he walked, thoughts raced through his mind.

Do not do this. It is unnatural, the guardians of the cave had told him when he first took the cup.

He rubbed his head as he recalled striking Teodorico, followed by Teodorico promising fire and brimstone.

As he came to the altar, the faces of today's victims whirled in his mind, bloody and questioning.

He fell to his knees at the communion rail at a spot made for him by kindly villagers before the altar. He did not feel deserving of their generosity. Quite the opposite, for he had done more than just bring a miracle to Greensprings; he had also brought death and destruction.

Besides Edmund, almost fifty villagers died today. Very few of Patrick's plans had gone well, and people had died for it. This was the burden of a leader. He did not like it, and wished it taken from him. He stared at the cup as he pressed his hands to his lips and prayed. He closed his eyes and for the thousandth time he begged forgiveness and asked that this all go away.

The whisper of a hundred prayers from refugees filled the church, lulling his weary soul to a place somewhat resembling calm. An indeterminate amount of time passed and he found himself slumping forward, only to jerk back to wakefulness. A keening noise filled his ears, increasing in intensity. When it had become too loud to ignore, he opened his eyes and drew a breath in shock at the sight before him.

The cup glowed golden, casting a hum along with its radiance. Its light, however, did not shine as brilliantly as the light above it. A light hanging over the cup burned like a white fire radiating from a sphere of darkness like a great eye. Despite its brilliance, it emitted no heat, and the only noise came from the growing hum.

Patrick turned to those around him to share in the magnificence of the sight, but they were still as statues. Even those who had their eyes open did not blink. The flames from the torches and votive candles did not flicker, but froze in mid-dance.

Patrick stood and looked around. Time had frozen.

The humming from the light increased, calling to him.

He stepped through the communion rail gate and approached the altar. His eyes hurt to look at the light, and the hum turned to a high-pitched buzz in his ear. Despite the discomfort, he felt compelled to come forward.

He stood face-to-face with the light, shielding his eyes with one hand. At this distance he saw the circular darkness was in fact a window, and it roughly equaled the size and shape of the host priests used at Mass. Still feeling no heat, Patrick placed his hands on either side of the window and leaned into the wall of fire, placing an eye to the window to look inside.

His vision swam, and then cleared.

A solemn bearded man sat at table with many other bearded men in colorful robes. The man, Jesus, held a round piece of bread aloft. This bread caught Patrick's eye, drawing him in deeper, acting as another window that revealed to him the same man hanging from a cross. In turn, the body of Jesus in this image acted as another window, drawing Patrick's eye in further, bringing him back to the scene at the table. Sucked in yet again through the bread-window, the process happened anew in a ceaseless cycle, each one faster than the previous. The rapidly changing images turned to a pulsating light of their own.

Patrick swallowed hard, his eye glued to the window, unable to dislodge himself. He cried out as he pushed against the wall of fire, and tears streamed from his trapped eye. The buzz in his ear threatened to explode his head.

Just when he thought he couldn't take it anymore, he managed to blink, breaking the bond. He fell to the stone floor of the dais, gasping.

"Hurts, doesn't it?" a voice asked him.

Patrick stood, breathing heavily, and faced the speaker.

The Other stood there, contemplating him with his own face.

The room had gone quiet, and the buzzing was gone. The refugees remained, still frozen in place, and so too the brilliant wall of fire.

"Truth, that is," the Other clarified. "Truth always hurts when faced directly."

"You talk," Patrick said, stumbling forward. "Is that my voice? Is that how I sound?"

"Does it matter?"

Patrick shook his head and blinked. "No, it doesn't, but can you help me?"

"How?"

"You are a ghost or a spirit, or some such," Patrick explained. "The cup is spirit, so can you grasp it and take it from here? Take it back to the cave? Please, I beg of you."

A profound sadness came over the Other's face. "I'm sorry. I can only point out the obvious."

"But you've helped in the past," Patrick pleaded.

"That was then, this is now."

"What must I do?" Patrick asked. "Please tell me, I will do it. I will do anything to make the pain and suffering stop."

"After casting a stone into water, can a man stop the ripples that spread in every direction?" The Other shrugged sadly. "It is good you take responsibility for your actions, that you are repentant, but what is done is done. Do not compound the matter by dwelling on guilt. Guilt is an illusion."

Patrick fell to his knees and beat his breast, shouting, "But I am guilty, and I will give up my life to fix it! Take my life! Take it!"

"Oh, a life will be taken," the Other said, and every word that came from him came sadder than the last, "for certainly that is what is needed to restore the balance you disrupted. The girl was not meant to live."

"So take mine!" Patrick shouted, beating his breast again.

"It will not be yours," the Other continued. "You see, consequences are not necessarily about what happens to you because of what you did—but what happens to others, because of what you did."

A chill went up Patrick's spine and he swallowed hard. "What do you mean?"

"Remember the sermon Teodorico gave the day Chansonne held the cup?" Patrick's own face came close to his. "Remember the story of King David? How he sinned? How, overcome by the beauty of Bathsheba, he had her husband killed, and took her for his own? Even after David repented with all his heart, it was too late. You see, though he was forgiven, the wages of sin are still death."

Patrick frowned, struggling to remember the scripture through the pounding pressure against his skull. Who died in that tale? Not David, not Bathsheba, but...

Patrick's heart leaped into his throat.

"No," he choked.

The Other disappeared.

Patrick looked around. The brilliant light had disappeared, the torches and votive candles flickered normally, and the refugees stared at him.

"NO!" Patrick cried and ran to the entrance.

#

Aimeé tucked Chansonne into bed and kissed her gently on the forehead. The other children already snored peacefully away.

"Go to sleep now," she purred. "Tomorrow is a new day."

Chansonne grabbed her as Aimeé rose to leave.

"There, there little one," Aimeé reassured, "I'll just be in the next room. I've checked under the beds and in all the closets, there are no monsters. I will only be in the next room, and Sir Geoffrey stands guard down the hall. You are safe."

Chansonne leaned back into her pillow and Aimeé kissed her one last time and departed.

Closing the door between her chamber and the children's dormitory, she moved to the little bureau and exchanged her clothes for a nightgown and slipped under the bedcovers. She left a candle burning in case the children needed her in the middle of the night, which happened often. She wished Katherina helped more in this one duty: assisting with the frequent late night walks to the water closet, fetching glasses of water, and explaining away frightening shadows. But the princess slept peacefully in her bed several floors above.

Exhaling gently and letting the day drain from her limbs, Aimeé closed her eyes. Before long, sleep began to overtake her, and she felt the now familiar brushes on her cheeks accompanied by children laughing in the distance. Normally, the distant giggles faded as sleep overtook her, but tonight they grew louder and more discordant, turning more to wails and sobbing.

Aimeé opened her eyes, or thought she did. A whiteness engulfed her like a mist.

"Am I dreaming?" she said out loud, again not sure for no sound came from her.

She figured she must be, because she could not move. Her arms were pinned at her sides in a nightmare's paralysis. The distant wailing intensified and the whiteness collected around her like falling snow. No, not snow, little flowers. Little white flowers that fell in her mouth and nose and choked her. Every breath she exhaled sent the little florets fountaining above her, just to be sucked back in when she struggled to inhale. She coughed and choked and fought to sit up, but could not. A heavy warmth rested on her chest, pinning her down like a pool of molten lead. The wails and sobs became louder and louder.

A pair of amber cat's eyes appeared in the mist above her, glittering with pleasure. More of the flowers she exhaled disappeared into the creature's mouth.

Aimeé struggled to rise, to breathe, to call for help, to do anything, but could not.

Panic overtook her as she felt her dream-self dislodging from her body, slowly slipping away in the form of a stream of flowers down the throat of the evil cat.

A sound broke through the mist and mournful wails.

Suddenly, the cat stopped robbing her of breath. The creature's head snapped in the direction of the sound, and Aimeé's eyes followed as well.

In the mist, a tall, willowy figure stood at the center of the room, singing.

Hush little sister don't you cry,
Because in the morning we're going bye-bye,
But first we're going to close our eyes...

Katherina?

No, the voice was younger, unknown.

The cat growled from deep in its throat. Aimeé coughed flowers and found she could breathe again, but could not rise from the weight on her chest.

The mist began to lift as the song continued. The cat's claws dug into her flesh as its growls and hisses protested against the chant. The animal shifted and faced the singer, and now that the air had cleared, Aimeé could see the glossy black cat clearly.

Also, she could clearly see her savior.

"Chansonne?" she wheezed.

The child stood in the center of the room, not so tall as the blurry image in the mist, but just as fearless as she sang. The words escalated in tone and the cat seemed to wince at them. It laid back its ears in fury, baring its teeth.

The song finished and the cat and girl faced off.

The cat launched itself from Aimeé's chest, relieving her of the invisible bonds. She rose, but a scream from Chansonne sent a palpable shock wave throughout the room and knocked Aimeé down again. The same shock hit the cat in midair, sending it flying, writhing, and twisting. It transformed and grew in the air, becoming some sort of giant bat that fluttered to the ceiling and clung to the wooden beams.

At that moment, Patrick and Geoffrey burst into the room with swords drawn.

"What the—" They cried out at the sight of the creature hanging from the beams.

It turned its head towards them and hissed a mouthful of fangs. Blazing yellow eyes with slits for pupils set in a vaguely female face glared hate at them. The creature dropped and took flight on webbed wings and targeted Chansonne in a flurry of claws, fur, and scales.

Chansonne screamed again, and the shock wave of her voice caught the monster in mid-flight like a fly slamming into a spider's web. The scream turned into a coherent rendition of the sung *Gloria* and the beginning long note emanated from the child like a wall of air washing in every direction, picking up Patrick and Geoffrey, their capes, the bed and its sheets, Aimeé's hair, and the bureau and candle.

Every loose item in the room hung suspended in air, temporarily frozen in space like insects in amber. Even the air took on a hazy quality, as if folded in on itself.

The monster screeched in pain, fought against the invisible web, and grabbed at its ears. By the time Chansonne had reached *In Excelsis Deo* the creature had disappeared in an explosion of silent lightning. When they opened their eyes and they could see again, a screaming comet was shooting out an open window.

Sheets of gossamer material gently floated in the air, falling to earth. Geoffrey let a large sheet come to rest in his outstretched hand and to his surprise he held the wispy skin that had always fascinated Father Wulfric at the murder scenes. This particular skin held a face imprinted on it.

"Lilliana?" he said in shock and disbelief.

"I made Lilly go bye-bye," Chansonne whispered. "I sang her a Lilly-bye."

Patrick and Geoffrey looked with amazement at the child.

"Patrick," Aimeé said, her voice cracking in fear, "something's wrong."

Patrick looked to her sitting up in bed, a crimson color spreading from between her legs across the white sheets.

Chapter Seventeen

Lilliana's skin burned, but not nearly as much as her anger. Both disrupted her rest as she tried to regain her strength in the darkness. Voices came, muffled as if from behind a door.

The voice was Philip's. "If time is of the essence, as you say, then this is the best course. I know you would rather I assault the keep every waking moment, but I have found everything I need to know from the first assault. My plan is the preferred way."

"Time *is* of the essence," came Teodorico's reply. "When a rescuing army arrives, we must be gone and this place a smoldering pile of rocks, hmm, yes?"

"And so it shall be," Philip assured, but he sounded as if he struggled to be cordial. "My men's time and effort are best applied to assembling the engines."

"Shouldn't you at least be wearing their defenses down, or something, hmm?"

"Your Holiness, please," Philip said, a growl starting to creep into his voice, "leave the matters of battle to me. I promise you will have the keep, girl, and cup."

"Oh very well, hmm?" Teodorico said. "Go prepare your toys."

After a pause, Lilliana could sense heavy footsteps departing.

Nearer, she felt a rhythmic tapping as if someone's leg bounced in an agitated manner. A grumbling belonging to Teodorico accompanied it.

"You can come out now. He's gone," Teodorico's voice said beside her.

Daylight filled her world, first in a thin horizontal line as she opened the lid, and then full brightness. From the trunk next to

Teodorico's chair, she slowly extracted herself, nude, like a flower reaching for sunlight. She examined her arms, noting how ghastly white she had become. Large patches of dead skin flaked from her body.

"How are you feeling, my love, hmm?" Teodorico asked, taking her by the chin.

Lilliana pulled away. "I need to feed."

"Are you still sore at me, hmm, yes?" he asked, hurt.

"You should have told me the extent of her powers," Lilliana said, anger in her voice as she tiredly peeled off a piece of skin hanging from her face.

"Perhaps you should have gone straight for the girl and grabbed her in her sleep; you could have covered her mouth, hmm?" Teodorico admonished. "Instead of wasting your time with the maidservant, hmm, yes?"

"She was in the way," Lilliana lied.

She scowled as she recalled how at the swimming hole the maidservant had recoiled from her outstretched hand.

Who's not having a baby now? Lilliana licked her lips.

"Honestly, I had no idea Chansonne had found her voice again, hmm?" Teodorico tsked. "And from what you told me, I doubted her voice was that powerful."

"You had better hope Philip's toy works," she said coldly, "because I will not go near that child again. I have not felt pain like that since... Well, for a very long time."

"I'm not placing all my eggs in Philip's basket, hmm?" Teodorico said. "While you were resting, a messenger brought us a little something, hmm, yes?"

He stroked a small and longish box on the table next to his chair.

Lilliana cocked an eyebrow. "So, the young King Henry finally made good on his promise. I told you he would."

"I didn't doubt it for a moment, hmm?" Teodorico said. "But I will need you to deliver it to Lucan."

Lilliana's mouth twitched.

"You needn't worry, hmm?" Teodorico assured, caressing her chin. "Wait until he is well away from the girl. There will be no need for you and Chansonne to cross paths."

Lilliana's mouth twitching turned into a sneer. "After I feed," she said, and turned to leave.

"Feed off of one of Philip's people, hmm?" Teodorico called after her. "I need to get my money's worth out of them."

#

Patrick paced outside the door of the room in which Father Hugh, Mother Superior, and a handful of nuns attended to Aimeé.

Every hour or so a nun would depart with an armload of bloody cloths, then return with fresh linens and hot water. Every time he asked what progress had been made, they placated or admonished him with kind but stern pleas for patience.

When the sounds of activity and cries of pain subsided, Patrick placed his ear to the door and listened: voices in low tones, occasional words that left him both relieved and distressed. "...lucky to be alive..." and "...may never have children again."

Footsteps approached the door and Patrick jumped back.

It opened and the room's occupants filed out looking as if they had experienced battle: weary, blood-splattered, and shutting their medical bags like knights sheathing swords.

"Is she going to live?" Patrick asked.

"Yes," Mother Superior replied. "She needs her rest, but I suppose it wouldn't hurt to stay for a bit, but only a bit."

"Yes, Mother Superior," Patrick said gratefully. "Thank you."

He slipped into the room. Daylight streamed through a window. The thick, metallic smell of blood still hung in the air and collected at the back of his throat. Aimeé and the bed on which she lay, however, were clean.

"Aimeé," he whispered.

Her eyes fluttered open and tried to discern if he were real.

"I'm sorry," he said. "I tried so hard to get to you, to help. It's all my fault."

She tiredly put a finger to his lips and hushed him. He sat on the edge of the bed.

"You need to stop that," she whispered. "You can't protect everyone all the time. It is what it is. I don't blame you. I blame... her. Lilliana? How? What is she?"

"I don't know, but I'm going to kill her." He took her finger and kissed it.

Aimeé smiled. "Good."

Rubbing her finger, he cleared his throat. "I need to tell you something."

She watched him, curious, and he had a hard time maintaining eye contact.

"You said I talked in my sleep about a woman named Paulette. Her name was not Paulette, but Yvette. She was a nun who accompanied a holy order that followed the crusaders to the Holy Land. Their plan was to pray the enemy into submission. To make Christians out of them. I know, crazy. But they were not the craziest people to join the Crusade." Patrick swallowed hard. "We... had a dalliance. I made her question her faith. I guess she felt it necessary to repent by throwing herself into her ideology. She convinced her people to contact the enemy directly. They were captured. I tried to rescue her, but it was too late."

Expressing no judgment, Aimeé touched his cheek.

"And you blame yourself for her death," she said, "letting it eat you up inside until it bleeds out in your dreams."

He pressed her hand to his face. "I do have a tendency to ruin women's lives."

"Stop," Aimeé said. "Let it go."

"How?"

"Stop squashing the things inside you needing to come out. For example, I know you love me, but you never say it."

Patrick smiled and kissed her hand. He leaned back, bracing himself with his free hand. "Is that all? That should be easy enough..." His expression fell as he lifted his bracing hand from the bed and stared at it. Blood covered it. "You're bleeding again," he said, panic rising in his voice. Another red spot bloomed between her legs.

He turned his attention to the blood on his skin and how it covered the thin scar running the length of his hand. The ghost of Yvette visited his memories.

"I'll get help," he stammered to Aimeé, who nodded and swallowed hard.

It did not take long for Mother Superior and the others to return. They tended to her and gave him reassurances, but implored him to leave the room.

As he stood in the hall helplessly watching the door, Geoffrey found him and urged him to the main gate.

"You need to see this," he said. "We have trouble."

Patrick nodded, moved to the exit, but Geoffrey stared at Aimeé's door.

"Is...?" Geoffrey asked, swallowing.

"There is no baby anymore," Patrick growled, "if that is what you're concerned about."

Geoffrey's brow furrowed in anger. "I meant, is she going to live?"

\#

"God, what a monster," Corbin said, looking out onto the field near the enemy camp.

"Aye," Patrick said, "judging from the footprint alone, the A-frame is going to stand almost as tall as our castle walls—nine, ten horses tall."

Waylan whistled, adding, "No wonder they haven't been attacking us. They must have every man working on it."

Onlookers crowded the Greensprings walls. Word had gone out that the Lost Boy camp worked on something massive. Theyspectators jostled to get a view of what disturbed the Avangarde so much.

"What is it?" Lady Katherina asked, wrinkling her nose at the pile of lumber with a multitude of men crawling over it with hammers, saws, ropes, and pulleys. "It doesn't look like much to me."

Patrick recalled that night in Philip's tent. The secret of what Philip hid underneath the tarp was now clear. He hadn't just been carving chess pieces, but most likely had been building a working model of this contraption.

"It will, Lass, it will," Corbin said with an air of trepidation. "It's called a trebuchet. It will make those catapults look like a child's slingshot. Patrick's right—if they build it to proportion with the frame they've already set in the ground, it's going to be the largest siege engine I've ever seen. They can fire horse-sized rocks at us from their camp, and there won't be a blessed thing we can do about it. Teodorico wasn't lying when he said he planned on leveling Greensprings."

"There's plenty we can do," Sir Brian said. "We can set it on fire."

Corbin nodded. "We're going to have to if we want to survive."

"Aye, and sooner rather than later," Patrick added, "judging by the progress they've made so far. It could be operational within a couple days. Maybe even tomorrow, if those other frames lying in the grass just need to be lifted into place. I see they've already fashioned their water wheels."

"Oh damn," Corbin said, scrutinizing the construction again. "Is that what those giant barrels are to the left?"

"Water wheels?" Katherina asked.

"Circles of wood, like barrels without lids, that are attached to the sides when the engine is finished," Patrick explained. "Men stand inside them and walk, turning the circles, like a water wheel at a grist mill. They spool rope, like a winch, raising the counterweight."

"Not all trebuchets use them," Corbin added, "but when they do, they're damn fast and can load and launch every ten minutes. Much faster than teams of men or oxen pulling on rope. Teodorico is wasting no time."

"All the more reason we need to do something now," Brian urged.

"I wish Wolfgang and Marcus knew of this," Sir Waylan said. "This changes everything. Before, we had half a chance of holding out. Now we're really running out of time. If they knew, I'm sure they'd redouble their efforts to get help."

The knights grumbled, speculated, and strategized. Patrick noticed Jon and Katherina exchanging whispers. Whatever they discussed did not seem to make Katherina happy and before long Jon broke away and approached Patrick.

"We should send word to Wolfgang and Marcus. If we send someone with a horse to the mainland, they can cross the Cornish peninsula and reach Glastonbury about the same time as the Avangarde arrive with their Guests."

Patrick nodded. "Not a bad idea if we could sneak a few men and horses to the Aesclinn docks."

"If we attack the trebuchet, that would make a wonderful diversion for someone to do just that." Jon grinned. "Two birds with one stone."

"Very well. Suggest it to Corbin; he'll pick someone to take the mission."

"He'd be more likely to go along with it if he heard it from you —and more likely to choose me if you suggested I am the one to go."

Patrick's mouth opened, but no words came out. Jon elbowed him and gestured with his eyes to Corbin. Katherina gave a pleading look to Patrick and gave a quick shake of her head.

"Jon, just say it. You don't need me to speak for you," Patrick finally said, avoiding Katherina's uncomfortable stare. "I'll support you."

"I don't want you to *support* me," Jon said angrily, stepping between him and Katherina with his back to her. "I want you to *champion* me. I want you to insist I be the messenger. Even if Corbin agrees to the plan, you know he won't choose me, unless you make the recommendation."

"Jon..."

"Don't 'Jon' me," his anger escalated. "I fought side-by-side with you against the goblins. I stood by you when *you* were looked upon as unfit for duty. You always got the girl. You've had your turn, Knight of Cups, now it's mine!"

"Gentlemen?" Corbin said, looking at the pair.

Patrick paused, his jaw muscle working back and forth as he ground his teeth.

"Jon has an idea," he said at last. "Waylan's right—we need to get word to the outside that things have changed here. Jon feels he can reach the Aesclinn harbor while we attack the trebuchet, distracting the enemy from him. He can make it to the mainland, ride cross-country to Glastonbury, and deliver a plea for faster help."

"Jon?" Corbin said, perhaps a bit more skeptically than he intended.

"Aye, it was his idea," Patrick pointed out, "he should be the one to go. He's capable and eager."

Corbin pursed his lips and looked between Sir Jon and Sir Patrick. "It's not the craziest plan I've heard lately, and it just might prove helpful."

With that, the knights gathered around to form their strategy.

Before joining the circle, Jon turned to Patrick and whispered, "Thank you, my friend."

"You're welcome, Jon," Patrick replied, and smiled wanly despite a sinking feeling in his gut. Katherina hung her head and stalked away.

#

When they had collected enough bladders of oil and torches for the attack, the knights marshaled in the courtyard. They huddled about braziers in the chill evening air in small groups, waiting for the right moment.

"This will be our first real combat," Jakob said to Patrick, holding his hands out to the flames. "Any advice?"

Patrick took his time answering. He struggled to put on an air of strength and attentiveness to the lads with whom he shared the fire, but other concerns weighed on him. Aimeé's bleeding had slowed, but had not stopped. Emilie had been sought to apply her healing gift, but the child now lay in her own sickbed, exhausted.

Sadness attempted to engulf him as he pictured his mother holding his baby for the first time, only to have it fade from her arms. Anger replaced the sadness, and Jakob's question focused him.

"Rely on your training." Patrick blew into his hands and wrapped his cape about him closer. "Keep a level head. I'm sure Sir Lucan is an excellent knight and must have been a good teacher. Therefore, do as he would command. Obey the horn signals we discussed, and all should go as planned. Speaking of Sir Lucan, where is he?"

"Praying before the cup," Jakob said.

Patrick recalled the rumors of how Lucan frequently prayed before the cup, showing an extraordinary passion when he did—so much that it disturbed the pilgrims, forcing them to leave the church. Before he could wonder again why Lucan felt so strongly, Josef spoke up.

"I think Jakob meant if you have any advice on preparing ourselves for death."

"Say your prayers, make your confessions, and make your world right with God," Patrick said, for there was little else to say. "Do those things, and fear and death have no power over you. The battle is in God's hands. It is a fine line between assuming you are already dead the moment you draw your sword, and maintaining hope you will accomplish your mission and make it out alive. To walk that line between recklessness and fearlessness is a difficult thing, and only comes with experience."

"I prefer to think God is with me, that the glass is half-full, not half-empty," Jon added. He shifted from one foot to the other, either to stay warm or to burn nervous energy. Probably both. "And He will protect me. If He doesn't, then it is as Patrick says—

meant to be. I won't worry about it until then. Besides, my mother always said heaven is our real home, where we belong. Dying is merely going home."

Patrick smiled and shrugged. "To each his own. There is no right way to face death, and you lads will have to choose your own."

"If what happens to us is entirely up to God," Josef said, brow furrowed deep in thought, "does that not then make us merely chess pieces with no say in the game?"

"We're chess pieces with free will," Patrick pointed out. "How we perform in the next square to which God moves us is entirely up to us. Do we perform admirably, or shamefully? Were we prepared, or unprepared? Did we inspire the other pieces to perform well when their turn came to move to their next square?"

"Still a pawn," Jakob grumbled.

"Well, perhaps we have some say in what square we land in, or how," Patrick amended, "but there is still only one direction to move—the direction God has sent us—and that is forward."

He paused, contemplating. Giving answers to a puzzle he hadn't quite sorted out himself didn't come easy, but he felt it important to try.

"Protecting this cup, this true relic of Jesus, from liars and pretenders," Jakob said, "that is something worth dying for. I'm happy for the opportunity."

"As I am," Josef agreed. Questions still played across his face. "Though I don't want to challenge God's reasons, I am curious as to why the cup needs protecting at all. Why doesn't God just snap his fingers and make it disappear—take it someplace safe?"

"I think you just answered your own question," Jon replied, staring solemnly into the fire. "The occasion offers us an opportunity to stand up for something. To believe in something. Pity the soul who has never had his faith tested, for how can he possibly know how strong it is until it has?" Jon continued to stare at the coals in the brazier, his eyes both vacant and thoughtful. "God has done so much for us, sent His son to die for us. Perhaps it is our turn to fight for Him. Maybe He needs us just as much as we need Him. Maybe He *needs* us to fight for the cup, just as he needed Noah to build the ark. Perhaps when this is done He will provide us with our own rainbow, our own promise."

Patrick's jaw dropped as he stared at Jon, never realizing the depths of his friend's poetic heart. Suddenly the time Katherina spent with Jon didn't seem so strange. Also, Jon may have just explained things better than the damnably enigmatic Other.

Activity grabbed their attention as Corbin and several others made their way through the groups of knights and braziers. Torches flared to life among the knights, spreading like the dawn's aurora.

"It's almost time," Corbin announced. "Head for the stables and mount up, but first we have some business to attend to." He stepped towards Jon, and Waylan handed a bundle of dark cloth to Corbin who in turn handed it to Jon. Jon shook it out. The dark cloth lengthened out to a surcoat and the white swan emblem shone brightly in the darkness.

"Congratulations, Jon. It's been a long time coming and you've earned it."

Cheers went up and all crowded around Jon to slap him on the back.

His smile lit up the courtyard.

#

Two hundred knights gathered in front of the main gate, as agitated as their horses. They awaited the inner and outer portals to open.

To increase the element of surprise, a group of men worked the winches slowly, and another group greased the gears and chains to minimize their squeak and rattle.

Sir Josef fidgeted more than most in his saddle.

"Nervous, Lad?" Patrick asked.

Josef looked about, then leaned towards the Irishman. He whispered, "I have to piss... bad."

Patrick chuckled, and couldn't help but feel the newly made knight looked like a twelve-year-old boy in armor.

"Let your water run in the saddle. I'm certain you won't be the only one."

Josef nodded, let his shoulders droop, and moaned in relief.

Patrick shook his head, smiling.

Eventually the signal came to prepare to sortie.

With a silence-shattering clatter, the gates fell open and the knights thundered over the drawbridge. With the element of surprise gone, the knights shouted their battle cries and charged the trebuchet.

Within moments, an alarm horn blared in the enemy camp, and by the time the Avangarde reached the camp, they met a hasty, unprepared resistance. The lead knights carried no torches or oil bladders so they could concentrate their efforts on plowing a path with lance and sword for those who did. They accomplished this easily enough as they trampled, lanced, and cut down half-dressed and sleepy Lost Boys stumbling from their tents. They swept through the camp like a deadly wind, hurling toward the trebuchet frames silhouetted against the night sky.

When they reached them, two things struck Patrick as significant: one, that the monstrosity's sheer size could only truly be appreciated when you stood next to it, and two, the surprising lack of defenses around the engine.

Also, the thing was nearer completion than they had guessed.

"Something is wrong," Patrick called to Corbin as he tossed aside his shattered lance, the tip of which was still embedded in some unlucky soul's breast. "Philip would post at least a company of soldiers to guard his investment."

"Let's just count our blessings, get the job done, and be gone." Corbin commanded the bladders broken against the wood and the torches cast.

Men and horses wheeled about, their breath coming out in misty puffs in the cool air. Patrick hung his shield in his harness, stood in the saddle and jumped to the chest-high base of the trebuchet. The smell of freshly milled oak filled his nostrils as he drew his sword and approached the engine's central, long launch-trench. He raised his sword to cut the launch cable of the throwing arm, but paused and cursed loudly.

"What's wrong?" Corbin asked.

"The launch cable, it's not rope," Patrick replied. "It's chain."

Corbin also cursed, but for another reason. "The fires aren't taking. It's not burning fast enough."

Patrick approached the A-frame and put his nose up to the wood as thick as an entire ancient oak tree. Not only did it smell of freshly cut wood, but also incredibly moist.

"They soaked it with water!" Patrick cursed.

A roar of shouts came from the tree line of the forest and a small army of foot soldiers descended upon them. With the sound of clashing steel, they engaged.

Corbin cursed and commanded the retreat horn sounded.

As the horn blared, Patrick jumped into Siegfried's saddle and fitted his shield to his arm just in time to fend off a sword. The blow still managed to knock him from the saddle. Cursing, he rolled to his feet and prepared to meet his attacker. The sound of combat pressed around him.

A dark shape lunged at him, and they joined in a deadly dance to the tune of metal and shouts. His opponent was skilled enough to shatter Patrick's shield in short order. Patrick shook off the shards, gripped his sword hilt two-handed, and then windmilled ahead. While his adversary struggled to fend off his blows, Patrick rotated to a backward grip, spun, and thrust the blade behind him.

His attacker froze, impaled on Patrick's blade, then fell gurgling.

Through the thickening smoke, Corbin rode up with Siegfried in tow and tossed the reins to Patrick.

"We've run this bunch off," he said, "but two thousand more are on their way. We need to go. Are you wounded?"

"Just my pride," Patrick replied, climbing into the saddle. "I can't believe I let my guard down."

"Well, then you're doing better than this fellow." Corbin pointed with his chin.

Patrick looked down, and in the sputtering firelight and smoke, the Lost Boy Jean-Jean stared back at him with vacant eyes.

#

They rode back into Greensprings under halfhearted pursuit by the enemy. They made no shouts of joy or triumph.

Once inside, stable hands took their horses and monks attended the dead. They had only lost six Avangarde, but within an order as small as theirs, any death was a tragedy. Patrick felt relieved he did not know any of them very well, but also regretted he hadn't made more of an effort to know them while they lived. Whether they were Corbin's friends, the knight did not show. He cut the notches in his gauntlet and turned away. Patrick noted a slight tremor in his hands.

After inspecting Siegfried for wounds, Patrick turned him over to the stablehands and found Jakob and Josef. Both were wide-eyed and flushed.

"Are you well?" he asked them.

Jakob nodded. "That was both frightening and exhilarating."

Josef plucked at something splashed across his forehead. He held up the squishy white substance and made a face.

"Looks like a bit of someone's brains," Patrick said.

Josef's eyes crossed and he fell unconscious backwards. Jakob caught him.

Patrick approached Corbin who now stood with fists on hips, staring at the walls as if his eyes could penetrate them.

"We have to do something," he said, chewing his lower lip, "though I have no idea what. They'll be even better prepared next time."

"We'll think of something," Patrick assured, "and I'm told Jon made it through, so there is hope."

#

Lucan cringed at the sound he had dreaded to hear, but knew it would come eventually. A "thud" hit the roof of his chamber, followed by skittering noises across the ceiling. He approached his window, cast open the wood shutters, and returned to the center of his room with his back to the window. Wind washed over him, ruffling his hair.

"It's time," Lilliana said.

Lucan turned to face her. Aside from tousled hair, she made the picture of a noblewoman in maroon velvet gown. She held a long box of polished wood, no longer than her forearm.

"It is there?" Lucan said, eyeing the box suspiciously.

She set it on a table and took a quick step away as if glad to be free of it. "I told you so."

Still frowning with skepticism he picked up the box and undid the simple latch. When he opened it, his eyes widened at the contents.

"I can't believe it," Lucan breathed, withdrawing the chunk of metal.

Lilliana backed up another step, keeping a wary distance from the long antique spearhead he now turned over in his hand. An age-old design: rolled iron, pounded to a leaf-shaped blade. The bottom portion curled the metal into an opening to accommodate a wooden shaft. This fluted to the center of the blade, lending the weapon both lightness and strength. Though still sharp at the edges, the spearhead was ragged and pitted with dark red rust, which also gave the impression of dried blood. Its tip was missing.

"I don't think Emperor Henry would be very happy to know we are holding his property." Lucan shook his head, continuing to turn the thing over as he examined it. "The Spear of Destiny."

"If all goes well, it will be returned soon enough that it won't even be missed—or maybe we'll just keep it." Her voice was playful.

Lucan scoffed and set the item into its bed of crushed velvet and snapped the lid shut. "First, it has to work."

"Teo believes with this relic, this spear that pierced the side of Jesus, you will be able to do just that. It is the cause for the blood that spilled into the cup now resting in yonder church. Teo believes by bringing them back together, especially in your hands, wondrous things will happen. He was right about the girl, wasn't he?"

Lucan grumbled his concession.

"Obtain the cup, and take it to the northeast wall. It is the least-guarded position. You can let yourself down with a rope and find your way to Teodorico's tent from there."

"A rope?" Lucan said, frowning. "You can't meet me and, you know..."

He flapped his arms.

"I have no intention of coming anywhere near this place again," she responded, lips twitching, "and I definitely have no wish to be anywhere near that cup."

Lucan looked away, saying bitterly, "Right, I'm your tool."

Anger rose in her face. "A tool of your own choosing, and with a common goal. You're not losing your conviction, are you?"

"I admit I have my doubts." He stared long at the box next to a flagon of wine, not sure which one he wanted to pick up more. "Lilly, have you ever wondered if what we're doing is right? I had thought this was a simple mission of taking the cup and putting it in an ambitious man's hands. Why do so many innocents have to die? When did it become so complicated? I am tired."

The anger faded from her face and she came close to stroke his cheek.

"Do not lose faith now," she said, gentleness softening her voice. "We are so close, and it has always been a rule of the universe that for great things to happen, there must be a great price."

Lucan took her hand, pressed it to his face, and closed his eyes. "We could just run away. Things have moved along enough on their own now they don't need us anymore. We could watch from a distance. Together. Like in the old days."

Her smile was bittersweet. "The sun has set on you and me, all that is left is the mission. Focus on you, not on 'us.' This is the only way to take matters into your own hands. Furthermore, who is to say it wasn't always you who was meant to usher in the end times? Perhaps that is why God cursed you with your existence; to act as His agent, His hand, His tool."

She withdrew her hand and stood at a distance.

He drew a deep breath and nodded.

Smiling with satisfaction she moved toward the window, but before she departed she turned to him and said with narrowed eyes, "Just out of curiosity, Emperor Henry sent you to Antioch when the crusaders captured the city. You were to fetch the missing spear tip. Your exploits to save the crusaders from siege using the tip has become legend, but what indeed happened to it?"

Lucan's eyes narrowed at her in return. "It is as I originally reported: after the battle, the tip was assumed into heaven by angels."

"Indeed?" Lilliana said, eyes narrowing even more. She turned back to the window. Wind whipped through the room and she was gone.

Lucan retrieved the spear from its box, reached over the collar of his tunic, and pulled out the shard which hung from a leather thong around his neck. He held up the bit of metal to the spear.

The jagged piece fit perfectly.

#

Patrick gingerly made his way up the church's flying buttress and landed solidly on the roof. He went to the edge and surveyed the trebuchet, which neared completion across the field. Though now scorched and blackened, it was sound. From here it did not look so imposing until you realized the little ant-sized figures moving about it were people.

Presently, an ant-sized figure walked inside each of the water wheels, turning them, and simultaneously the cabin-sized counterweight full of rocks at its front slowly rose until it came to rest. The wheels locked in place and the ants exited, followed by a shout. A figure standing to the side of the engine pulled a lever and the wheels quickly spun in reverse, dropping the counter weight in a free fall. In response, the launch arm shot skywards and a thunderous rattle filled the air: the swinging arm dragged a chain along the bottom of the device until the chain whipped over the top of the engine with a *ker-whoosh!* A group of people standing too close to the backside of the engine ducked, missing the chain by a hair.

The chain flailed about for some time before coming to rest at the end of the bobbing launch arm. The construction crew cheered at their successful test.

Patrick shook his head. The enemy needed only to attach the launch basket.

Greensprings had considered long and hard what kind of attack could disable the thing, excluding a costly full-frontal assault. Nothing came to mind. Even Patrick, here in his "thinking place," had no answers. The only good news from their strategic council was the agreement that because the girl and the cup remained inside the keep, Teodorico would not allow Greensprings leveled until after their removal. He and Philip would likely concentrate the trebuchet attacks on the keep walls, creating breaches where Lost boys could enter with portable bridges spanning the moat. The enemy would spill into Greensprings like death poured into a bottle. That process would take longer, though, offering a glimmer of hope for a rescuing army to arrive.

As Patrick pondered this, he noticed people leaving the church in large numbers. His brow furrowed as he leaned over the edge to see another group leave.

Curious, he walked over to the stained-glass dome. Lucan stood near the altar, staring uncomfortably at the worshippers until they stood and left. Eventually, he remained alone with the cup, and Patrick did not like how he looked at it.

#

Patrick quietly made his way from one pillar to the next, keeping out of Lucan's line of sight.

Lucan still pondered the cup, arms halfway crossed while he chewed a thumbnail. Eventually, he leaned towards the cup and passed his hand through it.

The room filled with the fragrance of roses. Patrick made one last quiet jump to the pillar nearest Lucan.

The knight produced what looked like an old, broken spearhead and again he leaned towards the cup, hovering the old weapon near the vessel. After a pause, he touched the two metals.

An audible ting filled the emptiness of the church.

Patrick's eyes widened, and they widened further when Lucan tipped the entire cup with the spearhead.

When Lucan reached with his free hand to grasp the cup, Patrick stepped out from the shadows.

"Stop," he said. "What are you doing?"

Lucan stiffened and looked over his shoulder.

"Stay out of this, Patrick," he warned, and moved to grasp the cup.

Patrick drew his sword and took a step forward. "I said stop!"

Lucan spun and struck Patrick's sword with the spearhead.

As if made of pottery, Patrick's blade easily snapped off at mid-length and clattered noisily across the stone floor of the church. Patrick looked at the jagged remnant in his hand with disbelief.

"I said stay out of this," Lucan said sternly, and the spearhead glowed faintly in his hand.

He turned and reached for the cup a third time, but Patrick tackled him from behind, pinning his arms to his sides in a bear hug.

Lucan squatted, preventing Patrick from lifting or throwing him, and violently threw his head back. The blow caught Patrick on the cheek, and an explosion of stars stunned him. In that brief moment of pain and disorientation, Lucan pivoted and punched Patrick square in the stomach. Regardless of his chain mail, the blow knocked the wind out of him. He doubled over with a grunt. Lucan caught him by the throat and lifted him into the air just high enough to slam him back down to earth onto his back.

Lucan blew a wisp of hair out of his face.

"Stay," he said simply and turned yet again.

Coughing, Patrick sat up and lunged at Lucan's leg and latched on to it. Lucan dragged him for a step before turning.

"Damn you, Irishman," he growled, "you're a persistent fellow, I'll give you that, but you must let go."

With that he viciously kicked Patrick in the ribs and sent him rolling. Patrick used the momentum to roll to his feet and pull out his dagger.

"Too much has happened," Patrick wheezed, wavering on his feet, "and too many people have died already for you just to walk off with it."

Lucan raised the strange piece of metal and replied sadly, "I'm sorry, Sir Patrick, but if this is how it has to be, then so be it."

He lunged forward and swiped. Patrick bobbed and dodged and they circled each other, coming together in brief but fierce clashes alternating between slashes, jabs, and fist blows. Each of them made little progress in penetrating the other's defenses, expertly blocking with forearms at just the right moments.

Patrick's vision swam from his previous injuries, his breath labored, and he had no doubt that the special nature of Lucan's blade held the advantage and would cut through his armor as if it were butter. He had to be clever.

He feigned a stumble and remained down just long enough for Lucan to do just what he hoped he would: strike down with an overhand blow. Patrick caught Lucan's forearm on his own, then drove his dagger up into his sternum.

Lucan's eyes went wide and he staggered back, dropping his weapon. He reached for the blade protruding from his chest, pawing at it.

Pained and exhausted, Patrick leaned on his knees. After regaining his breath he looked up to watch Lucan's final moments, but shock filled him when he saw something else.

Wide-eyed, Patrick watched the man painfully extract the blade from his heart with only the smallest amount of blood to show for it. When finished, he regarded the blade oddly and dropped it with a clatter to the floor.

"That," he said, regarding Patrick angrily, "hurt."

"What are you?" Patrick said, not sure whether to run or try for his dagger. Lucan made no immediate move.

"I'm cursed," Lucan responded with a half-hearted smile, "but I hope you don't hold that against me."

Patrick snorted. "No, I hold the fact you just tried to kill me against you."

"I gave you every chance to leave," Lucan replied, scowling, and then gestured to his chest. "And, excuse me?" The anger suddenly left Lucan and he paced back and forth, running his hands through his hair, mumbling, "What am I doing?"

"What *are* you doing?" Patrick asked, his muscles still taut.

Lucan put his back against a pillar and slid to a sitting position.

"Trying to bring an end to the world," he admitted.

Lucan's changed demeanor eased Patrick's coiled nerves, and no longer sensing a threat, Patrick took a knee near him.

"How? What does the cup have to do with it?"

"I think you can imagine what will happen if Teodorico obtains the relic," Lucan explained, "but let me spell it out just the same; with a relic like that, Teodorico can become the sole recognized pope, consolidate his power in Western Christendom, and perhaps even combine all fragmented Christians—from the Catholics to the Orthodox to the Coptics—but his vision of Christianity would be a dark and twisted thing, with an emphasis on power and control, snuffing out the light of God. If Teodorico did not do this himself, certainly his successors would. Within a hundred years, all the reasons for God to unleash the Four Horsemen would arise, and the end times would commence."

Patrick frowned deeply, his mind reeling. "Why would you be a part of this?"

"Because I want the end to come," Lucan confessed. "I cannot die, cannot rest in peace, until Jesus returns. There is only one time that will happen, and that is when the events of the Book of Revelation play out, and that won't happen until the world is in such a hopeless state God unleashes the Four Horsemen."

"You are immortal?" Patrick breathed.

Lucan scoffed. "I cannot die, or age, if that is what you mean. Existing is not the same as living. There is little joy in my continued presence."

"But how?"

"How is it I can't die? I think you know your Bible better than most, and the legends surrounding it," Lucan continued. "You know the scene where the centurion is commanded to thrust his lance into the side of Christ? That was I."

"Longinus," Patrick said, appraising the man anew.

Lucan laughed. "That is not my name. 'Longinus' means 'Lancer,' or 'Lanceman.' That was attributed to me much later. My name is Lucien Gaius Aurelius. I was a centurion of the First Syrian Legion of Rome, and I had a life. All that changed and was taken from me the day I was commanded to ensure the Nazarene troublemaker was dead by stabbing him with a spear. The mixture of blood and water pouring over me that day transformed me. A baptism of sorts, but I have no special blessings—just a continued existence that goes on and on with no explanation."

"God has never told you why you cannot die?" Patrick asked.

"No," Lucan replied with bitterness. "All the mystics and saints I have consulted say I am cursed for daring to harm the flesh of God, and the curse will not lift until Jesus returns."

This revelation was enthralling, and Patrick temporarily forgot the impending battle outside. "But you were only doing your duty."

"So was the Israelite in scripture who put out his hand to steady the Ark of the Covenant when it started to tumble from its cart," Lucan reasoned, shrugging. Moisture glinted in his eyes. "Look what that got him: death. He was lucky, if you ask me."

"Still, that gives you no right to jeopardize our safety."

The sadness in Lucan's face shifted to anger. "If you had lived my life you would understand!"

"You don't think I've experienced loss? Suffered? Questioned God's plan for me?" Patrick scoffed. "You don't see me trying to end the world!"

Lucan's eyes narrowed at Patrick. "Why is that? You of all people should understand! You lost a child! You should be angry! You should be helping me! Why do you defend the cup?"

Patrick rose angrily. "Because I believe! I believe in hope. I believe in goodness. Even when I struggle to find it in me, I can't stop believing there has to be good in the world! I can't believe God lets the cup stay here purely for my punishment. There has to be a greater reason, even if I don't see it!"

In a rush, his feelings finally came clear to him.

"I am angry! But I have to recognize God made a natural order of things, which I broke. God created the sun, but should I blame Him for what happens to my eyes if I stare too long at it? The blame is mine!" His voice echoed. He chuckled to himself as a dozen images crossed his mind; from Aimeé to Yvette to his mother and beyond. "Wise people have tried to explain to me that the trick is not to wallow in the blame. But I must admit, I haven't quite sorted out how to accomplish that."

He rubbed his temple, attempting to massage more memories of Yvette to the surface so he could confront them. Few came.

Lucan stared at him nonplussed, fascinated. Patrick returned his stare, clenching and unclenching his fists as he considered this lost soul who had put Aimeé and others at risk.

"I'm sorry for your situation," Patrick continued, voice escalating from a growl, "I can't imagine what it must be like, but I do know everything has a purpose. Your life is a long and extraordinary one. It only stands to reason your purpose will be just as extraordinary and just as long in revealing itself. So, sit tall in the saddle and help, or get out of the way!"

Lucan gazed at him thoughtfully. "You are one of those people, aren't you?"

"What kind is that?"

Lucan grunted. "One of those who infect people with hope."

Patrick blinked and tensed, not sure what Lucan meant to do next. "Are you through? Or do you still wish to put the cup in Teodorico's hands?"

"I'm done," Lucan replied, "and I will help."

Patrick thrust out his hand. "Do I have your word on that?"

Lucan smiled tiredly, but genuinely.

"You have my word as a former centurion, a knight, and gentlemen. Fight strong," he said, beating his breast and then clasping Patrick's hand.

"Live stronger," Patrick said, and added, "We could use the skills of a Roman officer."

"Former officer," Lucan corrected as he bent over to pick up the spearhead. "That too was taken from me the day I failed to keep the body of the Nazarene in its tomb."

"You were one of the guards at the tomb of Christ?"

"Yes, until a brilliant light blinded me, and the earth shook, knocking me to the ground," he said, examining the spearhead. "But do you think Pilate believed any of that? Do you think he cared? No, he only cared the body went missing. I took the money the Jews gave me to keep my mouth shut and ran before Pilate could take my head."

"And that?" Patrick asked, pointing to the spearhead.

"This," he replied, holding it up, "is the Spear of Destiny as they call it these days. It was the one I took from the hundred in the Praetorian armory that fateful morning. It became more than a piece of metal the moment it pierced the side of Christ."

Patrick regarded it with fascination. "You've kept it all these years?"

Lucan laughed. "No, it was lost to me early on. It's been traveling the world almost as much as I, but on a separate path. I had heard it came to rest in the hands of the German kings, but I didn't believe it until the German kings became the emperors of the Holy Roman Empire—for it is said any who wield the spear will be undefeated. The empire grew at an incredible rate. So I offered myself into the empire's employ to help usher in the end of the world.

"And I waited... and waited. When the Salian Dynasty came to the throne, the spear no longer helped in battle. The emperors kept this a secret, but still managed to use it as a threat in negotiations. By the time Emperor Henry Salian took the throne, he had come to see the relic as a quaint antique, a useless symbol, which he squandered. Last I knew it rested in his treasury. His son snuck it out to give to Teodorico to give to me in the hopes it would help me take the cup."

"It worked," Patrick pointed out. "Until now, only Chansonne could touch it. Now you can. Perhaps we could use that to our advantage."

"The spear touched it, not I," Lucan argued. "You prevented me from following through on my experiment."

Patrick motioned for him to try again and they approached the altar.

Lucan tapped the cup again, making the tinging noise, but still his hand passed through it, even while holding the spearhead. The smell of roses filled the air.

"I was afraid of that," Lucan said. "I still cannot hold the cup. It only teases."

"I guess a broken spear just doesn't hold the same power over destiny as a complete spear," Patrick mused out loud.

Lucan's head snapped up.

"I think you may have something there," he said, and reached inside his tunic and pulled out an object affixed to his neck by a leather strap.

"Is that what I think it is?" Patrick gasped, eyes widening at the sight of the jagged piece of metal.

Lucan matched the two pieces together. "Perhaps if we complete it, destiny will be on our side."

"You've had it all this time." Patrick shook his head. "It wasn't 'assumed' into heaven as you claimed. Why?"

Lucan turned the bit of metal over in his hand, smiling ruefully. "I was in the employ of the Empire long enough to see they had become bogged down in politics and were not going to bring the apocalypse I hoped. When Emperor Henry sent me to Antioch to retrieve the tip, I had already decided not to give it to him. I had planned to wait for a better emperor to come along. Unfortunately, his son, the younger Henry, was no more promising."

Lucan's smile turned roguish. "But then Lilith found me and told me of Teodorico's plan and I knew I had found my man. The power of an empire coupled with religious fervor around the cup? That I believed." He shook his head. "It wasn't hard for her to convince me. She found me at my lowest. Also, I guess it was a way of having control in a world where I felt none. It was my way of telling the emperor to toss off."

"Lillith?" Patrick frowned.

"Lilliana," Lucan explained. "Lilith is her real name."

"What is she? How does she fit into all this?" Patrick asked, newly angry.

"She is immortal," Lucan said, "and far older a creature than I. She has existed since the dawn of time, and she, too, finds no peace until the world ends. Her motives are almost identical to mine."

"She is a demon?"

Lucan mulled that over, taking his time to respond. "Something else. She was once human. *She* is cursed. Did you know in the Garden of Eden, Adam had a wife before Eve?"

Patrick shook his head.

"God fashioned a woman from clay and breathed life into her, just as Adam," Lucan continued. "God named her Lilith. Adam was the first creature to have free will, and Lilith had an abundance of it. She was to be the mother of the world, to be a companion to Adam. Though she wanted children well enough, she was much too independent and wanted her own identity, separate from Adam's."

Lucan screwed up his lip and raised his eyebrows. "Apparently, when your gift is to help start a world and you turn your back on it, God takes offense. So, she was cast out of Eden and cursed with immortality so she could ponder her rebelliousness for all time. God also cursed her with barrenness, giving her immortal life but with no ability to make it. The years twisted her, turning her into a monster. They say the Devil found her and made her an offer; gave her powers like a demon so she could exact her vengeance on mankind, especially women, the daughters of Eve. She has a particular hatred for women who can bear children."

Patrick watched the play of emotions across Lucan's face and thought he recognized them.

"You love her, don't you?" Patrick said.

"Once, but no longer." He hung his head. "We had our time, and because we did, I know there is still goodness deep down inside her. There is, as you say, hope."

Patrick wanted to scoff at that notion, considering what she had done, but suppressed it and changed the subject.

"And she found an instrument to manipulate in Teodorico?" Patrick surmised.

Lucan nodded. "We are the willing damned, chasing each other in circles."

"No," Patrick said confidently and clapped Lucan on the shoulder, "we will break that circle. Come with me to the council chambers. Let's see if we can reforge the spear, and forge our destinies."

#

Within the hour, Patrick presented Lucan to Father Hugh, Sir Corbin, and Mother Superior and explained the situation.

"After some vigorous discussions," Patrick vouched, rubbing his swollen cheek, "I'm certain Lucan is truly in our camp."

To reinforce this, Lucan laid the spear and tip on the table in the council chamber. He took a knee, hung his head, and begged forgiveness. The council regarded the fragments and him with open mouths. Father Hugh reverently touched the relics.

"You are Longinus?" Father Hugh said in wonder. "So the legends are true. You walk the earth still, and now you are here."

Only Mother Superior seemed to have moved beyond her awe. "It makes sense. Avalon attracts the supernatural like a flame among moths."

Corbin shook with excitement. "Yes, we can use this. This is the miracle we've been waiting for. With these we can lead a successful assault on the trebuchet. Patrick, did you not say it was the tip alone that led the crusaders to victory at Antioch? Imagine what we can do with both pieces."

"With a little work first, perhaps," Patrick cautioned.

"What do you mean?"

Patrick nodded to Lucan who stood and addressed the council, explaining the true nature of Lilliana.

"She has the power of a demon," he finished his summary to the shocked faces. "If a battle for the trebuchet swings in Greensprings's favor, she undoubtedly will enter the battle in her monster form, and the spear pieces will not stop her."

"But a reforged spear will," Patrick added.

Lucan nodded in agreement. "It will not kill her, but it will harm her, evening the odds."

"Long enough for the spear to shatter the trebuchet launch chain into pieces."

"Chansonne's voice will keep Lilith back from our walls," Corbin mused out loud, "and a reforged spear will give us a battlefield advantage. Both will buy us time."

The assembled leaders looked to one another and nodded.

"How long will it take to reforge the spear?" Mother Superior asked.

"Hours, no more than a day I reckon," Corbin replied.

"Make it so," she commanded, and she kissed the blade.

#

Not surprisingly, the keep smith was named Smith.

He assessed the metal in his hand and stated, "It can be done, but it won't be quite the same. There will be a weld-scar at the seam, and it could be weak at that location as well."

"But it can be done," Corbin confirmed, pulling at his collar to relieve the heat from standing so near the forge. "How long?"

Smith chewed his lower lip. "Four hours?"

"Excellent," Corbin said, "Set to it then and—"

Before he could finish, a rumbling filled the air and a shout went up from the wall.

They exited the smithy's forge just in time to watch in shock as a fiery meteor shot through the sky, just clearing the keep's tallest tower. Even from the sky, it still bathed them in its heat. It disappeared over the western wall and sent a rumble through the dirt as it landed.

"Greek fire," Corbin breathed, despair creeping into his voice. "We're out of time. The trebuchet is operational."

"Not quite," Patrick pointed out. "That was a test shot. The engine is too close and overshot us. They will need to move the engine back at least five hundred paces, which will be no easy feat with an engine that size. We have time, perhaps just enough."

Corbin nodded and turned to Smith. "Hurry, but don't take any risks. We need that spear solid and in one piece."

Sir Waylan and Sir Brian rushed up then.

"We have a problem," they said.

"Clearly," Corbin replied, jerking his thumb in the direction of the fireball.

"Not just that," Brian elaborated with deep sadness. He and Waylan exchanged a pained glance. "They've captured Sir Jon."

Chapter Eighteen

When they mounted the wall, they found Philip standing just within shouting distance and a group of Lost Boys behind him, making a wall of shields.

When Patrick and Corbin appeared, Philip gestured to his men and they parted to reveal a bedraggled Sir Jon on his knees with hands tied behind his back. His face was bloody and beaten, and his new Avangarde surcoat was dirty and torn at the collar.

"What do you want?" Corbin called.

"You know what I want, but I don't expect you to give it to me over one knight," Philip called back.

"Then, why bother?"

Patrick turned to Fletcher at his side. The archer predicted his question and shook his head.

"Because you've angered me," Philip answered coldly, "and I wish to demonstrate my displeasure."

"That won't be necessary, Philip," Corbin argued. "Hang on to Jon, and after a battle or two, we'll undoubtedly have some of your men as prisoners and we can make an exchange."

"If you ever capture my men," Philip replied, taking out his dagger, "feel free to kill them for me for their failure. I would expect no less. This is about communication. This is about communicating to you exactly what you can expect when you defy me. When you try to sneak around me. When you trample my men in their tents after a long day's work."

He sauntered up to Jon.

Fletcher nocked an arrow and took aim, but bit his lip and shook his head in frustration.

Philip's men readied their shields.

Philip grabbed Jon by the hair and the half-conscious knight moaned.

"Philip!" Patrick shouted when he raised the blade. "We both know what you really want! Release Jon and I will come down to you!"

"Patrick!" Corbin hissed.

Though his helmet's visor covered his eyes, Philip's wicked smile conveyed a world of malice. "Oh no, Patrick. You will be the last to die. After you see everyone you care about die first. You will know what it means to be helpless. To fail."

Philip jerked Jon's head up and bared his throat.

"Patrick," Jon called weakly, "it's okay. I'm going home now."

Philip and the Lost Boys laughed.

With Jon's words, the bottom fell out of Patrick's stomach and he moaned. Nevertheless, he still hoped somehow...

Philip ran the blade across Jon's throat. A crimson chasm formed, gushing blood.

A berserker's rage engulfed Patrick and his vision turned as red as the blood spouting onto the earth. "Damn! No! Jon!" A long string of nonsense frothed out of Patrick's mouth. He lost all sense and it barely registered in his mind his comrades struggled to restrain him as he attempted to jump over the wall in his passion.

Philip's smile did not waver as he let Jon's twitching body slump to the side. He bent over and used the edge of Jon's cape to wipe his blade.

As the immediate rage subsided, Patrick could not believe his ears at what he heard next.

"Philip," Corbin called, "you've communicated well to me just now the difficulty of our situation. I have a certain perspective I didn't have a moment ago. Perhaps it's time we talk about how we can all get what we want."

Patrick shook his head as if the act would make him understand better. Surely Corbin could not be suggesting what he thought? He distantly noted how remarkably calm Corbin remained.

Philip shrugged. "Send over the girl in the white dress to negotiate with the pope."

"No," Corbin explained, "this discussion will be just for us soldiers. The men who matter."

"Very well, I'm listening," Philip returned.

"No," Corbin continued. "I will not shout at you like this, among so many ears."

"You can't negotiate with him! Not after what he just did!"

Corbin waved Patrick off, keeping his eyes on Philip as he continued, "Five of us will come down to you unarmed, and five of you can meet us halfway, unarmed. Have a group of horsemen behind you. They can cut us down if our archers start to fire on you."

Philip bobbed his helmed head. "Agreed. Twenty minutes."

"You can't be serious!" Patrick shouted in disbelief.

Corbin turned on Patrick and drew his dagger and growled. "Listen! I need you to trust me right now!"

Corbin lifted his hands and attempted to cut another mark in his gauntlet. His hands shook. Patrick saw the number of marks cut stretched from the tip of his thumb to his wrist.

"Do you think I want to do this?" Corbin said between clenched teeth, and gave up trying to cut the mark. "Do you think I enjoy watching my friends die? I never asked to be Steward of Greensprings, nor to be leader, but the duty fell to me. Sometimes we must make the best of what lot we cast. I have a plan, so please, just go down there with me. All will make sense soon."

He said this last while giving Patrick a piercing stare.

Patrick ground his teeth, hoping Corbin's plan was good enough. Together, they descended to the gate and handed their swords and daggers over to their comrades.

"Fletcher, I don't think I need to tell you what needs done if they don't hold up their end of the bargain," Corbin said.

The tall archer nodded.

When Philip's horsemen had arrived, the gates rattled open. Woodenly, Patrick followed Corbin and three others out to parley. Among them Patrick recognized Jeremie Le Beau and Jon de Lorraine. When they came within a few paces of each other, they stopped. Patrick looked away, so angry he had to cross his arms to keep his hands from striking out at Jon's murderers.

"I'd like to make you an offer, but I don't think Teodorico will like it," Corbin declared.

"If you're trying to bribe me, it won't work," Philip replied. "I assure you the pope has made it very clear what will happen to me if I don't put the cup in his hands."

"He will have the cup. You see, I plan on giving it to him."

Patrick grew dizzy with disbelief. "What! You can't do that! How could—!"

"Patrick! I am in charge here. It is my decision. Do not question my authority. I don't need to explain myself. Trust me!" Corbin shouted, stabbing a finger at Patrick.

Patrick felt the blood drain out of his face and the paralysis of shock overcame him. Philip smiled at the reaction.

"I don't see how Teodorico obtaining the cup will disappoint him," he said.

"Because you are going to refuse to destroy Greensprings once he has it," Corbin replied. "You see, I don't care for the cup anymore and the troubles it has brought us. I care for the lives of the people behind these walls. When Teodorico has the cup, he is still going to order you to destroy us to satisfy his petty ego. You may very well be successful, but it will cost you, I promise. You can avoid all that by taking Greensprings's considerable treasures without a fight because we handed it to you. Just leave us in peace."

Philip's lip curled. "I've already escaped one excommunication. I don't care to have another because I refused a pope's demands."

"There is enough treasure in Greensprings to pay off Teodorico and soothe his anger," Corbin explained, "with enough left over to buy your father's kingdom back. You shouldn't have any trouble changing Teodorico's mind. He is a greedy politician, I'm sure you know the type. Every day he keeps you in his employ is a day he has to feed and supply you, which I'm sure is a costly affair. If he has the cup, which is all he really wants, he will go back to the mainland merry, and with more coin in his purse to show for it. Besides, flattening an unknown castle on an island no one believes exists does not benefit him politically, so why would he bother?"

Philip pursed his lips and his head bobbed.

"I think I like this plan," he said at last.

Patrick felt blood return to his face, this time threatening to boil out his eyes. He opened his mouth to protest, but Corbin spun on him.

"Shut it! Now!" he shouted.

"Ja, Patrick," Philip jeered, "listen to your betters."

"Are we agreed, Philip?" Corbin asked.

"Agreed."

"Very well, then. Is that Teodorico's tent there, on that hillock?" Corbin said, pointing to a large white canopy.

"Ja, it is," Philip said. "You can bring the girl and cup there."

"Not the girl," Corbin clarified. "We captured Lucan trying to sneak out with the cup. For whatever reason, he can hold it."

Philip froze, pondering the veracity of this news, looking for a ruse.

"You can confirm with Teodorico when you give him the news," Corbin assured. "I'm sure he will tell you that is precisely why Lucan joined our side, to act as a spy and thief."

"Very well. We'll see you at the tent soon."

Corbin nodded and turned to leave. Philip and his men did likewise. Patrick stood his ground, his gaze snapping back and forth between the two departing groups. Even now he held out hope for an explanation. For the bite of the jest to reveal itself. When none came, he exploded.

"No!" he cried, removing his helmet and throwing it at Philip as hard as he could. The helmet bounced off the back of Philip's helmet with the sound of a bell tolling with a broken clapper.

"Patrick!" Corbin warned.

Philip froze in place and his men's eyes widened at the brazen attack, but after clenching and unclenching his hands a few times, Philip continued on his way.

"Damn you, Philip!" Patrick shouted at him. "And damn you, Corbin!"

"Go home, Patrick. Be a good little dog and do what you're told," Philip called over his shoulder.

"You're worse than a dog! You're a murderous, lying, filthy piece of shit! And Brutus is going to be just like you!"

Philip froze again, but this time his clenched fists did not release. Moisture glistened from underneath his visor, trailing along the right side of his nose.

Within a heartbeat, he spun and hurled his own helmet at Patrick, making him duck. When he did, Philip closed the short distance between them, tackling Patrick to the ground. They rolled in a flurry of capes and flailing arms, screaming and striking at each other like a pair of fighting boys on a playground.

The Avangarde looked amongst themselves as did the Lost Boys, then the groups looked at each other, shrugging nervously. The archers did not fire, nor did the horseman make a move. After many tense minutes, Patrick finally managed to get behind Philip. He wrapped his legs around Philip's torso, hooked a finger in his mouth, and started to pull viciously. A muffled cry issued from Philip and he reached into his boot. When he pulled out a dagger, both Lost Boys and Avangarde dove on the pair and wrestled them apart.

"That's enough Patrick!" Corbin shouted. "We're leaving now."

Patrick and Philip still fought to get at one another, cursing each other, but when sufficiently apart they turned on the soldiers who held them. Philip's men, apparently more afraid of him, released the frothing man. He shot back towards Patrick as his fellow Avangarde dragged him away, but Corbin barred his path. They locked eyes.

"Corbin," Philip hissed, looking Corbin up and down with the most contemptuous of looks, "don't fool yourself. There have been three men in this world who've ever frightened me, and you're not one of them." Jon de Lorraine tugged on Philip's arm, urging him to leave. Philip shook him off, but left just the same.

They deposited a furious Patrick on the cobblestones of Greensprings's courtyard. Not too far away they also laid out Jon's body. The gates closed.

Patrick shot to his feet. "Corbin, how can you just give them the cup?"

"Oh, I'm going to give them a cup all right, but I don't plan on giving them *the* cup."

Patrick froze. "You mean...?"

"Yes, Patrick, I lied to him."

A mixture of relief, confusion, and some embarrassment flooded him. "But, why didn't you just tell me?"

"Because I needed Philip to believe me, and you're a poor actor," Corbin explained. His shoulders slouched and exhaustion shown on his face. "I think Philip knows you well enough to recognize when you're truly angry. You did a fantastic job just being you. He is now convinced we mean to hand the cup over."

Patrick leaned over on his knees, emotional exhaustion taking its toll. "I'm sorry. I understand now you've bought us the time to reforge the spear."

"Yes, and I also have a better plan than throwing a suicide attack against the trebuchet," Corbin added as Avangarde returned his weapons. "Did you notice that arrogant fool Teodorico set up his tent on the edge of the enemy camp?"

Patrick nodded. "Yes, probably so he could have a nice view."

"Aye, and he's now within charging distance of our gates," Corbin continued, drawing his dagger. "We're going to march right up to Teodorico with Lucan holding a cup from the kitchen in one hand, and the Spear of Destiny behind his back. We're going to put that blade to Teodorico's throat, hold him hostage, and make him tell the Lost Boys to pack up and leave."

"It just might work," Patrick acknowledged.

"It better, because we're out of time," Corbin said. "Speaking of which, I'm going to check on the progress of the spear."

He left and Patrick turned to have a moment with Jon, but froze. Katherina and Chansonne were among those gathered about his body. When Katherina saw him, she stood from stroking Jon's muddy blond hair and slapped Patrick hard across the face.

Surprised, but not really, Patrick put up his arms to defend himself. She threw more blows at him, red blossoming in her face. The blows quickly subsided to weak flailing and after a half-hearted but angry attempt to prevent him from holding her, she acquiesced and held him back, weeping.

"All you had to do was say no," she sobbed.

"You're right," Patrick agreed, choking, "I should have told Jon no. It would have hurt him terribly and he would have hated me, but you're right, he would still be alive."

"He was so proud," Katherina whispered, "so proud."

They held each other for a while, then Patrick noticed Chansonne standing by with a concerned look.

"Why are you here?" Patrick asked. "Word couldn't have reached you about Jon already."

Katherina disentangled herself from his arms and wiped her eyes.

"It's Aimeé," she said, regaining some of her composure. "She is not getting better. The bleeding has slowed, but won't stop. We thought you should know."

"What of Emilie?"

"She is still exhausted from healing the wounded," Katherina replied. "The men love her for it, but she is now bedridden herself. I'm worried about her."

Patrick threw back his head and gazed at the sky, wondering how this day could get any worse.

As if to answer his questions, Corbin returned. "The spear is not ready," he said angrily, "and probably won't be for another couple hours."

"I don't think they'll wait on us," Patrick lamented. "The trebuchet should be in its new position any moment now."

"I know," Corbin agreed, punching a palm with his fist. "We can still proceed without the spear. The plan still might work."

Patrick sucked air between his teeth. "That is going to be difficult to pull off without the power of a relic, especially if Lilliana is there."

Corbin held out his hands. "I'm open to suggestions."

An unlikely one came from an equally unlikely source: in a small voice, Chansonne asked, "Would you like me to hurt the bad men?"

#

Lilliana poured herself a drink and took a seat on the litter under the canopy, foot tapping almost as impatiently as Teodorico's fingers on the arm of his chair.

"You believe him, hmm?"

"I am familiar with Patrick's hotheaded Irish rages," Philip answered, rubbing his cheek, "and I can tell you he did not take the news lightly. Ja, Corbin will be marching over here with the cup with your man, Lucan."

"Lucan," Teodorico sniffed derisively. "I cannot believe he got caught. At least he still managed to complete his mission, after a fashion, hmm?"

Lilliana's foot bobbing intensified. "This feels much too easy; something is wrong." She took a deep drink, not looking at any of them.

"You are too suspicious, my dear, hmm?" Teodorico said. "They merely see the futility of their situation. The fact they tried to bribe Sir Philip shows the extent of their desperation. Though I must admit, crushing them now will seem almost unfair."

Philip smiled. "I still will receive all the wealth of Greensprings?"

"Of course, hmm?" Teodorico said. "So long as you kill every occupant in the keep and leave no stone standing, hmm, yes?"

"My pleasure."

"I would advise against this," Lilliana protested. "Something just doesn't feel right. Continue with the original plan: destroy the walls first, attack, and then take Lucan or the girl and the cup."

Teodorico tsked. "And what? Run the risk of accidentally burying them underneath rubble? This is a fortuitous opportunity, hmm? Plus, there is no harm in entertaining their desperation, hmm? And I have enough men here to seize the messengers, and they can watch Philip's trebuchet turn their home to dust."

Lilliana slammed her drink down, threw her scarf about her neck, and moved to leave.

"Dearest, you don't wish to watch, hmm?"

"If they are indeed bringing the cup," she replied over her shoulder, "I do not care to be here. The thing makes me uncomfortable."

She left, leaving Philip and Teodorico to plot their next move.

#

Teodorico's restlessness escalated so much he poured himself a drink. When he had emptied the flagon's contents, he shoved it into Victor's hands, splashing the last of it on Victor's robe. Agitation flashed across Victor's normally smug countenance.

"More," Teodorico ordered.

As Victor bowed and left, Teodorico walked to the far edge of the canopy to watch the progress of the trebuchet.

"Are they not in position yet, hmm?".

"Almost, your Holiness," Philip replied. His finger tapping on the pommel of his broadsword showed his only sign of impatience.

"If the messengers do not come by the time the engine is in place, start launching anyway," Teodorico commanded.

"They come," Philip said, gesturing with his chin towards Greensprings. "They're on foot. I imagine by the time they arrive, we will launch the first missile."

"On foot?" Teodorico scowled, squinting in the direction of the keep. "What do you see? Tell me, young man with a young man's eyes."

"I see Patrick and Corbin in the front," Philip described. "There is a tall man in gray tunic behind them. I imagine that is Lucan—his hands are bound, but he carries a golden cup. Two more knights march behind him."

Teodorico raised an eyebrow thoughtfully as he took a drink. Lilliana was right. Something didn't feel right.

"Send men to intercept them," he said.

"Your Holiness?" Philip asked, raising his own eyebrow.

"You heard me—do it."

Philip selected a handful of men from the twenty or so who surrounded the canopy, and ordered them across the grass toward the representatives from Greensprings.

"What do you see?" Teodorico asked. "What do their faces say?"

Philip shrugged. "They're surprised, look none too happy about it, but still they come."

Teodorico drained the last of his wine and looked at the empty vessel with irritation. He looked for Victor, but his assistant hadn't returned.

Philip grunted a small gesture of surprise. "They brought the girl after all. They stepped aside and she came out from behind Lucan."

Teodorico trembled. "Tell your men to kill them! Now!"

Philip frowned in confusion. "What on earth for? It's just a child..."

"Do it! Do it now! Kill them all!" Teodorico raged in a panic.

But it was too late.

#

"Now," Corbin said.

He hadn't wanted to trigger the plan so prematurely, but the five Lost Boys were marching towards them. There was no turning back. They stepped aside, crouched, squeezed their eyes shut, and covered their ears.

The approaching Lost Boys only chuckled amongst themselves at the sight of the little girl in a white dress who regarded them impassively. They became vaguely aware of shouting from behind them when the girl started to sing, but soon all other sound became drowned out as her voice slowly escalated from a single musical note to a high-pitched scream.

The capes and hair of the Lost Boys at first fluttered in an unlikely wind. This buffeting air turned to a gale, and grew denser, like water hitting them as if from a waterfall. Pressure built in their ears and their eyes twitched. The lead pair of men tried to draw their swords and rush forward, but they fell to their knees and joined their comrades on the ground, holding their hands to their ears, crying out in pain. Their cries disappeared in the invisible hurricane engulfing them.

Blood gushed from their mouths, eyes, and noses, and it oozed between the fingers pressed against their ears. The blood floated away in droplets. Their writhing forms rose in the air. Capes, weapons, hair, and any other loose objects on them traveled skyward.

Their heads exploded in blossoms of red gore.

When Corbin looked up, bodies rained down. The canopy had blown away, and even the trees behind swayed as if brushed by a passing giant. Teodorico and all those near him had fallen to the ground and rolled from side to side in pain, holding their heads.

Beyond them, the enemy camp's fringe was flattened. Already, however, the Lost Boys from deeper in the camp mobilized to come to the pope's aid.

"Chansonne, do it again," Corbin shouted to the girl.

Chansonne looked in the direction of the gathering men and opened her mouth.

Nothing came out but a choking cough.

Her eyes went wide and she grasped her throat with her hands, struggling to make a sound.

"Dammit," Corbin cursed, standing and drawing his sword. "Lucan! Take her back to safety, now! Patrick, Brian, Bisch... with me!"

He charged Teodorico and his entourage. The other Avangarde joined him with a war cry. Their heavy armor made the distance feel like leagues, however, and by the time they arrived at their target, Philip and several others waited with drawn weapons.

Corbin tackled Philip and knocked him over. He used the momentum to roll and continue on his way to the crawling Teodorico. He didn't get far when Philip grabbed his leg from behind. Corbin turned just in time to fend off a sword blow. The Rhinelander swung again, but Patrick's blade deflected it.

"Get Teodorico!" Patrick called, and engaged Philip with furious swings.

Corbin stood and stumbled towards the pope, cutting down two dazed Cardinal Guards barring his path. The sound of hand-to-hand combat rose all around him as he reached for the old man. Before he could grab Teodorico and hold a blade to him, his attention flicked to the onrushing mob of Lost Boys.

#

Patrick was wild and angry with his sword, sending Philip staggering. Chansonne's voice had dazed the man, but he managed to deflect every one of Patrick's blows.

Between swings, Patrick snatched a glance at the battlefield. Brian had just cleaved one opponent in two in a shower of blood, only to have another stand in his path. Bisch windmilled his two-handed sword against three Cardinal Guardsmen. Corbin almost stood over their prize, but had to brace himself against a new onslaught of soldiers.

Patrick cursed their luck. Philip found his footing and took the offensive, planting his boot in Patrick's gut. In a heartbeat he was on the ground and Philip stood over him. All around, the tide of Lost Boys and Cardinal Guardsmen washed closer, eroding hope.

"Goodbye, Patrick!" Philip cried, raising his sword. His green eyes blazed.

Before the blade could fall, Philip hurtled back in a shower of splintering wood. A flash of horse's flank shot overhead, bearing a rider whose surcoat colors Patrick recognized.

"Jakob," he murmured thankfully.

More reinforcements from Greensprings raced through on horseback, breaking up the press of enemy soldiers. Patrick hacked at the air just to make room to stand up and breathe. Nearby, Jakob wheeled his horse around and tossed a broken lance aside for his sword, and then fought his way back towards Patrick.

Philip stumbled to his feet and ripped off a disfigured shoulder guard. Before he could retrieve his sword, a new battle cry went up. Josef was riding at him from the other direction, a lance leveled at his chest. Rather than run or duck, Philip crouched and waited with nerves as tempered as a sword's steel. When the right moment arrived, he side-stepped and dropped his weight on the shaft of the passing weapon, cradling it underneath his arm. The maneuver sent the tip of the lance into the ground.

Even before Patrick could form the thought, *Let go!* Josef was flung from the saddle. The young knight came crashing down, and his helmet bounced away.

Patrick cried out and redoubled his efforts to fight his way past the five men who separated him from Philip and the boy.

Jakob diverted his mount to come to Josef's assistance. Philip was quick; he picked up the lance tip and hurled it at the rider, striking him square in the chest, and knocking him from the saddle. Philip bent to retrieve one of the many weapons littering the battlefield and returned his attention to Josef.

Patrick crushed one man's face with the pommel of his sword, ducked another's swing, and pierced another through with his blade. By the time he extracted it, another two men blocked his path and Josef and Philip exchanged blows. Jakob reappeared and joined his friend in fighting the Rhinelander.

They attacked Philip with youth and exuberance, but Philip moved between them and deflected their blows with the grace and power of an experienced warrior.

An Avangarde horn sounded a retreat and the ferocious action around Patrick became frenetic. He deflected a blow from a Lost Boy, nearly severed the leg of a Cardinal Guardsman, ducked the slash of another, spun away from a slash to his back, and continued his way toward the battling trio.

Philip dropped Josef with a blow to the neck. The blade did not penetrate Josef's chain mail hood, but the grotesque angle at which Josef's head flopped left no doubt at the result.

Rage erupted in Patrick, sending his skin to tingling as if his anger tried to claw its way out of his body. He took out his wrath on the next Cardinal Guardsman to block his path, hacking him to pieces. Hot blood washed over his face, temporarily blinding him. The act of savagery did nothing to quell the rising panic. He could not reach the surviving boy. By the time he had finished the Guard and cleared his eyes, Jakob had fallen to his knees with his back to Philip, but facing Patrick. He cradled a forearm, at the end of which dangled a hand facing the wrong direction. Philip drew back his sword and shoved the blade into his back, exploding the tip out the front of Jakob's chest in a spew of chain links and gore.

"Philip!" A clear path opened and Patrick charged forward.

A malicious smile spread across Philip's lips.

Suddenly a horse blocked Patrick's charge. "Patrick, we must go!" Sir Waylan shouted, offering a hand to pull him up into the saddle. The Irishman hesitated, and Waylan urged him again.

Behind Philip, a hundred or more enemy horsemen were galloping toward them.

Cursing, Patrick took Waylan's hand. They bolted towards the Avangarde with the horn.

"Blow it again!" Waylan commanded.

The knight blew three blasts, each one longer than the last.

"Corbin! It is lost! We must go!" Waylan shouted.

Corbin paused in swinging his sword just long enough to look around, but it was too long. Two opponents jumped him.

Bisch swatted them away with his giant sword and picked his friend up by the cape.

"Go!" Bisch shouted, waving Corbin off. "Bad-bad!"

When he protested, Bisch planted his sword in the ground and threw Corbin over his shoulder. He carried him behind the horn blower and set him down. "Go! Bad-bad!" he bellowed, taking his sword up again and charging the enemy.

Corbin cried after him in vain.

Bisch swung his mighty blade, taking out a half-dozen enemy soldiers.

A smallish figure came forward and pulled two short swords from scabbards strapped to his back. He faced off with Bisch and the enemy mob paused to watch.

"Now! We need to go while they're distracted!" Waylan shouted.

As he, Patrick, and the horn blower struggled to keep Corbin on the horse and flee, Bisch bought them time.

The short Lost Boy, Diego, dodged and danced around the hulking Bisch like an angry squirrel. He lunged in to swipe at Bisch's meaty thighs, then would pull back just out of range of the long blade. Bleeding from a dozen wounds, Bisch's swings came slower and slower, making it easier for Diego to make his frustrating attacks. Finally, he shoved his blades under each of

Bisch's armpits, causing the giant to drop his weapon. He fell to his knees and Diego pounced on him, swinging his double blades in a scissor-like fashion.

Bisch's head came away from his shoulders in a geyser of blood. His hulking body fell to the side with hands twitching. Diego laughed gleefully and the Lost Boys swarmed over Bisch's body in pursuit.

Corbin slumped where he sat, his protests ended.

The Avangarde retreated.

Patrick and Waylan entered Greensprings last, just as a rumbling grabbed their attention: a fireball struck the ground just before the keep walls. Rocks, earth, and cinders exploded in a fountain of destruction, spilling across the earth like liquid fire. The flames leaped across the chasm-moat and splashed against the wall, sticking to the stone like burning pitch.

"Now the trebuchet is too far," Patrick said, wiping sweat and blood from his face. "They'll have to move it again, but only one more time, and only a little ways."

Dark smoke roiled into the air.

Chapter Nineteen

Patrick slid off the back of Waylan's horse. An invisible giant held his head in its grip, squeezing.

"Boys..." he whispered to himself. "They were just boys."

He drew himself up, took a deep breath, and told himself Jakob and Josef were also knights, and a knight's duty is often to die.

Yet the squeezing sensation intensified. His skull swarmed with thoughts of Jon, Bisch, the dead villagers at the pit, Yvette, and Aimeé. He shut his eyes and tucked the images away in a dark corner of his mind, promising himself he'd face them later.

The courtyard, already buzzing with the newly returned Avangarde, erupted when Corbin exclaimed, "Twenty? Are you sure?"

The knight nodded solemnly, responding, "Or thereabouts. We could not retrieve the bodies to make a proper account, but Philip will put them on display. We'll know then."

Corbin grabbed his curly hair and paced, looking about as if trying to find somewhere to run. His face alternated between determination to give orders and spasms of impotent grief.

"That is a grave dishonor to leave so many of our comrades on the field," he moaned, the light dimming in his eyes. "It's my fault. All my fault. Bisch, Bisch..."

He plucked at the gouges he had made on his gauntlets. The crowd of Avangarde started to look from one to another with concern.

"We had no choice. It was all we could do to retrieve you," Waylan consoled.

"And without Teodorico as a prisoner..." Corbin mumbled, looking as if he might retch any moment.

"We had to do something," Waylan continued. "We couldn't just wait here to be smashed to bits. Your plan was sound. If the girl's voice hadn't failed..."

"The girl," Corbin hissed, looking around furiously, "where is she? I demand to know what happened!"

"Er, I saw her enter the church..." Waylan stammered, then moved to change the subject. "Sir, we need to prepare our next move. We need..."

Corbin ignored him and shot towards the church.

Before Patrick could chase after him, an excited Lucan approached with Smith, holding up a newly formed spearhead.

"Where is Corbin going?" Lucan asked, some of the excitement leaving his face.

"To do something rash, I think," Patrick responded, a new concern constricting his heart.

#

A crowd followed Corbin as he marched up to the altar, where Chansonne stood.

"You!" he railed at the child, pushing his way through the usual crowd of pilgrims and refugees. "What happened? Why did your voice fail?"

Chansonne backed away, fear in her eyes.

"Corbin, I don't see how this helps anything," Patrick shouted, close behind. "Leave her alone so we can plan."

"Plan?" Corbin said scornfully, turning on Patrick. "I had a plan! It would have worked! That is, until she let us down! Now I want to know why my friends are dead!"

Chansonne ran to the far side of the altar and hid.

"She doesn't know why," Patrick continued. "You saw her. She strained her voice just as if you or I had strained our sword arm. Now, let us go. The trebuchet will be in its final position soon and we have to do something. There are other options."

"Why?" Corbin continued to fume. "So we can delay the inevitable? Any minute now the largest siege engine I've ever seen, funded by a rat of a pope and his imperial supporters, is going to smash our walls so two thousand murderers and rapists can overwhelm us. They will bring that soul-sucking she-demon, as well. Jon did not make it to the mainland to warn Wolfgang and Marcus. There will be no rescuing army. We are alone!"

As Corbin paced, he gestured wildly to the gawking spectators in the room. More people streamed into the building—Father Hugh, Mother Superior, and Geoffrey among them. The severity of the situation dawned on Patrick as he looked around the room at the faces. Despair began to spread through the room like a creeping fog, climbing people's legs and swirling around their torsos, coming to rest on their faces, smothering them. Some started to cry. Fear and hopelessness infected each new person who entered the church. A knot formed in Patrick's stomach and threatened to climb into his throat to choke him.

"Corbin, what is wrong with you?" Patrick said, trying to keep his voice low so as not to travel too far in the echoing room. "Get it together. We need you."

"What's wrong with me?" Corbin shouted, disregarding Patrick's attempt at civility. "My eyes are opened, that's what's 'wrong' with me!"

The knot in Patrick's stomach twisted like a nest of snakes as Corbin's darkness slowly crept towards him, accelerating when he saw Aimeé limp into the room under the assistance of Katherina and Candace. Rather than speculate why they had allowed her out of bed, Patrick moved to stop the poisoning despair filling the room before it could reach her.

"Corbin, there is hope," Patrick said loudly, shaking the darkness off. "The spear is finished."

"It's a little late," Corbin scoffed. "Does it still have miraculous powers? Can Lucan hold the cup now?"

Lucan looked down, abashed. "It was the first thing I tried when Smith found me. I still cannot hold the cup."

"Then so what?" Corbin laughed bitterly.

"It can still rally the men," Patrick retorted, "as it did at Antioch. And now that it's complete, it can act as a weapon against Lilith; it can balance the battlefield."

"For what purpose?" Corbin continued to rail.

"It can cut the trebuchet launch chain," Waylan pointed out.

"And how many more good people will we lose this time?" Corbin raised his hands in frustration, showing the marks on his gauntlets. "Maybe all of us will die this time. Even if we successfully destroyed the engine, they would just rebuild it before an army came to our aid. We should just give them the damn cup! Who cares, anyway? What has it done but cause us misery."

"You can't mean that," Patrick said, scowling, "not after everyone who has died for it."

"Yes, look at how many people have fought and died for it," Waylan added, "and that is just here. Imagine what it will be like when it reaches Christendom under the control of a pretender pope. He will force that little girl to use it to his ends."

"Precisely," Brian interjected, stepping forward. "If he can bring the dead back to life, then what is to stop him from raising dead soldiers just so he can send them back into battle again and again?"

"Or bring the wealthy back to life who paid for it at the highest bid?" Father Hugh concluded.

"I don't care!" Corbin snarled. "Do you hear me? *I don't care anymore!* Throw the thing and the girl over the wall and be done with it!"

With that Corbin dove for Chansonne.

"Take it!" he cried at her. "Take it and throw it over the wall!"

Chansonne fled the altar and ran into Patrick's arms. Corbin came to rest on the far side of the altar and slammed his hand on the marble, breathing hard.

"I just want it to end," he moaned, looking at the faces staring at him. "I just want things to go back to the way they were!"

He swept the candles, flowers, and scriptural texts onto the floor in a cacophony of sound. He swiped last at the source of all the drama, but his hand passed futilely through the cup. He drew his dagger.

"Bisch..." he mumbled, searching for a spot on his gauntlet.

In frustration he ripped them off and hovered the blade over his bare hand. A gasp rippled through the room when all saw a series of cuts in his flesh. Some older, red and puffy, some recent and still oozing blood.

A chill traveled up Patrick's spine. He held up his own hand, examining the scar along his own palm.

"Corbin, please stop," Patrick said, compassion in his voice. He disentangled himself from Chansonne and stepped forward, placing a gentle restraining hand on Corbin's wrist. "Don't do this. Trust me, swallowing all the responsibility will only swallow you."

"Really?" Corbin sniffed a derisive laugh. "Because from where I'm standing, I'm feeling all alone, with each death hanging from my neck like a millstone."

"I know," Patrick whispered, "and trust me, it will only get worse and drown you. Don't let it. You are not alone."

"How do I keep it from drowning me?" Corbin almost shouted, and his face screwed up to near tears.

Patrick froze. Yvette flashed across his mind for the thousandth time. He desperately wanted to know the answer to that question himself, yet it eluded him. At this most crucial of moments, however, he had to say something.

Glancing again at the scar on his hand and feeling the weight of the stares of all assembled in the church, Patrick motioned Lucan forward.

"By looking to the future for hope, and letting go of the darkness of the past," he said, nodding to Lucan. "Miracles can happen."

Lucan held up the relic, now polished and sharpened. It gleamed silver, though it had a jagged dark scar worming its way across the upper third of the blade. Sunlight caught it, reflecting into Corbin's face, creating a shimmering patch on his countenance.

Corbin regarded it with fascination. Slowly, the pain and hopelessness melted from his face as he reached out and grasped the bottom portion. When he drew it near him, he peered long into the reflective surface. A hum filled the air, and the cup shimmered with sunlight.

A smile spread across Corbin's face and the darkness truly fled from him. He stood straighter.

"Hope," he whispered, and the light reflecting on his face turned red, then blue, then yellow. "God has sent a sign. A promise like that unto Noah after the flood."

"Corbin?" Patrick said, frowning quizzically.

Corbin pointed up and behind him to the upper clerestory windows of the church while still looking into the mirror surface of the spearhead.

All followed his finger to a brilliant rainbow hanging in the sky.

Gasps filled the room.

Corbin looked up to the crowd as if noticing them for the first time, like a waking sleepwalker.

"Forgive me," he said, chin held high. Though his voice held a tone of contrition, it came loud and strong so all could hear him. "I let despair get the best of me. You deserve better and I promise you I will not let it happen again. As God is my witness."

He pointed to the rainbow with the spearhead.

Sighs of relief whispered through the room accompanied by a palpable release of tension.

"That is more than a promise," Patrick said, though not to Corbin. He regarded the rainbow. "That is a beacon—see—that is no ordinary rainbow. This is an Avalon rainbow."

"And?" Waylan asked.

"In my home country, rainbows point to hidden treasure. A rainbow appearing in Avalon on a cloudless day can only point to one thing: the cave of treasure where I found the cup," Patrick said.

"What difference does that make?" Brian asked.

"I've always argued the cup should be returned," Patrick explained, "I believe now it can. It is as Corbin says, a promise from God. If we return it, peace will return, and it will truly be out of Teodorico's grasp."

A light shone in Brian's face. "The girl, she can take it!"

"No!" Mother Superior protested. "She is just a child."

"A child whose voice can level a kingdom," Brian argued.

"And we need that voice to protect the keep from Lilith," Geoffrey pointed out. "If she left, we would be exposed to that demoness."

Mother Superior shook her head in exasperation. "Her voice is strained from the attack on Teodorico's tent. We don't know if she can defend herself during a run for the cave, let alone defend Greensprings."

"The enemy doesn't know that," Waylan countered.

Arguing ensued and fingers started to point.

Patrick clenched his jaw, wanting to jump into the argument, but a disturbance at the edge of the crowd drew his attention.

Corbin's spectacle, the rainbow, and then the argument had distracted Patrick from Aimeé. Now he fought his way through the crowd to her side as she collapsed, pale as a ghost.

"Whatever you do," Katherina said angrily, "send Chansonne over here with the cup, first! We sent her for it ages ago!"

The girl darted up the stairs, grabbed the cup as if it were the most ordinary of objects, and brought it to Aimeé. At first Aimeé hesitated, but after urging from Chansonne, she took the cup and drank.

At first Patrick felt trepidation, recalling what troubles had ensued the last time the cup had touched her lips, but this quickly gave away to relief when color returned to her face and her eyes brightened. Without assistance, she stood on firm feet, back and shoulders straight and strong.

"Thank you," she said to Chansonne.

She breathed deeply as she looked at the shocked faces staring at her.

"What is wrong?" she asked. "It is only healing. It is not as if I were raised from the dead again."

The implications hit Patrick like a rockslide.

"Child," Mother Superior pointed out, "you're holding the cup."

Aimeé's eyes widened as she realized the truth; she held the vessel in her hand.

"It's her!" Brian declared. "She will return the cup to the cave!"

"What?" Patrick exclaimed, his head snapping towards Brian. "She can't."

"It can't be a coincidence," Waylan added, "not with the rainbow appearing when it did."

Patrick tried to find a counter argument. Panic rose in him, seeing hope in all the faces around him. Yet he found no argument.

"It was I who brought it here," Patrick said, dipping his head in resignation, "so, if she is the one to return the cup, then I must go, too, and protect her."

Throughout much of the current debate, Corbin had remained silent, but now he spoke with calm logic. "No. The minute that madman Philip sees you enter the forest he will know something is afoot and come after you with a vengeance."

"So we will take a hundred men and protect her," Patrick reasoned.

Corbin shook his head. "That trebuchet is going to fire any moment. There is no telling how long it will take to return the cup. We will need every fighting man to stop the engine." He swallowed hard, but set his chin firm. "However many of us die in the process."

Patrick paced. "But if we..."

"But nothing," Corbin cut him off. "If Philip sees anyone making a run for the forest, he should only see, at most, two random people fleeing the fighting. Not you. You must lead the charge on the trebuchet with Lucan and the spear, drawing all of Philip's attention to give Aimeé any hope of slipping away unnoticed."

"Unnoticed?" Patrick cried. "Like Jon? No. There must be another way."

"Patrick, I will do this," Aimeé said.

"No," Patrick all but shouted as he came towards her. "Find another way."

"Like what?" Aimeé asked. "Send Chansonne? You know I cannot allow that."

"I can't let you go." Patrick's voice fell to a whisper.

Aimeé leveled a sharp gaze at him, bordering on anger. "You 'forbid' it? This is not your decision to make. I have benefitted unnaturally from an object that was never meant to be among us. I should be the one to take it back. Only when the balance of nature has been reset will our fortunes change for the better."

"That's not what I mean," Patrick confessed, coming even closer to her. He looked her in the eyes and his lips trembled. "I can live without you. I have most of my life. I've already been sad and lonely for so long I know it's possible to go on living without you..." Aimeé frowned, confused by the argument, but then Patrick fell to his knees and took her free hand with his two shaking ones. Tears welled up in his eyes and his voice quavered. "But I don't want to. I don't want to live without you. I love you. I want to marry you, have thousands of children with you, whether they're mine or not, and spend the rest of my life with you. I can't do that if you die today."

Tears welled up in her eyes and a bittersweet smile spread across her face. She stroked his dark hair.

"My dearest Patrick, how I love thee," she said between laughing tears. She kissed him on the lips. "We are all going to die this day unless I take the cup to where it belongs, and unless you stop that machine from crushing everything we love. We must do these things. We must play our parts."

After a heartbeat, Patrick nodded, conceding.

"Still, someone must go with you to protect you. Corbin?"

"Not I." Corbin gripped his sword hilt. "I have a rendezvous with a Spaniard."

"I will do it," Geoffrey said, stepping forward.

Patrick stood and placed himself between Aimeé and Geoffrey, scowling.

A hurt look crossed Geoffrey's face. "I know I am undeserving," he admitted, looking around Patrick to Aimeé's face. "I have wronged you, and I cannot change that. All I can say is that I am sorry, and I am willing to die for you to prove it." He took a knee before her and lowered his head. "I beg your forgiveness. Will you give me the chance to prove it?"

Aimeé's mouth hung open, a bewildered look on her face.

"Yes," she whispered after a pause. Her tone sounded more like a question.

"Aimeé..." Patrick started to say, but Fletcher ran into the church then, shouting.

"The trebuchet is almost in position," he cried.

"We're out of time," Corbin said, and though he was every inch the confident leader again, he looked to Patrick. "What would you have us do?"

All eyes in the room fell on him. He met Aimeé's determined gaze, then he nodded and addressed the crowd. "We will attack the engine! Corbin is right, if Aimeé has any chance of returning the cup, we must draw all attention to us. Geoffrey, take Aimeé and the cup to the end of the rainbow after all have sortied out the gate. Smith, affix the spearhead to a shaft and bring it to Lucan, who will carry it into battle just as at Antioch. Fletcher, if your men are up for it, they are welcome to join us on the battlefield with swords after they have spent every last arrow. Father Hugh, Mother Superior, and all the clergy of Greensprings; pray. Loudly.

Finally..." Smiles bloomed across the faces of all in the building when he beat his chest. "Fight strong!"

"Live stronger!" came the roaring response.

Even as the echo from the mantra faded it became replaced by the sound of marching boots, jangling spurs, clinking armor, and creaking leather as the knights poured out of the church.

Patrick intercepted Geoffrey.

"I know, you'll kill me if I let her down," Geoffrey preempted.

But Patrick thrust out his hand. "I meant to say thank you, and Godspeed."

Geoffrey tentatively took his hand, then shook vigorously when he saw Patrick's sincerity.

#

Not long after assembling in the courtyard, dark clouds started to fill the sky.

Patrick kissed Aimeé long and deeply before lifting her onto the back of Geoffrey's horse, Samson.

"Come back to me," he said, squeezing her hand.

She nodded and returned the squeeze. Patrick finally broke away, letting their touch linger as long as possible.

When he arrived at the front of the assembled Avangarde and mounted Siegfried before the gate, Smith stood nearby with the reins of Lucan's white horse in one hand, and the Spear of Destiny on a fresh shaft of ash wood in the other.

"Where is Lucan?" Patrick asked.

"He'll be here soon," Corbin said as he approached with two long swords, one resting on each shoulder. "He said he had a more comfortable suit of armor in his room. What do you think?" Corbin asked this last part while slashing at the air with the two swords. "I think your little friend out there has the right idea using two swords, but he's too small to wield the grown-up-sized ones."

"Excellent," Patrick responded, happy to see Corbin's spirit back.

Lucan arrived then, wearing a bronze breastplate with elaborate artwork, a blue cape, and a bronze helmet with cheek guards and a red crest. Armored greaves covered his forearms and shins.

"Who are you supposed to be?" Corbin asked, admiring Lucan's regalia.

Lucan snatched the spear from Smith and responded, "I am Lucien Gaius Aurelius."

"Very well," Corbin said, nodding favorably. "Mount up, centurion."

The three of them mounted up and guided their horses toward the gate.

"I must know something," Patrick said, leaning towards Lucan. "When it comes to Lilith, can you do what needs to be done?"

"I can't kill her simply because she cannot die," he admitted, but his lips curled into a roguish smile as he hefted the spear, "but I'll be very happy to hurt her."

Satisfied, Patrick nodded.

The gates rattled open just as the bells of the church tolled. They could hear the monks and nuns begin their hymns.

#

Teodorico winced as Victor applied healing balm to a cut above his eye.

"That will be quite enough," Teodorico said irritably, pushing Victor away. "Just get me a glass of wine, hmm, yes?"

Victor bowed, smiling his smug smile, and left with the medical box.

"It's only a scratch, my love," Lilliana quipped. "You act as if you lost a limb."

"A scratch I wouldn't have received in the first place if you had been present when they attacked," Teodorico snapped.

"Sorry, my love," she pouted. "Count on me to be of more direct help now."

"Help?" Philip der Rhinelander scoffed, plucking at a bandage that covered one of his own wounds. "How could you possibly have been helpful?"

Teodorico scowled and turned to Philip. "Sir Philip, I should have told you about the girl and her powers. That was my mistake. I underestimated the depths of our enemy's desperation, hmm? Imagine that—using a child on the battlefield? You were unprepared for the possibility, and that was my mistake. Likewise, there is something you should know about our Lilliana. She is not what she seems, hmm, yes?"

Philip frowned, looking the beautiful women up and down.

"She is an Amazon?" He sniggered.

Lilliana's eyes flickered between the amber eyes of an attractive woman and the yellow slits of a monster.

To his credit, Philip merely backed up a step. He regarded her with suspicion.

"You needn't worry, hmm?" Teodorico chuckled. "She is firmly on our side and can be a great asset on the battlefield should the need arise, but you and your men should be prepared to witness an extraordinary sight should she take to the field in her true form, hmm, yes?"

"Her true form? What are you?" Philip's left hand rested on the hilt of his sword. squeezing the pommel.

Lilliana smiled as she received a wine goblet from the returning Victor.

Teodorico took a goblet from Victor, too. "Let's just say there are all kinds of angels, and to gaze upon one in their true form with human eyes can be... confusing, hmm? God used a giant sea-beast to teach Jonah a lesson. I, too, have wondrous creatures at my disposal to achieve what I want. So, inform your men, hmm, yes?"

"I don't care what sort of sorcery you use," Philip said, his lip curling at the edge, "so long as I get what I want. If she is going to take to the battlefield in any form, natural or unnatural, I'd appreciate her keeping her distance."

Bells started to ring from Greensprings, drawing Philip's attention to the gate.

"Starting now," he said, strapping on his helmet.

#

When the last of the Avangarde thundered out the gate, Geoffrey's great white warhorse reared and pawed at the air before bolting across the drawbridge. Aimeé almost fell off the back, her grip complicated by the chalice in her hand, and by the alien and odious sensation of clinging to the man who had raped her.

She didn't know how to feel. Things had happened so fast and her mind whirled.

She bounced and slid from side to side, feeling the pain torturing her body afresh. Heedless, the horse sped across the field toward the forest where the rainbow disappeared. Geoffrey reached down and touched her where her free hand clasped the wrist of the hand holding the cup. She almost recoiled, but he was only urging her to hold on tighter.

"Are we being followed?" he shouted over the thunder of hooves and wind.

Behind, the diamond-shaped Avangarde regiment smashed into a wall of mounted Lost Boys. Despite being outnumbered, the Avangarde plowed through the cavalry, trampled the infantry that came next, and continued to the giant wood machine. Aimeé thought she perceived a brightness at the tip of the arrow the Avangarde formed. She hoped Patrick always stayed close to that light.

"Well?" Geoffrey groused, and then, "Never mind, I see them."

As Geoffrey put spurs to Samson again, Aimeé saw what she had missed during her first glance: horsemen had peeled away from the battle and pursued them, about five in all. Unencumbered, and on fleeter horses, they quickly made up ground on them.

Rain started to fall. First a fine mist, then a downpour. Mud kicked up by Samson's hooves began to plaster Aimeé's backside. Yet the rainbow still shone brightly against the thunderheads, leading them on like a torch. Even after they entered the forest, it appeared and disappeared through openings in the canopy, eventually bringing them to a wide meadow. The rainbow met the forest just beyond the clearing, so bright it seemed to push aside the branches like a solid band of light. Aimeé's heart jumped at the sight of it, realizing how close it and the cave must be.

Geoffrey crossed the meadow and pulled up just short of the tree line.

"This is as far as I go," he said, and took Aimeé by the wrist and gently let her down from the horse.

"What are you doing?" Aimeé almost shouted, looking around fearfully for their pursuers.

"The rainbow ends very near," Geoffrey explained, setting his lance against Samson's neck while he tightened the straps on his helmet, "and the forest is thick. You will make better time alone than with an armored knight and his horse. The enemy is close, and our tracks in the mud leave no doubt about our path. Our best chance is for me to stay and fight, and buy you as much time as possible."

"Geoffrey," Aimeé said, reaching up and touching his leg, "there are at least five of them, you will not survive."

Geoffrey laughed, flashing his perfect teeth. "My lady, you wound me. I can handle seven on a good day, six with my eyes closed." He took his shield from where it hung on the saddle and pulled it onto his forearm. "Besides, I'd gladly fight ten if it meant dying a holy and glorious death."

"Geoffrey, if this is some sort of misguided attempt at redemption, it is wholly unnecessary." She met his eyes. "Come, I need you to accompany me to the cave."

"It is necessary," Geoffrey responded somberly, taking up his lance again. "Do you understand me, my lady?"

"I'd be more inclined to believe you if you would stop calling me that. Do not mock me in such an hour," Aimeé replied.

Geoffrey's brow furrowed in puzzlement. "Call you what?"

"'My lady,'" Aimeé said. "You know I am low-born."

Geoffrey's smile was free of its old malicious humor. "Some women are born into nobility," he explained, "and others are simply born noble. I believe you are the latter. Now, do I truly have your forgiveness, Lady Aimeé?"

Emotions played across Geoffrey's face as if his heart might break at any moment.

A knot choked Aimeé's throat. "Yes," she whispered. "You have my forgiveness."

It seemed then a weight lifted from Geoffrey, taking with it a dark shadow.

"You best go now, Lady Aimeé," he said.

When she had passed back into the tree line, she glanced over her shoulder. Five horsemen appeared in the clearing. They reined their horses to a stop, taken aback by the scene. They looked around, then from one to the other. They then spread out as they slowly approached, as if anticipating a trap.

"Goodbye, Sir Geoffrey, and Godspeed," Aimeé said, and ran into the forest.

"Dragonetti," Geoffrey called to one of the men who came towards him, "I can't tell you how pleased I am you're here. You just made my day."

He put spurs to his horse and charged.

#

The Lost Boys expected the Avangarde to make another attempt on the trebuchet, even so soon after the attack on the pontiff's tent. Therefore, they were already lined up in battle formation about the engine. The ferocity with which the Avangarde attacked, however, came as a surprise.

The spear did not light up, nor did lightning flash from it. Patrick claimed no visions of a host of angels, such as what he believed he saw at Antioch. None of that seemed to matter, however, because its mere presence made the Avangarde feel righteous and invincible.

The cavalry met them head-on, lance for lance, yet could not stop the wave of white swans breaking through their ranks. The Lost Boys who survived the wave had to turn and chase the Avangarde who now rampaged through the infantrymen.

Bodies bounced off Siegfried's armor as the horse barreled through the mercenaries. Patrick stabbed at the occasional enemy who slipped between him and Lucan. Lucan held his right hand high, holding the spear. Together they dug a channel to the trebuchet whose water wheels were turning again, spooling chain. The counterweight hung high in the air, almost in a position to allow the launching arm to cast its deadly load.

When they arrived, the majority of Avangarde raced their mounts around the engine in a continuous and circular fashion. A knight is most effective when on horse, and even more so on a moving horse. Therefore, to keep the mercenary army at bay, they formed a ring of whirling blades about the trebuchet, acting as a meat grinder when the enemy came near. While doing so, others would permanently disable the device.

A company of Lost Boys, however, had already positioned itself against the engine to protect the vulnerable water wheels and the launching mechanism.

Waylan changed his grip on his lance and hurled it like a spear into one of the turning wheels. The weapon slipped just between the moving spokes and impaled the walking man inside who turned the contraption. The wheel on the opposite side continued to move the counterweight, but at a slower rate.

Regardless, the counterweight had nearly reached its position.

Brian tossed his lance as well, striking down a Lost Boy who ran with a torch toward the missile sitting in the trench.

"Cut the launch chain," Patrick called to Lucan. "I'll guard the launch mechanism."

Lucan nodded and they urged their horses closer to the device.

As they pulled up next to the base to step from their saddles, a mob of Lost Boys tackled them, knocking them to the ground. Siegfried went wild, kicking and biting. The big horse brained two of them before they could plunge their pikes into Patrick's prone body. The rescue bought time for Patrick to struggle to his feet. He set to hacking a path back to the engine.

Just then, Siegfried let out a shriek of pain.

Patrick turned in time to see several adversaries lasso Siegfried with whips. Others dove on the horse, driving pikes into the beast.

"No!" Patrick cried.

Siegfried stumbled to his front knees, struggled to rise while kicking with his rear hooves, but succumbed to the pikes driven into his flanks and shoulders. Bloody froth hung in strands from his muzzle as his cries turned to whimpers, then to a labored wheeze. He fell to his side.

Patrick leaped forward and hacked to death anyone who had touched his horse, but it came too late to save his oldest friend in Avalon. Siegfried lifted his head one last time, rolling his eye to Patrick one last time before he lay down forever. There would never again be a loving nuzzle from him.

Patrick set his jaw and turned back to the battle.

"Amigo!" Diego cried, standing before him. The little Spaniard twirled his twin short swords and swung at Patrick, taking advantage of his pain.

Before his swords could make their full arcs, however, a pair of blades scissored Diego's head off in a fountain of blood.

Corbin stood behind the falling body, his twin long swords dripping gore. He winked and turned to find new victims.

Patrick made his way toward the engine again, taking stock of the battle.

Lucan had recovered from the tumble and fought toward the engine, as well. The Avangarde's "ring of blades" around the trebuchet grew tighter and thinner as the enemy pressed in. The number of unhorsed Avangarde fighting on foot matched the number still in the saddle. Too many swans lay on the ground. The smell of blood and waste hung in the air, heralding death. The counterweight hung in position. The launch basket was full of Greek fire begging to be ignited. The launch lever needed nothing but a pull before it flung its deadly mass at Greensprings.

Rain started to fall.

A Lost Boy raced towards the barrel with a lighted torch. Lucan raised the Spear of Destiny to hurl at the man, but multiple arrows feathered the Lost Boy's back, stopping him in his tracks.

A cheer rose from the Avangarde host as more arrows flew through the scene, followed by brown-garbed villagers in leather and brass armor joining the fray.

Patrick opened his mouth to add his cheer, but it died in his throat when he realized the Lost Boy holding the torch did not drop like a rock; rather he teetered forward and landed on top of the oily barrel in the iron launch basket. The torch fell into the incendiary material and ignited it with a *whoosh!* It flared, sending a rush of heat over Patrick.

"Lucan! Cut the cable!" Patrick climbed the frame and ran for the launch lever.

Lucan heaved himself onto the trebuchet, but his head snapped back suddenly as a cord of boiled leather wrapped around his neck and pulled him down into the mud.

From horseback, Philip pulled the whip around Lucan's neck taut. He tied his end of the whip to the saddle, slid to his feet, and smacked his horse on the flank, sending it running. Still holding the spear, Lucan was dragged out of sight in a heartbeat.

Philip drew his sword and came forward.

#

Aimeé stumbled through thickets, pausing only to disentangle her hair and skirt from brambles. Yet in circumventing obstacles, she became disoriented and lost track of the rainbow. After what seemed like hours, she rested against a mossy tree, panicking.

The canopy here grew so thick little sunlight penetrated, giving the impression of night. Though the trees grew large and healthy and an abundance of toadstools and ferns carpeted the forest floor, the darkness gave the place a sinister aspect.

"Where is it?" she wondered aloud.

Patrick had spoken of a group of gray rocks surrounded by aspen trees. She saw no such thing, only giant oaks, ash, and yew. She'd passed plenty of knolls that might hide a cave, but they'd been fenced with brambles.

She turned about, searching for the rainbow.

When she made one final turn, she came face to face with a bloodied Dragonetti.

"Hello, wench," he hissed, grabbing her by the throat.

Aimeé screamed and fought out of his grasp, stumbling away. She ran but tripped over a branch, then crawled on all fours as fast as she could.

Dragonetti staggered after her, holding one mangled arm close to his chest.

"Oh, no you don't," he said, snagging her by a foot.

She turned onto her back as he dragged her toward him, and kicked him hard in his gashed face. He lost his grip on her and cursed, holding his bleeding nose. When he did, Aimeé kicked him in the crotch and ran.

She didn't get very far when he leaped on her. Her head struck a rock.

Stars flashed across her vision and sound slid away to a muffled distance.

He climbed onto her body and started to rip at her dress.

"You like to play games, do you? Well, I have a new game for you!"

#

Patrick slashed one Lost Boy's throat and pierced another clear through the chest with his sword. He pulled his blade out and kicked the body from the trebuchet frame. For the time being, he stood alone next to the launch lever.

"You want me?" he taunted Philip who fought his way towards him. "Then come and get me!"

Aesclinn villagers courageously threw themselves at Philip, but they did not realize they faced a warrior god—all of them fell to his sword. But they slowed him down. Patrick had a moment to wonder how Aimeé and Geoffrey fared, and to hope maybe if he kept the enemy away from the launch lever long enough, the blazing missile just might do the job for them, burning the machine down around it if it stayed in place long enough.

Something heavy landed behind him, shaking the engine. When he turned, a creature of nightmare stood there.

On the far side of the flames perched a batwinged monster, its giant pinions spanning the siege engine. She stepped over the flaming missile, impervious to the heat licking at her scaly legs. A long sinewy tail narrowed to a scorpion's barb. Even in his shock, a corner of Patrick's mind still thought surely Homer had this creature in mind when he described the harpies of Greek legend.

For despite her fangs, pointy ears, slitted yellow eyes, and horns, Patrick recognized the face.

"Lilliana," he breathed. *Lilith.*

She lunged and swatted at him with great clawed hands.

Backing away, he ducked and slashed at her, but he may as well have hacked at the trunk of an oak tree. In his retreat he nearly lost his balance; he realized he was at the back edge of the trebuchet, straddling the end of the launch channel. He windmilled his arms to regain his balance, but Lilith took advantage of the moment to deliver a backhand that sent him flying into the mud—and his sword spinning away.

The ground shook when Lilith landed astride him, scorpion tail poised over her back, directed at him.

"You should have taken the first kiss I offered you." Her voice dripped with malevolence. "Because I guarantee you this one won't be so sweet."

#

Though still dazed, Aimeé fought the brute who pawed at her.

She tried to focus her efforts, but her senses were blurry. Stars flickering across her vision started to truly dance, bobbing and weaving around Dragonetti's head. Rather than dissipate over time, more appeared, forming a constellation among the tree boughs. A singsong hum filled the air.

When the lights buzzed Dragonetti's face he swatted at them in agitation. Aimeé used the distraction to try and rise, but he slapped her face.

"Oh, no you don't!" he growled.

The slap focused her.

"Fight!" a tiny and familiar voice at her ear said.

Dragonetti struggled with her corset. Memories of past assaults flashed across her mind, and her hand gripped a rock. With all her strength she smashed it into Dragonetti's temple.

He fell to his back, but immediately tried to rise. "Run all you want, I'll still—"

"Who says I'm running?" Aimeé struck him again.

He fell back and Aimeé straddled his torso, pounding his face repeatedly with the rock.

The forest echoed with savage cries. The cries were hers, but she lost all sense of time and only stopped when her wrist gave out and the bloodied rock slipped from her grasp. When it fell away, a weight also seemed to fall from her shoulders.

Wide-eyed and sucking air through clenched teeth, she looked into the ruin of Dragonetti's face. She also realized a tiny voice squeaked in her ear, urging her to stop. A mote of light danced around her head.

Aimeé picked up the cup and stood, looking around in wonder at the dancing lights illuminating the forest. Blues and whites bobbed and pulsated around her, casting her in an ethereal glow. Beautiful, but indistinct music filled her ears.

The mote that had spoken in her ear transformed into a familiar face.

"Talia!" she cried happily.

The little fairy girl buzzed to Aimeé's ear as her comrades also revealed themselves. They formed a Fairy Kingdom carousel rotating around her head, comprising all manner of tiny creatures.

"What's that?" Aimeé said, leaning her head to one side to hear better. "Yes, yes, a very bad man. No, no, I think he was the only one here, but there are many more out there, and they are going to do bad things to my friends if I don't find the end of the rainbow. Can you help me?"

Talia danced away and looped through the air, urging her to follow. Aimeé followed the beat of dragonfly wings. When they had gone a fair distance, Talia pointed out into the darkness.

"It's this way?" Aimeé asked.

Talia nodded. With that, she flew to Aimeé's cheek, gave the tiniest of kisses, and shot away like a miniature falling star. In a blink, the others left as well, leaving the forest almost completely dark.

"Wait," Aimeé called after her, "I don't see the way."

No sooner had she said this than the ground at her feet lit up. Glowing flowers sprang up in the shape of a footprint. They grew out of the green moss, winding and twirling as they grew to finger's height. Another batch grew in the shape of another footprint, then another, and another, leading in one direction like an invisible guide.

She followed them and sure enough they brought her to a pile of gray rocks with a clear cave entrance. The footprints ended there.

Aimeé peered into the darkness. A torch flared to life at the entrance, then another farther down the tunnel, then another.

She followed the path lined with breezy cobwebs and ancient hand paintings.

Eventually she came to a cavernous chamber filled with magnificent, golden treasures, just as Patrick had described.

Aimeé turned in circles. "Hello?"

"We are here," a woman's voice said.

Aimeé turned to see three women, tall and willowy, with porcelain features. They had eyes like Patrick's mother. Aimeé sighed with relief.

"I have returned the cup," Aimeé said quickly, lifting the vessel for them to see. "Thank you for taking it back. Please tell me my friends will be safe now."

"We will take the cup," declared the lead woman, then in unison they all said, "but we cannot help your friends."

#

The scorpion tail rose, but paused when a familiar voice bellowed from the side.

"Keep away from the Irishman!" Philip cried. "He's mine!"

The Rhinelander marched forward unimpeded by opponents, blood dripping from his sword.

"Keep your distance!" Lilith returned, giving Philip an acid glare. "Or I'll suck the soul from your corpse!"

Patrick groped in the mud for his weapon, but to no avail. He raised his arms against the stinger's strike.

But just then, a thunderous creak shattered the air and the counterweight dropped in a free-fall. The launch chain rattled between Lilith's legs, dragged at high speed in the trench underneath her.

At the noise, Lilith turned with a squawk of surprise just in time to see the flaming launch basket smash into her as it scooped her up and flung her toward Greensprings along with its fiery missile to the sound of *ker-whoosh!*

"Suck that," Philip quipped, removing his hand from the launch lever and continuing toward Patrick.

#

"What do you mean?" Aimeé choked out. "That can't be. The rainbow led me here. I've returned the cup." She held it out again for emphasis. "Will you not help?"

One of the maidens gently lifted the cup from Aimeé's hands. "We are no longer of this world. We can only help by guarding the cup again."

"But not long ago goblins of Avalon attacked Greensprings—they were enough of the world to do that much. And the wee fairies? Twice they have attacked those who would hurt me," Aimeé argued.

"We are mostly shadows now," the third woman said. "Even the goblins have faded. As for the pixies and their kind, they can act as pests at best. It would take a miracle for us to intervene in a battle."

"Yes!" Aimeé cried. "A miracle! That is what I hoped for when I followed the rainbow."

"The Creator placed it in the sky to guide the cup here, and avert any greater tragedies," the first woman explained, "but many choices have set current events in motion, and they must play themselves out. If the Creator were to intervene, then He would be dishonoring those choices made freely."

"But we want intervention," Aimeé protested, frustration mounting. "We're asking for help. We're praying for a miracle."

"I'm sorry, Child," the second said sadly.

"No!" Aimeé wailed, falling to her knees. "It can't be! Did not Mother Mary ask her own son to turn water into wine? Did he not agree? Is there nothing I can ask for? I will do anything!"

The ethereal creatures gazed upon her compassionately. "Then you must pray to the Creator directly," the foremost maiden said, gesturing. "There you may find your miracle."

She pointed to the wall of the cave where another tunnel led into a room shrouded in mist that glowed from within.

"What is this place?" Aimeé asked.

"That is beyond our domain," the maiden responded. "There lies your hope. Good luck, Child."

Aimeé rose and approached the mist. She could not see through it, but stepped into the swirling mist. It was both crisp and soft as it caressed her skin. Something crossed her path in the mist, no higher than her waist. Distant laughter echoed. Another form ran across her path, but from the other direction, giggling. More movement came from behind her, and above her, and all around her. The laughter came louder, and from many sources, as if from a playground.

Airy hands brushed across her face, though she could not see their owners. They touched her forehead, cheek, and lips.

"Hello?" she called out into the mist.

The brushes on her face subsided, as did the laughter, and the place slowly brightened to a dazzling white.

"Welcome Aimeé de la Chasse," came a feminine voice.

A single form walked towards her out of the mist, materializing into a tall woman in a white gown. Her face had simple features, but beautiful ones, though somehow also indistinct. In fact, they seemed to shift as she spoke.

Aimeé regarded her sharply, then looked around. Because of the mist she could not tell if she stood in a cave, a room, or an open field. "What is this place?"

"This is your prayer," the woman responded simply. "It is not a 'place,' exactly. I apologize for my choice of words. Language can be inadequate when it comes to the human plane. We are neither here nor there, nor are we now, nor ever."

Aimeé closed her eyes and shook her head. "I'm sorry, I don't understand."

"You're praying," the woman explained. "What would you call where you mind goes when you pray? Especially in deep prayer that touches the face of God?"

"This is the face of God?" Aimeé asked incredulously, looking around again.

The woman smiled kindly. "In a manner of speaking. Moses conversed with a burning bush, did he not?"

"I see," Aimeé responded. "And you are?"

Again the kind smile. "Not important. You are what is important. You have a difficult path ahead of you."

"Yes," Aimeé agreed. "Everything I care about is about to be destroyed. Many of my friends may already be dead. We thought bringing the chalice back would end all that. We thought the rainbow meant something. Were we wrong?"

"No," the woman replied, and her smile turned bittersweet, "but things rarely are exactly as they might appear."

"Is there nothing I can do or say? Cannot I save my friends? Was the rainbow just a false hope?"

"It was a real sign," the woman conceded, her sad smile deepening. "Returning the chalice atoned for having taken it in the first place; an admirable act that many would never have attempted, but what you are asking now, to alter both the present and the future, is something different. It requires... more."

"Like what?" Aimeé's asked. A chill came over her.

"Faith," the woman explained. "God created order from chaos. He created natural laws to maintain that order and cannot break them lightly, or chaos will return. He is not blind to suffering, however, and would risk chaos for those who have faith."

But she felt doubt. She imagined the Lost Boys stepping over Patrick's body to corner a frightened Chansonne. "I've said it before, I'll say it again; I'll do anything," Aimeé said, voice trembling.

The woman's smile disappeared. "People always insist on 'doing' something, when God only asks that people believe."

"God doesn't want proof?" Aimeé said, her nose crinkling. "Did He not ask Abraham to sacrifice his son? Did not God sacrifice his own son?"

"Is that your concern, that you feel your faith must be accompanied by a sacrifice to make it feel 'real'?" The stranger asked, leaning forward with eyes narrowing sternly. "What if you were asked to sacrifice your child, like Abraham. Would that be 'real' enough for you?"

"But I can't have children, not anymore," Aimeé responded.

"In this place all things are possible," the woman said, waving a hand in a broad stroke to the surrounding mist. "Perhaps you are asking the wrong question. Perhaps you should be asking yourself, 'What prayer would I sacrifice to win a miracle for my friends?' What would be the 'hard' choice?"

Aimeé remained silent. The mist turned colder, sending a shiver up her spine.

The woman answered for her, and to Aimeé it seemed the woman's features turned almost sinister. "What if your prayer to have children again were answered, in place of saving your friends? What harm would there be in that? Your friends might yet survive without the intervention of a miracle."

"No," Aimeé said, shaking her head resolutely. "I came here for one reason, to save Greensprings."

The woman smiled slyly, and she gestured into the mist. "Ah, easy to say 'no' when the opportunity is abstract, but what if it were here before you?"

Laughter pealed from the mist and a small form walked towards her: a boy of no more than seven. He wore a tunic. His hair was dark, his skin light, and his eyes—hazel with halos of gold about the pupils. He looked up at her and smiled sweetly.

"Your child," the woman explained.

At the sight of the boy Aimeé's heart fell into her stomach. She bit her lower lip and knelt before him. He touched her face—her forehead, cheek, and lips. Aimeé drew a sharp breath and tears brimmed in her eyes. She touched his face back.

"Please don't do this to me," Aimeé said, turning to the stranger. "Make it stop."

The hard look in the woman's face softened. "This is your prayer, you can make it stop any time."

The child tugged on Aimeé's hair. "Can you tell me a story?"

The brimming tears in Aimeé's eyes now overflowed and she broke down. She held the child, sobbing.

#

Patrick's fingers finally brushed the hilt of his sword in a puddle. He rose to his knees, but the pain temporarily paralyzed him; Lilith's attack had at least broken some of his ribs. Worse, with a sinking heart, the trebuchet missile struck the tallest tower of Greensprings. It exploded in a shower of cinders, collapsing the top portion into an inferno of sputtering flames. A chill came over him. How many people had died in the destruction, and how many more would in the resulting blaze? Who would they be? Katherina? Chansonne? Trent? Willy?

Philip fell upon him now, his sword cutting a wide arc at his head. No preamble, no attempt to gloat before achieving his revenge. Just a rush to murder.

Given time, Patrick would have told Philip not to bother, for the light that imbued Patrick's spirit had extinguished just as the light of the flames engulfing Greensprings flared brighter.

Patrick's sword arm drooped.

#

"Not again," Aimeé sobbed, clinging to the child. "I can't lose you again."

Time passed, an indistinct period during which the boy returned her embrace. Eventually, she wiped her tears and looked at the woman. "Is there no other way?"

The woman sighed and her features shimmered, making it difficult for Aimeé to discern whether anything sinister had ever marred her beautiful features, or if she had only imagined it.

"You see," the woman said, "so easily, you humans fall into the trap of believing a sacrifice is necessary. You only need believe your prayer will be answered."

"It doesn't make sense," Aimeé protested, brow creasing as she struggled with the idea. "It can't be that simple."

The woman smiled. "Love doesn't always make sense, but there it is."

Aimeé nodded slowly, letting the words sink in. A warmth blossomed across her heart. "It's a gift."

"Yes," the woman agreed as her smile broadened, "a free gift."

The warmth growing in Aimeé turned bittersweet.

"Then you're not real," she said to the boy, stroking his face sadly. "You're a dream. A lesson."

"Of course I'm real," the boy laughed, then touched her breast. "I'm here."

Aimeé hiccuped a sob in her attempt to suppress it. The boy touched her necklace. "I have to go now, but would you play for me first?"

Wiping away tears, Aimeé put the tiny instrument to her lips and played, letting her fingers dance lightly along the holes. The music came easily, melting pain in her heart along with the mist around them to reveal natural sunlight and a brilliant blue Avalon sky. They stood not in a cave, but in an open field. Both the child and woman tilted their heads to the sky with smiles and closed eyes, letting sunlight bathe their faces. A breeze stirred the woman's dress, sweeping it behind her like gauzy wings.

When Aimeé finished, the boy wiped her tears. "Goodbye, Mummy. I love you."

"I love you too, Baby," Aimeé choked out, hugging him.

He faded, leaving her holding emptiness. She pulled in her arms, hugging herself. After a long shuddering exhale, she turned to the woman and asked, "Now what do I do?"

"You have faith. You can 'do' anything," the woman explained. "Play the other tune on your flute. You just might be surprised what comes to your aid now."

Aimeé raised her eyebrows, returned the flute to her lips and played the music. It came powerfully, echoing like an anthem, and she wondered how she ever could have confused this tune for the healing one.

Something blocked out the sunlight. She looked up expecting to see the woman standing closer, but she had disappeared.

In her place stood a king.

Chapter Twenty

Patrick staggered back, grabbing his head, his vision returning to normal.

"Do you see now, Patrick?" the Other asked. "You did nothing wrong. You were not alone in causing all this to happen. In so many instances, your guilt is an illusion, holding you prisoner. Now, will you lift your sword arm and continue the fight?"

Patrick stopped his staggering and came to rest, looking about the frozen battlefield. Though he understood the sights better now, nothing had really changed since the Other took him on his vision-journey. Greensprings still burned. Philip's sword still came precariously close to his head, and many of his friends lay dead, dying, or about to die all around him.

"I believe you," Patrick said, "but I'm still struggling to see how I can break these chains of guilt so I can do as you ask."

"Just let go. Recognize the truth," the Other counseled. "Recognize that life is a river down which we're all carried. How we choose to float, swim, or sink determines who we are when we arrive at our final destination. Swim and keep your head above water so those struggling next to you in the river will be inspired to stay afloat. Letting guilt weigh you down will only drag others down with you."

"I've already dragged so many down," Patrick whispered, extending an arm and holding out a bloodied hand to an image shimmering into existence before him.

A petite blonde in a blood-smeared habit regarded him with large blue eyes.

"It is an illusion," the Other insisted. "Even pain can become so familiar it becomes comfortable, but you must let it go."

"I want to," Patrick struggled to say, tears choking his voice, "but..."

Then he heard the music.

Flute music floated to him on the wind. It was the tune his mother had played for him as a child, but the tempo differed. A tempo that belonged to Aimeé and the sound sparked a light in his heart; the music meant she still lived. He latched onto that light and let it grow, even when he felt a familiar darkness try to smother it. Rather than help the darkness as he had done so many times... he let go. He let the music engulf him, filling him with peace.

When the music finished, he opened his eyes, not realizing he had even closed them. The blood on his outstretched hand fell away like a scattering of crimson butterflies and a smile bloomed across Yvette's face as she faded into nothingness.

"I will fight," Patrick said, clenching his cleansed hand into a fist.

The Other smiled and motioned him back to frozen Patrick. "Come, take your place and see this through."

Patrick stood behind his kneeling form. "What do I do?"

"Just kneel into yourself," the Other explained.

Patrick positioned himself, but turned one more time to the Other.

"I know what you are now," he said.

"Oh?" the Other returned.

"You are me," Patrick explained, "but it is I who am the doppelgänger; the creature that would usurp the life of the good Patrick and bring ruin to all those he loves. You have also shown me it doesn't have to be so. I have a choice. I can choose to be the good Patrick, and not the doppelgänger. Isn't that so?"

The Other nodded.

Patrick smiled, dipped, and merged into himself like a hand into a glove.

The Other turned and started to leave, but hesitated and came back. He leaned over and lifted Patrick's sword arm, positioning the blade to meet Philip's.

With that, he turned again and walked away, lifting his hand and snapping his fingers.

#

The blow bounced off his sword and he used its force to get to his feet.

Both he and Philip looked to their weapons, taking a moment to wonder at the suddenness at which Patrick had deflected the assault. But only for a moment.

They set to attacking each other—hacking, slashing, piercing.

The pain in his ribs went numb with battle-passion, and Patrick frustrated Philip's plans for revenge. He focused all his attention on fighting to the end, as the Other had counseled. Meanwhile, Philip gripped his sword with both hands and redoubled his attack. Spittle flew from between his gritted teeth, and through his visor, his green eyes bulged in rage.

With three successive double-handed blows, Philip sent Patrick's sword flying. Patrick ducked the next swing and dove for his weapon. Recovering it in a roll, he came to his feet to see Philip raising his sword. Philip froze, however, when a long barb protruded from his chest.

The great mercenary leader dropped his sword. Blood trickled from the corner of his mouth. And then his body flew to the side like a rag doll. In his place stood Lilith with smoke rolling off her blackened skin.

"Damn you!" Patrick cried and rushed forward to attack before she could extract her tail-barb from Philip's body.

She struck him, sending him sprawling. When he rolled to a sitting position, he noted the odd angle at which his left forearm hung, wondering why he couldn't feel it.

Lilith casually, but deliberately, marched forward, whipping her scorpion's tail about. With her blackened skin, she looked even more like a vision from hell, and though her hair smoked, the long skeins webbed her face and stuck to her teeth.

She opened her fanged maw and cackled. Her tongue darted over the air like a snake's. Spreading her wings wide in triumph, she arched her barbed towards Patrick.

Before she could take another step, a tremendous blow sent her stumbling to the side. Lucan stood there in a muddy blue cape.

"Sorry it took so long," he panted, "but that horse just wouldn't stop."

He turned his attention to the furious Lilith. Her tail whipped at him and her claws windmilled. As she rushed him, Lucan whirled the spear and thrust it at her head.

She dodged, and her stinger punctured his breastplate.

Lucan cried out in pain, but returned the favor by ramming the spear into her chest. It penetrated deeply, and for the first time she screamed in something other than rage. She raked Lucan with her claws from forehead to groin, leaving bloody gouges across the soft places between his armor plates. He withdrew the spear and slashed it across her chest, opening a valley of black ichor and bone. She staggered back, taking her stinger with her.

Lucan spun the spear, crouched, and readied for another attack.

She didn't take the invitation. Instead, she spread her wings and flew away, screeching and wobbling through the air.

Lucan planted the spear and leaned heavily on it, holding his side. "God, that hurt."

"She is defeated, then?" Patrick asked, struggling to his feet. His arm hurt again, and so intensely that he expected to vomit.

"No, she will be back," Lucan replied, trying to catch his breath, "but we have other things to worry about."

Patrick looked around. The fighting was in a lull. Fewer than fifty Avangarde remained, and with them, a handful of villagers. They slowly backed their way into a small circle around Patrick.

Though surprisingly few Lost Boys remained, they still outnumbered the Avangarde four to one.

The enemy slowly closed in.

#

Lilith crashed among the tents, rolling to a stop.

Smoke still seethed off her flesh and blackness oozed from her wounds. She shrieked in angry pain.

"I take it things are not going well, hmm?" Teodorico fumed from his canopy.

"Lucan wields a reforged Spear of Destiny," Lilith growled, straightening to her full height as her wounds closed up. "It is a complication."

Teodorico leaned forward and growled back, "Then you'd best get back in there and 'uncomplicate' it. That damn fool Philip again miscalculated his ridiculous toy's trajectory, and now Greensprings burns. We need to get in there quickly to keep the girl and cup from burning too, hmm, yes?"

Lilith cast a hesitant glance to the battlefield.

"Just distract him long enough, hmm?" Teodorico purred, sitting back in his chair. "He is just one durable man with a very sharp blade. We can still overwhelm him with my final play. Trust me, my dear—we are very close, hmm, yes?"

Lilith hissed at him, but nevertheless took to the air.

Teodorico turned to Victor. "Send the signal and let's end this, hmm?"

#

Patrick limped over to Philip and knelt over him. He was immobile in a growing pool of blood.

"Hold!" a voice among the Lost Boys shouted. "They have Philip captive!"

A tense calm hung over the battlefield—the sort of calm before the trap door on a gallows opened.

"It would appear you have won," Philip choked, blood spilling from his mouth.

"Nobody wins in our business," Patrick said.

"Das ist true," Philip conceded and coughed more blood. "So, now what?"

Patrick undid the strap to Philip's helmet and flung it away, revealing his mop of blond hair. He glared down at him, remembering Jon, Josef, Jakob... and many more.

Philip's mouth curled into a sly smile. "Go on. Do it. You want to."

Patrick drew his dagger from his belt with his good hand and held it suspended over Philip's face. Shouts erupted around him, urging him to kill or not kill him. Some wanted revenge. Cooler minds wanted a prisoner.

"Do it!" Philip shouted in a spray of bloody spittle.

Patrick squeezed the dagger until his knuckles turned white. He raised the blade, but stopped. "I will not fall into this trap," he said, lowering it. To himself, to the Other, he murmured, "I didn't learn to forgive myself just so I could fall into darkness all over again."

Philip sneered at him. "Coward."

Patrick blinked and shook his head. "You wouldn't understand, but it takes more courage to give forgiveness than to take revenge."

"Forgiveness?" Philip's sneer turned into a bloody, coughing scoff. "What business do you have giving forgiveness? You hypocrite! I don't want your forgiveness—I want my brother back!"

The accusation stung. While he spoke of not falling into one trap, he had fallen into another. Whether receiving it or giving it to yourself or others, forgiveness remained incomplete unless you asked for it.

The Avangarde and Lost Boys were getting unruly. Soon the killing would recommence unless Patrick did something.

Patrick pursed his lips, nodding. "Yes, I caused Karl's death. I didn't ask him for help, but I should have known he might try. It was a suicide mission." Patrick met Philip's green eyes, which were clouded with pain. "My foolishness took him from you, from Brutus, and from Sigirid. He is no longer around to take care of his family. I'm sorry for that. I'd die in his place if I could, as God is my witness. I beg your forgiveness."

They stared at one another for a time. Patrick's eye twitched as the shouts around him escalated.

"I don't believe you," Philip spat.

Patrick took Philip's hand and slapped the dagger into his palm, then held the blade to his own chest. The sounds of agitation turned to a collective gasp of shock. "There, you want your revenge? Take it! Just swear to me on Karl's name you will call off the Boys and tell Teodorico to shove it up his arse! Tell me you forgive me, and I will give you my life."

Philip stared wide-eyed. He breathed heavily through blood-soaked teeth. Shouts erupted again, now directed at Philip.

"Your word, in Karl's name!" Patrick insisted.

Philip grabbed the dagger with both hands and his body tensed.

"Phht!" he said at last. He tossed the blade aside and his body relaxed. "You take all the fun out of this. Asshole."

Patrick let out a breath he didn't realize he held. The shouts and agitations around them quietly died under a blanket of new gasps.

"Karl loved you," Philip continued. "He wouldn't want this. Besides, I am dying. I just wish I could be there to see Teodorico's face when he learns I told the Lost Boys to stand down."

Patrick slumped with relief, then laughed. "I'd like that, too."

"You know what I'd really like?" Philip added, beckoning with a hand to Jon de Lorraine and Jeremie Le Beau who hovered on the edges of the Avangarde circle. "To see Brutus and Sigirid one last time, to explain to them why I can't watch over them."

Patrick called to Corbin and Waylan to let the two Lost Boys through their defenses. Lucan followed them, keeping a cautious eye.

"You still can," Patrick said, "just as a guardian soul."

"Bah, there is no going to heaven for the likes of me," Philip scoffed, urging his lieutenants to kneel down when they arrived.

"Not true," Patrick replied, making room for Lorraine and Le Beau. "If you can forgive me, you can ask forgiveness from God."

Lorraine and Le Beau looked between them quizzically, having arrived in the middle of the conversation.

Philip barked a cynical laugh that turned into a cough and more blood trickled from the corner of his mouth.

"You know my deeds," Patrick continued, "and I can tell you there is hope for everyone. I found it here in Avalon. I'm still far from perfect, but I am no longer lost. I made my peace with God, and you can, too."

Philip's eyes softened and he regarded Patrick with something like curiosity. He touched Patrick's face. "Ja, you are different. At first I thought it weakness, but now I see otherwise. You think it's possible... even for me?"

Patrick nodded, squeezing his hand.

"You were always good with words," Philip said, frowning. "What do I say?"

Patrick shrugged. "Don't say anything. Just use your heart."

At first Philip frown deepened, but eventually he nodded and closed his eyes. A quiet moment passed. Lucan watched intensely, caught between skepticism and wonder.

When Philip opened his eyes, much of the anger and hardness had melted away.

"Thank you, my brother," Philip whispered, "and now I'd like to return the favor."

He turned to his lieutenants and gave them quiet orders.

Patrick stood and looked around, making a quick assessment. Corbin, Waylan, Brian, Lucan, and forty some other Avangarde and villagers survived, crouched and holding weapons ready to fight to the end. Not a horse among them. The trebuchet smoldered from small fires, but was intact. Bodies lay everywhere. Blood soaked the ground and every puddle glinted crimson. Arms, hands, and heads lay side-by-side with the weapons, helmets, and shields to which they had belonged. Spent spears, pikes, banners, and javelins made a macabre forest among which crows and ravens already swarmed.

"We are done. The Lost Boys will stand down," Jon de Lorraine said, standing and clasping Patrick on the shoulder. Professional disappointment filled his voice, but personal relief filled his eyes. He jerked his head towards Philip. "He wishes to speak to you."

Lorraine ran to inform the Lost Boys. Jeremie remained near his dying leader.

"Thank you, my brother," Patrick said, taking a knee near Philip.

"I have one more thing to give you," Philip said, and his face screwed up with some effort, "to remember me by."

He grunted, and a horrible noise came from his bowels followed by an even more horrible smell. He laughed.

"Oh, God, Philip, that's awful," Patrick said, covering his nose.

"Nein, das ist gut," Philip said, his entire body shaking with laughter.

Patrick joined him in laughing, though his laughter came out nasally as he pinched his nose.

Philip's shaking laughs turned to convulsing gurgles. His back arched one last time, and the pain in his face melted away. The light in his green eyes faded, and his pupils relaxed, dilating to twice their size.

"Goodbye, my brother," Patrick said, closing Philip's staring eyes with his good hand. He stood, gripping his broken arm.

"What do we do now?" Jeremie asked, as if Patrick now led the Lost Boys.

Before Patrick could respond, a horn blared at the edge of the forest where the harbor road came.

All eyes turned towards the sound to witness a river of red surcoats and flowing banners carrying the heraldry of Teodorico's former cardinal office. An endless line of soldiers marched, keeping pace to drums. They must have numbered as many as the Lost Boys had when at full strength.

"What the—?" Jeremie exclaimed, squinting at the new arrivals who split in two like a serpent's tongue to surround them.

"I'm guessing by your reaction you knew nothing of this," Patrick said.

Jeremie shook his head.

"Lucan?" Patrick asked.

"No, but I'm not surprised," Lucan admitted while watching the fresh army advance with glittering weapons and armor. "It explains how Teodorico could afford such expensive mercenaries."

"What's that supposed to mean?" Jeremie asked, frowning.

"Teodorico had no intention of ever paying you," Lucan explained dryly. "That's his personal army from Albano. I'm guessing he planned on the Lost Boys doing all the hard work, then have his men sweep in and take the credit. Of course that would require 'eliminating' the Lost Boys."

Jeremie's face turned to a mask of anger. "We are with you. What do we do?"

"Phalanx," Lucan said simply.

"Shield wall," Patrick translated, and the Lost Boy turned to his comrades and shouted the command.

As Corbin coordinated the Avangarde with them into a defense, Patrick leaned down and picked up a sword, not sure what kind of help he could offer in his condition.

A shadow engulfed them from above, followed by an object falling from the sky, crushing Lucan and sending his helmet and spear flying.

Lilith stood on his back, then used it to launch herself at Patrick.

#

Patrick stabbed at her with his sword, connecting solidly, but the force of her assault still sent him sprawling. Pain shot through his arm like lightning.

Lilith wrapped sinewy talons around his blade, which protruded from her chest. She extracted the weapon with only the slightest of grunts and tossed it aside.

In a fog of pain, Patrick fumbled through the mud for a weapon, but could not find one within reach. The new enemy crashed against the joined shields of Avangarde and Lost Boys. Lilith spread her wings and in the blink of an eye she stood over Patrick, grabbing him by the throat and lifting him into the air.

"Beautiful fool," she said, and opened her mouth near his.

The sensation of ice water vomiting out of his mouth engulfed him, leaving a growing emptiness inside him. A white mist flowed from his throat into Lilith's. He felt as if his flesh were slowly deflating, soon to be an empty bag of skin dangling from her hand.

He clawed at the iron grip at his throat, but to no avail. From the corner of his vision he saw the Spear of Destiny resting on the ground, broken at the shaft, but too far out of his reach. The sounds of battle raged around him.

His vision swam and his senses reeled. His heartbeat slowed and his feeble strength ebbed. After one last attempt to claw free, his head lolled back skyward. At death's door, his mind was almost feverish.

Through the swirling mass of dark storm clouds, he thought he glimpsed bat-winged monsters clashing with bright-feathered angels in gleaming armor and flashing swords. Their collision rent the heavens with thunder.

Rain pelted his face.

Is this your will, God? he thought, too tired to ponder whether it was fair. *I don't understand, but I will trust.*

Just as the last bit of his resistance drained away, and he sighed out the last of the mist his body had to offer, Aimeé's music seemed closer, stronger. It turned to a horn's blare, bursting in his ears and shaking the earth.

Lilith faltered, stumbling.

The earth did indeed shake, but something else was causing the familiar tremor.

Horse hooves, from cavalry.

Sunlight burst forth, parting the dark clouds. Out of the forest to his left a group of knights descended upon the field. Patrick did not know these thirty knights who charged with such precision— but surely they had to be men of renown. The bannerman's long flowing pennon did seem familiar, though. Its red dragon stretched the entire length of the fabric, and it stirred boyhood stories. Next to the bannerman rode a leader in a gold-crown-crested helm. In his hand, held high, he carried a sword with an hourglass hilt Patrick had no trouble recognizing, for he had borrowed it for a brief time.

To Patrick's right another group of knights came, this one from the direction of the harbor, carrying heraldry and banners he recognized. The leading men wore the black and white swans of the Avangarde: Sir Wolfgang and Sir Marcus. Between them came Sir Charles, carrying the banner of the Papal Guard, and behind them rode a hundred knights in gold and white.

The flute music, the horn blasts, and the sound of trembling earth were drowned out by another music: glorious music Patrick could barely describe. In his fevered state he thought he surely imagined it, just as he imagined the fantastical sights accompanying the music. The forest came alive, lumbering forth on roots and crushing the enemy. Every bird and beast of Avalon flowed among their trunks, pouring over the red surcoats. Here a bear dragged a soldier down, there a pack of wolves scattered a squad of spearmen. Raptors dove from the sky to gouge eyes from those attacking the shield wall of defenders. Fairy creatures joined the fray. A giant ogre picked up two red-clad soldiers and banged them together like cymbals. A company of goblins matched swords with startled humans, moss covered trolls waded through the melee swinging massive wooden clubs. Among all flowed fireflies, blinding the enemy.

Yet Lilith still sucked at his soul, eyes rolled into the back of her head as if the intimate nature of the attack sent her into a state of ecstasy. She fell to her knees, allowing Patrick to touch earth as well. The Spear of Destiny rested almost within reach, but Patrick could not even summon the strength to reach for it.

Time to go, he thought, and this time the sentiment was not a matter of quitting, but accepting.

He had no regrets. He had done as the Other had urged; hold out and give hope to his comrades. He had accomplished that much.

From the corner of his eye a small hand grasped the broken shaft of the Spear of Destiny and lifted it from the earth.

Lilith's head suddenly jerked back, disrupting the transfer of mist. Aimeé stood behind her, a handful of Lilith's hair bunched up in her fist.

"I don't think so, Bitch!" she hissed in Lilith's ear, and made a thrusting gesture.

The Spear of Destiny burst from between Lilith's breasts, spewing ichor and gore.

She shrieked in agony, releasing Patrick.

As if in slow motion, Patrick fell to earth and dirt and pebbles bounced as his head struck the ground. His vision narrowed and darkness started to close in around him. His breath came in struggling gasps. His hands twitched uncontrollably.

Lilith writhed nearby, trying to staunch the flow of dark blood from her wound. Lucan struggled to sit up, though his legs beneath his hips turned at an odd angle compared to his torso. He reached out to Lilith.

"Lilly, stop," Patrick heard him plead, though the sound came muffled and surreal in his ears. "Just let go, it's never too late to find peace. Come with me."

For a brief moment, Lilith's demonic visage shimmered away to reveal a normal woman. A beautiful woman, nude and vulnerable. She reached out to Lucan, but before their fingers touched, the demoness returned.

"No!" she cried, and took to the air to fly away in an erratic pattern like a stunned bat, fountaining black blood.

Aimeé was next to him now, shouting his name, but she sounded a thousand miles away. She lifted his head and forced her fingers into his mouth, and she moved them about as if clearing some obstruction there. When she lifted his head, he saw the aftermath of the battle.

The enemy defeated. The sky clear. The survivors took a knee and bowed to the leader of the mysterious knights who had ridden from the forest.

Patrick smiled weakly.

Aimeé was safe. The day was won.

Darkness closed in, and he knew no more.

Chapter Twenty-One

Golden sunlight streamed into the room, waking Patrick with its warmth on his face. After a few moments, that caress turned to a stifling heat baking him under the mountains of blankets that covered him. Between that and the headache pounding the inside of his skull, he wished he hadn't woken at all. He wished to sleep again, but someone in the room snored.

Corbin leaned back in a chair with his boots kicked up on Patrick's bed. His head, bandaged with much padding packed against one of his ears, lolled over the back of the chair. His curly blondish locks spilled over the linen wraps.

Patrick kicked at his boots. "Oi, do you mind? I'm trying to sleep here."

Corbin snorted to wakefulness, almost falling over in the chair.

"You're awake," he said sleepily.

"Thanks to you, wanker."

"You've been asleep for days," Corbin pointed out. "We didn't think you were going to make it, but you pulled through."

Patrick wiggled the fingers of his left hand, the only part of his entire left arm that wasn't splinted. "Aimeé?"

"She is well," Corbin assured. "She would not leave your side for the first few days. Only after it was clear you would survive did she allow herself to go help others. Ever since then, we've been taking turns watching over you."

"Geoffrey?" Patrick continued.

Corbin shook his head sadly. "Aimeé said he acquitted himself well. A true Avangarde. The cup was returned."

Corbin explained all that had happened, filling in the gaps in Patrick's memory and knowledge. Though never confirmed, the knights who had come to their aid out of the Avalon forests must have been King Arthur and his knights. Patrick had no doubt about it. Though legend stated they would not awaken from their slumber until all of Britain needed them, they had come to the aid of Greensprings.

"Who is left among us?" Patrick asked.

Corbin listed the Avangarde who remained, among which were himself, Waylan, Brian, Gregory, Jeremiah, Wolfgang, Marcus, and twenty others.

Patrick bit his lip and sadly shook his head that only aggravated his headache.

After a moment of silence, he looked around and frowned. "Where am I?"

"What?" Corbin laughed. "Rumor has it you snuck in here enough times. You're in the Hall for Lady Guests."

Patrick scoffed. "Damned lies. It was only once. Maybe twice. Why here?"

"During the battle, Candace went into a panic and started screaming that everyone needed to go to the Hall for Lady Guests. Katherina convinced everyone to do so. Virtually everyone was saved because they were spared from the keep fire."

"Katherina and the children are well?"

"Aye," Corbin said, "but Greensprings will never be the same again. This building and the Hall for Guests are about all that survive. Every other building is at least half burnt to the ground. The Lost Boys didn't leave Aesclinn in much better shape."

"The Lost Boys? What has become of them?"

"There are about one hundred left." Corbin said sadly. "They walk about freely. They did make a final stand with us and denounced the pretender pope. Teodorico, by the way, is locked up on a boat in the harbor. His tent was untouched by the battle, but his people abandoned him. Sir Charles will be taking him back to Rome in chains."

Patrick nodded, satisfied.

"Abbot Herewinus is here again with several of the other former benefactors," Corbin continued. "They've decided to officially close the Greensprings school. The cost to rebuild, plus the fact we tend to attract all manner of villains, suggest that it's time."

Patrick laughed ironically, just short of bitterness. "How do you feel about that? What will become of us, the Avangarde?"

"It was a dream. A glorious dream," Corbin replied, "but dreams must end and we must come back to the real world. Many of us, myself included, are going to start a new order to protect Saint Peter's Orphanage. We'll be escorting the children back there soon. Wolfgang is going to hang up his sword and return to his home for a deserved rest. Marcus and some others will take up positions in Paschal's Papal Guard, along with many of the Lost Boys."

"What?" Patrick almost shouted, wincing when he almost sat up in bed.

Corbin smiled. "Aye, Jeremie Le Beau and Jon de Lorraine lead the company. They mentioned Philip had a talk with you. Any idea what that was?"

Patrick shrugged, smiling.

"You know, you're welcome to come with us to Saint Peter's."

"Maybe," Patrick said, and struggled to sit up, "but first I must see Aimeé."

Brother Ambrosius—Brobrosius—burst into the room. "I'm taller than you!"

Patrick returned his smile. "My friend, you always will be. Do you mind giving me a hand?" With his smile lighting up the room brighter than the sun, Brobrosius helped Patrick dress and then assisted him out the door.

Just outside the hall, Patrick encountered the Lady Katherina overseeing the packing of several wagons. Willy and Trent assisted her.

Patrick gave up using Brobrosius as a crutch long enough to embrace the young men and exchange kind words. When they returned to packing the wagon, he limped over to Katherina and leaned heavily on the wagon. Its cargo was a long box.

"I'm taking Jon home," she said, touching the casket. "His family should know he was a hero. The reason he was captured was because he held the Lost Boys off at the docks while the fishermen cast off. It was the fishermen who finally delivered word to Wolfgang to bring the army sooner."

A glow burned in Patrick's heart. He laid his hand on the warm wood. "Good for you, Jon. I'll miss you my friend, but I'm glad you're going home. Say hello to everyone when you get there."

Patrick turned to Katherina. "And you? What will you do after?"

She squared her shoulders. "I will go to see my mother in Rome, to inform her of my intentions. I plan on going back to our home country to face my uncle. It is time I reclaimed my rightful crown."

Patrick froze at the news.

"It is what I want," Katherina insisted, "and I must do it alone, with my people. My supporters. I am ready."

Patrick nodded somberly. "I wish you the best of luck. I will miss you."

They stared at one another for a long while. "Thank you, Patrick—for everything," she said at last, eyes sparkling with tears. "You rescued me more than once, and in more than one way. I will never forget you. Thank you for your friendship."

Patrick's vision blurred, as well. "In a certain way, I will always love you."

She nodded, and a bittersweet laugh escaped her lips as they embraced. He kissed the top of her head. Even though her fierce hug hurt his broken ribs, he held on to her. His tears ran into her hair.

"I can't tell you how happy I am to see finally you can shed tears," she confessed.

"It wasn't an easy road, making that happen."

"I know, I know," she said.

Eventually they disentangled, and with Brobrosius' assistance he limped past the blackened, skeletal ruins of Greensprings.

Next he came across Sir Charles, who distributed orders among knights in gold and white surcoats marked with the papal sigil. The lanky young man no longer seemed the awkward squire. "I see you've found employment already," Patrick said, surprised such a young man would be given such a position of authority so soon.

Charles smiled and clasped hands with Patrick. "Only temporarily. I'll be moving on soon to fulfill my family duties."

"Oh?" Patrick said, brow furrowed in curiosity.

"I must go home to the Danemark. I'm a grown man now. A knight. I've been in exile far too long at my uncle's court in Flanders. It's time to win my father's throne back."

Patrick blinked, jaw dropping. "Throne?"

"Yes," Charles explained with a humble smile. "My father was King Canute, assassinated when I was a child."

Patrick looked anew at the young man, shaking his head in wonder. He had known Greensprings as a haven for nobles in exile, but today drove the point home.

"Good thing I didn't know that, otherwise I'd stumble all over myself making a bad impression," Patrick said.

"You made just the right impression," Charles said, smiling.

Patrick hugged the young man, said his goodbyes, and moved on.

He and Brobrosius crossed the drawbridge and made their way across the grass towards the medical tents. Halfway there, Abbot Herewinus and Father Hugh met them.

"You are looking well, all things considered," the abbot commented.

"I understand the school and the Avangarde are finished," Patrick said.

"Yes, we discussed it long and passionately while you were unconscious. Father Hugh and his monks will be coming home to Glastonbury, as will Mother Superior and her nuns. I'm sorry if our ultimate decision saddens or inconveniences you."

Patrick patted the man's shoulder. "It is probably for the best. It is as someone told me—we did seem to cause more trouble than anything else."

Herewinus laughed. "I don't know about that, but it is my hope all the work here was not in vain. I hope we touched enough lives that there will be real change in the world. I hope we planted enough seeds of what peace should look like that they will take root and grow, if only centuries from now."

"I hope so, too," Patrick agreed. "To teach peace in one place is admirable, but perhaps we should now concentrate on taking peace to where it is needed."

The elderly men nodded in agreement.

"You know, Sir Patrick," Father Hugh added, looking Patrick up and down. "I've been told the natives of Avalon fought for us in the battle, but they made it clear that it's time we leave them in peace, and since Aesclinn is all but destroyed, the surviving villagers and Greensprings staff will settle near Glastonbury. We will need a lord to administer the land. Do you know anyone who cares for the opportunity? A fair and good leader?"

"Why, yes!" Herewinus interjected, also looking Patrick over. "We already have a sizable community of your countrymen at the monastery. Many a fine monk has come from your Green Isle. Why, once upon a time the abbot of Glastonbury was none other than Saint Patrick himself."

Patrick's mouth dropped; butterflies turned in his stomach.

"I could like this idea," he said nervously, "but I first need to discuss it with someone."

Father Hugh smiled and jerked his head towards the tents. "She's inside, helping Mother Superior."

The priests left him and Patrick continued on his way until a horse's hooves rumbled from behind. Lucan reined up next to him. His centurion armor was gone, but he still wore his light blue cape.

"Lo, Lucan, you are well," Patrick said, studying the man. "You did not look so good the last time."

Lucan threw back his head and laughed. "You know what they say: it's hard to keep a good man down. Even a man with his back broken in half."

"And Lilith? Is she gone for good?" Patrick asked.

"No. Her last days are up to God. When that may be, I cannot say, but I don't think she will trouble you again."

"And you?" Patrick noted the bulging saddlebags.

Lucan looked to the horizon. "I feel lighter—born again. Perhaps I should go out into the world and do some good, and patiently wait for the end times. Maybe by doing that, I will cause less trouble for myself."

"Sounds like an excellent plan," Patrick agreed. "I wish you well with it. Don't take this wrong, but I hope we don't meet again, because if we do, I'm afraid there might be four horsemen behind you."

They laughed together.

"What will you do, Patrick?" he asked.

Patrick shrugged. "I have many options I'm considering."

Lucan smiled. "Then I wish you the best. Take care, Irishman."

With that Lucan wheeled his horse about and moved to depart.

"Lucan," Patrick called after him, "what became of the spear?"

"I gave it to King Arthur to take back to his cave. He can use it when he wakes from his slumber in the next time of need."

"Truly?"

Lucan winked with a sly smile and galloped off on his horse. Within moments he became a dot on the horizon.

At last they entered the tent, and after a few inquiries, Patrick found Aimeé among the cots, tending the wounded men. She put aside the bandages she had been cleaning and rushed forward. For a moment Patrick reacted to the sight of the blood on her apron, but the sensation passed, soon forgotten.

They embraced strongly and kissed deeply.

Through the wide-open doorway Brobrosius found his orphanage comrades, Candace, Emilie, Stuart, Martin, and Chansonne. He chased them in circles on the grass, laughing happily.

"You shouldn't be out of bed," Aimeé scolded him.

"I couldn't wait to see you," Patrick said, refusing to let go of her. "I had to tell you how much I love you."

Her smile grew larger than he'd ever seen.

"And I wanted to say that everything is going to be fine," Patrick said, "God has it all planned out."

"As long as there are no cups, spears, demons, demigods, or what have you in our future, I will be happy."

"No worries there," Patrick replied. "The cup was my fault. God simply made the best of the situation. He taught me a lesson from my mistake."

"And what was that?" she asked.

"Faith is in the heart, not in a cup. Holy objects are tangible reminders of the miraculous, meant to increase our faith, not be the focus of it. God wants us to embrace the love the cup represents, rather than what its powers can do for us."

Aimeé kissed him.

"The next cup I want to see is just a regular communion chalice at our wedding," he added. "That will be plenty enough miracle for me."

Aimeé's eyes looked downcast, and she said, "You know I cannot have children. Does that change anything?"

Patrick kissed her deeply and called Chansonne over. When she came, he bent down and picked her up with his good arm.

"Chansonne? How would you like to come live with Aimeé and me?" he asked.

A giant smile spread across the child's face. Almost as big as Aimeé's.

Together, the three of them held each other silhouetted against the doorway, watching the sunrise.

Epilogue

Victor waited in the darkness outside the stout wooden door. He smoothed out the front of his new gold and white cassock, reflecting on how he rather liked these new colors. At last the door opened with a noisy turn of the lock. An older man in white robes exited.

"Cardinal Giacomo, I trust you found our guest to your satisfaction?"

"It is as you say," the cardinal replied as they moved toward daylight at the end of the corridor. "He shows no signs of torture or poisoning. The pope will be pleased to hear that. My report will simply show his afflictions are a result of his advanced years and natural causes."

"Good, good," Victor said. "It pains me to think Paschal might think, after his public sentence of house arrest for Teodorico, we might have disregarded his call for compassion and abused our guest."

"Oh, Paschal didn't think so, but when Teodorico's health took a turn for the worse, we had to investigate, you understand?"

"Of course," Victor replied. "Paschal's compassion must be real and without suspicion for the good of the public order. I know that personally well."

"Ah, yes," Giacomo said, stopping to assess his guide. "You received full clemency. Paschal is truly compassionate."

"Yes, he certainly is," Victor acknowledged. "Now, will you be visiting us long enough to have midday meal? I think you'll find the cuisine in Salerno magnificent. The wines from La Cava alone are worth the trip..."

As their voices faded down the corridor, the withered old man who shivered in his bed twitched at every little sound.

Candlelight flickered, casting shadows against the stone walls.

At floor level, the shadow of a nebulous blob moved across the wall towards the man. As it progressed, it turned to that of a cat, then that of a nude woman sprouting bat-like wings.

As Lilith kneeled onto the bed, Teodorico jumped into a frenzy of twitches, but was too weak to do more than try to curl into a fetal position.

"Hello again, my love," she whispered. "Just a couple more nights, then your suffering will end."

He fought feebly, but her knees planted on either side of him prevented him from squirming. His frail hands scrabbled to cover his mouth, but she easily pulled them away.

"What's wrong, my love? Don't you like it when we kiss?" she said, her yellow eyes flaring in the dim light. "I told you long ago the price of failure would be steep... and I do need to feed."

She leaned closer and her embrace smothered his scream.

Her wings folded about them like a flower's petals closing for the night.

The End

Adam Copeland was born and raised in Silverton, Oregon. He attended Southern Oregon State College (now Southern Oregon University) in Ashland, Oregon. There he studied business, chemistry and French. He spent a year study abroad in France and has ever since been passionate about traveling internationally, going to such places as diverse as Asia, Africa and Mexico. He is an avid outdoorsman, enjoying hiking, backpacking, camping, mountain trekking and scuba diving. He is a co-founder of Northwest Independent Writers Association (NIWA), an organization dedicated to helping indie writers from the Pacific Northwest write, publish, and promote their work. Adam currently resides in Vancouver, Washington State where he is an active member of St. Joseph's Catholic Church.